INSURGENT

Books by Charles Sheehan-Miles

America's Future
Republic
Insurgent

The Thompson Sisters
A Song for Julia
Falling Stars
Just Remember to Breathe
The Last Hour

Rachel's Peril
Girl of Lies
Girl of Rage
Girl of Vengeance

Nocturne (with Andrea Randall)

Prayer at Rumayla
A Novel of the Gulf War

Saving the World on $30 a Day:
An Activist's Guide to Starting,
Organizing and Running
A Non-Profit Organization

INSURGENT

CHARLES SHEEHAN MILES

www.sheehanmiles.com

Published by Cincinnatus Press
PO Box 814
South Hadley, Massachusetts
United States of America

Copyright © 2012 Charles Sheehan-Miles.
Second edition Copyright © 2014 Charles Sheehan-Miles

Cover Design by Charles Sheehan-Miles

All rights reserved. No part of this book may be reproduced in any form or by any electronic or me-chanical means, including information storage and retrieval systems, without permission in writing from the publisher, except by a reviewer, who may quote brief passages in a review.

This is a work of fiction. Names, characters, places, and incidents either are the products of the author's imagination or are used fictitiously, and any resemblance to actual persons, living or dead is entirely coincidental.

ISBN: 978-1-63202-095-6

Cincinnatus Press
www.cincinnatuspress.com

v09152014

DEDICATION

In Memory of my father

Richard Edward Miles

1946 - 2010

ACKNOWLEDGEMENTS

THIS book has been in the works for a long time, and wouldn't have been possible without the help of a a great number of people. In particular, I want to give a shout-out to my fantastic editor Shakirah Dawud, who helped me shape it, and corrected my many errors, and found major inconsistencies, all at the last minute under significant deadline pressure. Shakirah: thank you. Any errors remaining are solely my responsibility.

To the fantastic beta readers who read multiple early drafts of the serialized ebook version of Insurgent: Darren Raynor, Patrick "Deuce the Two Cats" Patriarca, Matthew and Annaliese Cothron, Bryan James, Stephen Breuer, and Rowan Dow. You guys were patient, observant, fantastic. Thank you.

The editing was mostly paid for through a Kickstarter campaign. Thanks to the folks who backed that campaign and made the final book possible: Jeffery Fleischer, Rhonda Miles, Ashley Nicole Shelton, Paul Sullivan, Brett Lewis, Richard Miles, Chris Kornkven, John G. Hertzler, Michael and Heather Crider, Dave Wiener, Darren Raynor, Chris Gerrib, Annaliese Cothron, Patrick Kaeding, Bryce Touchstone, Donna Price, David Funsten, Lara Badges Kimber, Jackie Trippier Holt, Piotr Mierzejewski, John Burris, Michael Wasserman, Mike Bennett, Maria Pinkleton, Elizabeth Grace Brackman Kibert, Shayne Power, Cristi Carras, Sean O'Brien, Simon Cowlard, and William Foster.

DRAMATIS PERSONAE

WASHINGTON, DC
Wendell Price, President of the United States
Robert Hamilton, Vice President of the United States
Mark Skaggs, US Congressman
Carl Metzenberger, National Security Advisor

CHARLESTON
Valerie Murphy, Acting Secretary of West Virginia's Department of Law Enforcement and Military Affairs
Asa Vance Hatfield, Enforcement Division Chief
Wade Davis, Chief of Staff
Trooper Dennis Henry, State Patrol, Assigned as personal protection to Valerie Murphy
Detective Sergeant Billy Ray Corvath
JD Roberts, Charleston Station Chief, Department of Homeland Security

General Tom Murphy, Military Governor of West Virginia
Al Clark, Governor of West Virginia
Ambrose Hall, Special Prosecutor
Marissa Harmon, Secretary to the Governor
Lieutenant Aaron Thrasher, Aide-de-Camp to General Murphy

352 MILITARY INTELLIGENCE BATTALION
Lieutenant Colonel Cory Avedis, Commanding
Lieutenant Calvin Stewart
Private Karen Greenfield

WHITESVILLE
Bob Mays, Mayor of Whitesville
Zoe Mays, Bob Mays's wife
Rebecca Mays, daughter of Bob and Zoe
Dana Wilder, Rebecca's best friend
Jesse Turner, Rebecca's ex-boyfriend
Mandy Mays Blankenship

B COMPANY, 1st BATTALION 15th INFANTRY
Captain Mark Wellstone, Commanding
Lieutenant Jonathan Blake, Second Platoon Leader
Sergeant Larry Nguyen, Squad Leader

Corporal Jim Turville, Fire team leader
Private Karim Tilman
Private First Class Jesus Santiago
Private First Class Phil Nowell

Corporal Cantrell Meigs, Fire team leader
Private First Class Artur Gomez
Private First Class Matt Leo
Private Rodriguez

INSURGENTS
Joe Blankenship, leader of the Boone County insurgents
Reverend Roland Channing, pastor of the New World Pentacostal Church in Baughman Settlement
John Channing, former Marine officer, son of Roland Channing

HAMILTON BIOMEDICAL
Margaret Rutledge, public relations
Clifford Webb, contract programmer
Captain Matthew Floyd, US Army, head of security

ONE

New York Times, March 18
PRESIDENT EXPANDS STATE OF EMERGENCY
By Marcus Jennsen
Washington, DC – On Monday, the White House issued a statement expanding the current "state of insurrection" in West Virginia to include surrounding counties in Virginia, Pennsylvania,
Kentucky and Ohio. The statement formally suspended habeas
corpus in affected areas, and granted broad powers of authority to
military commanders.

L IEUTENANT Jonathan Blake leaned against the door
of his Humvee, eyes scanning the road and untouched
snow ahead as the convoy drifted forward. Two feet
deep, mostly unplowed, and some of the snowdrifts were three
or four times that high. High enough to hide a man, a squad—a
regiment, even.

Heavy timberland and mountains marched on either side
of the twisted road, an uninterrupted and threatening phalanx
of grizzled soldiers armed with storms and floods against the
unwary intruder. Gusts of wind sent a dusting of snow back
into the air in a swirling mist and cut visibility to nothing.
Almost two miles up the valley, towering over the town of
Whitesville, a nine-hundred-foot high earthen dam threatened
the town with annihilation.

At five feet, six inches, Blake had been the runt of his
ROTC detachment at University of Florida and compensated
for it with bodybuilding and a cavalier attitude marked by a

quirky sense of humor. The humor was little in evidence these days: he had dark circles under his eyes, and those circles had their own dark circles. His uniform was sweat-stained and filthy; the computer-generated camouflage pattern had lost its pixilated look after weeks of hard use. At least it didn't stink— he'd used so much soap in his last hand washing of the uniform that it still gave off antiseptic fumes. He'd sewn the tear in the crotch a couple weeks ago, but that repair job had begun to give out—along with his patience.

For weeks on end he'd rolled with his platoon from town to town, then back to the depot, then back to the towns, delivering supplies, trying to rebuild electricity, trying to rebuild... everything. Few of the tiny backwoods towns they'd visited had working electricity or phones. Local cops were mostly missing, and people were very quiet whenever the troops arrived. Ominously quiet.

Today's mission was no different: another tiny, one-light— if that—town in the middle of nowhere, at the end of a long, twisted mountain road. Along the road, they'd passed a startling billboard depicting a filthy gas station bathroom with the stark words, "No one thinks they'll lose their virginity here. Meth will change that." Further along the road, a dilapidated shack squatted in the woods, smoke curling from a chimney. A faded rebel flag hung in the window.

Power and phones were knocked out—presumably by the snow and ice. He'd never seen so much snow in his life, and every time he left the camp he asked himself the same question: Why did I ever leave Florida? A mountain back home would be ten feet above sea level, and a cold winter might mean a light jacket. Not this never-ending ice-bound world of hills and ice, teeming with wildlife, abandoned coalmines and inbred elementary school graduates. Wild and wonderful, my ass.

That was one attitude he had to keep to himself. Though his sense of the ridiculous had often gotten him into trouble in college and infantry training, he'd only once made the mistake of making a smart-ass comment in the hearing of Captain Wellstone, the new company commander. Wellstone didn't think new lieutenants were worthy of a sense of humor. Blake had a bad feeling he'd have more trouble with the Captain in the future.

Nor had Wellstone done a very good job of reintegrating the replacements with the folks who'd gone through the brief war three months earlier.

Blake's predecessor, his platoon sergeant, and half a dozen other members of his platoon were killed in January. Even more were injured. More than half the faces in his platoon were fresh replacements, most of them straight from Fort Benning's infantry training center. Whenever they had a few days of rest back at Camp Wingham, the tension in the barracks was palpable between the combat veterans and the replacements. Blake had wracked his brain for a solution to that problem with no luck. Instead, half the time he had to intervene in fights. After all, he was a replacement himself. A sniper had blown away Lieutenant Dale Wingham, namesake of their godforsaken camp outside Charleston.

Blake looked to his left. Behind the wheel of the Humvee sat Specialist Jim Turville. Turville had only been back with the unit for a week: he'd been shot through the throat and spent two months at Walter Reed Army Hospital in Washington. He seemed okay now, but he moved like an arthritic old man, and he probably wouldn't have been out on this mission if they weren't so shorthanded.

They moved slowly; the tires rustled in the soft, heavy snow. Four times now they'd had to dig the column out when they'd gotten buried in drifts too big to drive over even with the huge tires of the Humvees. Turville looked bored but alert as he stared out, eyes darting from place to place.

"You feeling all right, Turville?"

"Yes, sir. My throat's still a little achy, but I'll make it."

"All right. Just don't do anything I wouldn't do."

"No problem with that, sir. I'd just as soon stay right here warm in the truck."

Blake smiled. According to the platoon's non-commissioned officers, Turville had been in continual trouble for the first six months of his tenure in the Army, including an aborted move toward a court-martial: he'd accidentally killed a civilian in Charleston during the chaos last fall. Then, out of the blue, he'd shown remarkable heroism in combat. During the murderous fire when their unit had been ambushed, he'd run out into the open to rescue their wounded platoon sergeant. The move diverted fire from the rest of his platoon, allowing them to run to safety.

The platoon sergeant was killed anyway, and Turville was shot in the throat. The bullet missed the artery and windpipe, bruised one of the vertebrae, and passed out the side of his neck. Luckily it had been freezing cold then—like it was now. The cold had served to slow the escape of blood, so instead of bleeding to death, he'd half frozen instead.

Turville didn't know, but their former company commander had filed an award recommendation for the Silver Star. He wouldn't get it: they'd probably downgrade it to a Bronze Star or Soldier's Medal or something of the like. Standard operating procedure was to submit an award for a much higher level than was expected; everybody knew each grade in the chain of command would knock it down a level.

All that aside, Turville's miraculous survival had turned him into something of a good luck charm for the platoon. And, given the extreme shortage of decent replacements, that meant he was probably getting his own fire team whether he liked it or not.

Blake had emailed his wife Lana about Turville, telling a little about his story. She wrote back two simple sentences: "Turville is probably looking for redemption. Watch out for him."

Blake thought she was likely right. Ever since they'd met in college, she'd had an unerring eye for understanding people. He'd have done just about anything to be with her now, instead of here in this godforsaken wilderness. He couldn't help but worry about Turville as well: people looking for redemption were likely to do particularly stupid things.

Turville said, "Sir, I think I see somebody over there."

"In this snow? Where?"

"Look right over there, sir."

Blake looked. Two hundred meters ahead of them, to the side of the road, stood a man in white, baggy hunting gear, a rifle slung over his shoulder. The man waved at the convoy through the shroud of misty, blowing snow.

"Flash the lights at him and honk the horn, let him know we're coming."

"Yes, sir." Turville flashed the headlights. As they approached the man, Blake got a better look. He was well built: hair cut into a tight buzz cut, broken blood vessels in his face suggestive of a fair acquaintance with alcohol. Startling blue eyes stared back at Blake.

Turville slowed the Humvee to a stop a few feet from where the man stood.

Lieutenant Blake leaned out. "You need a ride somewhere?"

The man grinned, and his teeth gleamed.

"Oh, no, I don't need a ride. It's you who's gonna need a ride."

Blake recoiled, then his eyes widened.

At least twenty men stepped out of the woods, most of them armed with automatic rifles. All of them wore various patterns of camouflage, hunting clothes, all colors that blended with the woods. Most wore beards and looked haggard and weak, as if they'd been living in the woods even through this hard winter.

"Lieutenant, put your hands in the air. You too, over there, driver."

Turville didn't hesitate. He raised his hands, his face impassive.

Blake said, "I don't know what this is—"

"Shut up. Get out of the vehicle. We're commandeering this column for the West Virginia National Guard."

"The West Virginia National Guard? I don't think so—the National Guard is under Federal authority now."

The man smirked.

"Oh, is that so? Well, in that case, I guess I'm jes'confiscatin' it for me. I'm the head of the local militia."

Blake looked back and forth between Turville and the men. Turville's hands were in the air; he wasn't going to offer any resistance. They only had eight men on this convoy, and no escort. The trucks were loaded with supplies: water, generators. Well, this might be one of those times when discretion is the better part of valor.

Captain Wellstone was going to be pissed.

"Look, can I just call in, so you guys can get away, and I won't have to walk all the way to Charleston?"

"Well, the way I see it, you got two options. You can walk on into Whitesville. It'll take you about two hours, and you can call in from there. Or I could just shoot you dead right here, and then I won't have to worry about nobody coming after me. Understand?"

Blake raised his hands.

One of the men opened the door of the Humvee. Blake looked back at the other vehicles in the column. The two men in the other Humvee had been disarmed just as easily, as had the truck drivers.

"Got any weapons?"

"Just what you see."

Briskly, the men patted him down, confiscated his M-16 and the .45-caliber pistol at his belt. He also had two hand grenades in a pouch. They grabbed those, too. Not good.

"Check 'em for phones."

The search revealed his mobile phone. They took one from Turville as well. After the search was completed, the men got into the trucks. The leader waved with a grin and drove away into the snow.

The eight soldiers stood in a loose circle, seven of them looking to Blake for a solution—one he didn't have. Blake said, "All right, gentlemen, looks like we're going for a walk. We're screwed, but we might as well be warm while we're at it. Whitesville is four miles that way."

Blake pointed down the snow-covered road. "Let's move out."

"Uh, sir?" Turville said.

"What is it?" Blake asked, expecting a complaint, or at the very least some criticism.

"Do you think the Army will reimburse me for my phone?"

For some reason—and it was probably inappropriate—the question struck Blake as hysterical. He let loose a loud belly laugh as he turned toward the town.

"Why not, Turville? What's a few hand grenades and automatic rifles next to your missing cell phone?" Turville's blank stare just made Blake laugh even harder. "Come on, Turville. Let's get walking."

❧

"General, we just got a call from Second Brigade. We've run into some trouble in Boone County."

Brigadier General Tom Murphy looked up from the report he'd been reading and set it to the side on the utilitarian desk he'd installed in the governor's office three months before.

His aide-de-camp, Lieutenant Aaron Thrasher, stood in the door. Thrasher was a tall man in his early twenties with an immaculate uniform. He would have made a good model for a recruiting poster with his square chin, blue eyes and open, frank look.

"Trouble?"

"Sir, a relief column was accosted by a group of thirty men calling themselves the West Virginia militia. The column was relieved of weapons and trucks, as well as relief supplies."

Tom sat straight up in his seat. "Let's go down to the operations center."

As he stood, his phone rang, and he called to his administrative assistant. "Marissa, hold my calls."

"But sir, it's General Wells."

Tom muttered a curse. "Hold on." General Howard Wells, Commanding General of U.S. Northern Command, was many things, but patient wasn't one of them. This was one phone call he couldn't put off.

Tom picked up the phone. "General Murphy speaking, sir."

"Murphy, its Wells. I have good news for you."

"Yes sir?"

"We've located your niece and had a discussion with Homeland Security. They're releasing her today."

Tom relaxed in his seat and exhaled. He hadn't realized just how tense he was. For the last three months, he'd hounded Homeland Security over the disappearance of his niece, Valerie

Murphy. Chief of Staff to the then Secretary of State of West Virginia, she'd been arrested on the first day of hostilities and held without charges. Two weeks ago, Wells had promised he would approach the President about her.

"Thank God. Is there any way I can reach her?"

"I don't know anything about that. All they said was they promised to release her and Al Clark immediately." There was a noticeable pause, and then Wells continued, "Between you and me... the White House decided holding them any longer was too much of a political liability. They're hoping to cut them loose quietly, with a minimum of fuss."

"Whatever the reason," Tom replied, "We need him. Things are starting to get a little crazy here."

"I understand that. How are things going?"

"I was just heading down to the operations center to check, sir. One of our relief patrols was set upon by a group of armed men. They were relieved of all of their equipment. I don't know any details yet, sir. I'll let you know as soon as I find out."

"Relieved of their equipment? What the hell does that mean?"

Tom grimaced at Wells's response. "Again, sir, I don't have any details yet. I'll get them now and will get back to you with a report."

"Get back with me soon."

"Yes, sir. One more thing, sir."

"Yeah?"

Tom took a breath. "I've got three battalions of the state National Guard sitting around doing nothing as prisoners. I'd like to put them to use."

General Wells responded with a terse, "Go on."

"Look, sir. I've been saying for weeks I don't have enough troops here. State and local police have just about vanished, and we're having a nightmare getting even basic services going.

If I can get those troops delivering supplies, then my combat units can act as escorts or can be forward deployed in the towns. I think it will help."

Tom spoke in understatement. He'd told Wells the day he accepted the job of military governor that a reinforced brigade wouldn't be enough to do the job. The President had turned down the request of additional troops, a decision that had unnecessarily cost lives.

A few moments went by before Wells answered. "It won't look good politically, but I understand the issue. You make whatever preparations you need, and I'll tell you when and if you can pull the trigger on that."

"Yes, sir."

"Call me when you have a status on that patrol. And you need to give some thought to what you're going to do about officers for those National Guard battalions. No way in hell they'll let the officers come back. Out."

Wells hung up. Tom placed the handset back in its cradle and turned to Lieutenant Thrasher. "Let's go."

He marched to the operations center, the young Lieutenant half-skipping to keep up as they walked through the lushly carpeted halls of the governor's mansion.

The ops center was a large conference room converted to a military headquarters. Inside, two rows of tables were cluttered with laptops, papers and coffee cups. A large percolator sat against one wall, and coffee cups were scattered about the room. Another wall was covered with a giant map of West Virginia. The operations officer sat at the end, overseeing the battle captains who manned the radios and computers.

"Attention!" called the operations officer as Tom entered the room. Five seconds later, Colonel Jordan Bronner, the Chief of Staff, entered.

"As you were," Tom said. The officers relaxed. "What's going on?"

The operations officer, a young major, replied. "Sir, we received a call from one of the platoon leaders in 2/16 Infantry. Our relief convoy into Boone County encountered more than thirty well-armed men about two hours ago. We had eight men in the convoy, only light armed. They had to walk into Whitesville before they could call in."

"Anybody hurt?"

"No, sir. But they took both Humvees, as well as their weapons. They also got two trucks and all their supplies."

"What kind of weapons did they get?"

"They had eight M16s and a forty-five pistol. Half a dozen hand grenades. Gas masks."

"Humvees weren't armed?"

"No, sir, they weren't expecting any opposition. Nobody was locked and loaded, and they were surrounded before anyone had a chance to react."

"Christ."

Colonel Bonner looked at him and said, "You know what that reminds me of?"

"Yeah, you don't need to tell me what it reminds you of."

They looked at each other, thinking of the three months after the fall of Baghdad, when everything had seemed quiet. During that brief lull, the violence to come had merely been simmering in the under the surface. Tom had been afraid of that here. He'd been operating as military governor for three months. An unhappy situation to say the least, but he'd finally managed to convene the legislature three weeks before.

Of course, it figured that when they finally met, the legislature elected as their governor a man who had been held for months by the Department of Homeland Security under unspecified charges.

Tom had argued long and hard to get them to reverse their decision, but they'd held firm. He'd finally lobbied for the former congressman—now governor—to be released. He knew Clark hadn't done anything wrong. Clark and Valerie Murphy, Tom's niece, had been in Washington together trying to negotiate a peaceful settlement to the war when they'd been arrested.

"All right. I want to pull the battalion commanders together. We're going to have to come up with some new procedures. All of our convoys are going to have to be escorted."

"Yes, sir."

"We've also got those three National Guard battalions. They may be back on duty soon, minus their weapons. I want the staff to start working on contingency plans to use them for relief operations."

"Sir?" Bonner looked skeptical.

"Look, whoever set this up must have known there was a convoy on the way. They were well prepared, just sitting out there waiting for us. That means somebody gave them the information."

"Sir, my understanding is that this particular convoy went out because the phone and power lines had gone down, possibly because of the storm."

"Maybe they cut the lines. How did the platoon call in if the lines were down?"

"Satellite phone, sir, from a store in Whitesville."

"All right," Tom said. "Looks like we're going to have to do some investigation. Who's on their way out there?"

"A platoon from 28th MPs, sir. We sent two choppers as well, and they're heavily armed."

"All right, give me a report back."

"Yes, sir."

Tom turned around and walked back to his office.

"Marissa."

"Yes, sir."

The youthful admin assistant sat up when he called her name. She'd been Governor Slagter's assistant until January, when Slagter committed suicide. Tom had speculated more than once that the former Governor might have hired her for reasons other than her dictation ability, which was middling to poor. She was a contradiction, a puzzle he hadn't figured out. An extremely attractive, petite blonde with sea-green eyes, she dressed in a prim, business-like fashion. There were no photos on her desk—nothing to indicate a personal life of any kind other than the Bible she kept on the credenza. But her computer skills were nonexistent, and according to her personnel file this was her first job. In short, it appeared Frank Slagter had hired her because of her fantastic body and beautiful eyes.

Tom had little patience for men who hired women to function as eye candy. But he was stuck with her until the new governor took his seat—hopefully soon.

"My understanding is that the Department of Homeland Security is releasing two prisoners today: Al Clark and Valerie Murphy."

"Your niece, sir? That's wonderful news."

"Thank you. Find out where they are. I want to talk to them as soon as possible. You know Clark is taking over as governor here, so we can provide official transportation for him. I want to send a chopper to Washington to pick them up. Get Hatfield moving on that."

In the office, Tom sat down, and his eyes fell on the photograph on his desk. The picture showed two smiling men in their prime—Tom and Ken Murphy—in Iraq a lifetime ago. The frame was a cheap, two-dollar plastic frame from Wal-Mart that he'd bought maybe ten years before. The photo, however, was priceless. Ken Murphy, his big brother and lifelong hero, was gone—executed—leaving behind a gaping hole Tom knew would never be filled.

Somehow nothing seemed the same.

༨

The cheap cell phone sitting on the dash of Joe Blankenship's muddy pickup rang. Joe let it ring twice, then picked it up off the dash. His truck sat on a seldom-used, ice-covered road near the top of the ridge south of Whitesville. Below him, spread out like a moonscape, were the remains of Wright's Mountain: carved up, gutted to bedrock by mining companies, only rocky detritus filled in the hollow below the mountain.

A small community, Lorrie's Hollow, had existed in that tiny valley when Blankenship was a child. But the mine had closed, followed by most of the other small businesses in town. Pretty soon, no one was left but a few old, tired senior citizens in their trailers and shack. No one had been left to defend them when Montgomery Energy bought or stole their land.

"Yeah?" he said to the caller, his mind still shifting away from Lorrie's Hollow.

"We're in position," replied the man on the other end of the line.

"All right," Blankenship responded. "Army headquarters got the word. They're sending two choppers, followed by a platoon of MPs. Make your targets, and I want everyone out in ten minutes. No risks, all right? Not enough of us to go around as it is."

"No sweat, Boss. We're on it."

Blankenship hung up the phone with no further word. Everything he'd been working for since Mandy's murder hinged on the next thirty minutes. He trusted his own guys: they'd been through it together more than once. But his information from the Army headquarters in Charleston: that was different.

It came by way of Roland Channing, the leader of a Reconstructionist Christian group that had been sniffing around the rebels for a while. Promising information, resources, money.

This was a test of whether or not Channing could deliver on his promises. A dangerous test at that. Mandy would have said to trust his gut. His gut told him that with a core group of real patriots he could count on both hands, they just weren't going to accomplish a lot.

If he failed, Mandy's death would be for nothing. Dale Whitt had been assassinated because he believed in freedom. Dave Firkus gunned down the same day as his wife. Ken Murphy executed by the Feds after a trial so short it left most Americans gasping. If he failed, he'd be failing all of them. Spitting on their memories.

Blankenship would rather have died.

So he sat in the truck in the cold, waiting for word to come back. Either the rebels would fail here and it would be all over, or they would succeed and possibly open the door to saving the country.

Ironic, really, that the first shots would be fired right here in Whitesville, where it had all started for him and Mandy. Ironic and fitting.

✂

In Whitesville, the sun was just setting behind the ridge, leaving the woods above the town in darkness. The wind howled over the mountains, buffeting the town nestled in the constricted hollow.

Not much of a town, even when Turville compared it to other exciting locales in West Virginia. Here in "downtown," half a dozen or so businesses stretched on both sides of the narrow road. Drugstore, carwash, hardware store. There was no grocery store at all: Turville had no idea how far the residents had to drive to buy groceries. The carwash was closed, the hardware store boarded up. Hardly any traffic: they'd seen four moving vehicles in the last three hours, all of them trucks or SUVs, all of them built for this kind of nasty weather and terrain.

At least the town itself had been plowed—most likely by the residents, given that there wasn't much of a functioning county or state government. There was still no power or any operating phone lines. The LT borrowed a satellite phone from the clerk in the drug store in order to call in to headquarters.

Turville leaned, shivering, against the outside of the drugstore where he stood with Tillman, Nowell and Santiago, the members of his fire team.

Across the street, Corporal Meigs stood with his team. Until his injury in January, Turville had reported to him. It was a relief that was over—Meigs and Turville hadn't gotten along since the day Turville landed in Meigs's fire team after basic training. The mutual dislike between the two men had been both instant and visceral.

"Hey, hey, looky here," muttered Nowell, inclining his head down the street. Turville glanced in that direction. Two girls were walking toward them, both bundled up in heavy coats and snow boots. A wisp of dark hair had escaped the hood of the girl on the left.

"Knock it off, man," Turville said. "We're not supposed to bother the natives." But, he thought, the short one sure is pretty.

"Yeah, whatever. I still got eyes in my head, Turville. Got to use them for something."

Tillman, another rifleman right out of basic training, said, "Hey, do you hear that?"

Turville listened. He could just hear the fluttering of helicopter blades.

"Yeah. They're coming."

"It's 'bout time," said Nowell.

Turville opened the door to the drugstore and leaned inside. Lieutenant Blake was standing at the counter, grinning and chatting with the clerk.

"Sir, I hear a chopper," Turville said.

The lieutenant looked back at him, then walked to the door, waving to the clerk in the store. "Good. All right, everybody up. They'll be here shortly."

Turville looked around. The girls were about half a block away now as the men gathered in front of the drug store. They were a mismatched pair, one tall and blonde, and the other short, brunette. The blonde wore dark mascara and a heavy pink winter coat, giving her eyes a sunken appearance inside the hood. The dark-haired girl wore no makeup, a navy pea coat and matching knit cap. Short Girl and Tall Girl.

In the distance, Turville saw twin dots in the sky. Helicopters, coming in low over the mountains. Short Girl turned and pointed at the approaching helicopters.

They were older ones, Black Hawks, and the first one came in close over the town and started to descend. As the rotors flared, snow washed into the air from the street below.

Turville heard a whoosh, and a streak of flame lifted off from the woods, followed by another. He stared in disbelief, heart thumping rapidly.

Two more streams of smoke and flame appeared from the woods on the opposite side of the town. All of them sped into the sky toward the slowly moving helicopters.

Turville shouted, "They're firing at the helicopters. Get down! Get down!" He ran for the two girls, shouting. Tall Girl screamed, and Turville hauled both girls to the ground.

A moment later, both helicopters exploded and crashed to the street, spewing fire and metal parts all over the street. A metal fragment struck the building above Turville's head with a loud bang, and the street flooded with the acrid smell of burning plastic and explosives. Both of the girls screamed now, the short one grabbing him by the arm so hard it hurt.

Turville looked Short Girl in the eyes and grasped her other arm. "Get inside. Now."

He had trouble forming the words and realized at the rush of copper-tasting blood that he'd bitten his own tongue.

She nodded, eyes wide, face twisted in obvious terror; despite the fear, she grabbed her friend by the arm and hauled her toward the drug store entrance. Good.

The men in the two fire-teams had scattered around the intersection, taking cover behind various vehicles.

Turville ran toward the wreckage, but it was too hot to approach. No way anyone survived.

At that moment, he heard a pop, then another one. A cloud of snow scattered at his feet. A bullet. He felt a moment of sheer panic.

He looked around frantically and then shouted, "Somebody's shooting at us!" He ran for the drugstore, yelling to his team, "Come on!" More shots followed as they ran.

They got into the building as quickly as they could. The LT was shouting into the satellite phone, "They're shooting at us, I need backup now! We don't have any weapons!"

The two girls had crowded near the counter along with another terrified shopper.

Nowell looked over at Turville. "We got to get out of here before those assholes come down here."

Turville replied, "How? You know how to hot-wire a car?"

Short Girl interrupted him. "You can take my truck."

Turville looked at her. She'd taken her cap off, and her brown hair quivered a little from the static. Tiny green stones in her ears matched the green eyes that looked at him as she held out a set of keys.

"You sure?"

"Yes! You probably saved us out there—least I can do. I'll write down my number." She grabbed a napkin, scribbled her phone number on it, then pointed to where her car was parked across the street, an old Ford F-150 truck. Turville glanced at the note: Rebecca Mays, 413-9845—then stuffed it in his pocket.

"Sir," Turville said, tapping the Lieutenant on the arm.

"Yeah," the LT replied, covering the phone handset with his hand.

"I got us wheels; let's go."

Lieutenant Blake stared at him for about three endless seconds, then nodded and said, "Do it. Move out, men."

The squad ran out of the building. Across the street, the truck was parked, leaning on a snow bank. Turville jumped into the driver's seat, the Lieutenant next to him. The rest of the men piled into the bed of the truck.

"Get us out of here, Turville."

As if to punctuate the words, bullets slammed into the front of the truck with loud, popping cracks. Somebody in the back howled in pain.

"Where is that shooting coming from?"

"I don't know, sir. The tree line?"

A moment later, the engine roared to life and the radio turned on full blast. A newscaster blathering on about separatists in California. Turville put the truck in gear, switched off the radio, and raced out of town.

TWO

New York Times, March 19
VIOLENCE FLARES IN PHILADELPHIA PROTESTS
By Marcus Jennsen

Philadelphia, PA – More than 850 protestors were arrested in Pennsylvania Tuesday after protests there flared into violence. Three police officers were injured in the melee early in the morning after police attempted to eject protestors from the city center. Pennsylvania Governor Randall Abrams called for calm in a statement, further detailing the activation of the state National Guard to quell the protests that have continued in three cities since the beginning of March.

S H E no longer knew how long she had been in the cell.

It was a tiny cage, not much bigger than the bathroom in the apartment she could barely remember. This was nothing like that bathroom. In fact, it was nothing like anything she'd ever imagined, even in her darkest nightmares.

The walls received lackluster illumination from the single fluorescent bulb wrapped in a steel cage in the center of the ceiling. The walls were steel, the floor bare, polished concrete. A paper-thin mattress covered a cold shelf bolted to the wall. Merely twelve inches from what passed for a bed was a toilet and sink—one piece and seat-less.

A camera, built into the angle where one corner met the ceiling, offered no privacy. A thick door with a one-inch high slot faced the toilet and occasionally admitted food through a cramped, slotted portal.

The cell was cold most of the time, but when it wasn't, it was an oven. The heat lasted about a week, and despite the camera she'd stripped to nearly nothing in an effort to keep the conditions tolerable. By the end of it, the thin mattress, stained with streaks of salt, reeked of sweat.

Of course, that was just one more odor in a symphony of malodorous sensations that assaulted her from the first day she'd been in the cell. She remembered the thin, reedy pitch of antiseptic in the hall outside her cell. On entering the cell, she'd been overcome by the thick tones of old urine. Her predecessor, whoever he'd been and wherever he had gone, had been none too careful in his aim at the bowl. Nor had the stage been cleared before her arrival. An old stain of vomit near the sink gave of a cloying stench that resisted her efforts at scrubbing for days.

For the first few days in the cell, she'd raged, cajoled, and begged whenever that slot opened. When would she be allowed to see a lawyer? To call someone? What was happening outside? Would anyone talk to her?

No answers came through the tiny slot.

In the mornings—at least she assumed it was morning, because the light in the ceiling turned on—she would strip out of the prisoners' jumpsuit and wash herself in the sink above the toilet. Shivering with cold, she palmed the water off her body and then dressed. And waited.

The toilet had presented a problem. She was an inherently private person. The idea of using that filthy device to see to her needs under the watchful eyes of that camera made her want to vomit. She tried different arrangements with the prison jumpsuit to retain some privacy, some shred of dignity, but in the end there seemed to be little she could do. Waiting for so long to void her bladder caused her so much pain she'd had no choice but to give in.

Bastards.

She'd never been charged with a crime. She'd never even been told why they had detained her, though that was easy enough to deduce. No one asked any questions. They were tearing her apart without even the courtesy of telling her anything.

Sometime in the second week, she counted the fasteners in the steel walls. Each wall had two rows of notch-less bolts, extending from floor to ceiling, with a bolt spaced every six inches, fifteen per column.

Sometimes she crouched down beside the slot in the door and waited for it to open, just to get a glimpse of what was outside.

There was nothing.

She begged for something—anything—to read. Then, during her third week in the tiny cell, something followed the food tray into the room and thumped to the floor. A book!

She pounced on the tiny book. It was a Bible.

She was not religious. Other than the occasional wedding or funeral, she'd barely ever entered a church in her life. Her father and mother had never discussed religion much; when they had, it was to share their doubts and lack of understanding of religion. All the same, the book was her salvation.

She read it from the beginning. Her exposure to this volume had consisted of a single introduction to world religions class at Harvard long ago. To her, "people of the book"were the Crusaders. They were the Inquisition, the Ku Klux Klan, the religious zealots who denied science and evolution and a woman's right to her own body. They were the suicide bombers and killers who fought wars over their interpretation of scripture.

All the same, the book was nothing more and nothing less than a life preserver. Because in the silence of empty days and absolute solitude, there was nothing else. The choice between reading someone else's religion and insanity was little real choice at all.

Then one day she heard her father's voice. It sounded as clear as if he was standing in the room, his gruff southern accent more real to her than the cell.

He said, "I'm sorry, kiddo."

She wept.

The next night, as she lay in the absolute darkness and silence, she called out to him, again and again. Not just to her father, but to her long dead mother, to her old life.

No one answered.

Occasionally, she would hear noises. The sound of footsteps outside the cell door, or a cry in the night. But all too often, nothing at all. By her sixth week of isolation, she would sit for hours, eyes unfocused, mouth slack, unable to remember her father's name or where she had gone to school or anything before the cell that comprised her entire reality and the book that she had now read three times all the way through.

Sometimes, when she sat unfocused and staring, she could feel the floor vibrate. Not an earthquake vibration—she'd been through that a few times when visiting California during the life she could barely remember before the cell. This seemed more like the vibration of a heavy truck passing a building. But there was no sound. Nothing to hint at the cause of the occasional tremor.

Heat came into the cell by way of a one-inch wide grate in the ceiling. Sometimes the air, forcing itself into the cell through that narrow slot, hissed so loudly that she couldn't sleep. It sounded like the aspiration of a dying man, constricted and false in a way she couldn't pin down.

One night, she screamed and couldn't stop. She tore the mattress off the shelf, convinced that underneath it she would find snakes.

She stopped washing herself in the mornings. She slept until she awoke, then often fell asleep again moments later. Days and nights ran together, her thoughts dwelling on the book and its words of plagues and murder and death, its words of love and fear and rage. Sometimes she stared at the veins in her wrist and tried to figure out how to slice them open. Maybe then, someone would take her out of the cell.

She ate little, though meals continued to arrive through the slot. Each day, she pushed her tray back through, and it would later be replaced. Her jumpsuit seemed bigger than it should, but she couldn't remember how well it had fit the first time she put it on.

Then one day something else came through the slot, something so miraculous and frightening that she simply stared at it, her entire body shaking, in fear that it would disappear like the mirages of her mother and father.

A folded sheet from a newspaper lay just inside her door.

Trembling, she approached it and snatched it away from the door. She unfolded it, her eyes focusing on the photograph of her father. She remembered the photo—it had been taken when he'd testified in Congress... last year? Last century? She didn't know; time no longer had any meaning. But the headline did. Her eyes took in the words, but her brain would not accept them. Her heart could not accept them.

Then the meaning of the scrambled words became clear. Her father had been convicted of treason. She screamed and threw herself at the door until she was bloody.

ॐ

The day after the offending headline arrived through the slot, she lay in wait.

She heard the steps first and then the jangle of keys. Finally, the footsteps came to a halt outside her cell, followed by a metallic report, and with a rasp the slot slid open.

"Please," she said through the slot. "I have to talk to somebody. Anybody."

The first human voice she'd heard in weeks responded.

"Shut up in there."

༄

The clank of the outside door down the hall woke Valerie Murphy. She lay flat on the shelf that passed for a bed, staring up at the dirty ceiling.

She heard two sets of footsteps. That was unusual. The first sounded familiar: a jangle of keys, a slow limp. A guard. She didn't know which side he favored. She had heard but never seen her guards. This wasn't the one who had told her to shut up when she'd been losing her mind.

The second set of footsteps was harder to make out. They sounded as if they came from slippered or bare feet. Her sense of hearing had grown acute. At any given time, she could make out the creaks of the building, people walking in the halls—even traffic sometimes, although she didn't know where she was located.

The steps came closer, so she stood. She didn't know why—they'd never come through the door before. All the same, she stood and tried to arrange her matted, filthy hair. This was too unusual. They were coming only a couple of hours after a meal, and this time there were two of them. What could it mean?

A moment later there was a loud buzz and the door opened.

She stared. Her guard, whom she had heard day after day delivering meals to her, was short, fat, and ugly. Pretty much what she'd expected. He wore a gray uniform with a US Department of Justice patch on the shoulder. Department of Justice. Now there was a laugh.

Beside him stood someone unexpected, wearing nothing but prison overalls just as she wore. Al Clark, former congressman and, briefly, Secretary of State of West Virginia. Her old boss. Al didn't look so hot either. His hair had grown long, hanging dirty near his shoulders. She looked at him, wondering if she was hallucinating again.

"Al?"

"Valerie. It's me."

Her eyes watered, and she reached for him. They embraced, but the touch of another human being was too intense to bear. She backed off quickly.

"All right there, come on," the guard said. Not friendly.

"Where are we going?"

The officer didn't answer, but Clark spoke.

"We're getting you out of here, Valerie."

She couldn't quite place the words. Getting her out of here. What did that mean? Did it mean they were going to release her? Release her for what? She didn't know.

The guard walked away and they followed.

Down the hall, the guard opened another set of locked doors. A man and a woman in dark suits stood at the end of the hall. The diminutive woman offered a stark contrast to the tall, blonde, athletic man next to her.

"Ms. Murphy, come in here, please."

The woman indicated the room to the left.

Valerie looked in. Like the rest of the prison, it was drab, with a bare table, colorless floor, and cracked ceiling. But this room was different: it had a window.

She stepped in, disbelieving, walked past the table straight to the window and looked outside. She was stunned by what she saw, because she recognized it. Outside, far below, a crowded street was heavy with traffic, a riot of color and sound.

My God. She was still in Washington. This was the FBI headquarters. She couldn't be anywhere else. Why in God's name had she been held here all this time? She'd had no idea the FBI even had isolation cells in their headquarters. When she'd first been taken prisoner, she'd been carried in the back of a closed van for hours before being taken to a cell. That had been nothing more than a sham.

She turned back to face the others. They were all still standing.

"What is this?" she asked.

"Please have a seat, ma'am," the man in the suit said. His short hair and athletic build seemed almost fake to Valerie. He was nothing more than a mannequin in a suit. A plastic Ken doll that probably went out and played football on the weekends or went boating up the Potomac with an equally plastic Barbie doll. His Barbie doll would smile and vote Republican and probably went to church every Sunday.

All the same. ma'am, he'd said. No one had spoken to her with courtesy in a long time. She sat, folded her hands in her lap and waited.

"My name is Richard Higgins. I'm a special prosecutor for the Department of Justice. This is my assistant."

Valerie didn't respond.

"Last month I was given the task of investigating the charges of terrorism against you. You'll be happy to hear that you've been cleared. There won't be any grand jury, and no trial. I expect that within the hour you will be free to go."

Valerie was afraid to respond.

"However, we need to talk to you about a couple of things first."

"What things?"

The prosecutor and his assistant looked at each other for a moment, then at Clark. The assistant didn't seem plastic. In fact, she seemed anything but. The woman had deep lines in the creases of her eyes and radiated discomfiture. Valerie studied her and guessed that this woman, at least, had no desire to be here at all. Well, that made two of them.

"We're prepared to release you with no charges—nothing on your record—provided you remain silent about anything that has occurred since you've been here."

"I don't understand."

Higgins spoke. "It seems that some pressure has been brought to bear. I don't know who, but someone from the military had been pushing to have you released. I've been trying to complete my investigation as quickly as possible so you wouldn't be held any longer than necessary. That's the first issue. The second is that under West Virginia's constitution, the legislature is free to appoint the governor of their choice should the governor die. That new governor is Mr. Clark here."

Stunned, Valerie looked at Clark.

"You're kidding me."

"Apparently not. I don't know any more than you do about this; that's what they've told me."

"So you're going to go from being prisoner to being governor."

"It could be worse."

She smiled a bitter smile. "It certainly could. Why should I sign this piece of paper?"

"Because I need you, Valerie. I need you to come with me. I can't do this alone."

"What about my father?"

Clark looked over at the prosecutor. Higgins squirmed, and his face darkened a little. "I'm not sure..." He trailed off.

"What aren't you sure about?" Clark asked.

"I'm not sure I'm the person who should deliver this news."

Valerie's eyes watered. "Whatever news you have, it can't be any worse than what I'm afraid of, so you might as well just tell me."

"All right. General Murphy was tried for treason and executed."

She gasped. "But it's only been three months. What about the appeals?"

"I'm afraid that process went very quickly, ma'am. As I understood it, the General waived his right to an appeal. Again, he was executed, just a few days ago. I'm very sorry to give this news to you."

Valerie closed her eyes. Her father was dead. Executed. She saw his face as she had last seen him, right before Christmas. Smiling a bitter smile, knowing that at any moment the fighting might erupt. He'd already been dead by then; he just didn't know it.

"How?" she asked.

"What do you mean?"

"How was he executed?"

The prosecutor looked even more uncomfortable. "By lethal injection, ma'am. My understanding is that it was very quick. He probably didn't feel anything."

Abruptly, Valerie lurched out her seat and vomited the contents of her breakfast on the floor, leaving an acrid stink in the room. Clark reached for her, but she jerked away. She didn't want to be touched. Her father was dead, and there was nothing she could do about it.

"And what if I say no? That I won't sign your paper?"

Higgins looked at his assistant, his face disturbed, and said, "We'll continue to hold you indefinitely. As you know, West Virginia is in a state of insurrection. Accordingly, President Price suspended habeas corpus for all residents of the state effective January first. If you don't agree to remain silent, we'll make sure you never have the opportunity to talk." Higgins paused, distaste for his task clear on his face. "I never said that, but it's the bottom line."

"Valerie," Clark said. "Come with me. There's still good we can do. You can't make a decision like that—not after just hearing about your father. You'll need time."

She looked at him and said, "Time for what? I've known for three months that he was a dead man. It was just a question of when and how. I just wish he had died in combat. He would have been happy then."

Clark closed his eyes and said, "I understand."

"All right, then. Where do I sign?"

Higgins opened his briefcase and passed across a sheet of paper.

She scanned the lines. They were very simple, promising not to discuss the conditions of her imprisonment and waiving her right to sue the government. Who cared? What would be the point?

She signed the paper. She was free, but what did that mean? Could freedom bring her family back? Would freedom bring her any safety? Or just more risk?

Did it really matter if it did?

"Let's get out of here."

છ

Brigadier General Tom Murphy stood in the sunlight near the helicopter pad on the roof of the governor's mansion, chilled by the arctic wind and trying to absorb a little sunlight to offset it.

Though his temples had gone grey in the last year, Tom still looked young. His narrow face was clean-shaven, and he had a tendency to walk around with a half-smile that he knew sometimes seemed inappropriate for a senior military officer. That was fine with him: the smile disarmed people in a way he never quite understood. It made him trusted by subordinates and superiors alike. He might not understand the psychology of it, but he certainly understood the practical effect.

He'd spent all too many days trying to maintain that half-smile. In the last few weeks it hadn't felt appropriate at all. Behind the smile, he'd been torn by self-doubt and grief for his brother. Behind the smile, he'd been apprehensive that despite the quick conclusion of the brief war in West Virginia, the roots of the conflict had only been aggravated. And, despite everything he'd done, the situation continued to deteriorate.

The transport helicopter approached, the slapping rhythm of its rotary wings rattling the windows on the rooftop. It settled into its position on the roof, blowing a dusting of snow into the air, and the rotors began to slow.

Tom ran toward the chopper, followed by his aide-de-camp. Lieutenant Thrasher was a solid officer who had received high marks for his leadership during the ground invasion into West Virginia. A tour as a dog-robber to a general was a solid ticket punched for an officer with a promising career ahead of him, and Thrasher had jumped at the chance.

The side door to the chopper opened, and a crew chief in an olive-drab flight suit stepped out and then reached in to help the passengers disembark.

Tom almost stumbled when he saw his niece—Valerie had always been thin, but now she looked emaciated, her clothes ill-fitting, hair tangled. Her big eyes darted around like a hunted animal. Tom took her hand, walked her away from the chopper, and then turned to hug her.

She held on like he was a lifeline, and he was shocked by how much she had shrunken. She couldn't weigh more than a hundred pounds.

Behind her, Lieutenant Thrasher approached with the new governor, Al Clark. Clark didn't look much better than Valerie, though at least he seemed well fed. His suit was rumpled, and his hair hung below his collar. Tom released his niece and held out his hand. Clark gripped it.

"Welcome, sir," Tom said to the former congressman. "Let's get inside out of the cold."

Clark nodded, and the four of them entered the building.

"We're right in here," Lieutenant Thrasher said, leading the other three into what was now Al Clark's office. The smell of fresh paint was still strong in the large room.

A standard-issue government oak desk had replaced the one Frank Slagter had used as governor. There was no cleaning the blood out of the cracks and grooves of the desk, and Tom ordered it burned after the coroner completed his inquest. The wall behind the desk gleamed with fresh paint, and the carpet was brand new. He doubted Clark realized his predecessor had shot himself in this very room, and he supposed Clark didn't need to know.

"Can I get you coffee? Tea?" the lieutenant asked as he led them to a table next to a window overlooking downtown Charleston. Outside, they could see the rubble of the Byrd Federal Building, which had been bombed by terrorists six months before. It had been joined by rubble from several other buildings destroyed by cruise missiles during the brief war in January. Snow blanketed the ruins, softening the destruction a little, but it was still unmistakably a war zone.

It was hardly the beautiful city Tom had first visited a decade ago. But then again, it wasn't even the same country as it had been ten years ago. Everything had changed, too fast, and much of it for the worse.

Valerie and Clark both asked for coffee, and the lieutenant exited the room.

Tom sat down in one of the chairs and waved for them to sit as well. Valerie did, but Clark stood, looking out the window for almost a full minute. Finally he turned, and Tom could see in his eyes the same grief he himself felt every time he looked out.

Tom studied both of them. They were pale, and none too healthy. Valerie had shrunken in more ways than one: her eyes kept darting around the room nervously, and her hands lay flat against her skirt. She sat hunched over, shoulders bowed and head down. Overall, she gave the impression that at any moment she might get up and run. None of the confidence he'd learned to expect from her was evident.

"Have you been treated well?" Tom asked.

She just shrugged.

Clark looked grim as he answered. "As well as could be supposed. We've both been in solitary confinement for most of the last three months. No contact with anyone, at all. To be honest with you, all the changes... everything is a little overwhelming right now."

"I understand, I think," Tom said. "I appreciate you agreeing to come in on the chopper. I sent it as soon as I learned you were being released."

"Thank you, said Valerie. "I don't know where I would have gone if you hadn't sent it. I don't even know what happened to my apartment, my things."

"I hope I can relieve you on that score at least. Your dad asked me to take care of that; your rent was taken care of and the lease closed out. All your things are here in Charleston. For now, at least, you've got a room here at the governor's mansion until you find a place to live."

"Thank you."

Tom had to strain to hear her almost whispered words.

"Tell me a little more about the situation, General," Clark said.

Tom looked at his niece and sighed. His concern for Valerie and his desire to make this a personal reunion was outweighed by duty and the need to brief them on what had been happening in the state. But he didn't have to like it. He started to reply and was interrupted by the return of Lieutenant Thrasher, bearing coffee service on a tray.

Thrasher placed the tray on the table between them, then poured three cups of coffee. "I'm afraid we don't have any actual cream here, just the powdered stuff. I'll check with the house staff to get that corrected."

"Thank you, Lieutenant."

Valerie cradled the mug in her hands, absorbing the warmth, and seemed to savor the steam from the coffee. The action was so... normal, Tom could almost forget she'd just spent three months in solitary confinement. Thrasher took an unobtrusive position standing against the wall.

"Well," Tom said. "Here's the situation. I know the two of you were arrested the day hostilities began, so I'll walk you through it. Essentially, we had a three-day ground war here. The state National Guard put up a ferocious fight, but they were overwhelmed. On the third day, Governor Slagter shot himself, and I accepted your father's surrender, Valerie."

Tension tightened Valerie's expression. "Personally?"

Tom nodded very slowly. "Yes. I didn't think—well, let's just say I thought it would be best all around if it were he and I. He was taken into custody, and I suppose you know by now the results of that."

Tom blinked as his eyes watered involuntarily. The two people in front of him were momentarily superimposed by a vision of his brother's execution. The brother who had been his friend and his hero.

"Valerie, for what it's worth, I want you to know his last thoughts were of you. He… he asked me to look out for you, find out where you were being held and get you free. I've been doing everything I could to do just that."

She stared at him, her expression seeming to shift between grief and anger. He wasn't sure what was going through her thoughts, and it worried him.

"Go on," Clark said.

"Once we formally accepted the Guard's surrender, most of the federal troops were pulled out. I was appointed military governor, with the one reinforced brigade left behind. I've been working to get things back up and running ever since. I can't even begin to tell you what a challenge it's been.

"I'll be frank. West Virginia is bankrupt. Much of the state has gone through this winter with no power, minimal phone lines, and no services. Schools are still closed in a lot of counties because there is no money to pay the teachers and staff and no heat in the school buildings. The state police are only up to half the manning they should have, and that's pretty shaky. The three National Guard brigades are currently in custody here in Charleston, but all of their officers have been discharged, so we're not really in a position to put them to use any time soon."

Clark nodded, taking in the information. Tom only knew the former congressman by reputation—the two had never met before now. But Ken had always spoken very highly of him. How had the three months of imprisonment affected him? Would he be effective as governor? God only knew they needed a strong hand at the helm, but that hand had to be a civilian's.

"How is the economy?" Clark asked.

"It's a shamble," Tom replied. "We've had difficulty getting basic services back in place, particularly power. Business is still slow, and jobs are scarce. It's much worse in the cities; at least in the rural areas people are more prepared to deal with long periods without work. We've had riots in Charleston, and the mood is sometimes very ugly. Plus, half the legislature is still absorbed in the whole independence issue. It took me two months just to get a quorum to meet in the State House. As I'm sure you can imagine, the first order of business was to elect a new governor. The last thing I wanted was to be a long-standing military governor. You got stuck with the job."

"That must have created some difficulty in Washington."

Tom gave a wry smile. "You could say that. There were howls from the Justice Department and Homeland Security in particular. The media has been reporting dutifully every day on the fact that no charges had been pressed against the two of you. That's one of the reasons I flew you out here in a military transport. If you'd flown commercial, you'd have never made it through the cordon of reporters."

"I can only imagine," Clark said.

"So, that's the situation. To the extent we can, we've been running relief supplies all over the state. Food, water, generators. And that brings us to this morning. One of my supply columns was attacked by some locals claiming to be militia. They managed to make off with both weapons and supplies and shot down two helicopters. I don't know where they got surface-to-air missiles, but they have them."

"Dear Lord," Clark said. "Do you know who they are? Where did this happen?"

"No idea who they are. It happened in Whitesville—that's in Boone County, not too far south of here, on the Coal River. We don't know whether we're at risk of a wider insurgency or if they're just some disgruntled locals—and we have to assume the worst."

He watched Clark, gauging his reaction. He knew Clark had voted against the independence referendum last fall. At the same time, the then congressman had returned to Charleston to accept the position of Secretary of State in the briefly independent West Virginia. Where did his loyalties lie?

Clark's face betrayed nothing. "Who is investigating?"

"My provost marshal and the Criminal Investigative Division. You'll meet him later on. Unfortunately, we've got some serious gaps in the state police and military department, and frankly I don't trust the acting Secretary."

"Who is that?"

"Asa Hatfield. Do you know him?"

Clark shook his head. "We've met once or twice, that's it. I seem to remember he's a bit of a blowhard. I don't even know which way he went on independence."

"Nobody does—he plays his cards close to the vest. If you're up to recommendations from me, one of my first is that you need someone you can trust on that job, and I don't think he's it."

"I'll have to think about it," Clark said. "If I remember correctly, Hatfield's brother was Logan County sheriff, one of the brigade commanders in the Guard. Any idea what happened to him?"

"Captured. He's in Kansas, awaiting his court-martial."

"That can't make his brother happy."

"No, it certainly doesn't. He's one you want to keep an eye on."

There was a pause. Tom watched his niece, who had remained silent through most of the meeting.

"All right, what happens next?" Clark said finally.

Tom replied. "Tomorrow morning, the chief justice of the State Supreme Court will swear you in as governor. At the same time, I'll formally step down as military governor of West Virginia. I'll retain my status as an advisor and overall commander of the military here. If this were a foreign deployment, we'd negotiate a status of forces agreement, so we could clearly define responsibilities and accountability. I suggest we proceed as if that were the case.

"I've called for a cabinet meeting immediately after your inauguration, so you can meet your department heads. From there, it's up to you. I'll advise you and offer all the resources I can. The bottom line is, we've got to get this state up and running again, and quickly. As bad as things are, I'm very worried they could worsen. We're in a race against time."

As he spoke, Tom watched Valerie. Her face was closed, expressionless, and the more he watched her, the more uncomfortable he became.

"For now, I'll ask Lieutenant Thrasher to show you to your rooms so you can get cleaned up. I'll put him at your disposal for the next couple of days if you need anything at all. He can make arrangements for haircuts, clothes, whatever you need."

"Thank you, General."

Tom stood. "Governor, we've never known each other, but I know you were friends with my brother. I'd be honored if you'd just call me Tom."

Clark smiled. "Tom, then. Thank you."

Valerie stood without a word, and Lieutenant Thrasher said, "If you'll come this way, I'll show where you are staying."

The two started to follow the young Lieutenant; then Valerie stopped and turned back. Her face showed the first expression he'd seen since she'd stepped from the helicopter: grief etched in every line.

"Uncle Tom, you were the only person my dad listened to. Why couldn't you stop him?"

Tom flinched, and his half-smile slipped into a grimace. "Valerie, I don't think anyone could have changed Ken's mind about this. I tried. He was determined."

"I know," she whispered.

Tom Murphy was ten years younger than his brother had been, only ten years older than his niece. Looking at her now, he saw the kid he'd known twenty years ago: composed, serious, but fragile. She'd soon be thirty, and in just three years she'd lost her entire family—her brother and father in the last six months.

"Valerie, I can never replace your dad, but if you ever need someone to talk to, you know where to find me. I promised him I'd do whatever I could to take care of you."

She shrugged. "Sure. Whatever." Then she turned away.

Tom watched her go, trying to keep a grip on his emotions.

Ken, why didn't you appeal? Why did you go so meekly to your death? Those kinds of questions didn't lead anywhere. But Valerie was as wounded as any soldier he'd ever seen. Alongside his grief, he felt a flash of resentment for his older brother, who had left behind such a catastrophic mess for Tom to clean up.

Sure. Whatever.

He checked his watch. Ten minutes. He never had enough time these days. He left the room and walked back to the Operations Center.

Colonel Bonner was already there to meet him, towering over the battle captains as he stalked back and forth across the room, anger writ large on his face.

As Tom entered, the operations officer called out, "Attention!" The officers in the room jumped to their feet.

"As you were," Tom said. "Standing order: from now on, none of that when I come in. We may be going back into a war footing, and you've got more important things to do. Colonel Bonner? Is Colonel Sanchez here yet?"

Bonner shook his head. "He sent his XO, sir. Major Avedis, here." He pointed to a young major standing behind him, almost as tall as he was.

A flash of rage went through Tom, and he cursed. "Major, go on in the conference room there we'll be right in."

"Yes, sir."

Major Avedis stepped away, entering the conference room off the main operations center.

Tom strode over to Bonner and spoke in low tones. "Rick, what was Sanchez's excuse this time?"

Bonner's face twisted into a frown. "He says he's working an operation, sir."

"Not anymore," Tom said. "I'm relieving him."

Bonner's eyes widened. "You sure you want to do that, sir?"

Tom had known Rick Bonner for going on twenty years; his hesitation made Tom slow down and explain himself.

"Rick," he said, "I may have only had this star on my collar for a month, but I'll be damned if I'll have one of my battalion commanders ignore a direct order to report here. Who does he think he is? This is the second time! We've got what may be a full-blown insurgency blowing up in our face right now, and my Military Intelligence commander is off monitoring an operation? What the hell we do we have battle captains for?"

Colonel Bonner nodded. "I know, sir, and for what it's worth, I agree. Sanchez is a serious liability if we're actually going back on a war footing. But he's got a lot of friends in high places, General. You won't do yourself any favors with this one."

Tom shrugged. "I'll live. What do you know about his XO?"

Colonel Bonner knew when to stop pressing. He took the switch without pause. "Major Cory Avedis. Bowling Green '09. He's an up and comer: already made the Lieutenant Colonel's list—way too young for it. Two years in counterinsurgency as an advisor in Indonesia, followed by a stint as aide-de-camp to General Wells. He's been put in for a Silver Star from the war in January, but I don't know all the details behind that."

Tom grunted. "Okay, he'll do for now."

Without another word, he turned and walked into the conference room. Major Avedis jumped to his feet when he came in.

"Sir."

"Have a seat, Major. As of about five minutes ago, Colonel Sanchez is getting a transfer. You're going to be in command of the battalion for a while."

Tom thought if had whipped out a baseball bat and hit Major Avedis over the head, the major wouldn't have looked more startled.

"All right," Tom said. "What do we have?"

"Not much more information, sir," Colonel Bonner replied. "Whoever it was, they've got mucho balls. They could have taken out that squad easy and made off with the trucks. Instead, they waited, lured out the choppers, and took those out."

Tom nodded. "What does that tell us, Major?"

Avedis replied, "They wanted to make a statement, loud and clear. I'd guess by tonight they'll put out a press release or stick something up on the net. They want people to know that we're not invulnerable. It also says they've got significant planning capability. If I had to guess, I'd say whoever's running the show is former military."

"Agreed," Tom said. "Who is the audience for the message, though?"

Bonner looked thoughtful as Avedis replied. "It depends on their objective, sir, but I'd say almost certainly civilians. If they're following classic insurgent tactics, we'll see more attacks against our soft-points and against anyone who works with us."

"Right," Tom said. "Which raises the next question—and which is going to be your number one concern, Major."

"Yes, sir?"

"Someone in our command structure tipped them off. I'm guessing it was someone in the cabinet—some of those folks are pissed West Virginia lost the war. CID's going to be investigating from the inside, but your job is to work with them as you start collecting intelligence about the enemy. I want to know who these people are, yesterday. And I want to know who they're talking to on the inside."

"Yes, sir."

Tom looked at the young major, trying to gauge his ability to take on the intelligence battalion. He had the confidence, for sure. Bonner didn't hand out compliments, but he had spoken highly of Avedis, which spoke volumes. Well, if he were good enough for this, he'd already have some thoughts in mind and should be more than familiar with the capabilities of his unit.

"What's your plan?" Tom said.

Avedis responded without hesitating. "First thing is, we need to identify links. I'll want to put someone on my team together with CID so we can run down everybody who knew where that relief column was going to be and when. Any ideas how many people that might have been, sir?"

Tom looked over at Colonel Bonner.

Bonner shook his head. "Too many. Everyone on our team in the headquarters of course, plus the battalion command and supply folks. The cabinet members themselves, plus whoever they might have told. State police, what's left of 'em."

Avedis nodded. "That's what I thought. I'm assuming we're going to shift to a higher alert footing, in terms of who knows about operations? Need to know?"

"That's right."

"We run down that list of people who knew or might have known where the column was going. Run their credit reports, find out who they're related to, especially if they're from that part of the state. Political donations, public records. CID would have to do the bulk of that, or Homeland Security, I'm not sure which makes the most sense.

"While that's going on, we've been putting together a team on our side that's from the region—mostly Kentucky, some from West Virginia. They'll go undercover as much as they can here in Charleston and in the other cities. Where we'll have trouble is in the little towns. The attack was in Whitesville? Population there's about a thousand. They'll know any strangers. We'll be better off recruiting locals for information there."

"Agreed," Tom said.

"What I'd like to do, sir, is put together a good network. Not just in that area but across the entire state. Recruit folks in every town who can pass us information. It'll cost some money."

Tom sat back. Okay, the kid was thinking. That was the most important part. "Okay, do it. Let me worry about the money. Are you going to have any problems within the battalion? With you taking over command? It won't be permanent, but it might take a few weeks before we have a light Colonel who can take the slot."

Avedis nodded. "Yes, sir, I think I might, to be honest. Major Blake Harwood; he's the S3 and is senior to me by date of rank."

"All right," Tom answered, "I'll take care of Major Harwood."

"Thank you, sir."

A knock at the door interrupted him.

"Come!" Tom called.

The door opened, and the watch officer stuck his head inside.

"General, sorry to interrupt, but we just a got a report I thought you should know about right away."

"What is it?"

"Sir, call came in from the State Police as a heads up. The Boone County sheriff was found dead about an hour ago. Murdered."

Colonel Bonner let loose a long, slow whistle, and Tom sighed.

"Any details?"

"Yes, sir, that's why they called us. Whoever did it, they were petty thorough, tore his place apart. Tore him apart, too; at least twenty gunshot wounds. Machine gun, maybe. They left a note. Here's the fax from the State Police."

He handed a sheet of paper over. Tom lifted it to read, then passed it to Bonner, shaking his head. The note confirmed his worst fears.

It contained only one word, hand written in large block letters:

COLLABORATOR

THREE

New York Times, March 22
DEATH TOLL RISES IN AMTRAK DERAILMENT; INVESTIGATORS POINT TO DOMESTIC TERRORISTS
By Marcus Jennsen
Washington, DC – The Department of Homeland Security announced Friday it is opening an investigation into domestic terrorists investigators believe may have been responsible for the March 14th derailment of an Amtrak Accela train just south of Newark, New Jersey. Officials announced last night that the death toll in the accident is now more than 250 people, with hundreds more injured.

W HEN Joe Blankenship was growing up, the steep-roofed cabin had nestled in a clearing halfway up the slope of the mountain, surrounded by lush forest. The logs had settled over the decades, causing cracks to form in the mortar, which had, in turn, been patched several times over the years. A red-painted door with eight glass panes opened onto a view of the creek. The paint, much like the rest of the cabin, seemed to fight decades of atrophy and weathering, arrested occasionally by the periodic visits of Blankenship's father, and his father before him.

Joe's father, Lloyd Blankenship, had often brought him here, miles away from the nearest town. The trips decreased in frequency as his father grew both older and weary of disappointment in his only son. Lloyd was a loving man, but he was neither demonstrative nor affectionate. Blankenship had always turned to his mother for understanding, for affection. Later she became the buffer between them. His mother was probably the only thing that made it possible for Joe to continue a relationship with his father at all.

Blankenship still remembered the first time he'd brought down a buck: the flash of movement in the woods, the white tail. While his father looked on, he'd brought the rifle to bear, let out his breath, took his time, and gently, gently squeezed. Though he'd practiced, fired hundreds of rounds at mock targets under his father's careful eye, the recoil still shocked him. It knocked him back, right out of the blind, and he fell with a grunt.

His father laughed until tears ran down his face, but still lifted him to his feet, put his hand on the boy's shoulder, and then they went to claim his kill.

Later, as an adult, Joe had brought his love here, when she needed a place to get away from her own father. They'd been teenagers then, and life was difficult, often frightening, but they'd loved each other.

The cabin had been part of the thread of his life for decades.

Looking out the slightly warped window now, instead of rich forest he saw a moonscape. The mountain had been stripped, but Blankenship had refused to sell; he was the only holdout. A tiny island with two trees, the cabin and a few bushes surrounded by the devastated, bleeding earth.

It was still his. The only thing that was his. Mandy was dead and gone. Even the shock of her death had been wiped out of the consciousness of all but her closest family by the fighting and devastation that followed it. What was the death of one lovely young woman in the face of a civil war that claimed thousands of lives?

It was everything. It was nothing.

It was all he had.

Her picture sat on the desk in front of him. He leaned forward until his face was mere inches from her photo, and he studied her eyes. He'd never been a religious man, but he knew she was out there. And the one question he kept asking himself over and over was: would she approve? Would she support what he planned, or abhor it?

She was a good Christian. Perhaps she'd argue that he should turn the other cheek and let them get away with her murder. Or perhaps she'd say his greater responsibility was to defend his state, the freedom of his people. To follow through with what they'd all started a year before with a peaceful demonstration protesting the loss of jobs.

He didn't know. He'd begged for answers. He'd prayed for days at a time—he, a man who hadn't prayed in years. He received no answers, no burning bush, and no revelations. Only silence.

It was time to put the photo away. He would take it out again when he was done. For now, it was time to move forward. He would, for a time at least, close the door to the past, close the door to his love, his heart, and his life. He no longer had room for such things.

Outside, a pickup truck with Virginia plates pulled up the gravel driveway and came to a stop. Joe's guests from Baughman Settlement had arrived. He stood, slowly, gave a last glance at Mandy's photo, then walked to the door and opened it.

The driver of the truck was a young man in black slacks, white shirt and tie. He didn't really matter, Joe thought. Foot soldier. The passenger, however, was something else. The Reverend Roland Channing was a large man, built with powerful shoulders and arms, dressed in jeans and a flannel shirt and coat. He had a warm, round face, an easy smile with startling blue eyes and thinning blonde hair. He approached Joe with a hand held out to shake.

Joe shook his hand and said, "Thank you for coming to see me, Reverend."

Channing smiled and said, "Well, thank you for inviting me, Mr. Blankenship. You can call me Roland."

"All right, Roland, I'm Joe. Why don't you come on inside?"

Joe led the two men inside, and Channing said to the young driver, "Alex, why don't you wait in the kitchen while Joe and I talk? You can get us some coffee as well."

Joe frowned at the presumption. He hadn't offered coffee yet, or anything else.

"Yes, sir," the young man said.

Joe led Channing to the cabin's small living room. He gestured for Channing to take a seat next to the fireplace, and then took his own across from Channing.

"You'll have to forgive me, Reverend. My wife was very much a believer, but I've never been a churchgoer myself. It was Dale Whitt who told me about you."

"God Bless Mr. Whitt," Channing said. "A true martyr for the cause. And Joe, I see no reason to forgive. Not all of us serve God in the same ways. If I take my read correctly, you've served in your own ways, have you not?"

Blankenship nodded. "I suppose," he said. "I spent some years in the Army, mostly in Afghanistan and Iraq."

"And you are still fighting for your country."

Blankenship was more than a little uncomfortable with the way Channing was leading the conversation, but he nodded all the same.

"Tell me more," Channing said.

Blankenship took a deep breath, then said, "To put it bluntly, I'm looking for help. The federal government killed my wife for no reason."

"A good, God-fearing woman, from what Dale told me," Channing said.

"That's right. I led a company of irregulars, snipers mostly, during the war. We never really got a chance to do much, just tried to slow down the attacking forces. But to be honest, they moved so fast during the invasion we might as well have not been there at all. But I kept them together. We have three companies altogether, around a hundred and twenty men ready to fight. We've captured weapons and supplies."

Channing nodded and said, "Who handled the planning?"

"I did," Joe replied. "I've got plenty of counterinsurgency experience. This just flips the coin a little."

"What is your goal, Joe?"

"A free West Virginia."

Channing nodded, looked thoughtful for a moment, and then said, "Joe, I'd like to help you. I think we share the same goal. You're right that the federal government has gone off the track. You understand God guides me in everything, and I can't help but be appalled that our country has been taken over by the godless. It's all gold and sex and hedonism from Washington to Hollywood these days. How can we call ourselves a Christian nation when we have homosexuals getting married in our nation's capitol? How can we have any moral grounding when our children are forbidden from prayer in school?"

Blankenship nodded. He'd never cared much about gay marriage or the rest of it. But Channing was correct that America had drifted far from its founding principles.

"Now," Channing said, "let me tell you a little of my own goals. You see, I began shepherding my flock outside Baughman Settlement near enough to twenty years ago. Before that, my father was our religious guide, God bless his soul. Back then we were just an isolated compound in the middle of nowhere. My father led his family there when he saw the godless direction our country was taking in the 1960s. Hippies and drugs and free sex, you see. He had a vision, and he shared that vision with me: that one day we would lead a revival of the Christian values our nation was based on."

Blankenship nodded, wondering where this was going.

"Joe, here's what I can tell you. Today, we have grown and not by just a little. We have daughter fellowships in six different states and there are more than a thousand of us here in West Virginia. And not just in isolated settlements like what my father founded. We have prominent supporters in the legislature and throughout the state government. You see, when I took over the family, I came to realize that while my father was correct about many things, he was wrong about remaining isolated. How can we hope to influence the future of our country if we hide? Instead, we've worked to expand our reach."

Blankenship said, "Whoever you have in the state government is placed well. The information you passed us last week was right on target. Are you willing to offer your support on a more regular basis?"

"Not just support, Joe. God has guided us both to this meeting of the minds. I suggest it's time to become full partners. You have the military and insurgency experience. I have the resources, money, and networks in place. Together, with God guiding us, we can make miracles."

c✃ɔ

Valerie Murphy found the photo album at the bottom of a box in the back of the cold, musty storage room. Random piles of papers, books and old bills had been thrown haphazardly into the boxes, leaving no sense of order or organization at all. She could only guess what had happened; perhaps following her arrest, the feds had ransacked her apartment, looking for some thread of evidence to convict her.

It had taken her hours to find the few small articles she intended to remove from the storage unit. Clothing, of course, most of which would be ill-fitting until she regained some weight. Her laptop, chargers for her phone and tablet, and a few personal articles. She'd searched for nearly two hours before finding her old photo album.

Originally a simple three-ring notebook, her mother had quilted a cover for the photo album when Valerie was eight. The quilting was torn and stained. Many of the photos were loose, no longer bound to the pages, stained and torn.

She felt a stab of anger at the sight of one of her favorite photos. At six, she'd been sitting in front of a mirror while her mother braided her hair. Both of them were grinning. Her father had taken the photo. A dusty footprint was stamped right across both of their faces. She wasn't sure whether she had a digital copy, but the anger gripped her regardless.

Another photo, this one of her in her early twenties during a holiday visit home from Harvard. Kenny, Jr., her baby brother, was sitting in her lap, head thrown back in laughter. More photos of Kenny, on holidays and other visits.

She slid into a sitting position on the floor, ignoring the dust and dirt soiling her clothing. Paging through the album, she found herself wondering why she was bothering. Everyone in the album was dead. Her mother first, killed during a convenience store robbery. Her brother, dead of disease and federal budget cuts last fall. And her dad...

What would Ken Murphy do now, in her position? She'd often asked herself that during turning points in her life. But now, she couldn't imagine. Valerie's father had built a strong family, and his love for his family and his country had dominated his actions throughout his life, whether it was fighting in Iraq or nursing Kenny through a bad fever.

Valerie on the other hand, had no family any more, and increasingly she didn't know what to think about the country which had cut off medical aid for her brother and executed her father.

She shook her head in frustration and closed the album. One thing Ken Murphy would never have done was turn to self-pity, looking into the past. Right now, what she needed more than anything was a sense of grounded. It was time to go back to work, get on with her life, and move forward.

But toward what?

She had no idea.

അ

When Jim Turville joined the Army, he'd fully expected to find himself deployed in a war zone eventually. After all, the Army and Marine Corps had borne the brunt of the wars in Iraq and Afghanistan for most of his childhood. It was pretty much guaranteed that if anyone were foolish enough to sign up, and then even more foolishly ask to be assigned to the infantry, that someone was going to war. He'd never expected that war to be less than two hundred miles from home. But the last two years had changed his life beyond all recognition.

Two years ago, he'd been a senior at Thomas Jefferson High School in Fairfax County, Virginia, where he'd done well, if not outstandingly. He could have easily been accepted into George Mason or some other college, but not long after the beginning of his senior year, he'd announced his intention to join the Army instead.

His mother had tried to persuade him otherwise. He could do so much more with his life, she'd said. The military would send him far from home, and the odds of coming home wounded, either physically or psychologically, seemed all too high. Not to mention the fact that for more than ten years, soldiers had been churned in multiple tours in and out of Iraq and other countries.

This argument infuriated his father. Pat Turville was a firefighter, a brave man—and a drunk one—who had served a tour in Iraq with the National Guard. Turville's father argued the military wouldn't do him any harm.

Unfortunately, Dad was probably the strongest proof for his mother's argument. After his Iraq tour, he'd come home bitter, suffering from trauma, and consumed with anger at anyone he perceived as questioning the value or righteousness of the war in Iraq. Ten years wasn't enough time to even scratch the surface of that anger, let alone heal it.

Politics became a taboo subject in the house while Turville was in school. The alternatives—divorce or homicide—were unthinkable.

Turville graduated high school, spent the summer and early fall working odd jobs around town in Falls Church, then left for one-station unit training at Fort Benning, Georgia.

Basic training was uneventful as far as such things go. He'd breezed through the classroom and field training and enjoyed the challenges of them. Then he was assigned to the First Battalion, Fifteenth Infantry at Fort Meade, Maryland, where he managed to screw up during his first week with the company.

That would have blown over eventually, but when the Federal Building in Charleston, West Virginia was destroyed in a terrorist bombing last September, 1/15 Infantry was deployed to provide security at the site. Tensions were already far too high in the area when Turville accidentally killed a civilian.

It didn't take much effort for Turville to remember the kid. Short, but well built, he'd worn a baggy black raincoat and high-top shoes. His camera had been an expensive one—a gift, as it turned out, from his grandmother. Logan Jefferson was his name, and he'd been an honors student in high school and was expected to go to college to study filmmaking.

During Turville's two-month stay at Walter Reed Army Hospital in Washington, DC following his injury during the ground war, he'd spent a lot of time pondering the differences between Logan Jefferson and himself. Neither of them had grown up rich, and they'd both pursued similar interests in high school. Turville was a few years older, for sure, and white where Jefferson was black, but it wasn't too crazy to think that at one point their lives might have intersected. That is, if Logan Jefferson hadn't been killed.

Murdered, the sometimes cynical, self-critical voice inside Turville said.

Turville had been cleared in the investigation, but he knew who was at fault. If he hadn't disobeyed orders by loading his weapon, there would have been no accidental death.

All of which made him more determined than ever to never, ever screw up again. And made him more than a little uncomfortable with the news he had received this morning.

Just before chow, Sergeant Nguyen, his squad leader, appeared in the tent Turville shared with three other infantryman. Nguyen was an odd mix of genetics, the result of a tiny Vietnamese mother and a Kentucky-born and bred giant. The resulting mix of Asian facial features, rural Kentucky colloquialisms and oversized build and voice made him seem larger than life to the soldiers in his squad. The big Vietnamese-American sergeant seemed to fill the tiny tent, his gaze falling on each of the enlisted men before settling on Turville.

"Specialist Turville," he boomed.

Turville jumped to his feet.

"Got some news for you," Nguyen went on. He glanced at the other three soldiers—Tilman, Santiago, and Nowell—and went on. "These jokers might as well hear it as well. First, we're having a full company formation at 0900 hours—they're making some changes in our mission. We're going to be out in the field amongst the natives from now on. Turville, make sure you've got a clean uniform. They're giving you a Bronze Star for getting yourself shot trying to rescue Sergeant O'Donnell."

Turville nodded. "Yes, Sergeant."

"Second bit: you guys will not be getting a new fire team leader. You got the job, Turville. You're getting promoted."

Turville swallowed and glanced at the other three men in the tent. Then he said, "Sergeant, why me?"

Nguyen frowned. "What? Don't want the job?"

"It's not that, Sarge. It's—can we talk outside?"

"Fuck that, I'm not standing around in the cold. Privates! Get the hell out of the tent!"

Turville stood as the other three tent-mates groaned theatrically and cleared out of the tent. Once they were gone, he spoke.

"Sergeant, I'm honored. I'm just a little—well, you know, Sarge. I screwed up last fall and shot that kid. I don't know if I'm ready for this."

Nguyen nodded. "Yeah, I thought about that. I'll tell you what, Turville. Yeah, you screwed up. Big time. You're lucky not to be in prison, and sometimes you're so dumb you couldn't pour piss out of a boot with the directions printed on the bottom. But, on the other hand, you put your ass on the line to pull your Sergeant out. Then the other day when those choppers went down, you were the only person in the squad who thought to protect the civilians before yourself. That was the clincher as far as I'm concerned. I told the Lieutenant I wanted you to get the job after that happened."

Turville thought about that. He didn't know why he'd run for the two teenage girls when the choppers had gone down. It just made sense at the time. The Lieutenant had called Short

Girl—Rebecca Mays—and the military police had returned her truck. He wondered if he'd ever see her again. Probably not. But he still didn't think his instinctive move to protect the girls necessarily made him \ a leader.

"Will I be going to PLDC?" he asked, referring to the Primary Leadership Development Course, the first class given to new and rising non-commissioned officers.

Nguyen snorted. "Yeah, eventually. But right now, see, we're still in a war zone."

"All right, Sergeant."

Nguyen smiled. "In that case, congratulations, Corporal Turville. We'll make it official later today." He held out his hand.

Turville shook his hand, but he couldn't shake his doubts.

☙

"So what is your assessment?" Al Clark asked.

At the moment, Clark sat at the small conference table in the Governor's office, next to a window overlooking downtown Charleston. Valerie sat at his right hand. Only a few days had passed since their release, and she was still unusually quiet. The lack of her usual assertiveness made Clark nervous; he felt that if he said or did the wrong thing, she'd fall apart.

Asa Vance Hatfield sat across from Clark. Formidably built, the former soldier and cop had risen through the ranks of the State Police and had been acting Secretary of the Department of Military and Law Enforcement since the end of the war. Which led to this meeting. Clark was convinced Hatfield was the wrong man in the wrong job. While there was no evidence to indicate Hatfield was doing anything to inflame conflict, there was an equal lack of evidence to indicate he was doing anything to bring it to a stop.

Hatfield shrugged in response to Clark's question. "Governor, it's not so much a question of what is wrong as it is what is right. We're out of money. Right now I'm at less than one-third of our pre-war strength in the state patrol, and those that stayed are at half-pay. The Department has about three weeks reserve, and then we'll have to let most of those troopers go. I've already laid off virtually all of the administrative staff. On top of that, the feds have taken the entire state National Guard prisoner, so we have no capacity to respond to disasters, and frankly I don't think we'll get any help if we ask."

Clark frowned. "Why is that?"

"I wouldn't care to speculate on that, Governor. What I know is, it's been three months and we don't even have power through half the state. Charleston is a war zone, Governor. In 2016, we had thirty-seven murders in this city. It's April now, and so far this year there have been more than 250. We've got gangs moving in because there're no cops on the street. Businesses are closed, lights are out half the time, and there are no jobs. Street crime, theft, burglary, it's all through the roof. Bottom line, Governor, is we need help, and we need cash, and so far I've seen nothing from the feds."

"I see," Clark said. He leaned against the table, tenting his hands in front of his face. Hatfield was angry, but he had good reason to be. The question, of course, was whether he could do this job effectively.

"Have you talked to General Murphy about it?"

Hatfield scoffed. "No offense, Governer. I realize Ms. Murphy here is his niece, but Tom Murphy could care less. He ain't half the man his brother was. Yeah, I talked to him, way back in January, and at every cabinet meeting since. I need help, not more talk. And I don't trust a man who took his own brother prisoner and saw him executed."

Valerie flinched at the blunt words. Clearly the man had no diplomatic instincts. That did it. Tom was right about replacing Hatfield; he needed someone who could go to Washington and persuade Congress to part with cash. A lot of it. And the person best qualified to do that was sitting right next to him.

"I understand, Mr. Hatfield. Well, we're going to be making some changes, which I hope will get you some help. I'm shortly going to be making my appointment for the permanent Secretary position. The candidate I've got in mind right now has a lot of experience in Congress and ought to be able to get Washington to send some money our way."

Valerie tensed next to him. Hopefully she'd wait until Hatfield left before she blew her lid.

Hatfield's face turned bright red. The man was not very good at hiding his feelings.

"With all due respect, Governor, I can't think of anyone more qualified to run this department right now than me."

"On the operational level that's true, and I expect you'll continue to run the day-to-day affairs. But we need someone with some political savvy and Washington experience. You've just outlined the problem yourself, Mr. Hatfield. West Virginia is bankrupt, and without some emergency funding we can't get cops back out on the street. You stay focused on that. Thank you for stopping by."

Clark stood. He didn't have time to get drawn into a debate with Hatfield.

Hatfield stood stiffly, his hands bunched into fists at his sides. His face was still red, and one eyebrow twitched slightly. Despite his obvious difficulty controlling his rage, he kept his tone under control when he spoke.

"Well, Governor, I hope you're right about all this. Lord knows we need some help."

They shook hands all around, and Hatfield left.

Valerie spun toward him.

"Al, you aren't suggesting what I think you are."

Clark leaned against his desk. "Of course I am. I've never met a better organized or more motivated person than you. I intend to announce this afternoon that I'm nominating you for the job."

Valerie shook her head. "Al, I'm not ready for this. I have zero executive experience. I've been your chief of staff, and that's it. Don't you understand? Besides... I'm still—look, I'm still pretty messed up from the last few months. I don't want this job."

Clark tried to soften his tone. "Valerie, I understand. It's been a traumatic time. I've never been such a mess in my life. I'm right here with you. But we're both better off with something to sink our teeth into. I can't think of anyone who would better for this than you. I need you."

He knew she would respond that to that, if nothing else.

He shoulders slumped, and she whispered, "All right. I'll do it. I don't want it, I don't think I can do it, but if you insist, I'll take the job."

"Thank you, Valerie."

FOUR

"D amn!" Corporal Jim Turville said as the Humvee hit a deep pothole with a loud thump, splashing mud across the entire front of the vehicle.

"Sorry," Santiago said, jerking the wheel to the left. The streaks of mud on the windshield soon washed away under the heavy rain and the powerful rhythm of the wipers.

Turville leaned to his side so he could look up at the blue and black clouds marching across the sky. His throat didn't hurt as bad anymore—very much a relative state, unfortunately. Above him, the contrasts in the sky were dramatic as a strong northerly wind pushed thunderheads over them.

Behind them, standing on a small platform, PFC Tilman manned a machine gun. Nowell had his face buried in the latest Seth Harwood paperback.

"Turville, can I ask you a question?"

Turville looked over at Santiago. "Yeah, what's up?"

"What crawled up Corporal Meigs's ass?" As he asked the question, Santiago's usually civil face twisted in disgust.

"I don't know. What did he do?"

Santiago waved his hand, as if trying to scare away a bug. "Eggh ... Yesterday when we were headed back from chow—Tilman and me, anyway—out of the blue he comes up and starts messing with us. Uniform out of order, we're slouches. Man, I ain't no slouch. I bust my ass. Besides, he's not my corporal, you are. What the hell?"

Turville grinned. "Santiago, if I had a clue what was up with Meigs, I'd let you know. I don't. He's always on top of somebody—used to be me. I'll talk to Sergeant Nguyen about it if you want."

"Yeah, I want. If you don't mind."

"Sure."

They rode in silence for a few minutes. Then Nowell chimed in. Turville wished he hadn't almost immediately.

"He's pissed at you, Turville. It's about that Bronze Star—he doesn't think you should have gotten it."

Turville turned his head—too far—back toward Nowell. He let out a brief yelp of pain, and twisted his upper body around to reduce the pressure on his neck.

"What the hell are you talking about?"

Nowell shrugged. "I'm just saying, Turville. I heard him bitching about it right after the formation."

"Motherfucker," Santiago muttered.

Turville shrugged. "If it wasn't that, it'd be something else. Meigs is just a very angry dude. I don't think it has much to do with any of us. Anyway, let me know if you he gives you any trouble."

"Cool."

Turville carefully turned back to face the front. Ahead of them, the road continued to twist in hairpin turns up and over the mountains.

They weren't that far from where the platoon had been ambushed last week. However, they were arguably better prepared. The patrol—the entire platoon this time—was spread out in twelve Humvees, each driving more than fifty yards behind the one in front of it. Four squads of nine riflemen each, plus the heavy weapons squad with its twin M-240 machine guns. All in all, more than forty well-armed and pissed-off men. It would be a foolhardy militia-member that attacked this column.

Of course, that was just while they were on the move. Once they settled into Whitesville and its environs, things might change fast. The company was moving into Boone County to stay.

"Where you from, Santiago?" Turville asked.

"Me? Honduras."

"Yeah?" said Nowell, chuckling. "How come you're not in the Honduran Army?"

Santiago jerked a thumb back toward Nowell. "PFC Nowell thinks he's funny, yeah. It's no laughing matter. I make good money since I've been in the Army, and I can get my U.S. citizenship quickly. Once I have that, I can bring my wife and son to live with me."

Turville stared out the window in silence, but Nowell chimed in again. "Well, I'll be damned. You got a wife back home? You're always checking out the girls!"

Santiago looked in the rearview mirror. "I said I was married, my friend, not castrated."

Turville laughed.

A shout from Tilman, above them, cut that short.

"Heads up. Car!"

"Easy guys," Turville said. "Make sure you have your weapons, but don't do anything with them. Clear?"

The others murmured assent.

The vehicle, coming around a switchback toward them, was a brown-and-white pickup. Twenty years old, maybe more. Turville felt himself tense as it approached.

"All elements, this is Blue Six," they heard over the radio. "Maintain calm, report any problems. Blue Six, out."

"Yeah," Turville said. "Keep it chilled."

"And if it's some hillbilly terrorist?" Santiago replied. His voice was screwed up tight.

"Then we're fucked."

Santiago spat out the unzipped window. Scarcely a second later, the pickup passed them, headed in the opposite direction. The driver, a woman in her forties with deep lines her face, waved and smiled as she drove by.

"See?" Turville said, trying to keep his sigh of relief quiet enough the others couldn't hear. "Nothing to it."

He nearly jumped out of skin when Nowell leaned forward and shouted "Boo!" in his ear.

"Damn it, Nowell!"

Santiago chortled. "Corporal Turville, you're all right."

"Sorry, Turville," Nowell said, "I just couldn't help it."

Turville shook his head and laughed.

❧

Valerie Murphy frowned at herself in the mirror. Makeup couldn't disguise her pallor, and new clothes couldn't disguise her almost gaunt figure. She leaned in close, squinting her eyes, and noticed something that had escaped her up to this point: a long, fine white hair.

She shook her head. No surprise there. And nothing to be done to improve her prison-influenced appearance beyond what she'd already done. She wanted to make a good, solid first impression, but there was only so much she could do.

She walked over to the door of the small suite, straightened her jacket, slung her purse over her shoulder, then opened the door.

Outside, a state patrolman stood casually in the hallway. He held out a cup of steaming coffee in a travel mug.

"Morning, ma'am. I'm Trooper Dennis Henry. Lieutenant Thrasher suggested you'd be needing some coffee; I hope you like cream and sugar in it. Ready to go?"

She had to think for a moment, and then it clicked: Lieutenant Thrasher was Uncle Tommy's aide-de-camp. She smiled and accepted the cup. "Nice to meet you, Trooper Henry, and oh God, yes, I'm ready for coffee. Lead the way."

She followed him into the basement parking lot, where a government sedan waited. Exhaust from the car steamed out in a long trail of blue smoke, somehow giving the space a haunted, disturbing air. He opened the door for her, then got into the driver's seat. He passed a folder to her and said, "This is the agenda for today. Acting Secretary Hatfield asked Wade Davis—he's the acting chief of staff—to put together a schedule for you to give you an opportunity to familiarize yourself with the department."

"How thoughtful of Mr. Hatfield," she murmured sarcastically.

If Henry caught the mild sarcasm, he remained tactfully silent about it.

The car whisked her across town to the new headquarters of the Department of Military Affairs and Public Safety: a hundred-year-old pile of bricks and stone that looked like it had once been a bank. Two soldiers stood guard at a makeshift gate blocking the street; they waved the car through after swiping Henry and Valerie's driver's licenses.

Valerie followed Henry into the front lobby of the building. A long, stained marble counter stretched along one wall, resembling the check-in desk at a hotel. Two security guards with an x-ray machine and metal detectors blocked access to the elevators.

The guards were deferential after Henry introduced Valerie, and in moments they were in a slow-moving elevator.

Valerie took a moment to compose herself in the elevator. She could feel a tension headache coming on. Whatever else happened, she was determined to do a good job for Al Clark, her mentor and friend. But the truth was she didn't want this, wasn't ready for it; she wanted to run away and hide somewhere. She couldn't stand to be alone, but every time she was around anyone at all, she wanted to burst into tears. And that didn't even cover how she felt every time she thought of her father.

On the seventh floor, Henry led her to a suite of offices. Inside were two professionally dressed women and a man with short grey hair and a dark suit.

"Ms. Murphy," Henry said, "please allow me to introduce Wade Davis, the chief of staff."

The man in the suit gave her a broad smile. "Secretary Murphy, it's a pleasure to meet you. And please, allow me to offer my condolences regarding your father. He and I worked together for many years."

She felt a pang of regret at the fact that she'd never really know much about her dad's life outside what they'd shared. His professional peers, his friends, the things he enjoyed in his career, would always be lost to her.

"Thank you," she said, shaking his hand. "You were chief of staff when my father was alive?"

"Yes, ma'am."

"Well, then." She forced herself to close the door on her regrets and fears about Ken Murphy. "Let's get started."

"Right. To business, then," he replied. "Trooper Henry, thank you for fetching the secretary."

"Of course, sir. And ma'am, if you need anything, just ask for me. I've been assigned security for you full time., I'll be right in the outside office here."

"Thank you," she replied.

Davis led the way to her new office, a large room in the corner of the suite with windows overlooking the river and downtown area. Bookshelves lined one wall, a large walnut desk and credenza were on one side of the room, and a conference table occupied the other side of the room.

Valerie set her purse on the desk. Davis offered her a cup of coffee, and they sat at the conference table.

She looked at Davis, trying to gauge whether he would be an ally. After a moment, she said, "Wade... may I call you Wade?"

"Of course."

"Tell me about this agenda." She looked down at it and said, "I'm looking it over, and honestly I can't make any sense of it. Ribbon-cutting ceremony in Fairmont? Review of the Junior ROTC cadets in Moorefield? Not to be difficult, but I'm looking at three or four days of... fluff. I recognize that getting out and meeting people is important, but I also have a very brief window to get down to brass tacks before my confirmation hearing next Monday. How did this schedule come about?"

Davis looked startled for a moment, then a smile spread over his face and gave way to a chuckle.

"I'm sorry for the levity, ma'am, but just now you reminded me so much of your father, I ..."

Valerie was astonished as the man's eyes suddenly watered. He composed himself and then spoke again. "I apologize. Ken Murphy was a good man, and I think we'll all miss him, but I can only imagine how serious the loss is for you. The fact is, until this morning, Asa Hatfield was my boss. And he told me to put together a schedule that, um... kept you busy and out of the way. I believe that was the wording he used."

She nodded. "I had the feeling it was something like that. I take it from your response that you ... see things differently than Hatfield?"

Davis smiled. "You're the boss, ma'am, not Hatfield. While he makes a fine leader for the enforcement division, he... has failings in terms of seeing the big picture. I have the feeling you'll do just fine in this job. I'll do my best to support you in making that happen. Fair enough?"

Valerie heaved a sigh of relief. "I can't tell you how happy I am to hear that. I wasn't looking forward to firing someone on my first morning, and that's what would have happened had you given me the wrong answer to that question."

Davis laughed.

"All right, then. Here's what I would like: clear this awful schedule. Here's how I want to spend the next three days. First, get me access to email and the network here. I'll need my email on my portable, too. Second, within the hour I'd like a copy of whatever summary exists from each department on current activities, budget, challenges—you get the picture. I'll also want bios of each department head, and not the official stuff we put up on websites; I want to know details. Then set up one-on-one meetings with each department head, including our friend Mr. Hatfield. You'll sit in on those meetings with me. I'm going to ask your frank assessment of each individual. Each of them should be prepared with details on what they've been doing, what's planned, and what problems they are facing. Can you make that happen?"

Davis grinned. "Gladly, ma'am."

"One other thing, Wade... call me Valerie. Ma'am doesn't really suit me. Fair enough?"

Within minutes, a flurry of activity took over the office. Davis deputized the two administrative assistants, who began making calls to arrange the needed network access and schedule changes.

Valerie spent a few minutes arranging her desk. By the time she finished, Davis was approaching, carrying a thick folder.

"I thought you might find it useful to have a summary of activity within the department to begin with, ma'am." At her raised eyebrows, he quickly amended, "Um—Valerie. Anyway, up until Asa Hatfield took over, the old secretary used to hold twice weekly management meetings—usually never longer than an hour, but enough time to work out the big picture of the department. Before the meeting, the staff produced an executive summary of activity within the department. Even though we haven't been meeting, the summaries are still being written up. I've got the last several months printed out here for you."

She smiled. Davis was already proving a valuable ally. "Thank you. And the meetings? Let's go ahead and get those on the calendar for the foreseeable future."

He left the office, and she dove into the file. Details, both pedestrian and extraordinary, were laid out in the biweekly reports. Recent summaries noted that the department had less than twenty million dollars remaining in its coffers for the remainder of the year, that the temporary disaster relief staff in Mingo County had walked off the job a week earlier due to lack of power or clean water at their headquarters, and that a column of US Army tanks had inadvertently caused a bridge failure in Weston. Cost to repair would be nine million dollars. Local residents would be taking the long way around for a long time.

Valerie flipped through the reports, choosing to initially scan them for broad trends, returning to get finer details. A vague feeling that something was missing began to trouble her as she read, but she couldn't pin it down. The summaries seemed to be comprehensive, covering all the broad details of the department from budgeting to maintenance.

About twenty minutes later, her head jerked up suddenly. "Why isn't there anything in here about the Boone County sheriff? Or other possible insurgent incidents?"

She spread the papers out across the desk, frowning. Then she pressed the intercom button on her desk.

"Wade, there's no crime statistics here. Or anything about the murder of Boone County's sheriff. Why not?"

A heartbeat of silence, followed by a response. "I'll be right there."

Valerie waited, and a moment later Davis knocked lightly on the door and entered. Quietly, he said, "The former acting secretary ordered that crime statistics and anything related to possible insurgent activity be omitted from the bi-weekly summaries, Valerie."

She sat back in her chair, puzzled, becoming suspicious.

"Why? When? This related to our primary mission. Why in God's name would he not want it included?"

Davis shrugged. "I'm not sure I'd care to speculate what his motives were. But he made the order almost as soon as he took over as acting secretary back in mid-January."

Valerie sat back in her seat, considering the possible implications. Several possibilities ran through her mind, none of them at all reassuring.

One of the administrative assistants buzzed on the intercom. "Ms. Murphy, Mr. Hatfield is here to see you."

She hadn't finished the words before Asa Hatfield burst into the office. His face was apoplectic. Valerie stood up behind her desk instinctively. Davis stayed seated, but turned toward Hatfield, his eyebrows raised.

"Ms. Murphy, I want to know what's going on here. The whole schedule we worked out for you—cancelled? Who the hell do you think you are?"

Hatfield's words stunned Valerie. The arrogance!

"I think I'm the Secretary of this Department and your boss," she responded coldly. "I wasn't aware the enforcement division was concerned with whether or not the Secretary attended ribbon-cutting ceremonies and spent days on end meeting with elementary school teachers."

Hatfield backtracked. "Murphy, this schedule was worked out carefully to introduce you to the various activities of the department, and—"

"And keep me busy and out of the way," Valerie interrupted. "I'm quite sure this was carefully put together, Mr. Hatfield. Nonetheless, I have other things to do over the next several days, one of which is assessing the suitability of our department heads."

Hatfield's face went even redder at the implied threat. She continued, her tone cold.

"For that reason, I chose to reschedule. Now, I've instructed the Chief of Staff to arrange a meeting with you within the next day so we can cover the activities of the enforcement division, which I do believe is your job. I expect that we'll work together, Mr. Hatfield, and I hope you'll seriously reconsider your attitude. Do we understand each other?"

Hatfield's eyes narrowed. "You're sure as hell right we understand each other, Murphy. But don't think you'll get away with this. This is my department, and they might make you into some kind of pretty talking head, but I'm the one who runs things around here. You don't want to mess with me."

Davis came to his feet as Hatfield spoke.

"That will be quite enough, Mr. Hatfield."

"You're damned right!" he shouted. He turned and stormed out of the office, slamming the door behind him.

Valerie stood behind her desk, absolutely astonished. She met Davis's eyes. "I don't think I've ever seen such unprofessional behavior in my life."

Davis shook his head slightly. "Be careful, Valerie. Hatfield has a lot of friends in the legislature, a lot of allies. He won't be easy to dismiss."

Valerie sighed. She knew that and found it hard to believe she was willing to go to the mat over a job she didn't even want.

But she'd be damned if she'd let a man like that walk all over her. Now the real question was simple: where would the next attack come from? And would she be able to withstand it?

એ

As the line of Humvees pulled into the town, Turville thought Whitesville looked considerably better when he wasn't being shot at.

Getting shot at wasn't likely at this point. First squad had already split off from the column and begun setting up the TCP—tactical checkpoint, which was a fancy term for road-block—two hundred meters before reaching the town. Sergeant Nguyen, Turville, and their squad would be staying in town for the first week, acting as the quick reaction force if any problems came up at the other positions. The third squad would be setting up at the head of the dam overlooking the town. Finally, a fourth squad had been assigned to effectively act as the local police force, patrolling the town and its roads.

The tree-covered mountains towered over the town, which was small by any standard. Along the right side of the road was a short series of red-brick two-story buildings, including the drug store where they'd huddled after the ambush just a few days ago. Next to that, a small, cinderblock watering hole sported a confederate flag. Ironic, considering West Virginia had split from Virginia to stay with the Union back in 1861. Across the street were a few small houses and the river running behind them. Beyond the river were more mountains.

Also towering over the town, a quarter of a mile to the south, was an earthen dam more than nine hundred feet high. A small gravel road switch-backed up the sloped face of the dam, leading to a couple of small buildings that would house the security force there. The dam was the byproduct of mountaintop removal: as the coal companies sheared off the tops of the mountains, the refuse was washed, the coal removed and the dirt and rock piled up. Behind the dam were some five billion gallons of polluted, bracken water and coal slurry.

Directly across the narrow, two-lane street from the drug store was an abandoned house, which was to be their base of operations. The grey, weathered wooden steps to the door were splintering and ancient, and the clapboards, once white, didn't look as if they'd been painted since the twentieth century. Delightful.

The pavement was still blackened and buckled where the helicopters had crashed, and two cars that had been destroyed by the resulting fire still sat, abandoned. With the mountains towering over them, and barely thirty feet between the buildings on each side of the street, it felt claustrophobic.

Sergeant Nguyen, their squad leader, got out of his Humvee and directed the others where to park their vehicles. Out of the nine men in the squad, two would always be on duty at the machine-gun mounts in the hummers.

"Third squad, move out," Sergeant Nguyen called. Turville and the rest of his team jumped out of their vehicles, quickly moving to positions where they had their backs to the house, looking out at the street.

Lieutenant Blake stood in front of them. "All right, gentlemen. You know the deal. You'll be the quick reaction force for the next week and then rotate to the TCP. Everyone stays within sight of this building. We get a call, I want you rolling in two minutes, tops."

Turville kept one ear tuned—they'd been briefed on what was expected of them about ten times already, but his eye was fixed on the family coming out of the drug store just across the narrow street.

The father was about forty, balding, and had a bit of a paunch. He wore khakis and a white shirt and was talking with a pretty redheaded woman the same age.

Behind them was Short Girl. Now that it was warming up, she was dressed in a pair of jeans and a light sweater instead of the bulky peacoat she'd worn a week before. Her brown hair hung loose at her shoulders, and the breeze blew wisps of it loose. He hadn't noticed it the other night—probably because people were trying to kill him at the time—but she had a tiny mole on the left side of her face, just below her left eye.

When she stepped out the door, she let loose a sort of squeal and grabbed her father's arm. She pointed at the squad, speaking excitedly to her father, who looked over at them.

Then she waved at Turville. Oh, no, he thought. That's the last thing I need.

The family crossed the street, and the father said, "Excuse me?"

Lieutenant Blake turned around and said, "Yes, sir?"

"I'm Bob Mays. Mayor here. I made the arrangements with your Colonel for where your men would be situated."

"Oh, yes. It's good to meet you, sir. I'm Lieutenant Blake. We're just getting the men situated now. I understood we were meeting at four o'clock, sir? I'm happy to move it up, if you want, but I'll need to get our positions straightened out first."

The man shook his head and smiled. "No, that won't be necessary. I just came over because my daughter has pointed out one of your men who is responsible for saving her life last week."

Turville sucked a breath in.

"Oh …" Lieutenant Blake looked confused for a moment and then made the connection. "Corporal Turville."

Turville stepped forward. "Yes, sir."

"Mayor, this is Corporal Jim Turville. I believe he's the one who helped out your daughter and her friend."

The man's grin widened, and he reached out and grabbed Turville's right hand. Short Girl—Rebecca—actually winked at him.

"Son, anything you ever need, you just give me a call. The name is Turville, is it?"

"Uh…yes, sir. Although, I didn't actually save anyone, I just kind of shoved her over. If there hadn't been, you know, people shooting at us at the time, you'd have probably been pretty pissed…"

Lieutenant Blake interrupted. "That's probably enough, Corporal."

Turville could feel heat in his face. *Jim, you are such an ass sometimes.*

"He did, Dad. If he hadn't pushed us to the ground, I'd have been killed by the shrapnel."

The mayor wouldn't let go of Turville's hand. "I mean it, son. Rebecca's going off to college in the fall—well, if we can get the schools back open, anyway. I don't know what I would have done if I'd lost her. You can call on me for anything. Anything at all."

"Uh, thank you, sir. Um … I'd better be going, sir, we were just getting the guys in place."

"Oh, that's right. Well, I don't want to interfere with your duty. I will say I'm glad you men are here. I'll see you at four o'clock, Lieutenant?"

"Yes, sir."

The Mayor walked away, with his wife and daughter in tow. *She had to be at least eighteen,* Turville thought. *Life just wouldn't be fair otherwise.*

He got back in the formation.

Nowell elbowed him in the side. "You're my hero," he whispered, then made a smooching sound.

"Kiss my ass," Turville whispered back.

The Lieutenant wrapped up and rejoined the Humvees. Sergeant Nguyen took his place at the head of the squad.

"All right. Meigs, I want your fire team on security. Turville, you relieve him at 1800 hours; you've got the night shift. And next time, no talking in my formation. Got it?"

"Yes, sergeant," Turville replied as Santiago, Nowell and Tilman groaned. As the formation broke up, he glanced up at the dam. The Lieutenant and third squad Humvees were already driving up the face, back and forth in the narrow switchbacks. It looked ominous, hanging over the town like that.

Then he thought of Rebecca Mays and how she had looked when she winked at him.

FIVE

J OE Blankenship looked through the binoculars, scanning the facility in the valley ten miles south of Charleston. Just uphill from a deep bend in the Coal River, the buildings and surrounding grounds lay on a ten acre spread of land which had first been leveled, then surrounded with twenty foot high electrified fencing.

"Thoughts?" Channing asked.

Blankenship lowered the binoculars. He took his time before speaking.

"Looks like a full company of infantry guarding the site... figure at least one hundred and twenty soldiers. Not to mention

DHS, electronic monitoring, cameras. What's down there worth that kind of security?"

Channing answered, "It's a private research facility, owned by Hamilton Biomedical."

Blankenship raised his eyebrows. "Why all the security?"

"Government contracts. They study nasty stuff there... It's a biohazard research facility. Very serious bugs. Security is provided by the feds."

Blankenship thought about that. This raised questions he wasn't sure he was comfortable having the answers to. Why did Channing want to get inside the facility? Of what use could it be to their movement? He looked at the man sitting in the truck cab next to him. Channing seemed eager, determined to get in. But he hadn't discussed his motives.

"Okay... you said you've got a guy inside?"

Channing nodded. "Better... member of the security department. We've got access to the cameras and monitoring systems. But whoever goes in needs to be invisible and absolutely silent."

Blankenship nodded. "I know just the guys for that, don't worry. But I gotta ask you: why do we want in there? What's the payoff? If they're studying some kind of super bugs in there, that's the last thing we want out in the open. Freedom I'm interested in, but not suicide."

Channing grinned. "That's why I like you, Joe. Very practical. This isn't about actually getting our hands on something. It's about scaring them out of their minds. If the feds think we've got Ebola or something like that, they'll go nuts. Overreact. And that, my friend, plays right into our hands."

Blankenship nodded. Channing had a point: the more the feds overreacted, especially violently, the more supporters the revolution gained. This, though... he couldn't help but wonder if it was going too far. Channing had made it clear during their meetings that everything in his life was driven by his religious beliefs. Blankenship's relationship with Christianity was much more casual, and Channing's fervor made him very uncomfortable. But was he crazy enough to unleash a plague?

No. He wasn't crazy, just determined.

"All right," Blankenship said. "I want to talk to your inside guy. Let's set up a meet. We'll get some guys inside."

Channing grinned, his eyes unusually bright. Joe found he had to look away, his eyes drawn back to the research facility in the valley below them. He had the keys to Pandora's box in his hands. But would he be able to close it?

SIX

CLIFFORD Webb yawned as he scanned the remaining open bug reports. Nothing urgent, though one of the researchers was reporting a fault in level four. He didn't relish the idea of trying to debug in a biohazard suit, but like everything else in this place, the systems in level four operated completely independently. There wasn't even a wireless connection, because of the security risk.

Despite the snow piled up outside, the office was stifling. Someone had cranked the thermostats up to ninety degrees.

Webb checked the clock in the corner of his screen. Two hours left. Once he was out of here, he would have to rush home, shower and change, and get back out the door to pick up Margaret, who had finally agreed to have dinner with him.

It had taken Webb more than three months to work up the courage to ask her out. Margaret was a pretty, petite woman, athletic and smart. A junior supervisor in the PR department, she was responsible for relations with the local townspeople, who were understandably very concerned about the safety of the facility.

She was out of his league. But since the day he came on the contract, she'd been faultlessly kind to him; introducing him to the other staff in the lunchroom, even helping him find an apartment in south Charleston, pointing out which neighborhoods were safe and which ones less so. Occasionally she would stop by his spot in the cube farm and check in on how he was doing.

The truth was, Margaret was the only thing that made this contract tolerable. Webb was used to being a bit of an outsider: for the last five years, he'd been the temporary help, an IT architect who flew in for three or six months, helped design, build and test systems, then flew out. It could be a lonely life living in temporary apartments or hotel rooms, but the pay was great and he'd been able to travel.

This contract, though, was different. For one thing, so much of it was classified that even with his security clearance, he still didn't have a clear idea what they worked on. He knew Hamilton Biomedical had a federal contract to study deadly infectious diseases. But that didn't tell him much, and the written specs for programs, provided by a grim-faced federal program manager, didn't offer much more information. Badly written and badly defined, it was clear no one had ever explained that a requirements doc was supposed to tell the programmers what the requirements actually were.

The stress in the office was oppressive, overwhelming. Employees of Hamilton were in constant conflict with the feds, with their processes and regulations. The scientists lorded it over everyone, and everyone on the permanent staff looked down on the temporaries and contractors.

One of the main reasons Webb liked contracting was because it allowed him to stay clear of office politics. Unfortunately, in this environment it also made it impossible for him to get anything done.

Webb didn't look up at the sound of a woman in heels walking up behind him, until he heard Margaret's voice.

"Hey, you. Those must be some fascinating bug reports."

Webb turned toward her. She was about ten years younger than he was, probably in her mid-twenties. Dressed conservatively in a grey, skirted business suit, her only adornments were two plain stud earrings and a cross on a gold chain.

"Hey, Margaret."

"Are we still on for dinner tonight?"

Webb nodded, then broke into a smile. "I wasn't sure you would remember."

She rolled her bright, arresting blue eyes, then met his. "Silly. I was just going to get a cup of coffee. Join me?"

He sat up. "Sure," he said. "Give me just a minute, okay? Let me let Matt know where I'm going."

He stood, and she stepped out of the way, but only enough to let him squeeze by. He felt an almost electric tingle as he slid by her, then walked across the cube farm to his boss's office.

As he did so, he didn't realize he'd left his computer unlocked and logged in with administrative credentials. Nor did he notice Margaret lean in to the keyboard and type a few short commands.

By the time he returned to his desk, Margaret was standing where she'd been when he'd left, and his computer had been compromised with a keylogger and a trojan that allowed external control right through the company firewall.

SEVEN

Charleston Gazatte, March 24
MAN FOUND DEAD IN SOUTH CHARLESTON
By Bob Stoll
Charleston, WV – A 31-year-old man was found dead in his apartment in South Charleston Thursday, police spokesmen said. Clifford Webb, a short-term contractor with the Centers for Disease Control, had been renting the apartment for three months. After he failed to report to work for four days, supervisors with the CDC notified police, who forced entrance to Webb's apartment.
Police are tentatively ruling the death a suicide.

ALERIE Murphy leaned forward, listening to the police lieutenant who stood at the head of the conference table elaborating on crime statistics over the last three months in Charleston. The lieutenant spoke confidently, with the steady clip of someone intimately familiar with his subject matter. The details were more than a little disturbing: a massive rash of gang-related violence across the city; Little Cairo effectively blocked off by the residents after a series of apparent hate crimes; and a growing shanty town only a block from the capitol crowded with hundreds of people who had simply reached the end of the line of their resources.

"Thank you, Lieutenant," said Chief of Police Bill Keller. "I think that's it, Ms. Murphy. The bottom line is, we're hanging on by a thread. I've directed the police to simply ignore all but the most serious misdemeanors, because we just don't have the resources to go after everything."

Valerie nodded, then said, "I can't promise any quick fixes, but I'll stay in touch, and we'll see what we can do to get you some more funding."

They stood, and the chief said, "I haven't said so before, but... please accept my condolences for the loss of your father. He was a good man."

Valerie tried not to wince. Her father was still a gaping hole, and sometimes, especially when she was busy and hit by surprise, the shock of his passing left her unable to breath. She took a long, slow breath and nodded, then said, "I appreciate that, Chief."

The chief escorted her to the door of the conference room. Henry, the State Trooper, was waiting outside.

"Ms. Murphy," Henry said. "I got an emergency call from Asa Hatfield a few minutes ago; he's asking for an urgent meeting."

Murphy raised her eyebrows. An urgent meeting with Hatfield was not exactly at the top of her list of things to do. But she supposed there was little choice: as much as Hatfield's behavior during their last meeting appalled her, she was still responsible for the entire department.

"Let's not leave Mr. Hatfield waiting."

Fifteen minutes later, she walked into Hatfield's office. He sat behind his desk, which was stacked with filed and documents nearly a foot high. He looked up and closed a file when she entered.

His voice was conciliatory. "Morning, Ms. Murphy."

Valerie was surprised.

"Good morning, Mr. Hatfield."

"Thanks for coming so quickly. I didn't think you would."

A series of nasty responses ran through Valerie's mind, and as quickly as they came, she discarded them. Whatever else happened here, she needed to get some kind of a working relationship with him. That, or fire him, which she wasn't prepared to do yet. Finally, she replied, "Hatfield, why don't we talk for just a moment."

He nodded.

"Look," she said. "I get where you're coming from. You expected to be walking into this job. You've been a cop for decades, you know law enforcement, and the last thing you expected was some wet behind the ears female Harvard graduate former congressional aid as your boss. Am I on track so far?"

His face colored a little, but he nodded stiffly.

She leaned forward and said, "I didn't want this job either. Still don't. But I'm stuck with it, and we're stuck with each other. So I need to make you understand right up front: I'll do what's necessary to succeed. My father didn't raise any quitters, and he didn't raise me to take half-measures. I'd rather have you as an ally than an enemy."

He frowned, and the color on his face rose. His expression tightened for a moment, then he said, "Fair enough."

She stared at him a full twenty seconds, then stood. "Well, that's out of the way. What's this all about?"

All business now, he leaned forward and said, "Got a call from Homeland Security about an hour ago. They want us in for a special briefing at the Hamilton Biomedical lab. There's been a security breach there."

She shook her head. "I'm not familiar with it."

"It's a research lab, a contract with the Centers for Disease Control."

"And it's serious enough they're requesting the two of us?"

He nodded. "Yes… and that just about sets my hair on fire."

She nodded. "When?"

"Soon as we can get there."

"Let's get going, then."

Within a few minutes they were sitting uncomfortably together in the back of a government-issue Lincoln Town Car heading south out of Charleston. Valerie spent the time alternately reviewing her email and looking out the window at the depressing signs of poverty everywhere. Near the capitol was the growing shantytown where hundreds camped in tents and structures thrown together out of cardboard and scrap metal.

"How long has that been going on?" Valerie asked Hatfield.

Hatfield grimaced. "Started right after the surrender," he replied. "Lot of families of soldiers over there, people thrown out because they couldn't make their rent, or homes destroyed in the fighting. Some of them are just too lazy to find work. I don't know why they don't go to their families for help; they seem to think the government's going to have something for them."

Valerie refrained from answering. Not everybody had family to turn to, and she found it difficult to believe that such large numbers of people would be living in a shanty next to the state capitol unless they'd completely run out of options.

Thirty minutes later, Trooper Henry brought the car to a halt at the gated entrance. A large sign near the entrance read, "Hamilton Biomedical. Private property, No Trespassing." The two US Army guards underscored the warning.

After a lengthy check of their credentials, the guards searched the vehicle thoroughly before allowing them to proceed. Henry brought the car to a halt in the small parking lot, and they stepped out of the vehicle.

A man in a dark grey suit met them in the parking lot next to the low slung cinderblock building. He wore dark sunglasses, highly polished shoes, and a badge tucked into his lapel; his hair was shorn very close to bald.

Valerie extended a hand. "Good morning, I'm Secretary Murphy. This is Asa Hatfield, chief of the enforcement division, and Trooper Dennis Henry of the State Patrol."

The man shook her hand. "JD Roberts, Department of Homeland Security. If you'll follow me, please."

He turned and walked toward the entrance without another word. Valerie and Hatfield followed. Roberts swiped an access card, and they entered a lobby. Two more guards armed with automatic weapons sat behind a desk in the bare lobby.

Roberts handed over his ID, and gestured for the others to do so. "As you can see, we take security here very seriously."

Valerie couldn't help but think this was much like closing the barn door after the horse had already escaped.

She said nothing, handing over her ID to the guard at the desk, who said, "Please sign here," and presented a clipboard. She signed in, and the guard said, "I'll return your ID when you exit. In the meantime, please keep this guest pass visible at all times when in the facility. Visitors are not permitted beyond the office levels."

She nodded, and waited while Hatfield went through the same routine.

Roberts led them through another locked door and into a small conference room.

"Please have a seat," he said, gesturing to two of the seats on one side of the table closest to the door. "We'll be joined by Doctor Seeger in just a moment, along with Captain Matt Floyd, who is head of security here. But first, I want to make one thing clear. Due to the sensitive nature of this facility, we view this as purely a federal matter, and I am coordinating the investigation with the FBI. In short, I don't expect West Virginia authorities to be involved in any way. I'm giving this briefing as a professional courtesy only, at the request of General Murphy."

Beside her, Hatfield bristled. Valerie responded, "I understand that's your view, Mr. Roberts, but the fact is, if a crime has been committed, it falls under West Virginia's jurisdiction."

Roberts walked around to the other side of the table and sat sown. He laid his palms on the table, looked them both in the eyes and said bluntly, "Under normal circumstances I would agree, but there are two reasons this will remain a federal matter. First, the nature of the agents being studied here makes it a matter of national security, plain and simple. Second, it's clear that you have a highly placed leak in your own department. Possibly more than one. Until that matter is resolved, I refuse to have any state-level law enforcement involved in this investigation."

Valerie frowned, then said, "What exactly is being studied here?"

"I'm afraid that's classified—"

Hatfield interrupted, "Bullshit, Roberts. They're studying drug resistant bugs here. Staph, Spanish flu, God only knows what else."

She raised her eyebrows.

Roberts nodded once. "Your colorful head of enforcement is correct, Secretary Murphy. Hamilton Biomedical opened this facility a few years ago as a public-private partnership to study some of the most dangerous drug-resistant pathogens. This is one of five biocontainment level-four facilities currently operating in the United States."

"What exactly does that mean?"

Roberts explained, "Biomedical research facilities are classified based on the precautions taken to prevent escape of the research subjects to the outside. A level-four facility contains the worst of the worst: transmissible diseases, stuff like Ebola and smallpox. It also has the most sophisticated controls to prevent escape. Airlocks, reverse air pressure. The air that exits this building is superheated to prevent anything from escaping, and as a partner with the federal government, the facility is also guarded continually by a company of active duty infantry."

As Roberts spoke, the door opened. Two men came into the room. The first, a gaunt man in his fifties, smiled, revealing yellowing teeth. He wore a red ID tag that read "Seeger." The second man was much younger, and wore camouflage utilities and combat boots, with an embroidered name tag reading "Floyd."

Roberts stood and said, "Doctor Seeger, Captain Floyd, this is Secretary Valerie Murphy of the West Virginia Department of Military and Law Enforcement, and Asa Hatfield of the Law Enforcement Division."

They shook hands all around, then Roberts spoke again. "Captain Floyd, if you will brief the Secretary on the security breach."

Floyd nodded, then spoke in a crisp tone.

"At 2325 hours last night, a routine patrol discovered a maintenance panel on the exterior of the level-four facility was loose. The bolts had been removed and the panel replaced without them. At this point we put the facility on lockdown and alerted DHS, then began our initial investigation. We've identified footprints of at least two individuals coming from the direction of the south fence. Both wore boots; the tread pattern appears to indicate standard combat boots. The FBI lab is taking casts of the boot prints now and should be able to give us an indication of the weight of the intruders. Thus far we've been unable to identify where they entered the facility; there are no breaks in the fence, and surveillance video shows absolutely nothing."

Valerie leaned forward, and Hatfield spoke. "You have cameras inside and out?"

Floyd nodded. "We have surveillance cameras across the grounds, but none inside the labs. There is some indication, however, that the software managing the cameras has been tam-

pered with. We don't have any recordings from the last forty-eight hours. As best as we can determine, the system was
tampered with night before last, and while it's been displaying
current images, nothing is being recorded. Additionally, Clifford Webb, one of the programming consultants who developed the security system, turned up missing two weeks ago. He
was found in his apartment after we reported him as missing.
The police found him in his apartment, dead. It was ruled a
suicide, but given the security breach..." Floyd shrugged. "I'd
say anything is possible at this point."

Hatfield mumbled a curse. "Any indication of anything
missing?"

Doctor Seeger spoke. "We're conducting an inventory of
the labs and all samples at this time. So far nothing has turned
up missing, but the inventory is not complete."

Valerie looked at each of the men in the room, then asked
her question. "What's the worst-case scenario here?"

Seeger frowned, then answered, "I prefer not to deal in
hypotheticals."

Hatfield's face went bright red. "Doctor Seeger, our job is
to protect the people of West Virginia. You may not want to
deal in hypotheticals, but we have to. If these were terrorists
or insurgents, what's the worst case? What might they have
taken?"

Roberts interrupted. "Most of the work being done here is
classified."

Hatfield responded, "I don't give a rat's ass! Are we talking
Ebola? Something worse?"

Seeger finally answered, "The most likely is flu. Specifically
Spanish flu."

"As in the 1918 flu, doctor?" Valerie asked.

"That's correct. As you may know, samples of the flu virus
were recovered in Alaska in 1998, and a tremendous amount of

work has been done here and in other labs over the last two decades to understand it. This was a particularly serious pandemic. Somewhere between twenty and fifty million people were killed by it just at the end of the First World War. Our research here has been to identify ways of combating such pandemics."

Valerie paled. Twenty to fifty million. "You had live samples of the virus here?"

Doctor Seeger nodded. "Hamilton Biomedical is the only private facility in the world with the virus. It's being studied here on contract to the Centers for Disease Control. We study a variety of influenza types, primarily avian subtypes that can be transmitted to humans. Our work has been to identify the specific genetic changes which could cause varieties of bird flu to become easily transmissible in humans."

Valerie and Hatfield looked at each other, and Valerie knew he was thinking the same thing she was. They didn't have the resources to put cops on the street. How in god's name were they supposed to implement the types of measures needed to prevent spreading an epidemic?

Roberts spoke. "Look, I want to be absolutely clear about one thing. I've said it, but it bears repeating: this will remain a solely federal investigation. West Virginia will not be involved. Not at all. The only reason we're giving you this briefing—"

Hatfield interrupted. "Is because we're the ones who will have to contain the damage and deal with the fallout of whatever the hell it is you failed to secure."

"I hardly think that's a reasonable characterization," Roberts replied.

"What I want to know is this," Valerie said. "In the event of a worst-case scenario: home grown terrorists here have the flu, or some other pathogen from this lab, and they release it… what kind of resources will the federal government lend West Virginia to deal with the impact?"

"Obviously that's not a question I can answer," Roberts said.

"Of course not," Hatfield replied. "Because the answer is going to be none."

"At a minimum," Valerie said, "We need to set up a joint committee to plan to contain this thing if it blows up."

"We'll take your concerns under advisement," Roberts replied. His expression remained bland.

Hatfield stood. "Ms. Secretary, this is a waste of our time. I suggest we leave these gentlemen to cover their asses, and let's get to planning."

Valerie slowly stood. "I'm afraid I have to agree. Mr. Roberts, Doctor Seeger, Captain Floyd... Thank you for your time."

Back in the car, she said to Hatfield, "I think if it hasn't been closed, the investigation into this 'suicide' needs to be reopened. Quietly, though."

Hatfield nodded. "Yeah. I know just the guy to handle it; I'll have him report directly to me."

Valerie looked at him. "Mr. Hatfield, given the gravity of the situation ... we need to work together. I don't know the first thing about investigating something like this, but I'll do everything I can to give you political cover and whatever else you need. Fair enough?"

He met her eyes. "Agreed, Ms. Murphy. What do you have in mind?"

She thought for a moment, then said, "Your department investigates the suicide... Find out who this Clifford Webb knew, who might have had a reason to kill him. Who did he associate with? If he's responsible for hacking their security system, he had to have been working with someone. Meanwhile... I'll get the health department involved. We'll get contingency plans for an epidemic redrafted, start quietly pulling the resources together to deal with the worst-case scenario. I've still got a lot of contacts in Washington. If I can get some help on that end, it might make a big difference."

Hatfield nodded. The rest of the drive was quiet.

Two hours later, Wade Davis knocked, then entered Valerie's office.

"Valerie, I wanted to speak with you a moment about Hatfield. I understand you and he visited the Hamilton Biomedical facility earlier today?"

She nodded. "We did."

"Can you tell me why?"

Valerie frowned. "They requested the meeting; it was regarding a security breach there."

"Working with Hatfield is a terrible idea, Valerie."

As he spoke, he twisted a pen around in his hand, almost as if he were nervous. Valerie frowned and shook her head.

"I don't see why."

Outside, the sky was just beginning to turn a pale violet as the sun began to set over battered Charleston.

Davis approached, then took a seat across from her. "The bottom line is, you can't trust Hatfield. If he suggested to you that the sky was blue, I'd recommend you get an expert counsel to confirm the truth. He's trying to manipulate you on some level with this."

Valerie sighed and quickly considered Davis's words, then rejected them. "I agree, he can't be trusted. But the fact is, he's right about one thing. I have zero firsthand experience with this state. Not to mention this security breach could be a potential disaster bigger than anything we've faced yet."

Davis shrugged, apparently defeated. "It's your call, Valerie."

She nodded. "It is."

"Promise me this, please. Before you make any decisions, talk with me. I wouldn't put it past him to be using this as a way of somehow turning the tables on you. You understand?"

"Of course," she replied.

He gave a small nod, then stood and walked out.

Valerie turned toward the window, more than a little bit puzzled by Davis's behavior. Of course he didn't trust Hatfield; she didn't, either. But that certainly didn't negate the very real risk posed by the break-in at the lab. However much she might dislike or distrust Hatfield, she had to work with him. Surely Davis saw that?

Unless it was Wade she shouldn't trust. But that didn't make any sense. There was no doubt he'd genuinely grieved for her father, unless he was a far better actor than she gave him credit for. And of all the people she'd dealt with since arriving at the department, Wade had been the first to approach her as an equal and work with her, rather than put obstacles in her way.

She sighed. In reality, there was absolutely no one here she could trust. Someone in the department was leaking information to the insurgents, and she was the interloper, a political appointee in the midst of a crowd of career cops with their own loyalties, purposes and goals of which she knew nothing.

EIGHT

New York Times, April 2
SUPREME COURT AGREES TO HEAR ARGUMENTS ON ALABAMA SODOMY LAW
By Lawrence Jackson
Washington, DC – The Surpreme Court agreed on Monday to decide the fate of Alabama's 2016 law banning sodomy. In revisiting what legal scholars say is a replay of the 1986 Lawrence v. Texas case, when sodomy laws throughout the country were struck down by the high Court, gay rights advocates argue the case may represent the worst setback to gay rights in decades.

K EN Murphy stood in front of Valerie in his dress blue uniform, wearing full medals instead of the usual ribbons. His hands were relaxed at his side, and he had a strange smile on his face.

Valerie walked toward him. "Dad? What are you doing?"

Then suddenly, her father was flanked by Carl Metzenberger, the National Security advisor, on one side, and the President on the other.

Metzenberger spoke, his expression severe. "Mr. Murphy, it's time to say goodbye to your daughter."

"No," she said, stepping forward. She was stopped by a wall of glass. The President and Metzenberger led her father to a dentist's chair that hadn't been there before and leaned him back, strapping his arms and legs down. He kept the same damn smile on his face, like he was happy about it.

"No!" she screamed, uselessly banging her fists on the glass.

She watched helplessly as Metzenberger lifted a giant syringe. He held it up in the air, tapped the needle with the tip of his finger, and without hesitation plunged it into her father's chest.

Valerie woke up screaming.

❧

Two hours later Valerie looked at her handheld when it rang. A curse slipped involuntarily past her lips. David Brown. She stared at the phone for a moment. When had she last talked to David? It seemed like an eternity ago: before the war, before her father died, before she'd spent a lifetime in solitary confinement.

Her finger hovered over the Ignore button for just a moment, but at the last second she hit Answer and put the phone to her ear.

"Hello, David."

"Valerie! I was afraid this number wouldn't work anymore."

She leaned back in her office chair and looked out the window. The night sky was just beginning to lighten to rose. The sun would be up soon, and it wouldn't be long after that the shouts and chants of the protesters outside the building would begin.

Hearing his voice brought back a wash of memories. Life had been so much simpler a year ago, when she'd been dating David. She'd been on her way up, a star among congressional staffers, working to make a difference in people's lives. Her brother and father were still alive. She'd still been alive. She felt a yearning to go back to that life she'd never have again.

"I just got it turned back on," she responded quietly. "How are you, David?"

"I'm doing okay, Valerie. I just... I wanted to know if...well, if you were okay. You've had a rough time. And then I saw the article in the Post, and, well... I just wanted to check in."

Her eyes rolled toward the ceiling. Rough time.

"I'm all right." She was having difficulty controlling the shaking in her voice. The nightmare that had brought her screaming to wakefulness was still vivid in her mind.

"I'm coming to see you, Valerie."

She twitched. "David—"

"Don't say it," he interrupted. "I know you broke up with me. And I guess that's okay. But I'm still your friend, and... friends need to be there for each other. I've already bought my ticket; I get into Charleston at five o'clock."

Friends need to be there for each other. That seemed so far out an idea that it didn't even relate to her life right now.

Finally, she whispered, "All right, David. I'll be here until 7 or 8 probably. Send me a text to let me know where you're staying. We'll have dinner or something."

"Good! I'll see you then. You hang in there, Val."

She nodded. "I will. We'll talk later," she said quietly.

She hung up, and slowly put the phone down on her desk. She and David had dated for two years, even casually talked marriage. In the increasing tensions last fall, before the war, she'd unceremoniously dumped him—over the phone, at that. She didn't deserve friends who would talk to her after doing that.

What had he said? There was an article in the Post? She furrowed her brow. Leaning toward to her computer, she navigated to the Washington Post website.

The article was by a reporter she knew, though not well. Linda Monaghan had primarily covered economic policy when Valerie was on the hill, and she'd covered a number of stories Valerie had worked on.

"Former Congressional Aide Valerie Murphy In Too Deep, Say Aids." Despite the horrible headline, she scanned the article, growing increasingly angry the more she read. It was a hit piece, little more.

> "West Virginia Secretary-Elect of Law Enforcement and Military Affairs Valerie Murphy has been accused by a senior state government official of canceling a planned memorial service for an officer killed in the line of duty. Ms. Murphy, formerly chief of staff to West Virginia Governor Al Clark, was held by the Department of Homeland Security on unspecified charges related to the failed secessionist movement for more than three months earlier this year ... According to a senior West Virginia official, "Ms. Murphy is in over her head. She has no law enforcement experience at all, and canceling the memorial service shows she has no appreciation for the incredibly difficult job our public servants face every day..."

The article ended with the pathetic statement, "Ms. Murphy was unavailable for comment." She knew for a fact Monaghan had her cell number; the woman had called incessantly for details about Clark's opposition to the Fiscal Responsibility Act last year.

Valerie heard footsteps in the outside office, then there was a knock on her door.

"Come in," she said.

Davis poked his balding head in the doorway, then came in carrying two large cups of coffee. He placed one on her desk.

"Read the papers yet this morning?" he asked casually.

"Just the Post."

He nodded, then said, "It gets worse."

She frowned. "How?"

"Charleston Courier, Morgantown News, all the locals have their own versions. Unnamed sources in every case. It's character assassination, pure and simple. Hatfield's behind this; he's trying to stack the deck before your confirmation hearing. That doesn't even begin to cover what's floating around on the 'Net."

She frowned. "The 'Net?"

He shrugged. "Political blogs and the like. You don't want to look at it. Misogynist, hateful stuff."

Valerie sighed. "I didn't want this damn job in the first place. But I'll be damned if I'll let him yank the rug out from under me. We go on the offensive today."

He smiled. "That's the spirit. What's the plan?"

She braced herself.

"Proxy fight for today. It looks too defensive if I get out there. Al Clark got me into this; he'll be the anchor. I want him on CNN by noon. If you get any resistance, let me know, I'll call him. Al owes me, big-time. I've got a couple people in Washington who might go on record on this; I'll make some calls this morning. You'll talk to the press too... unnamed, I think. Make it clear this is not about me, it's about someone who wanted the job himself. Point some fingers, sling some mud. Fair?"

Wade grinned. "I like it."

"Anything in the papers about Hamilton Biomedical?"

"Nothing so far, but I wouldn't give it more than a few days."

Valerie nodded. "Meeting this morning. Pull in key people from enforcement and the National Guard Bureau. We need to start looking at containment options. I'll talk with the governor... we'll need a statewide response ready."

Valerie's phone rang. She looked at it and a big smile appeared on her face. Ambrose Hall had been then-Congressman Clark's chief of staff, and a good friend.

"I need to take this call," she said. "Let's get going on this, and I'll need a schedule for this morning's meetings as soon as you can."

"Already emailed it to you... I'll make adjustments and re-send," he said, waving.

She answered the phone. "Valerie Murphy."

"Well, hello, Valerie. Looks like you got sandbagged this morning."

She laughed. "Yes, I certainly did, Ambrose. God, it's good to hear from you."

"Well, dear, I'll not comment on the fact that you've been out of Homeland Security's clutches for almost two weeks and you haven't called. I'm sure you've been busy."

She sighed. "I'm sorry, Ambrose, I should have called. it's been... a nightmare."

"I'm sure, Valerie. Seriously... I wanted to offer my condolences regarding your father. Such a tragedy."

A stab of pain went through Valerie's chest. "Thank you, Ambrose."

"If there is anything at all I can do, please let me know."

She took a deep breath, and then said, "There actually is something."

"What is it? Anything at all, just ask."

"What are you doing these days?"

"Some consulting here and there, primarily for the Democratic National Committee."

She leaned forward. "I've got a job for you. A tough one."

"Not in West Virginia, I hope."

She chuckled. "I'm afraid so, Ambrose. But it's one you can sink your teeth into. I need a special prosecutor. Someone here has been leaking information... to the press, to possible insurgents. I need to find that person and put them away for a long time."

She heard Ambrose take a deep breath on the other end of the line. "You are serious."

"Of course I am. The governor will have to make the appointment, but I'm certain he'll do it."

She heard a sigh.

"I said 'ask anything,' didn't I? Foolish me."

"Ambrose... I need you on this one. I need someone I can trust."

"In that case... I'll be in Charleston by tomorrow."

She closed her eyes and breathed a sigh of relief. "Ambrose, I'd have your children for this."

He laughed. "That's hardly likely, dear. But all the same... for you, I'll do this. I'd better get off the phone before you ask me for anything else."

She laughed, too. "Ambrose... thank you. I'll see you soon."

She hung up, then pulled up her speed dial and dialed Al Clark. He agreed without hesitation to the appointment, as well as the press counteroffensive.

Turning back to her computer, she took a deep breath, knowing that it was a necessary step, but still reluctant. She googled her name.

The comments were the worst. "Traitor whore" was one of the milder comments. Conservative bloggers were on the attack, and there were dozens of hit pieces on the net.

Her personal email and Facebook page were full of very nasty comments. One comment on her Facebook page caught all of her attention. Written from an almost certainly fake account, it was brutal.

"You think you are such a smart Harvard whore, bitch, but I know where you live. Better watch where you walk alone at night, because I'll rape you in the ass and then gut you. If you don't like America go live somewhere else, fucking libtard traitor whore."

Bile rose in the back of her throat, and closed the window. Time to find something productive to do.

NINE

B ILLY Ray Corvath shut the door to the truck and leaned his head on the steering wheel, closing his eyes for a moment to shut out the sight of the parking lot and the long line of men and women waiting to get into the unemployment office.

"Maybe we should just go move in with my sister for a while," Faith said.

He shook his head, opened his eyes. He started the ignition and backed the truck out of the parking space. Mouth set in a thin line, he said, "I don't think so. They'll call soon. I'll put the extra TV up on eBay, maybe some other stuff. We'll get through."

Anxiety was written on her face. "I don't see how that's going to be enough, Billy. And what if they don't call? We can't go on like this forever; they're going to foreclose on the house."

He pulled out into traffic. The light at the next intersection was out, so he carefully nosed his way across it, then started toward home.

"Look," Corvath said, "It's not like things are going to be any better in Philadelphia. Your sister and her bonehead of a husband were locked down in their apartment for eight days during the riots last month."

Faith didn't have an answer for that. There wasn't one. Things might be bad here, but that didn't mean they weren't bad everywhere else.

They didn't speak during the rest of the drive home. He'd have preferred to have gone to the unemployment office on his own, but the grocery store was on the way, and going together meant saving a trip, and some gas. So she'd been there when he got the bad news he expected: even though he'd not worked since January or received a paycheck, he wasn't technically unemployed.

They wordlessly gathered the bags of groceries, mostly cheap generics and bulk items, and carried them into the too-big house he couldn't afford any more. He heard the phone ringing as he was unlocking the door, so he hurried into the kitchen and unceremoniously dumped the bags on the table, then picked up the phone.

"Hello?"

"Corvath? It's Asa Hatfield."

Corvath came to attention unconsciously.

"Yes, sir?"

"Got good news for you. I need you to come back to work. Today."

Corvath collapsed into one of the dining room chairs. "Yes, sir... I can be there in twenty minutes."

"Good. I'm assigning you directly to my office, so come straight here to see me."

"Will do, sir. Thank you."

Hatfield hung up unceremoniously. Corvath set the phone down and looked at Faith, who was staring at him, eyes wide.

"I have to report back in to work. Now."

She burst into tears.

౭ఎ

Thirty minutes later he was welcomed into Asa Hatfield's office. Hatfield closed the door, then sat down across the desk from him.

Corvath studied Hatfield for a moment. To the outside eye, a detective sergeant was pretty far down the food chain from the chief of law enforcement. But Corvath and Hatfield had served together in Iraq, and later—not long after his most recent promotion—Corvath had handled a particularly delicate case of corruption in the governor's office while reporting directly to Hatfield. The two men not only liked each other, but had built a certain level of trust between them.

Hatfield looked burdened now, with dark circles under his eyes. His bearing had a tension and energy to it that troubled Corvath.

"Welcome back, Corvath. Sorry we couldn't get you back on board earlier, but you know the situation."

Corvath didn't trust himself to speak on that topic. He simply nodded.

"Anyway, Corvath, I called you back because we've got a case. It's urgent, confidential... and very, very serious."

Corvath sat back to listen as Hatfield pushed a folder across the table to him.

"Three weeks ago, a consultant at Hamilton Biomedical was found dead in his apartment. Name was Clifford Webb. Thirty-two year old computer programmer, specialist in security systems. No known relationships in the state. He was renting a short-term-leased, furnished apartment in south Charleston. Charleston PD initially ruled it a suicide. Autopsy showed a high level of alcohol, but he died of strangulation... hung himself."

Corvath nodded. Obviously the suicide ruling wasn't the end of it.

"Here's the sensitive part. This is need-to-know only, Corvath. Hamilton Biomed specializes in studying some very dangerous diseases. Particularly the 1918 flu. Last week, there was a break-in at the facility, and we're having trouble getting any confirmation of what was stolen. The security system was hacked, and it was part of the system that Webb had access to."

Corvath muttered, "Holy shit."

"Yeah. You get the seriousness of it. We need to find out everything about Webb. Especially the last couple of weeks before his death. Who was he involved with? Finances? Where did he go for fun? Any secrets? Whatever you can find out. Especially whether he was responsible for the system hack, and if so, who he was working with."

Corvath nodded. "Right. Who's my contact at Hamilton Biomedical?"

Hatfield shook his head. "None. They refuse to cooperate with any state investigation; it's a turf battle with Homeland Security. You'll have to investigate it from the other end: his private life, family, finances, whatever you can dig up."

Corvath leaned back in his chair. "So, basically I need to learn everything I can about the guy and his work without learning anything about his work."

Hatfield shook his head. "Yeah, that's it. Why do you think I called you in on this?"

"All right, boss, I'm on it."

"Be careful, Sergeant. You don't want to get on DHS's wrong side. Actually, you don't even want to exist in their eyes. All right? Come to me quick if you find any issues on that end."

Corvath nodded. "Yeah, I will."

❧

Thirty minutes later, Corvath was at a hastily assigned desk, reviewing the file on Webb.

There wasn't much. Clifford Webb was a thirty-two year old computer programmer. Originally from Newark, he attended the New Jersey Institute of Technology, was an average student, and went on to work for Hewlett Packard as an IT consultant. That work took him to Washington, DC, where he'd done a lot of IT security consulting for various government agencies, including CDC. Corvath thought it was interesting that the contract that brought him to West Virginia was with the feds, not with Hamilton Biomedical, but given the nature of the facility, it made a certain amount of sense.

Single, never married. Webb's parents were divorced, the father estranged from the rest of the family. His mother still lived in Newark, and went by her maiden name. No known romantic interests, nor did it appear he'd made much in the way of friends during the three months he'd been in Charleston.

A quick Google search turned up Webb's blog, a painfully technical journal. Half the words in the titles of the entries made no sense to Corvath, much less the content. Corvath didn't expect to find anything of interest, but he reviewed the comments anyway: nothing incendiary, merely a continuation of technical discussions. It appeared Webb was a fairly well respected member of his field.

Webb had pages on Facebook and several other social networking sites. No posts about his work, but a lot of quasi-political posts, links to newspaper articles and political blogs. Webb leaned pretty far to the right, but not unusually so. He had 312 Facebook friends. If there were something there, it would take a while to find. Corvath made a note to cross-reference the Facebook connections with a listing of employees at Hamilton Biomedical... if he were ever able to get his hands on one.

Nothing on his blog or other online presences indicated unhappiness or depression. If anything, it gave an overall picture of someone deeply involved in his work, well respected, and consistently engaged with others. If Corvath were to tag anyone as suicidal, it wouldn't be Clifford Webb.

On the other hand, people presented exactly what they wanted to online. And the kind of depression that led to suicide was usually an intensely private experience.

A public records search turned up his mother's phone number in Newark. Corvath quickly dialed the number.

Three rings. "Hello?"

"Hello, is this Dianne Clarkson?"

"Yes. May I ask who is calling?"

"Yes, ma'am, my name is Detective Sergeant Billy Ray Corvath, with the West Virginia State Bureau of Investigation. I'm very sorry to bother you, but if you don't mind, I'd like to ask you a few questions about your son. And, I'd like to offer my condolences."

Her tone went cold. "Questions about Clifford? I... I understood his death was ruled a suicide."

"Yes, ma'am," he said in his most soothing tone. "Again, I'm very sorry to bother you with this, but it's routine, just to make sure we didn't miss anything."

"Of course," she replied.

"Ms. Clarkson, can you tell me anything at all about the weeks leading up to your son's death? Were there any signs of depression or other problems?"

She sighed on the other end of the line, and he could clearly hear her grief.

"I've gone over it... over and over again. Asking myself if there is something I missed, something... anything at all that would have given me a sign. But I can't think of a thing."

"When was the last time you and Mr. Webb spoke?"

"We spoke quite often through the winter As I'm sure you can imagine, he was very concerned about the war. In fact, for about three weeks in January he stayed at work around the clock, and slept there on a cot. There was some concern that rebels might try to... do something. I'm sure you know he worked at a very important CDC facility. I think the last time we talked was a week before he died."

"How did he sound?"

"Optimistic. There was a woman there he was thinking about asking out... I think her name was Maggie? He was seriously discussing staying in West Virginia for the long term."

Corvath scrawled "Maggie?" on his notepad.

"Do you know if he ended up going out with her?"

"I'm sorry, I... I don't."

"Ms. Clarkson... did he mention where he met Maggie?"

"Oh yes, he met her at work, of course. Clifford was never one for a very active social life; I'd expect work is the only place he met people."

"Thank you. I'll follow up with her as well."

"Sergeant... you don't think it was something to do with her, do you?"

"No, ma'am... like I said, this is an extra precaution we always take, it's just routine. And again, I'm really sorry to have bothered you with this."

They said goodbye, and he hung up the phone.

Who was Maggie? And why did a cheerful, optimistic guy at the top of his career suddenly hang himself without warning?

Back to the computer. No Maggie among his Facebook friends, but there was a Margaret Rutledge.

Bingo. Margaret Rutledge lived in Charleston, and listed her workplace as Hamilton Biomedical. She had even left a brief message on his Facebook page after he died. "I miss you, Cliff!"

Not the message he would've expect if there had been a budding romance between them. It was way too casual. Was she even upset?

Corvath needed to know more about Margaret Rutledge, and a lot more about Clifford Webb.

TEN

"Ambrose, it's such a relief to see you," Valerie said. She stood from behind the desk and hurried to hug her friend.

Ambrose Hall returned the embrace. As usual, the tall African-American former chief counsel to then-Congressman Al Clark wore an impeccably tailored double-breasted suit, highly polished shoes, and an unusual oiled and curled handlebar mustache.

"Valerie. It's very good to see you free."

She moved to the small conference table, sat, and nodded at the seat next to her. "Tell me how you've been," she said.

He smiled as he sat down. "To be perfectly honest, Valerie, I've been bored to tears. Most of the last two months I've been giving the democrats legal advice on their planned campaign ads. Watching paint dry would be much more interesting."

She returned the smile. "You won't be bored here."

"Indeed. Thus, I broke my promise to myself and have returned to the state of my birth. It was a challenge just getting into the building with the crowd of protestors outside. Now, tell me more about the plan here. I've spoken with Al. He's planning to make the appointment public later today, and I intend to jump in with both feet, so to speak."

She nodded, then slid a thick file folder across the table. "You'll find enough information to get started in here. Someone in the department is leaking information to insurgents. Troop locations, convoy movements, other information that probably only forty or fifty people have access to.

"Plus, the level of urgency on this: the Vice President is coming to speak in Charleston next week. It's top-secret for now, but if word gets out, he's going to be a target. We absolutely can't let anything happen to him. If you talk with Major Avedis—he's the military intelligence commander with the Army—he can brief you on what they've found thus far. But it's crazy to have the Army investigating this and not us. Plus, there've been other leaks which are purely politically motivated."

"Well," he said, "I'll review this information and we'll get things rolling. Will you put out some kind of a message to the top people in the department that I'll expect full cooperation?"

"Yes, of course."

Ambrose took her hand. "Now, Valerie, I want you to listen to me for a moment."

She met his eyes uncomfortably.

"Listen… How long have we known each other?"

Her eyes darted away. "Since my college internship with Al."

He nodded. "That's right. We've spent more time together, through more crises, than either of us have with partners, lovers, family. I probably know you better than you know yourself."

She nodded, not trusting herself enough to answer.

"Then I need you to hear me. I've never seen you this... rattled. Valerie. Your hands are shaking. You're pale. You've lost your father, spent three months in solitary confinement, had mud slung at you in the news media, been handed an impossible job. You need to make sure you are taking care of you. You understand me? I know you throw everything you've got into taking care of Al, your father before he died, and your job. But one of these days, if you don't take care of yourself, all that is going to catch up with you. I don't want to see you fall apart or have a nervous breakdown. You understand?"

Valerie nodded. "All I can do right now to hold myself together is take things as they come."

"Of course. I'll do what I can to help."

"Thank you."

They stood, and he gathered the files. Valerie opened the door to the office, and her assistant said, "Ms. Murphy, I know it's probably nothing, but there is apparently a teenage boy at the gate claiming you're expecting him? He claims he's family."

Valerie cocked an eyebrow, looked at Ambrose then back to the admin assistant. "I'm not expecting any teenagers here— what's his name?"

"Bobby Wright."

She frowned. Bobby! Her sixteen-year-old cousin lived in Atlanta. What was he doing here?

"Well... I do have a cousin from Atlanta with that name. Send him up, let's find out what this is about."

Ambrose looked amused. He winked at Valerie, then said, "I'll leave you to your domestic crisis, Secretary Murphy."

Valerie rolled her eyes, returned to her office and opened the first of the stack of files on her desk. A few minutes later a knock on the door disturbed her concentration. The door opened, and her assistant opened the door and said, "He's here, Miss Secretary."

"I'll see him."

Valerie looked at her young cousin as he came into the room. He was disheveled, clothes rumpled as if he'd slept in them, hair spiky and uncombed. He also had a black eye.

She stood and walked over to him. The last time she'd seen Bobby was at her little brother's funeral in the fall. A lifetime ago, really.

"Bobby," she said, her voice low. "Are you all right? What in God's name brought you all the way here?"

Despite the black eye, he grinned at her. "Good to see you, cuz. You got all thin while you were in jail... not that you weren't thin enough before."

Valerie closed her eyes and tried to count to ten. She made it to three. Almost.

"I see you haven't learned much tact since we saw each other last. What's going on?"

He shrugged, walked over to one of the chairs at the conference table and slumped into it unceremoniously. "Um... my Dad and I had a fight. Big one. And, well... here I am. I know it's not exactly kosher to just drop in like this, but... can I stay with you for a couple months? Maybe I can help out here, be an intern or something?" For a moment, his face lost its cocky composure, looking almost vulnerable. "I don't have anyone else I can ask. Um... please?"

She sat down at the table across from him. "Bobby... you're family. But you have absolutely no idea how incredibly bad an idea that is. How did you get here, anyway?"

He shrugged. "Greyhound most of the way, but the buses weren't running in West Virginia, so I hitched the rest of the way."

She closed her eyes, suppressing a shudder. "Have you any idea how crazy that is? West Virginia is a war zone." *Are you absolutely nuts?* she wondered.

He nodded. "Yeah, yeah, I know. I read all about it."

"And you still came here?" she asked in disbelief.

"Valerie," he said, his voice dropping. "I didn't have any-where else to go. It's not like I can go to Uncle Tom, I mean, he's in the Army. I know you think I'm a freak, but... come on... please?"

Valerie deflated. "I don't think you're a freak, Bobby. Judg-ment-impaired, maybe, but not a freak."

"Then I can stay?"

"Do your parents know where you are?"

He met her eyes, shook his head.

Valerie sighed, then took out her phone and dialed her least favorite relative. A moment later, Bobby Wright, Senior, an-swered the phone.

"This is Bobby Wright."

"Bobby, this is Valerie."

She could almost hear the gears turning in his head. A mo-ment later he said, "Valerie Murphy?"

"Yeah. It seems I have something that belongs to you."

"Oh, holy shit! Is Bobby there? In West Virginia?"

"Yes."

"His mother's been frantic. The little shit ran away three days ago."

She looked at Bobby, her eyes falling on his still-swollen black eye.

She took a deep breath, then said, "Look, Bobby, obviously it's not my place to get involved in a family argument, and I don't really know what any of this is about. But he's asked if he can stay here with me for a couple months, and if I'd put him to work here at the department. If it works for you, I'm willing to do it. Maybe a cool-down period would be appropriate."

Bobby pressed his hands together in mock prayer, then mouthed, "Thank you."

His dad breathed on the line for a moment, then said, "Yeah, maybe that is a good idea. Would it be safe?"

"No reason it shouldn't be. He'd be here in an office, and I've got 'round the clock security."

"Jesus H. Christ. You should seriously quit that job, Valerie. Come work for me, I could use a good agent."

Valerie shook her head even though she knew he couldn't see the motion. Be a real estate agent in Atlanta, working for her philandering uncle? Not in a million years.

"I'm pretty committed here, Bobby, but thank you for the offer," she said. "Look, I'll do my best to keep Bobby out of trouble. For the time being, I'm staying in a secure apartment building, and I have armed guards everywhere I go. There's some risk, but more to me than him."

"Well... the experience would probably do the little shit some good. He's throwing away his life down here."

She winced at her uncle's characterization of his son.

Her uncle continued, oblivious to her hostility. "Yeah, he can stay there with you. Nothing I can do to stop him anyway. Just make sure he calls his mother, okay? She's a basket case over this."

"I will."

They said goodbye and she hung up the phone, then eyed her young cousin. "All right, Bobby. I've got a meeting in five minutes, which I've now lost the time to prepare for. I'm turning you over to my assistant, and she'll find something for you to do. You can stay, but give me any trouble and I'll pack you up back to Georgia in a heartbeat. Clear?"

He nodded. "Thank you, Val," he said very quietly.

ELEVEN

D ETECTIVE Sergeant Corvath took a sip of his coffee, then sat up as he saw the young blonde woman walking across the parking lot. She appeared to be twenty-something, and wore a below-knee-length green skirt and matching blouse. She crossed the parking lot and entered the apartment building quickly.

Once she was inside the building, he opened the door and got out of his truck, then walked across the lot and into the building behind her. She would just be putting down her bag when he knocked.

Corvath rapped on the door with his knuckles. He waited a few moments, then knocked again.

A moment later he saw the security peephole darken. A tremulous voice inside asked, "Who is it?"

"Miss Rutledge? I'm Detective Sergeant Billy Ray Corvath with the state bureau of investigation. I'd like to ask you some questions, please."

A pause, then he heard the chain on the door click into place, followed by the sound of the deadbolt sliding open. She opened the door two inches.

"Can I see some identification?"

Careful girl. Smart. He held his badge and identification out to her through the door opening. She took it a moment, then apparently decided it was genuine. A moment later she closed the door, unlatched the chain, opened it wide, and returned his ID.

A cautious expression on her face, she said, "May I ask what this is about, Detective?"

"Yes, ma'am. I'm doing a routine follow-up on the death of a co-worker of yours. Clifford Webb. I believe you were acquainted with him?"

She nodded, looking troubled now. "Of course. Come in, I'll be happy to answer any questions. Can I get you anything to drink? A glass of water?"

"No thanks," he said, following her into the apartment.

She gestured toward the kitchen table. "Have a seat." She sat down across from him. "What can I do for you? I... I'm afraid I didn't know Cliff very well; I was stunned when he killed himself."

Corvath studied her expression as she spoke. Appropriately sad, but not grief-stricken. Concerned. Nothing more or less than what he would have expected.

"Can you tell me a little about your relationship with him?"

She shrugged. "To be honest, there wasn't much of one. We knew each other from work, and had lunch together a couple of times a week. He did ask me out, just a few days before he died. We went to dinner and a movie. I think he read rather more into the relationship than I did, or at least he wanted to. He was a nice guy, but not really my type."

"Oh? How so?"

She frowned. "This will sound quaint I'm sure, but my faith is very important to me. He had little interest in such things."

"I see," he replied. "Did you see any signs of... depression? Unhappiness? Anything to indicate he was likely to commit suicide?"

She shook her head emphatically. "No, not a thing." Her eyes dropped to the floor. "Well...."

Corvath leaned forward. "What is it?"

She met his eyes and blushed a little.

"He was a very lonely man, Detective. And... I told you he was considerable more attracted to me than...." She fumbled for words. "Detective, I'm afraid I may... I mean... I feel somewhat responsible. I was pretty firm in telling him... we weren't going to go out again. He was disappointed."

Corvath was stunned. She believed he killed himself over her rejection after one date? Was this some colossal arrogance? Or was there more to it? Some people were just neurotic, and blamed themselves for a lot of things, but this seemed extreme.

He struggled to frame his next question, then just blurted it out. "Did he do or say anything to indicate suicide was likely?"

"I didn't see him again after our date. We went out on Saturday night. He didn't show up for work on Monday."

"He wasn't reported missing until Wednesday."

"Actually, I talked with my supervisor about it on Tuesday morning, when he didn't come in for the second day in a row. I'm not sure why they waited another day before reporting anything."

"Were you concerned?"

"Yes, of course. He was a nice man, even if he wasn't really for me. I considered him a friend."

"As best as we can determine, Mr. Webb died early on Sunday morning. You may be the last person who saw him alive. You're aware he left no note? No diary, nothing to indicate he was considering suicide or why. Nothing online. In fact, his last blog entry on Saturday afternoon was perfectly normal."

She sat up straight. "Detective, what are you trying to imply?"

He didn't want to say it outright, but subtlety was never Corvath's thing.

"I don't think it was a suicide at all."

She blinked, and her eyes suddenly watered. If she was acting, she was damn good. "You think he was murdered?"

Corvath nodded. "I think there is a strong possibility of it. No offense, Miss Rutledge, you're an attractive lady, but I find it difficult to believe that a successful, apparently self-satisfied man at the height of his career killed himself after one date with you."

She blushed. "You're becoming offensive, Detective."

"Not trying to be offensive, ma'am, but it's my job to dig these things up. What time did you last see him?"

"He drove me home at about midnight."

Corvath wished they had a more precise time of death. Unfortunately, Webb had been dead four days by the time he was found. The best the coroner had been able to do was place it between midnight and six a.m.

"What did you discuss in the car?"

She sighed. "Not much... I'd already made it clear I didn't want to see him outside of work again, and he took it pretty hard. He was very quiet."

"Can you tell me anything about his work?"

The quick change in subject threw her off balance.

"I didn't know much about it... He was a security consultant, did something with computers. I don't really know much about computers; I couldn't tell you more than that."

"Did he have an office? Is it an open floor plan?"

She looked puzzled.

"It's mostly open, but the security staff had closed offices. And yes, I had one or two occasions to talk with him in his office."

"About?"

She shrugged. "I work in the Communications Department, and we've done several media campaigns focused on the security at the facility. I met Cliff while working on one of those."

"Was he cooperative? Enthusiastic?"

She leaned back, looking at Corvath as if she was starting to get annoyed… or possibly defensive.

"I don't understand where all these questions are leading, Detective."

"Ms. Rutledge, part of my job is to understand as much about Mr. Wells as I can. His state of mind, his activities during and outside of work, and especially what was on his mind during the last two weeks of his life. Fair enough?"

"I didn't really know Cliff well enough to know the answers to any of that."

"Just answer the question, okay? Was he enthusiastic about it?"

She nodded. "Yes, Cliff loved talking about his work. He wrote about it in his blog; he would go on about it at length to just about anyone who would listen."

Corvath looked at her for a few moments. Then he said, "Something doesn't ring true here, Margaret. You're telling me you think he killed himself because you rejected him, but at the same time you're saying you didn't know him very well, that you were just acquaintances. It doesn't make any sense."

She was unperturbed. "I didn't say he killed himself because of me. I said… I felt guilty that I might have contributed to it. How am I supposed to know what else was going on in his life? I'm sure there are plenty of other things there I know nothing about. He was close enough to being an atheist. Maybe he just felt empty."

Corvath frowned. "Can you suggest anyone else I can speak with? Any close friends or co-workers who spent more time with him?"

"Matt Burris maybe, he's another security contractor; they worked pretty closely together."

"Thank you. I'd like you to remain available for more questions if they come up."

"Of course."

Corvath left, not at all satisfied with the answers he was getting.

&

Bud Johnson crushed the note and tossed it into the wastebasket.

"I'm tired of the threats, Mary. I won't stand for this."

His wife stared at him from across the table, and said, "Bud, I'm afraid."

He reached out and took her hands between his. "Mary, let the fear pass. God's will be done, not ours. I won't knuckle under to these people. They're no better than terrorists."

She sniffed, and said, "I know, Bud. But you're more than a minister. You're a husband and father. And... I need you. Please don't do this."

He stood and took his wife in his arms. "I love you, Mary Beth. But I must do what I must do. Pray for us."

He parted from her and gently kissed her on the forehead. He straightened his tie and buttoned his coat. "It's time to go."

"Children!" she called.

Bud, Junior and Eli came out of their room. Both wore neatly arranged suits, though Eli's hair was getting a little long.

"Don't you think it's time to get a haircut, Eli?" Bud said. "Those curls would look beautiful on a girl."

Eli blushed, said "I'll get a haircut this weekend, Dad."

Bud smiled, and led his family out of the house and toward the church.

❧

The noise of more than a thousand congregants began to settle as they took their seats. In the background, he could hear the large diesel generators outside, which gave power to the church. Power had been out in the town almost continuously for weeks, but the church should be a tower of light.

Bud took his position at the pulpit and the crowd began to quiet. He looked out at them, gave a beatific smile, and began.

"My friends, tonight I wish to speak about many of the things which have been on all of our minds in recent days and months. We live in a time of strife and trouble, here at home and abroad, and I've spent much of the last several weeks praying and listening for God to give me a sign. What is the proper course for our future, when everything is so certain?"

"Six months ago, I stood at this pulpit and I told you that I was choosing to vote for independence for West Virginia. I explained my reasons to you, and my concerns for the greater United States of America. I told you, we've left God behind, and left God out of our lives. We've allowed the liberals and socialists to dominate our political discussions. We've opened the door to sinners and homosexuals in our military and in our government."

Bud took a sip of water, then spoke again. "We lost! I don't know why we lost; perhaps that was the inevitable result. Perhaps we didn't have enough faith. Perhaps, as with Job, God felt that we must be tested even more. And now, we are facing that test. There are those of you out there who are even now arguing that we must continue the struggle, that we must fight on, secretly, and from hiding.

"As many of you know, I've worked closely with the federal troops here in Morgantown in recent weeks. Our people need decent water and power and medical care, and I have worked with the soldiers—men and woman like ourselves—in order to help our community recover. And just in the last day I've myself been warned... threatened in fact... that we must not co-operate with the federal occupiers who are spread throughout our state.

"My friends, I say no. In prayer and in meditation I have sought the answers, and what I believe is that while God may support an honorable struggle for our rights, he would not support skulking in the darkness, striking and killing and hiding. I believe it is time to move on from this discussion. Move on to arguing and fighting within the system, not without it. We must do what we can to rebuild our state, which means that whether we would choose to or not, we must ignore the threats, we must invite the occupiers into our homes, we must cooperate with them and rebuild our state."

Bud's eyes fell on his wife and two sons, sitting in the front row. Mary Beth looked frightened, but proud. His sons looked uncomfortable, as they often did sitting in the front row of the church.

"Let us pray," he said.

There was a murmur as hundreds of worshippers repositioned themselves.

"Dear Lord," he called out, "in this time of trouble and tribulations, we ask you for guidance! We ask—"

His words were cut off by a loud crack, then another. The first bullet, a high-velocity rifle shot, entered his forehead, passed through his brain and broke out the back of his skull without slowing down. The second hit a moment later through the bottom of his chin as his head was thrown back, and blew out the top of his skull, splattering most of Bud Johnson's brain across the wall behind the altar. A woman screamed as he slumped to the floor.

The screams rose to a thunderous pitch the crowd realized what had happened. Most of them were in shock, men holding their children and wives near the floor. During the chaos that followed, no one noticed as a large man in the very back of the room gently set his rifle on the floor next to front door and slipped outside.

TWELVE

THE entrance to Hamilton Biomedical was set a hundred yards back from the road, and Corvath would have missed it had he not been navigating by GPS. As it was, he drove by it and had to do a U-turn on the narrow two-lane black top, then come back down the road and turn right into the long driveway.

At the end of the driveway stood a twenty-foot-high fence and gatehouse manned by two men who looked suspiciously like U.S. Army soldiers, right down the M16 rifles, Kevlar helmets and other assorted combat gear.

Corvath came to a stop and rolled down his window as one of the soldiers approached. A sergeant, he wore the combat patch of the Eighty-second Airborne Division.

"Can I help you, sir?" the sergeant asked.

Corvath held out his credentials. "Detective Sergeant Billy Ray Corvath, State Bureau of Investigation. I'd like to see Captain Floyd, please."

The soldier took the credentials and stepped back into the guard shack, while his partner continued to stand watch. Not the normal greeting for a research facility. But considering what they studied here, better to be safe than sorry, Corvath supposed.

They kept him cooling his heels for nearly ten minutes while the sergeant spoke on the phone. Checking whether he was who he said he was? Probably. Which might not be a good thing. Corvath remembered Hatfield's emphatic warning: he didn't even want to exist in the eyes of Homeland Security.

After an excruciatingly long wait, the Sergeant returned to the vehicle and handed Corvath his credentials.

"I'm sorry, sir, but I can't help you. You can back up, there's a vehicle turn-around right over there," he said, pointing back in the direction of the main road.

Corvath frowned. "What do you mean, you can't help me? Is Captain Floyd not available? He's the head of security, correct?"

"Sir, this is a federal facility, and you may not enter. I'm not at liberty to tell you anything else. Please turn your vehicle around, and have a nice day. Somewhere else."

Irritation creeping into his voice, Corvath said, "I'm investigating a murder here, soldier. You can't just run me off. I'd like to speak with your superior officer right now."

The sergeant stood up straight, then looked at his partner and gave a nod. The other soldier unslung his rifle and held it ready.

"Sir, I repeat, you are criminally trespassing on a top-secret federal installation. If you do not remove yourself and your vehicle within the next thirty seconds, I'll be forced to place you under arrest. If you resist, I am authorized to use whatever force necessary to obtain your cooperation. Am I clear, sir?"

Holy shit! Corvath looked at the soldier in shock, then said the only thing he could. "Fine. I'm gone."

The sergeant and his partner stood watching as Corvath put the truck in reverse and backed up to the turn-around. He put the truck in drive, made a U-turn, and drove out.

He shook his head. He had expected some resistance, maybe some jurisdictional back and forth. Threats of arrest—or deadly force—had not been anywhere in his expectations. Being serious about security was one thing. But this was just crazy.

Corvath jerked when his newly reactivated cell phone rang. He glanced down at the screen. Detective Mays. Though not involved in the January war, Mays had been injured when a cruise missile struck the old Military and Law Enforcement building in Charleston. With two broken legs, he wasn't going to spend much time out in the field, but he could run credit checks and make phone calls.

Corvath pressed the Talk button, then held the phone between his ear and shoulder as he drove.

"Corvath speaking."

"Corvath, it's Mays. Got some interesting news for you."

"Go ahead."

"Okay... first thing, I wasn't able to cross reference your pal's online friends with a list of employees at Hamilton, because Hamilton refuses to release anything. They referred me to CDC, who referred me to DHS, who told me politely to go suck wind."

Corvath sighed.

"Go on," he said.

"Okay. Here's where it gets interesting. I ran a credit and backgrounder on Margaret Rutledge. She comes up clean as a whistle. No arrests, not even a speeding ticket. Goes to church every Sunday and Wednesday night. School records... none for high school; she was home-schooled. Graduated with a double degree in divinity and communications from Oral Roberts University. Four-point-oh."

"Odd combination for someone working at a big scientific project," Corvath replied.

"Yeah, I suppose. Anyway, there was nothing there. She's kind of a poster child for the perfect Christian girl. Except for one tiny thing."

Corvath waited. When he didn't, Corvath said, "All right, Mays, don't drag it out. What is it?"

Mays said, "She drives a 2018 Ford Focus, and apparently didn't have the credit for it. The co-signer on the note is William Channing. Channing's father is Roland Channing... the Reverend Roland Channing, who heads the New World Pentacostal Church in Baughman Settlement. Reverend Channing's other son, John Channing, was briefly detained as a suspect in the Arlington bombing last spring."

Corvath nearly dropped the phone, and quickly pulled to a stop on the shoulder. He didn't notice the blue Ford sedan half a mile back on the road that also pulled over a moment later.

"Say again, Mays? She's linked to a suspect in the Arlington bombing?"

"Not exactly. John Channing was initially a suspect, then he morphed into a 'person of interest,' then finally DHS stopped investigating him altogether. I haven't been able to get my hands on any of the records from the investigation, but a friend of mine at the FBI tells me that the investigation in Channing was dropped on two fronts: first, the evidence was extremely flimsy. Second, congressional pressure."

"Congressional pressure? From whom?"

"My friend wouldn't say, but apparently there's still a lot of questions and unhappiness in the FBI. Seems DHS stepped in and basically pushed them out of the investigation entirely, so he never got an answer that satisfied him."

"Hmmm... Do we know where John Channing is now?"

"No. But that doesn't really mean anything. I did some checking. The New World Pentacostal Church isn't just a church. They've got a huge compound outside of town, somewhere around two hundred residents, and almost nine hundred acres of land. They don't really mix with the town much at all, except a few select people who do the shopping and whatnot. Kids in the compound are all home-schooled. That's where Margaret Rutledge grew up. Other than her birth certificate and high-school equivalency, she basically just popped out into the world whole six years ago, with almost no record of her existence prior to that. I don't know if there's any family relationship between Channing and Rutledge."

"They're close enough he'll cosign on her loans, though," Corvath replied.

"Right. And Channing is wealthy... extremely wealthy, from what I can find out. His operation sells sermons, books, videos, all kinds of stuff. He's pretty influential in some very conservative Christian circles."

"Nothing wrong with that."

"There is if his son is involved with a terrorist act."

"Gotcha. See what else you can find out about Channing and his family. But Mays... be careful. I already had a rifle stuck in my face today. This case is looking more complicated than I thought."

"Son of a bitch. You gonna tell me what it's about? Why are you interested in Rutledge?"

"You don't want to know."

"Damn. How did I know you were going to say that?"

☙

Three hours later, Corvath was sitting at the dinner table with Faith and their six-year-old son Corey. At that moment,

Corey was doing a particularly funny imitation of a bronto-saurus.

Faith, sensitive to her husband's moods as usual, remained quiet during dinner, and didn't ask him much about his day. He was brooding about the case.

The connection between Margaret Rutledge and John Channing scared the crap out of him. It turned a simple sui-cide—possibly murder—into something much bigger and much more frightening. But there simply wasn't enough infor-mation to go anywhere with it yet. Hopefully Mays would be able to come up with some background on Channing in the morning. Corvath would be reporting in to Hatfield tomorrow anyway, to let him know the progress of the case.

All three of them jumped at the sudden pounding at the door.

Corvath stood and automatically felt for his sidearm. He wasn't wearing it, of course; he never did at home. Faith's face went pale when he reached up to the top cabinet, took down the pistol and clipped it to his belt.

Whoever was out there pounded on the door again. Loud, as if hitting it with a fist.

Corvath walked to the door and looked through the peep-hole. Three men in suits outside, suit jackets unbuttoned and open. He didn't know them.

"Who is it?" he called through the door.

"Department of Homeland Security. Open up, Corvath."

Son of a bitch.

Corvath unlocked the door and opened it. He kept a hand resting on his sidearm.

"You got credentials?" he asked.

The apparent leader of the trio handed over a folder. JD Roberts, Special Agent in Charge.

"We've got some questions for you, Corvath," Roberts said. His eyes turned toward Faith, who had entered the room behind Corvath, anxiety written on her face. "Please come with us."

Corvath swallowed. If he refused, there was nothing to stop them from just grabbing him. He was all too aware that habeus corpus had been suspended in West Virginia, not to mention any other legal protections. Better to just cooperate.

He turned to Faith, tried to maintain a casual expression and failed miserably. "I'll be back in a bit, honey. Can you put Corey to bed tonight?"

"Okay," she said, a quiver in her voice. She was frightened, all right, but standing tall. In that moment, Corvath fell in love with his wife all over again. "See you in a little while?"

"Yeah," he replied, his mouth dry. He took his coat off the rack and put it on, then said, "Let's go, gentlemen."

Roberts glanced down at Corvath's sidearm with a sneer, then turned bacto the outside. A large black SUV with deeply tinted windows sat at the curb. Roberts opened the door to the back seat and said, "Get in, Detective Sergeant Corvath."

Corvath hesitated. Their neighbor, Bob Reynolds, used to work on the staff of the adjutant general of the state National Guard. At the end of January, he'd disappeared. Rumor had it he'd gotten into a similar SUV with suited men.

Roberts repeated himself. "Get in, Detective Sergeant Corvath. We're going to have a talk, drive around, see the neighborhood a bit, then we'll drop you off. Nothing to be frightened of, yet."

Yet.

Corvath shook his head minutely, then got into the vehicle. Faith was no doubt looking out the window. He didn't know what they would do if he didn't obey, but whatever it was, she didn't need to see it.

Once seated, Roberts slammed the door closed, then walked around the vehicle and slid into the back seat beside him as the two unnamed DHS agents jumped into the front seat. The SUV took off with a screech of tires.

Roberts didn't speak. Corvath sat, claustrophobic and silent, but noting that there was no door handle on the inside of the back seat. Just like a police car. They hadn't taken his sidearm, but he had no illusion that he would be using it.

The agent drove onto a main road, then onto the highway.

Corvath was determined not to open the conversation. Eventually Roberts would tell him what the hell was going on.

After about ten minutes, he realized where they were going: up the mountain road, above Charleston. He kept silent, and eventually the SUV came to a stop at an overlook. In the darkness, he could see the lights of the city spread out below them. Large patches had no streetlights, no electricity at all.

"Look down there, Corvath," Roberts said. He pointed to a black patch, roughly downtown. "Do you know what that is?"

It was obvious. "That's where the Byrd Federal Building used to stand."

Roberts nodded. "That's right. You know what my job is, correct?"

Corvath frowned. "Scaring the crap out of the wives of honest cops?"

One of the agents in the front seat snickered.

Roberts smiled. "My job," he said, in a tone of voice that sounded if it was directed at a six-year-old, "Is to protect the nation against bad guys. I'm basically a cop, just like you. Except on a much bigger stage. You go after murderers and thieves. I go after mass murderers. See? We're on the same side."

Corvath shook his head. "You could have fooled me. A phone call would have done just fine."

Roberts shook his head. "No, a phone call would have failed to make the impression I wish to make. Do we agree that first impressions are important?"

"I agree that you give a great first impression of a jack-booted fascist."

"I'm sorry you feel that way, Corvath." He seemed to consider for a second, then said, "No, actually I'm not. I don't really give a shit how you feel. What I want to know is, why you were at the Hamilton Biomedical facility today. What's your interest?"

"I'm investigating the death of Clifford Webb."

"Clifford Webb committed suicide."

"Possibly. The evidence doesn't point that way as clearly as the Charleston police thought."

"Perhaps. What have you found so far?"

Corvath raised his eyebrows. "Not a lot. No reason for Webb to kill himself. But ..."

"But, what?"

"I'm pretty sure Webb was murdered. And the reasons had something to do with Hamilton Biomedical."

Roberts nodded. "You are correct, Corvath."

Surprised, Corvath responded, "I am? You know?"

"Of course I know. We're investigating it ourselves. And you're stumbling all over our investigation, in a very clumsy way. Sergeant, you're going to end up getting someone killed if you keep this up."

Corvath narrowed his eyes. "Then what am I missing? Fill me in."

"I don't think so. I am, however, going to make myself very clear. You are to drop your investigation, and turn over everything you have to me."

"Why would I do that? Are you bored? I thought you said murder isn't a big enough crime for you."

"I'm not asking, Corvath. You're impeding a very serious investigation into some very serious terrorists. If you don't drop it, we're going to take you into custody. You're not going to like that, Corvath. This isn't the world of nice little arrests and arraignments and prosecutions, you know. We take you into custody, you just disappear. Indefinitely."

Corvath took a deep breath. Roberts wasn't making an empty threat. They could detain him as long as they wanted, and there was no legal response, no challenge he could mount. Faith and Corey would be left with no support. No husband, no father.

"I thought you said we were on the same side, Roberts. How does that fit with your threats?"

"Big picture, Sergeant. You don't have it, and I do. Do we have an understanding?"

Corvath swallowed. "I need to talk with Hatfield. I was brought back on duty for this investigation. He's not going to sit idle while I just quit."

Roberts shrugged. "Hatfield is not my problem. You go talk to him. I want you in my office by noon tomorrow, with all of your files and notes from the investigation. And if I don't get all of them, you won't be leaving through the front door, nor will you see your wife and child again any time soon. Do I make myself absolutely fucking clear?"

Corvath nodded. He had no choice.

THIRTEEN

ARRY'S Hog House was a popular barbecue three blocks from the temporary headquarters of the Military and Law Enforcement Department. Popular before the war, anyway: the lack of a functioning economy in West Virginia had hurt business across the board, and Harry's was one of the few downtown restaurants still open at all. When Valerie walked into the dark restaurant with booths that could seat six comfortably, she saw only two patrons in the back.

She walked in their direction, then slid into the booth across from Asa Hatfield without a word. Henry stayed near the door, eyes scanning the place. She noticed him nod to the man with Hatfield.

Hatfield nodded, then spoke.

"Miss Murphy, this is Detective Sergeant Billy Ray Corvath. He works for me in the enforcement division."

Valerie nodded. "Nice to meet you, Detective."

Corvath was clearly uncomfortable. "You too, Miss Secretary."

"What's this about, Hatfield? Odd place to meet, don't you think?"

Hatfield frowned. "At this point, I don't trust anyone. And Corvath has stumbled onto a hornet's nest. Best we talk in private."

"All right."

Hatfield turned to Corvath. "All right, fill her in, Detective."

Corvath leaned forward and spoke barely above a whisper. Valerie had to lean in to make out his words.

He outlined his investigation, starting with his interview with Clifford Webb's mother, former co-workers, apartment manager, everyone who knew anything about him. He moved on from there to the interview with Margaret Rutledge, and her claim that maybe Webb killed himself because she had rejected him.

"They only dated once?" Valerie asked.

"That's right. It doesn't really stand up to close examination. But we found a very troubling link between her and one of the original suspects in the Arlington bombing."

Corvath went on to detail connection between Margaret Rutledge and the Channing family.

Valerie closed her eyes. Memory of the Arlington bombing was still very clear to her. It had been close enough to rattle the windows of then-Congressman Clark's office on Capitol Hill—close enough for her to see the huge plume of smoke rising from the burning buildings in Crystal City. The second worst terrorist attack ever conducted on American soil, and no trace had been found of the perpetrators.

"So... you're suggesting that John Channing may have been involved in the Arlington bombing after all. And that there's at least a link to the break-in at Hamilton Biomedical."

"Yeah, that's about it."

She looked at Hatfield. "This is... very serious."

Hatfield interjected. "You aren't kidding. And that's not the worst of it. Corvath, tell her about your friendly visit from DHS."

Valerie listened as Corvath related the nighttime visit from JD Roberts to his home, and the threats he had made. "When

I got home," he said, "I… my personal computer had been tampered with."

"Tampered with?"

"It was riddled with child porn. Enough to put me away for forty years. Fucking had to format my hard drives to get rid of everything. And the thing is, my wife was home when they put it on there. Had to have been done remotely." He was sweating as he told the story. "Which means they could do exactly what they said they could, even out in the open. Who would believe me?"

She was shaking with rage. "I assume you did as he said, and turned everything over?"

Corvath nodded. "I'm not a fool, Secretary Murphy. My family needs me. I turned over everything. But I kept copies. I don't know what Roberts's problem is, but there is no way I'm dropping the investigation now."

Hatfield said, "You need to be very, very careful, Corvath. If DHS is watching you, they could pick you up any time."

"That's right," Valerie said. "And there's nothing to stop them from holding you forever, Detective."

"Or just killing him," Hatfield said.

"Why would they do that?" she asked.

"How the hell should I know, Murphy? But they've got the legal authority to detain or kill U.S. Citizens on the President's say-so, and no one can say 'boo.'"

She sat back, closed her eyes. She knew that was true. "But why wouldn't DHS want this investigated? It doesn't make any sense."

Corvath said, quietly, "Detective Mays won't discuss the case with me at all now… but before Roberts visited him, he told me something disturbing. Right after the Arlington bombing, there was a joint investigation. DHS, FBI, Army Intelligence. DHS pushed everyone out, over the loud objections of the FBI. The thing is, DHS forced the investigation to stop investigating Channing. Word was, there wasn't enough evidence to implicate him, and a lot of congressional pressure. This is going to sound crazy, but who's to say that Channing doesn't have ties to DHS? They operate in their own little world. No oversight—they can pretty much do anything they want. Maybe someone in DHS didn't want the Arlington bombing to be solved."

She shook her head. "I can't see that. Why wouldn't they want it solved?"

Corvath frowned. "Who really gained from the Arlington bombing? Sure as hell wasn't anyone in West Virginia. No known terrorist group took credit. I'm no terrorism specialist, but don't they take credit when they blow the hell out of something? Isn't that the whole point? But DHS got all kinds of shiny new toys and powers out of it. Huge budget increase, and no one knows what they actually spend any of it on."

"That's... I'm sorry, but that's like the worst of the conspiracy theories I've seen on the web."

Hatfield said, "Maybe not. But that doesn't mean there aren't one or two of them in that bunch who might look the other way when it benefits them. They don't have to be involved in a conspiracy... Maybe it's more of a case of protecting the terrorists they like versus killing the ones they don't."

She signed. "What do we know about Channing?"

Corvath said, "I did a lot of digging. Roland Channing is considered a bit of a fringe case by most of the mainline Pentecostal groups, but in some ways he's very influential. You ever heard of Rousas John Rushdoony?"

She shook her head. "No, but I'm not really up on religious groups."

"Rushdoony was a bit of a nutcase, if a brilliant one. He died in 2001. Basically, he argued that Christians were required to unite the government and the church. He recommended Old Testament style courts and punishment, all under the rule of God. Stoning for adultery, hanging homosexuals, keep women at home popping out babies, and more. Huge following in the Christian homeschooling community: his entire goal was to reformat American government to fit under the Ten Commandments. He's considered somewhat of a heretic by a lot of the Pentecostals, but he had a great deal of influence in some key areas. Channing shared much of his philosophy. Channing's father founded their group as an isolated, apolitical isolationist group—a cult, really. Bought hundreds of acres near Front Royal back in the late sixties. Home-schooled all the kids— no one really knows anything about them—until the old man passed away and Roland Channing took over in 1981."

"What happened then?"

"Channing wrote a tract which circulated very widely in those days, not just with the Pentacostals, but also with the Christian Identity movement, bunch of other really right-wing groups. His argument was simple: isolation puts off salvation. Instead, he recommended effectively taking over the government. Giving a rigorous education to the kids, putting them all through college, then working to place them in positions of power and influence. Judges, government officials, the police, anywhere. Kids from his compound, and some other related ones, started hitting the mainline divinity schools and other colleges around that time. And not just religious colleges... from what I've been able to find, they've had people through MIT, Georgetown, Princeton. Its quiet, but Channing has ties with mid and high-level government officials throughout the federal and state government."

"What, like moles from a foreign country?"

"Yes, exactly. Who is to say that Channing doesn't have a son-in-law or cousin or something in charge of DHS's investigation? What do we really know about how they work internally?"

Silence fell at the table. Then Hatfield said, "Murphy, got a question for you. What do you know about JD Roberts?"

She shook her head. "Almost nothing."

Hatfield pulled a printout from his pocket. It was Roberts's official bio on DHS website.

"Take a look."

She did. JD Roberts grew up in Front Royal, Virginia. Almost directly across the state line from Baughman Settlement.

જી

That evening, Valerie walked into the bar in the Charleston Ritz-Carlton Hotel. It was extremely quiet: a few small groups sat murmuring over drinks. In the back corner, a youngish man in a tuxedo played very quietly on a baby grand piano.

The maitre'd approached her. "Good evening, madam, a seat for one? Or are you meeting someone?"

She glanced around the bar, but didn't see David. "I'm meeting someone, thank you. David Brown?"

He smiled. "Mr. Brown made reservations. Please, this way."

He led the way to a table near an open fireplace and held her chair for her as she sat.

"Thank you," she said. She ordered a drink and checked her email while she waited. The budget battles in the department were going to get bloody unless she could secure some federal funding, and soon. A trip to Washington was in order the moment her confirmation was completed. She'd spoken earlier today with an assistant secretary in Homeland Security who had not exactly made promises, but at least made it seem possible that some policing grants might be made available.

She was so absorbed in her email that she didn't notice David approach until he was standing right next to her.

"Valerie," he said quietly.

She jerked a little, then blushed and stood.

David was an unusually tall man, half again past six feet, muscular, a regular visitor to the gym in the basement at 16 Wall Street. They'd met and had been close friends at Harvard, before she went to Washington and he went into investment banking.

He leaned close, kissed her on the cheek, and said, "It's good to see you."

She smiled, awkwardly. "Thank you, David."

They sat down across from each other. A waiter appeared almost instantly, took David's drink order, then vanished.

David stared at her openly, his eyes full of concern. Valerie fought not to squirm in her seat, knowing he was noting her pallor, weight-loss, the dark circles under her eyes.

"You've had a tough year," he said.

She nodded. "I'm getting through it."

"Are you? I was terribly worried, Valerie. I..." he took a deep breath, then said, "I was afraid I'd never see you again. You just... vanished. The news kept saying you were being kept at some undisclosed location. What did they do to you?"

She shrugged. "Not much. I was in solitary confinement virtually the entire time. I can't... I can't really talk about it."

He frowned. "No offense, but you look like they were keeping you in a dungeon. A gentle breeze would blow you away."

A half smile, not genuine, passed across her face. "Anything to lose weight, right?"

He grunted. "You couldn't really afford to lose it."

Shut up, David. Just shut up. She met his eyes. "I don't really want to talk about all that, David. I need to move on."

He nodded. "That's fine. I'm just... worried about you. I couldn't believe it when you got out and immediately jumped into... this. Are you sure you don't want to take some time?"

She looked away, then said, "David, I don't really know what I want, to be honest. But I've made a commitment here."

He shrugged. "I get it. But listen, if you need it—I have to offer. If you want to get away from all this and take some time just for yourself, you've always got a place with me in New York. Do you understand? No pressure—I'm not asking you to get back together with me, though there's nothing in the world I want more. What I'm offering is some space. Your brother and father died. And you can't tell me being suddenly locked up wasn't a traumatic experience. If you need a place to go... to just heal. Please... take care of yourself."

Valerie tried to picture it. What would she do in New York? Sleep in? Nothing at all? It was incredibly tempting to just... walk away, lose the pressure, the pain, the gaping grief that her father's execution left behind.

Tears brimmed in her eyes just in time for the waiter to return. She quickly rubbed her eyes dry, pulled herself back together, and they placed their orders.

The waiter gone again, she said, "David, I'm grateful for the offer. But I've made commitments here. My confirmation hearing is in less than a week. And... people's lives depend on me doing a good job. I can't walk away from that."

Sadness passed across his face, and his lips turned up in wry smile. "I guess I expected you to say that. Maybe that's why I love you... Because you put your misguided sense of duty in front of everything else."

She exhaled in half of a laugh. "I'm my father's daughter, I guess."

Tears were suddenly running down her face as her mind turned to Ken Murphy. Duty. To his family, to his country— that was what mattered to him. He'd held to it right to the end, when everything else was falling apart.

She missed her father terribly.

David reached across the table and took her hand. She returned the light pressure, then used her other hand to wipe her tears.

"Look at me," she said. "I'm sure the papers would love a picture of me sitting here sniffling... it would play right into their 'Valerie Murphy is in over her head' theme.'"

He tilted his head, looked her in the eyes and said, "Are you sure you aren't?"

Of course not, she thought. I'm in so deep I have no idea how to get out. But that didn't mean he had any right to point it out.

"I doesn't really matter, David. Life is what it is. I'm not going to walk away, no matter how tempting your offer is. Thank you, but no. I'm going to tough it out as long as I can. This is where I belong."

He smiled grimly, and said, "I would never forgive myself if I didn't at least try. The offer remains open. If things get too hot here, you've always got a place to run."

She took his hand in both of hers and said, "I was never a very good girlfriend, was I? Always too busy with work."

He gave her a reassuring look. "You were the best, Valerie. I was... gifted with the time we had together."

At that moment her phone rang. Without looking at it, she reached into her purse and pressed the Ignore button. Fifteen seconds later the phone chimed with incoming text messages. Then it rang again.

She frowned, opened her purse and looked at the phone just as Henry entered the restaurant and scanned the room, obviously looking for her.

The text message on her phone made it clear why: Major baptist minister assassinated by insurgents while giving sermon in Morgantown. Call asap. Wade Davis.

She muttered, "Oh, shit," and saw the caller was her uncle, General Murphy.

"Hello?"

"Did you get the word?"

"Yes. What happened, exactly?"

Tom Murphy quickly related the details of the incident.

"I'm certain you'll be very busy the next little while, but I want to extend an invitation to you or someone on your staff you can trust; we're pulling together an emergency meeting at 0600."

"All right; I'll have someone there. Thank you for the heads up. I'm headed back into the office now. I'll be in touch first thing in the morning or before then."

David's face fell at the words. Two additional state troopers had entered the room, now flanking the door.

She hung up and said, "David, I'm very sorry, but I have to go. It's an emergency."

He waved a hand. "Go, take care of business. Just... call me soon. I'm headed back to New York in the morning."

"I will," she said. His expression was so disappointed, and she paused and kissed him on the forehead as she left the table. "Let's go," she said to Henry, then headed for the door.

FOURTEEN

L IEUTENANT Aaron Thrasher put his phone away.

"Sir, General Wells's chopper is coming into Charleston airspace now; he should be on the ground in ten minutes."

Tom Murphy frowned, then shoved the loose papers on his desk into a drawer. He stood, gave a brisk tug on his uniform blouse, picked up his cap and handheld, and said, "Well, let's not leave the general waiting, Lieutenant. Everything ready for the briefing?"

"Yes, sir."

As Murphy exited the office and started down the hall, Thrasher fell into step to Murphy's right and a half-step behind.

"Before the briefing begins, I'd like to see Major Avedis for a few minutes, along with Colonel Todd."

"Yes, sir. Colonel Todd already mentioned that possibility to me, sir, it's all set up."

Murphy grinned. "You've passed one of the major tests of a good dog robber, Thrasher."

Lieutenant Thrasher chuckled. "I'm grateful to hear that, sir."

They reached the stairs and headed up the flight of stairs to the rooftop helipad.

On the roof, Thrasher kept fidgeting rather than standing an invisible several feet away until needed. Murphy frowned.

Finally he asked, "What's going on with you today, Thrasher, you seem... pensive."

Thrasher's eyes widened a little, and he finally said, "Sir... my apologies. I was actually going to ask you... what is the likelihood of me being clear of duty Friday evening?"

"You have plans? Or hoping to?"

"Yes, sir. With Marissa Harmon, actually. Dinner, and hopefully dancing afterward."

Murphy grinned. His inherited administrative assistant wasn't a rocket scientist, but she was extremely attractive.

"By all means, Lieutenant. Take Friday night off. Young officers need... um... challenges."

Thrasher smiled. "Yes, sir."

Murphy heard the chopper before he saw it. Coming up low from the south, it was a standard Army transport helicopter, differentiated only by the red plate attached to the window carrying the four white stars of a four-star general. The pilot landed expertly on the roof, and the moment the pitch of the turbines dropped, the ground crew ran out and began tying down the wheels.

The doors opened, and General Howard Wells stepped down, followed by his aides.

Murphy approached and saluted. Wells returned it the salute. He was a small man, built like a terrier, with a florid complexion and grey eyes that wandered everywhere. Murphy didn't know the commander of Northern Command well: due to their differing assignments over the years, he'd never worked under Wells until the beginning of the war in West Virginia. Wells had a reputation for being very difficult to work with.

"Welcome to Charleston, General," Murphy said. He started to turn to lead Wells back downstairs, but Wells reached out and touched his arm.

"Hold up just a moment, General Murphy. Let's chat privately for a moment before we go face the bullshit brigade."

"Yes, sir. Thrasher, why don't you go show General Wells's aids where they can work."

"Yes, sir," Thrasher said. He quickly led Wells's aids, a bulky captain and a very young lieutenant, downstairs.

Once alone, Wells turned to look out over the city. In the distance to the east, the sky was just beginning to pale with the earliest morning light. He rubbed his hand against his chin, then said, "Murphy, I know this visit was extremely short notice. The bottom line is, the President ordered me to get the straight poop as quickly as possible. I'm sure your staff will have a pile of pretty power points to look through, but I'd like the bottom line now. How serious is it?"

Murphy carefully avoided looking at Wells. He was all too aware that in terms of Pentagon-level politics, a one-star general was utterly expendable. Whatever he said in the next sixty seconds might well determine the course of his career.

"No bullshit, sir?"

"I want it straight."

Murphy nodded. "Worst case right now? Picture Iraq in May of 2003, but with much worse terrain and much more skilled and knowledgeable insurgents. If we don't cap this thing in the next six weeks, we'll be fighting it for years. And to be honest, sir, I don't have anything close to the assets I need to do that."

Wells raised an eyebrow. "General Varley told me, and I quote, 'You can take Tom Murphy's assessment to the bank.'"

Lieutenant General Varley was the Eighteenth Airborne Commanding General, and had been Murphy's commander for three years at Fort Campbell.

"That's very kind of General Varley to say, sir."

"All right. Let's get the dog-and-pony show on the road. I've learned everything I need for now. Except one question: If this thing escalates... and based on what you are telling me... can you ride it to the finish?"

"Of course, sir."

Wells looked closely at Murphy's face, doubt written on his features. Finally he nodded.

"Then let's go."

⟡

Valerie entered the briefing room with Davis at her side and took a seat at the long conference cable. She had the beginnings of a severe headache riding just behind her brow, and had struggled to get moving this morning. Her limbs feeling as if they had weights, and it had taken three cups of coffee before she even felt marginally alive.

Hatfield entered the room just behind them, walked the long way around the table and sat as far away from them as he could. Wade raised an eyebrow at Valerie, then opened his notebook and began writing. Valerie reached into her purse and switched her phone to vibrate and sat down.

A moment later, two men entered the room. The first, an Army Colonel with the military intelligence crest on his collar, walked into the room and set a stack of papers at the end. His hair was ruffled, slightly longer than she was used to seeing on soldiers, and his eyes were framed by thick glasses with dark brown plastic frames. Next to him sat a very young, gangly Army Major, also military intelligence.

The Colonel leaned across the table and extended a hand toward Valerie. "You must be Valerie Murphy. I'm Colonel Richard Roth, the brigade intelligence officer. I think you've met Major Avedis, commander of our intelligence battalion."

Valerie stood and shook his hand. "Nice to meet you, Colonel. I assume you know Wade Davis and Asa Hatfield?"

"Yes, ma'am, we've worked together extensively."

Davis said, "I suppose Congratulations are in order then, Major Avedis? I thought Colonel Sanchez was commander of the MI battalion?"

His face unreadable, Avedis replied, "Thank you, Mr. Davis; it's actually acting commander, for the time being. Colonel Sanchez transferred to Washington, so I'm more or less babysitting until they appoint a new commander."

Hatfield, ever diplomatic, leaned forward and said, "So tell me, Major, are you going to be a carbon copy of Sanchez, or are you actually going to do something to help us?"

Valerie looked at Hatfield. Had he seriously just said that in an official meeting? Uncle Tommy had implied Hatfield couldn't be trusted, and might be their leak to the insurgency. Regardless of whether that was true, the man had no finesse.

Avedis turned red. "Mr. Hatfield, I intend to do everything I can to help, within the limits of the resources I have."

"Well, Major, I hope that's true. Sorry if I sound skeptical, but we've got a long way to go," Hatfield said.

Valerie felt her phone vibrate. She reached into her purse and pulled it out. David Brown. She declined the call, then quickly texted, "MEETING. CANT TALK NOW. VAL."

The door opened a moment later. Thrasher stepped into the room and held the door open. Her uncle came in, followed by a four-star general. Several other officers came in on his heels.

The Army officers in the room jumped to their feet, followed a bit more slowly by the civilians in the room. Four more men, two of them in civilian clothes, entered the room behind the two generals.

"Please be seated," Wells said. "Tom? It's your show."

"Thank you, General." Murphy began by introducing the people in the room.

Next to Tom was General Howard Wells, who reported directly to the President. She'd never met General Wells in person, but knew him by reputation as a blunt, plainspoken man. Wells had been involved in some scandal or other about five years before. A quick Google search on her handheld turned up the story: He'd recommended in internal emails several years earlier that northern command manage a registry of foreign-born citizens and resident aliens in an effort to more closely track the flow of money out of he United States to terrorist groups. President Obama at the time had been forced to deal with considerable outrage from a fickle public, which had screamed for just such a database in the years after September 11. Wells had been forced to make an obviously insincere apology to the public, but no harm appeared to have stuck to his career.

To Wells's right was JD Roberts, the director of the Charleston office of the Department of Homeland Security. Valerie had met his predecessor, Justin Hagarty, on several occasions. Hagarty had been anything but a recruiting model: short, with rounded shoulders, he'd looked like an accountant, and had probably done more to bring about the West Virginia war than any other single individual.

Valerie reminded herself not to underestimate JD Roberts's potential for harm. In the last few days she'd been unable to get any more information from him regarding the security breach at Hamilton Biomedical, and she didn't expect that to change.

Hatfield at to Roberts's right, then beyond him, Ashia Farhan, the SAC, or Special Agent in Charge, from the FBI's Charleston office. She was extremely tall, with extremely dark skin, wearing an expensive burgundy suit. When Murphy introduced her, she spoke with a slight East African accent. Valerie wondered if she could enlist Farhan in her efforts to get some cooperation from the feds? There was a natural rivalry between the FBI and DHS: maybe Farhan could get her some cooperation.

Arrayed along the walls were several additional staff officers from Murphy's headquarters.

Introductions complete, Murphy said, "I think you all know why we're here. Last night, a popular Baptist minister in West Virginia was assassinated while giving a sermon recommending cooperation with the authorities and reconciliation with the United States. It's my belief that we are facing a growing and potentially very dangerous insurgency here in West Virginia. What we're going to cover this morning is what we believe are the capabilities of that insurgency and discuss courses of action. We're going to start with Colonel Richard Roth, from brigade Intelligence. Go ahead, Colonel."

Roth stood, picked up stack of papers and began passing them out to the meeting participants. Valerie took hers and glanced through it. The top page was an executive summary, followed by a number of annotated maps, then a fairly thick report. The maps showed locations of a series of attacks and violent incidents. As she settled the papers, her phone vibrated again. She glanced at it.

"Enjoy your meeting. Please remember my offer: you have a place to run if you need it. David."

She looked up from the phone as Colonel Roth returned to the end of the table and began speaking.

"Thank you, General Murphy. I'm the brigade intelligence officer here, and a counterinsurgency specialist. If you'll turn to page 3 of your report, you'll find an overview map of specific incidents that we believe to be insurgent acts. The following page lays them out on a timeline. What I want to make clear here is two things. First, we have effectively three areas which appear to have significant activity: along the Coal River in the southern part of the state, including the edges of Charleston; second, in and around Morgantown, and finally the Harpers Ferry area."

Roth's eyes darted at the others in the room, taking in reactions. The two general officers were poker-faced, studying the graphs. Hatfield had a skeptical expression on his face.

"The second point I want to raise here is that the incidents have been increasing in frequency and effectiveness. In the first six weeks after the conclusion of hostilities, we saw five incidents of sabotage of military equipment, which were initially simply seen as vandalism. The following six weeks saw more than thirty incidents, including the theft of a number of weapons. In mid-March, we had our first casualty, when an AT-4 rocket was fired into the ammo dump at the Eighth Support Company headquarters in Jefferson County. Two soldiers were badly burned, and one of the bunkers was destroyed, along with something over two-hundred thousand rounds of ammunition that cooked off for more than three days before the fire could be controlled. We have reason to believe that, among other items, surface-to-air missiles were stolen from the inventory during the fire."

Roth paced a little as he spoke. Face pensive, he continued. "Following the ammo dump incident, General Murphy ordered a serious assessment of the likelihood of a general insurgency. I'll present our conclusions shortly. But by now the answer is obvious, because in March, we had three direct force-on-force attacks. An infantry platoon was ambushed in a fairly coordinated attack in Boone County, and two Black Hawk helicopters were shot down when they attempted to relieve the infantry position. Less than a week later, attackers killed four MPs with sniper fire in Morgantown, and the very same day a rocket attack on a convoy killed two soldiers near the Maryland border. Additionally, we've had at least two targeted assassinations directly attributable to insurgent activity."

Roth halted his pacing, put his hands behind his back, and said, "Based on the pattern of attacks, we've concluded that we're dealing with at least three groups of insurgents, company sized or larger, as well as a significant number of sympathizers who are providing shelter. We suspect, and this is merely an educated guess, that the core of these groups were formed out of the civilian militia, which West Virginia organized in the final days prior to the ground conflict. A number of these guerrilla groups were detailed as support to maneuver battalions of the West Virginia National Guard. We believe their leadership has significant experience: most likely former soldiers, veterans of Afghanistan and Iraq, with significant counter-insurgency expertise."

General Wells leaned forward. "Elaborate on that."

Roth took a deep breath. "First, per capita, West Virginia has more military veterans than any other state in the nation. Second, the planning of the attacks reflects significant experience and expertise. Bad guys may get in a lucky shot or two, but bringing down two Black Hawks in their first major engagement? I don't buy it. They planned that mission for maximum shock value, and waited until the relief forces came on the scene."

Wells nodded. "Concur. Go on."

Roth continued. "The key question is: what is the enemy trying to accomplish? I think the answer is simple: they want federal forces out of West Virginia. In order to accomplish that, they'll take a standard insurgent approach: harass the occupying forces, recruit as many sympathizers as they can, and frighten the rest of the populace into non-compliance with the US. The assassinations of the Boone County Sheriff and Reverend Johnson accomplish the final goal pretty effectively. There will be more incidents, likely many more. Anyone who works with or cooperates with federal forces will be targets. Our troops in the field, especially more isolated units, will be targets. I would expect to see a significant online campaign to spread disinformation and propaganda within a matter of weeks."

"Recommendations?" asked Murphy.

Roth said, "I can speak to strategy, but understand sir, most of my recommendations are unlikely given the current political climate. We need to call a spade a spade and make it clear that there is a war on here, and devote the necessary resources. The obvious comes first. We don't have anything like enough troops to contain a full-fledged insurgency. A reinforced brigade isn't going to be able to effectively contain anything. I would push for two divisions at a minimum. A major push for better intelligence, which means more resources and more money. We have a list of former officers of the West Virginia Guard we'd like to spring from wherever they are, and put them to work helping us identify likely insurgents."

Wells raised his eyebrows.

Roth responded to his expression. "General, understand that to an extent we're dealing with very clannish people here. It's likely that some of the former commanders of the state guard will be able to break through much more effectively."

Wells nodded. "Go on."

"We need to seal the borders. As it stands, our insurgents could be staying in motels or with friends or family in Kentucky or Virginia, Maryland or Ohio. All they need to do is load up some cars, come across the border, do their thing, then disappear."

Hatfield jerked up straight in his seat. "Are you nuts?" he blurted. "Do you have any idea what that would do to West Virginia's economy?"

Roth narrowed his eyes. "I'm quite aware of that, Mr. Hatfield. On the other hand, it will probably do less economic harm than a prolonged and bloody war would do."

Hatfield shook his head. "You're talking about turning West Virginia into a police state."

Roth nodded. "I am. My next recommendation is going to be nearly that: we need effective tracking of the populace. Which means police and military checkpoints on all major roads, tracking of people by state-issued identification, a full database of who belongs where and when. It's a must that we isolate the insurgents from the rest of the population. We have to force them out into the open, away from potential hiding places, and especially away from civilians. We can't afford any more incidents like the one in Whitesville. It's a minor miracle no civilians were killed during that ambush."

Hatfield's face was red. "What you are describing will push more people into the insurgency, not away from it. This is America, damn it! You want to make people have to show their papers every time they go to the grocery store? Close the borders? It's a damn fool idea!"

General Murphy leaned forward. "Now is not really the time to discuss this. Most of these decisions will be made at a level far higher than any of us, so I'd advise we keep cool heads. Colonel Roth, do you have anything else?"

Murphy's interjection had its intended effect. Hatfield leaned back in his chair, crossed his arms over his chest and looked at the wall. Valerie shook her head, then looked back at Roth.

"One final comment, General. As you know, we're working closely with Homeland Security to identify who is leaking information to the insurgents. That effort continues, and I believe we'll have some breakthroughs soon."

Murphy nodded. "We can discuss the particulars of that in private. Thank you, Colonel."

Colonel Roth sat down. Murphy leaned forward again. "Is there anyone in this room who will make an argument that we are not facing a significant and growing threat of insurgency?"

Hatfield leaned forward again. "You left one thing out: Hamilton Biomedical. That changes everything."

Roberts jerked his head up., "That's classified information, Hatfield."

Hatfield raised his eyebrows. "I think the people in this room are the very definition of need to know."

Roberts said, "That's beside the point—"

"No, Mr. Roberts, it's not. We're talking about a possible pandemic here in the hands of terrorists! You don't compartmentalize that shit, you start dealing with the response! So far, all I've seen your office do is threaten to make my detectives disappear just for doing their jobs!"

Murphy leaned forward and held up a hand for silence. "I've not been briefed on whatever this is. Have you, General?"

Wells shook his head.

Looking back at Roberts, Murphy said, "Hatfield has a point, Mr. Roberts. We'll talk after; I want to know what this is about. In the meantime, does anyone else have anything to add?"

Silence followed the question. Valerie looked at Wade Davis, then at Hatfield. Then she leaned forward and said, "I do need to make one point clear."

Murphy looked surprised, then said, "Go ahead."

Valerie swallowed. "I agree the seriousness of this can't be overstated. That said, we've got other problems—serious ones—which parallel the violent insurgency issue, but in some cases overshadow it. Nothing you do to counter the insurgency is going to be effective if we don't have basic law enforcement and basic services. We've still got large areas of the state with no electricity, most local law enforcement is out of commission or locked up with the National Guard, and crime is up to astro-nomical levels—everything from simple theft to violent crime and gang violence. If we don't address those issues, your coun-terinsurgency efforts will be completely undermined."

Wells frowned. "Can you clarify? You said most local law enforcement is locked up?"

Valerie nodded. She consulted her handheld, then said, "As I understand it, a total of 614 police officers and firefighters were serving in the state National Guard at the beginning of hostili-ties. This includes the state police, local sheriff's departments, and so on. Of those 614, 12 were killed in action, and the other 602 are in custody. A fairly extreme example: Jefferson County had a total of forty-two sheriff's deputies. Thirty-seven of those were in the National Guard. Two were killed, four are simply missing, and thirty-one are in custody. As a result, a county with a population of 200,000 now has a total of five sheriff's deputies."

Wells nodded. "You recommend we release them? They committed treason."

She nodded. "Of course they should be released. While I'd argue that treason is very much a debatable term, the fact is that on a practical level, without basic law enforcement and govern-ment services, West Virginia is effectively a third-world country. You have to go beyond the political questions and ask yourself: do you want retribution? Or do you want success?"

A faint smile crossed Wells's face. "Noted. Thank you."

Roberts leaned forward. "While I recognize the difficulties West Virginia faces with regards to manpower, we absolutely recommend against releasing anyone who was involved with the conflict. The bottom line is, you are talking about people who committed treason—took up arms against their own govern-ment. These people are not to be trusted."

Hatfield snorted and rolled his eyes.

Valerie straightened in her seat. "Do you have an alternative in mind? One that will allow us to put some cops on the street?"

Roberts shrugged. "Not really my area of responsibility, Ms. Murphy. To be perfectly frank, had it been up to me, both you and the Governor would still be in detention as well. I'm hardly shocked that you would recommend the wholesale release of traitors, given your own role in the war."

Valerie stared back at Roberts. "You must be referring to the role I played doing everything I possibly could to stop the war in the first place."

Roberts smirked. "Not my fault you chose to represent the losing side, Ms. Murphy."

Wells's eyes darted back and forth between Valerie and Roberts, then he interjected, "Do you have anything constructive to offer here, Mr. Roberts? Whether you like it or not, Secretary Murphy is the duly appointed representative of the state here."

Roberts turned to the General. "Yes, sir, I do. I would urge a deterrent action: swift, expeditious trials for treason for all those who took up arms against their government, followed by the death penalty for enough of them that no one considers taking such an action ever again."

Silence fell across the room like a blow. Valerie found herself shaking. Her father had faced just such a swift, expeditious trial and execution. So swift that it could be seen as nothing but a miscarriage of justice.

Hatfield exploded. "Roberts, why the hell do you think we went to war in the first place? Because of the bullheaded attitudes of the people in your department! What absolute bullshit!"

Roberts crossed his arms. "The fact is, DHS is conducting its own investigation into these so-called insurgents, and we have no intention of sharing any information with anyone in the West Virginia government, which is suspect. General, I'm happy to work directly with the military headquarters here, but that will be the extent of our involvement with this group. But if we learn that anyone in the West Virginia government, at any level, is sharing information with these terrorists and murderers, rest assured that the result will be far worse than a mere three months in solitary confinement."

Wells slapped his hand flat on the table with a loud crack. "Enough!"

Silence settled in the room. There wasn't a person present who didn't know that Wells was the only person in the room who could pick up a phone and get the President of the United States on the line whenever necessary. Right now, he was clearly angry.

"Let me make myself absolutely clear," he said. "Our objective is not to fight the last war. It is done. Whoever felt whatever about it, West Virginia's secession is over. Our job now is to re-establish public safety in this state, which means I want cooperation and productive proposals for how to deal with this insurgency. Am I clear?"

There were nods around the room. Murphy said, "It's clear our most urgent needs are funding and manpower. General, it's my intent to establish a joint headquarters, so we can better coordinate. In the last two weeks, we've been working to establish boots on the ground in key areas, but it's been tenuous, due to the manning situation."

Wells nodded. "I agree, Tom. In the immediate term, I can get you troops from Fort Campbell and Benning. Say two brigades of infantry, which will turn this into a pocket division, really. More than that soon after, but you and I will need to go to the President for approval. We'll get warning orders to the relevant commands this morning. That will get you more coverage on the ground."

Murphy nodded. "Yes, sir."

"Be prepared to brief the National Security Council within forty-eight hours. We're behind the curve on this, and it's time to ramp up."

Wells looked at the FBI and DHS representatives. "Please get us an idea ASAP of what resources your agencies can bring to bear."

At their nods, Wells stood. "I think we've done all we can here this morning; let's wrap up. Secretary Murphy, I'd like to meet with you, Mr. Roberts, Mr. Hatfield and General Murphy alone for a few moments."

Once the others had cleared the room, Wells told them to sit again. Valerie took a seat across from Roberts and next to her uncle. Hatfield stayed several seats away.

"All right… What is this about?" General Wells asked.

"General, I'm not at liberty to disclose any details; the incident is classified," Roberts said immediately.

Hatfield muttered a curse.

"General, there's a been a security breach at Hamilton Biomedical. It's a level-four biohazard research station under contract to the CDC. They've got nasty super-bugs there."

The two Army Generals looked at each other in shock. Wells leaned forward. "Why the hell wasn't I briefed on this? Roberts?"

"General, I'm not authorized to—"

"Bullshit. In case you missed it, Roberts, I'm in charge of Northern Command, which is the primary military command concerned with domestic security. By definition, this falls under my authority. If DHS is holding this under wraps, Roberts, you have overstepped yourself."

Roberts narrowed his eyes. "You'll need to take that up with the Secretary of Homeland Security, General. I report to him, not you."

"By God, I'll take it up with the President!"

Roberts shrugged.

"General," Hatfield said, "It goes beyond that. Roberts is actively trying to suppress any investigation of related issues. One of our state investigators has been investigating the suicide of a contract worker about two weeks before the security breach. He's been making significant progress—enough to indicate that it was no suicide at all, and might well be related to the security breach. Roberts and his DHS pals swept in yanked my investigator out of his house, then threatened to take him under indefinite detention."

Wells muttered under his breath. "Roberts? Do you dispute this?"

"Of course not, General. Detective Corvath was interfering in a federal investigation. I made it absolutely clear to him he was to back off or be considered an accessory."

Wells closed his eyes. "General Murphy, is this what you've been dealing with all along? I don't believe I've ever encountered such obstructionism before."

Murphy responded, "It's fairly characteristic, General."

Wells looked at Roberts . "Mr. Roberts, the minute we're finished here, I'm placing a call to the President of the United States, asking that you be removed from this office and replaced with someone who understands interagency cooperation. I'm absolutely appalled."

Roberts looked smug. "I have no concerns there, sir. Why should I, when the military commander on the scene is the younger brother of a convicted traitor, and the secretary of the state law enforcement bureau is the daughter of the same traitor? With all due respect, General, you are kidding yourself if you think this is the group that will accomplish anything. I'd be stunned to find out they weren't both actively aiding the insurgents."

Wells stood. "This meeting is over. Secretary Murphy, I'd recommend you take whatever steps you find necessary to protect your detective."

"We are, sir," Valerie responded. "He's being reassigned to the special prosecutor's office to work a different case. I hesitate to drop the investigation, but I can't ask him to actively investigate a case which would result in his kidnap by the federal government."

Roberts stood, looked at Valerie with an amused expression on his face, then said, "Does she not demonstrate my point, General?"

His eyes swept over them all, and he stood and walked out of the room.

FIFTEEN

T HE phone rang several times before it was answered. The scratchy voice of an elderly woman answered. Ambrose Hall tensed as she answered the phone, and unconsciously sat straight in his chair.

"Hello?"

"Mother? It's Ambrose."

"Ambrose! Dear, it's so nice to hear from you."

There was an awkward silence. After about fifteen seconds, he said, "Mother, I wanted to let you know I'm in Charleston for work. I've been appointed special prosecutor on an important case."

He waited for an invitation. There was only silence.

Ambrose sighed. "I thought while I was in town, I might stop in and see you. It's been nearly ten years."

Ambrose clenched his right fist, during another long wait, already knowing the response was not going to be worth hearing.

"Ambrose dear, it's always good to hear from you. I wonder if you've decided to settle down and get married?"

He sighed. She was nothing if not predictable.

"Mother, I think you know the answer to that. I fully intend to get married to Mitch, as soon as it is legal to do so."

The silence on the other end lasted a full thirty seconds. Finally she spoke, and he could hear grief in her voice. "Son, I'll always love you. But I think it best you not come visit until you are ready to leave your life of wickedness."

He closed his eyes, but it did nothing to stop the rest of his body from shaking.

"Well," he replied. "You take care, then, Mother."

"You too, my son," she sobbed on the other end of the line.

Ambrose hung up the phone. He sat at his desk, back perfectly straight, eyes staring straight ahead. He took a deep breath, trying to calm himself. He didn't know why he'd expected anything different from this phone call: it had played out exactly the same as the last time he'd called, and the time before that, and fifty other times. Better to focus on work, and moving forward. He knew coming back to West Virginia had been a mistake.

When he finally turned back to his work, his eyes strayed back to the last email he'd received from Valerie. She suggested that he pay particular attention to any suspects from the Front Royal area, or anyone who had attended a seminary. Odd, that.

❧

"Have a seat, Mr. Davis," Ambrose said.

Wade Davis took a seat across the table from him. They were in a small conference room with a view across downtown Charleston. To the side of the table, a court reporter sat with a Dictaphone.

"Mr. Davis, I appreciate your taking the time to come see me."

"Of course, Mr. Hall; whatever I can do to assist."

"Let me get the formalities out of the way. As you know, I've been appointed by the governor as special prosecutor to investigate the leaks from the West Virginia government to the insurgency and the press. In that capacity, among other things, I've assembled a list of individuals who had knowledge in particular of six US Army convoys, all of which were ambushed in three different counties. That list has thirty-nine members, most of them either in the US Army headquarters or the West Virginia Department of Military and Law Enforcement. You understand?"

"Yes, Mr. Hall." Davis's tone was cooperative, but somewhat bored.

"All right. You are one of those thirty-nine individuals. This doesn't mean you are a suspect in any way, however it does mean I have to ask you a number of questions. Some of them may be difficult. At this time I'd like to place you under oath for your deposition. Any objections?"

"None, sir."

"Please raise your right hand."

Davis did so.

"Do you solemnly state that the testimony you will give in this deposition will be the truth, the whole truth, and nothing but the truth?"

"I do."

"Let us proceed, then. For the record, please state your name, occupation and place of residence."

"My name is Wade Lloyd Davis. I am Chief of Staff of the West Virginia Department of Military Affairs and Law Enforcement, and a resident of Charleston, West Virginia."

"Thank you."

Ambrose studied Davis for a moment. Should he start with the softball questions? Lull him into relaxing? At this point he didn't have any real reason to think Davis was a suspect in any way. But nothing ruled him out. And there were a number of concerning discrepancies in his phone and financial records. Ambrose decided on his approach, then spoke.

"Mr. Davis, on March 2, a relief convoy of the US Army was surrounded by suspected insurgents in Boone County. The soldiers in the convoy were disarmed and left beside the road, and subsequently attacked in the town of Whitesville. Are you familiar with the incident in question?"

Davis nodded. "Yes, I am."

"Can you tell me when you first became aware of the existence of that convoy?"

"I believe it was at the cabinet meeting that morning. There was some discussion of it, because phone lines were down in Whitesville, which is in an area that had particularly nasty weather that week. With no power, we were concerned about the welfare of the residents. The convoy was dispatched to take food and fuel to the town, as well as a set of satellite phones for the Mayor and volunteer fire department."

Ambrose nodded. "I see. And when did you become aware that the convoy had been attacked?"

"I think it was sometime the next day. Mr. Hatfield told me about it. He was the acting Secretary of the department at that time."

"Tell me how you feel about Mr. Hatfield."

Davis blinked several times. He opened his mouth to speak, then hesitated.

"Please," Ambrose said. "be frank. The records of the investigation won't be public, except those related to any indictment we go forward with. Whatever you tell me is confidential."

Davis leaned forward and said, "I... I'm afraid I don't trust Mr. Hatfield. If you ask me, he is the most likely source of our leaks."

"Why is that?"

"Isn't it obvious? His elder brother is a brigade commander in the National Guard, and is currently under detention pending court martial for treason."

"That would be Colonel David Hatfield, former Logan County Sheriff? He was commander of the 501st Artillery during the war?"

"Yes, sir."

"Hatfield was passed over for command of the war effort in favor of General Murphy, even though Hatfield was considerably senior at the time. Isn't that correct?"

Davis nodded. "Yes."

"Why is that?"

Davis shifted in his seat, uncomfortably. "It was at least partly based on my own recommendation, Mr. Hall. I recommended to the governor that he appoint Colonel Murphy, because I didn't feel Hatfield had sufficient combat experience to successfully command the Guard during that time."

"Asa Hatfield was acting Secretary at that time?"

"Yes, the previous secretary had resigned."

"Did he agree with your assessment?"

David frowned. "He wasn't aware of it. I went directly to the governor, feeling that the acting Secretary would have a conflict of interest."

"Because his brother was being considered for command?"

"That's right."

Ambrose leaned forward. "So, Mr. Davis, do you feel that under the right circumstances, working outside of channels is the necessary or correct thing to do?"

Davis's eyes went cold. "It appears you have trapped me into saying so, Mr. Hall."

"How did you vote on the issue of West Virginia's independence?"

"I believe, sir," Davis said, his tone icy, "You are aware of the secret ballot system?"

Ambrose smiled. "Allow me to rephrase. Did you support independence?"

"I did."

"Why?"

"It's a complex issue. But the bottom line is, I felt strongly that the Federal government has long since overstepped the bounds defined in the Constitution."

Ambrose opened a folder and leafed through the papers inside. He took his time looking through the folder, not thinking about the contents: his objective was to continue to keep Davis off balance.

Finally, he took out three sheets of paper, stapled to each other, and slid them across the table to Davis.

"Mr. Davis, do you recognize these documents?"

Davis nodded, and answered slowly. "Yes… that's my financial disclosure documents."

"According to the disclosure, your total assets, including your house, are $275,000? And your total debt, including your mortgage, plus assorted credit cards, is $295,000. Correct?"

"Yes."

Ambrose frowned. He then took another set of papers out of the folder. "This is a copy of your credit report, pulled last Monday. According to this, your total debt is more than $400,000. Can you explain the discrepancy?"

Davis raised an eyebrow. "The financial disclosure was filed April of last year, just after I completed my taxes. This credit report is obviously much more recent."

Ambrose nodded. "Yes... nine months. In nine months, you've accumulated more than one hundred thousand dollars in debt. Where did the money go?"

Davis leaned back in his chair, his face expressionless. He met Ambrose's eyes. "I don't really wish to discuss it, but since you seem to have dug up my entire personal life already, perhaps you already know the answer to that?"

"Please enlighten me."

Davis sighed. "Last May I took a personal loan of $100,000. My intent was to purchase, refurbish and flip a townhouse here in Charleston. It was an investment. Before I finished, of course, we had a war, and as you can imagine, housing prices have zeroed. I'm likely going to be financially ruined."

Ambrose made some notes, than said, "As I said before, Mr. Davis, you aren't at this time a suspect. That said, what you've just described is a powerful motive."

Davis dismissed the comment, an edge of anger in his tone. "Perhaps it would if I had any money coming in. I presume you have my banking records as well? Simple enough to see I get a little money from personal investments, and from my salary, but little else. I'm sinking fast, Mr. Ambrose. I've had no secret infusions of cash."

Ambrose nodded. What Davis said was true. Which didn't mean he wasn't the leak, and which didn't mean he wasn't taking money for it. It simply meant there was no proof at this point.

"How close were you to Governor Slagter?"

Davis frowned. "The former Governor was a self-centered opportunist who believed in nothing but his career prospects. I'm sure his suicide was a tragedy for someone, but I'm not sorry to see him gone."

Ambrose was taken aback by the vehemence of the response. "Yet, you advised him, at least in some matters."

"That's my job, Mr. Hall. It doesn't mean Slagter and I were drinking buddies."

"He supported independence for the state, as you did."

Davis sneered. "Not out of any genuine political conviction. Slagter blew whichever way the polls went. At that time, the vast majority of West Virginians supported independence."

"What was your reaction when he committed suicide?"

Davis didn't hesitate to answer brutally. "Contempt. He abandoned a sinking ship. It would have been far better had he stood up like a man, like General Murphy did. Frankly, I wish Slagter had done it sooner. If Ken Murphy had been our governor, West Virginia would be an independent state today, most likely."

Ambrose raised his eyebrows. That conclusion was hardly likely; the independence movement in West Virginia had been doomed from the beginning. But Davis's admiring tone of Murphy was interesting. Ambrose decided he would follow that line.

"You speak highly of Ken Murphy. You admired him?"

"I did. He was a highly principled man, who stood up for what he believed in."

"What about Valerie Murphy?"

Davis sat back. "Ms. Murphy is... not her father. She is admirable in her own way, but different."

"How so?"

Davis thought about the question for a few minutes, then said, "I believe she has the same courage as her father. But I don't think she knows yet what she believes in."

Interesting. Ambrose thought that was a remarkably keen observation, especially given that Davis had only known Valerie for a couple of weeks. He decided to change the subject again. Without pause, he took several more sheets of paper out of the folder, and laid them out next to each other in a row.

"Mr. Davis, these are the record of phone calls made from your personal cell phone over the last eight weeks. I'd like to ask you some questions about some of these numbers."

Davis rolled his eyes. "Fine, Mr. Ambrose. Whatever you wish to discuss."

Ambrose continued. "The numbers highlighted in yellow we have cross-referenced against various government officials, restaurants, as well as family members. Do you see the phone number highlighted in blue?"

Davis studied the papers in front of him. He nodded. "Yes."

"Can you tell me what that phone number is?"

"Not off the top of my head. May I consult my phone for the answer?"

"Please do."

Davis took out his phone, then began paging through it. Finally he responded. "I'm sorry, I don't recognize the number."

Ambrose shook his head.

"You've called that number six times in the last six weeks. Always on a Thursday morning around eleven. According to your calendar in the department computer system, you've taken a long lunch on all six Thursdays. Would you like to reconsider your previous answer?"

Davis's face flushed, and his eyes flashed angrily, but he said, "No."

Ambrose shook his head and decided to push further. "Mr. Davis, that phone number is registered to the Moonlight Spa in downtown Charleston, two blocks from this building. It's known by the police as an active place of prostitution. The pattern of phone calls, followed by long lunches, would tend to suggest that you are spending your lunch breaks on Thursday with a prostitute. Are you absolutely sure you don't want to reconsider your answer?"

Wade Davis was shaking now. He shook his head stiffly, then said in a monotone, "I refuse to answer on the grounds of the fifth amendment."

Ambrose sighed. "That is your right, Mr. Davis. Even under West Virginia's constitution, were it, in fact, an independent state. Let's move on, then. Do you recognize the phone number highlighted in yellow?"

Davis shook his head. "No, I don't."

"The phone number is registered to a disposable cell phone. It was purchased in Cincinnati on January fifth at Wal-Mart. I've subpoenaed the security video from the Walmart in question, and we have the list of every phone number which called into that phone, and every number it called to. So, before very long, we'll have identified the person anyway. You understand, Mr. Davis? Maybe you should just come clean and tell me who the phone belongs to."

"I have no idea who the number belongs to. I'll check, and get back with you." His throat sounded dry.

"Thank you, Mr. Davis. I think that will be all for now."

SIXTEEN

ETECTIVE Sergeant Corvath walked into the office on the seventh floor of the office building across from the new headquarters of the Military and Law Enforcement Department. The office building was mostly vacant and had been for some time since the economic downturn and the war. This office was obviously still incomplete: there was fresh paint and carpet, but little in the way of furniture, and boxes were everywhere.

A receptionist sat behind the desk at the door. A little over forty, wearing conservative clothing, she was on the phone when he entered. Her eyebrows were almost quivering with anger, and a deep wrinkle of irritation ran between her eyes.

"I'm sorry," she said in a tone of voice most people reserved for small, petulant children, "Mr. Hall is not taking any calls from the press. I don't know how to explain that to you any other way."

She listened to the phone for a minute more, irritation growing on her face. "No, sir, he's made his instructions very clear. He won't take your call, so there's no point in me asking. You're welcome to talk to the governor's public affairs office. Have a nice day."

Corvath could just hear the voice on the other end of the phone speaking urgently as she set the phone down.

She looked up at him and smiled. "Hello, how can I help you?"

Corvath grinned and said, "I'm not a reporter."

She burst into laughter. "Thank God," she said.

"I'm Detective Sergeant Corvath, from the state Bureau of Investigation. I've been temporarily reassigned to the special prosecutor's office."

"Oh, yes," she said. "Have a seat, I'll let Mr. Hall know you're here. I'm Molly, by the way."

"Nice to meet you, Molly," he said.

He sat in one of the uncomfortable waiting chairs while she picked up the phone and spoke into it briefly. Just a moment later she gestured toward one of the doors behind her and said, "You can go on in."

Corvath stood and walked to the door and opened it. Ambrose Hall was just standing as he entered.

The two men looked at each other, and for a moment Corvath was a bit taken aback by Hall's appearance. A tall African American in an impeccably tailored coat, Hall also wore a well-groomed handlebar mustache. Corvath didn't think he'd ever actually seen a man wearing one.

"Sergeant Corvath, come in, have a seat." Hall said, stepping forward and holding out a hand to shake.

Corvath shook, then sat where Hall indicated.

Hall sat down across from him and came right to business.

"Valerie Murphy called me yesterday. She briefed me on your situation and asked me if I could take you on over here. She tells me you're one of the best investigators the department has."

"It's very kind of her to say so."

Hall grinned. "Sergeant Corvath, if you have the opportunity to get to know Valerie, you'll find she doesn't say things like that when she doesn't mean them. I'm very pleased to have you aboard. I've been working with a hodgepodge of local detectives and attorneys, and to be perfectly frank, I've desperately needed an experienced investigator assigned to the team."

"Thank you," Corvath responded.

"Tell me a little of the trouble you ran into over there?"

Corvath filled in some of the details of the case, including the threats from Homeland Security.

When he finished, Ambrose said, "I wish I could say I was surprised. But I'm not. To a large extent, it was DHS that precipitated the war in the first place, and it seems they've learned very little from the experience."

Corvath nodded.

"Valerie tells me you intend to continue to pursue your leads on the case, if a bit more circumspectly."

"Yeah. To be blunt, I'm pissed that DHS stepped in the way they did."

Ambrose nodded. "I don't have to tell you to be careful. Do keep me informed, however. Based on what Valerie told me, there may well be some common threads between your case and this investigation."

Corvath leaned forward, interested.

"What we've been working on so far has been largely a matter of the process of elimination. My task is to investigate who is leaking information to the insurgents. The six specific incidents of convoys that were ambushed are our primary cases. All six of them were well-planned ambushes: the insurgents appeared to know the exact timing of the convoys, their strength, and how to attack them most effectively. The Army has gone into a much tighter mode of secrecy in the last few weeks, and while there have been more attacks, none of them had the same aspect of pre-planning and information. So our pool of suspects is limited to people who had knowledge of the first six convoys, but who were cut out of the loop with subsequent Army operations."

Corvath nodded. "All right. Who are our suspects?"

Ambrose passed a list across to Corvath.

"We started out with thirty-nine people. I've ruled out General Murphy and his aide-de-camp, though if it comes down to it we may re-open that line of inquiry. Out of the remaining thirty-seven, twenty of them are US Army, assigned to the headquarters planning staff. Again, I see them as secondary suspects, though we are following routine inquiries in those cases."

"Who is left?"

"Our final seventeen suspects are ten members of the governor's cabinet, all of whom I consider in the primary pool of suspects. JD Roberts, the special agent in charge of Homeland Security. Ashia Farhan, the SAC of the FBI's Charleston field office. Marissa Harmer, the governor's administrative assistant. Asa Hatfield, who you know, of course. Wade Davis. And their administrative assistants."

"Who do you consider likely?"

"Wade Davis and Hatfield are my two top suspects. I'm intrigued by the idea of Roberts being behind it, but I think it unlikely. The governor's assistant may or may not have had full access to the information, but based on what I've seen, it seems likely. We've just about ruled out Ashia Farhan: based on her personal history, it seems highly unlikely.

"Hatfield? I wouldn't have thought him a suspect."

"Why not?"

"Strong law and order type. He's been a cop his whole life."

"True. On the other hand, his brother is pending trial for treason. It seems to me that makes for a strong motive."

Corvath nodded. He respected Hatfield, and found that it troubled him a great deal to doubt him. He said, "My gut inclination is to rule him out. So... I'll look very closely at him. I don't want to let personal likes and dislikes get in the way."

"Good. What do you think of Davis?"

"Don't know much about him, other than what I've read in the papers. He's basically a politician."

Ambrose smiled. "That makes you distrust him."

Corvath nodded.

"You'll be interested to know that Davis has some irregularities in both his finances and personal conduct. Neither of which make him an insurgent sympathizer, but both of which make either blackmail or greed a possible motive. He spends his Thursday lunch break at an Asian massage parlor here in Charleston."

"Damn," Corvath said. "I worked a joint case with the FBI about ten years ago, a crackdown on those places. Mostly young women trafficked from South Korea. We shut a bunch of them down."

"Apparently they've reopened. If it became public Davis was indulging in sex with girls smuggled from South Asia—that would be the end of his career. I think blackmail is a definite possibility." Ambrose said.

"What else about Davis?"

"Bad real estate investment last spring, before the war. It's put him hundreds of thousands in debt. We know the insurgents are well funded, though we don't have any sources for the money. Maybe he's angling for cash."

Corvath nodded. "Could be." He took another look at the list. "What about the governor's secretary?"

Ambrose shrugged. "Not much on her. Single, though it seems she's been on a couple of dates recently with General Murphy's aide-de-camp. No blemishes on her record. She was recommended to Governor Slagter by the state representative from Morgantown; it's her first job. She grew up outside Cincinnati. Home schooled, attended Virginia Theological Seminary."

Corvath could practically feel the hair on the back of his neck stand up. He sat up straight. "How long has she been in the job?"

"Two years."

Corvath rubbed his chin for a moment. "It's… interesting. The case I was working… Clifford Webb was a computer security contractor at Hamilton Biomedical. He supposedly committed suicide two weeks before the security breach there. I think it was murder."

"Go on."

"Right before he committed suicide, he briefly dated a woman named Maggie Rutledge. Rutledge was also home-schooled, and went to a seminary. Perfectly clean record, but she's linked indirectly with John Channing, who was the prime suspect in the Arlington bombing last year. DHS stepped in when I began following that line of investigation."

Ambrose muttered. "Channing… I've seen that name recently. Hold on a second." He turned to his computer and began typing rapidly. A moment later, he muttered, "Well, I'll be damned."

He turned the monitor on his computer toward Corvath. "Take a look at this."

Corvath leaned forward. The monitor showed a scan of a cancelled check, written to Virginia Theological Seminary, for twelve thousand dollars. The check was drawn on the account of Roland Channing, Jr.

He looked from the check to Ambrose.

"Channing paid Marissa Harmer's college tuition. All of it," Ambrose said.

Corvath exhaled slowly, then said, "Looks like we need to take a closer look at Ms. Harmer. And Roland Channing."

ᘒ

Corvath spent the rest of the day sitting at his new desk in the special prosecutor's office, following up all the information he could find about Marissa Harmer, John Channing and Roland Channing.

There wasn't much on Harmer. She'd finished college two years ago; she wasn't a remarkable student, but had above-average grades. Very little on her credit report, though it was remarkable for the lack of student loans. But they already knew the answer to that: her attendance at Virginia Theological Seminary had been entirely bankrolled by Roland Channing.

Roland Channing, on the other hand, increasingly appeared to own a small empire. As head of the New World Pentecostal Church, he published a huge number of books, which were heavily sold throughout the country to various evangelical churches. In 2015, he'd invested nearly five million dollars in founding the New World Pentecostal Radio Network, a chain of radio stations across the country that had unusually high ratings and some ten million listeners. Channing also managed a scholarship fund, greatly expanded in the last ten years, that put nearly four hundred students a year through seminaries across the country.

The entire enterprise had come under scrutiny briefly following the Arlington bombing. But the investigation had come to a screeching halt after only a couple of months, and gone in an entirely different direction.

Why had DHS stopped the investigation into Channing? It didn't make any sense.

John Channing, one of Roland Channing's sons, was a different character entirely. Instead of a seminary, he'd attended Georgia Tech, then gone on to the Marine Corps, where he'd served in Iraq and Afghanistan. His military records indicated a serious but impulsive young man. He'd been reprimanded for insubordination to his battalion commander while in Iraq. Corvath made a note to follow up with the battalion commander and find out what that had been about: the written reprimand included few details.

After five years in the Marines, Channing went back to Baughman Settlement, and there was no record of what he did for the next three years. Then, in 2014, he'd been convicted of assault and battery in Washington, DC. It was an ugly case: Channing had been in a popular bar on Capitol Hill where he was approached by a transgender woman named Tiffany Arsenault. Apparently the two had hit it off, and Channing had taken her back to his hotel. Unfortunately for the girl, she revealed her past as a man to Channing before the encounter went any further. Channing beat her nearly to death. She'd been hospitalized for three months.

Channing served fourteen months on a felony conviction, then returned home to Baughman Settlement. Corvath frowned. Tiffany Arsenault had almost certainly spent more than fourteen months in physical therapy after her assault. Sad.

There was no indication in the record of why Channing had been in DC at the time, but Corvath couldn't help but wonder if it had any bearing on the case. Because last year, when the Arlington bombing took place, Channing had been pulled over for speeding on I-66 headed out of Washington. He'd been arrested by the Virginia State Police for going over a hundred miles per hour in a fifty-five zone. He promptly became a suspect in the bombing, because hidden in the back of his truck were four electronic kitchen timers. Kitchen timers that could be easily modified as bomb timers.

Unfortunately, no further evidence linked him to the bombing, and eventually DHS had forced the investigation to move on to other avenues, primarily Muslim Americans.

Channing pled guilty to speeding and reckless driving, paid a three-hundred dollar fine, and disappeared back to Baughman settlement.

There was little more about him, except one item in his credit report. In February, an apartment complex in Charleston had run his credit.

It took nearly an hour for Corvath to track down the whereabouts of Colonel Barry Welsh, Channing's former commanding officer in Iraq. He was now assigned to the US Embassy in London as a military attaché.

It wasn't quite four in the afternoon yet in London. Corvath dialed the embassy, not expecting to reach Welsh, and was pleasantly surprised to be connected with him right away.

"Colonel Welsh, I'm Detective Sergeant Billy Ray Corvath. I'm with the Special Prosecutor's office in Charleston, West Virginia."

"What can I do for you, Detective?"

"Sir, I'm currently working on a confidential investigation; I can't get into the details. But your name came up in the context of a man we are interested in. Do you recall a Lieutenant John Channing?"

"I do... Channing served in my battalion in Iraq. What about him?"

"Sir, can you tell me anything about him? What he was like?"

"Sure. To be honest, Detective, Channing was a bit of a hothead. A very motivated platoon leader, he pushed his men very hard. In a lot of ways, he was the ideal Lieutenant: patriotic, keen attention to detail, had the respect of the men."

"Sir, can you tell me the circumstances of his reprimand?"

"In general terms. How familiar are you with the second battle of Fallujah?"

"Only vaguely, sir."

"It was likely the largest urban battle fought by the United States since the fall of Hue in Vietnam. When we first took Iraq, Fallujah was fairly friendly to coalition forces, you understand. But, to be blunt, the Army screwed it up. Killed a bunch of civilians in a demonstration. That was followed by insurgents killing American contractors, burning the bodies and hanging them from a bridge. You probably remember the footage, it aired worldwide."

"Yeah, I remember it," Corvath said. "It was outrageous."

"No question. Our intent from that point was to pacify the city with strategic counterinsurgent operations. Lots of boots on the ground, foot patrols, outreach to the local community. But the politicians ordered otherwise. Instead, we went in force, put the city under siege. It turned into a major clusterfuck, and finally they called in the Marine Corps to clean it up. We had to take the city block by block, building by building. Insurgents had booby-trapped the entire city—bombs inside buildings, snipers in the towers of mosques. It was a giant bloody maze. We lost more than fifty marines in the battle."

Corvath said, "I remember some of the media coverage."

"Okay, so you can imagine the potential for chaos. Everything had to be tightly managed—especially the movement of our troops. Channing had a platoon. Overall, he was a good Marine, a good officer. But sometimes he was way too aggressive. We had a situation where his platoon was preparing to assault a building, and there was some confusion at that point whether the building was already occupied by British troops. I ordered a cease-fire so we could clear up positions. Channing ordered the assault anyway. It was pure dumb luck he didn't kill any friendlies."

Corvath thought about that for a moment, then said, "Why only a reprimand? I would have thought ignoring an order in combat would result in more serious punishment."

"Two reasons. First, a written reprimand in an officer's jacket is more serious than you might realize. It effectively killed his chances of ever becoming a company commander. The Marine

Corps won't promote hotheads who ignore orders to senior positions."

"I see. What was your other reason?"

"Simple enough: he was a damn good Marine, a damn
good platoon commander. Yeah, he screwed up. But sometimes
you take the evil you know. We were in the middle of some of
the most serious fighting the Marine Corps had been involved
in in years. I wasn't about to replace an experienced combat
commander with some wet-behind-the ears officer who had
never heard a weapon fired in anger. Plus... I can't say enough
in praise of the heroism of our young Marines in that conflict.
It was the ugliest fight you can possibly imagine. They took it
on the chin and kept going forward, no matter how ugly it was.
When I think of the sacrifices those young men made..." He
trailed off, unable to continue.

"Gotcha... That makes perfect sense. Anything else you
can tell me about Channing? His personal life?"

"I didn't know much about it. I know he was extremely devout. Led Bible study sessions with the battalion chaplain. I'm
not sure he was cut out for real counterinsurgency operations:
that takes a certain level of sympathy with the local population, and he hated Muslims with a passion. I know he's a damn
smart man—Engineering degree from Georgia Tech. Very
sharp. But very driven by his passions. A good officer needs
to have firm control of himself, and I sometimes doubted his
control."

"Thank you, Colonel. You've helped a great deal in giving
me a clearer picture."

"No problem, Sergeant. Good luck in your investigation. I
do hope Channing isn't involved in anything serious."

"As I said, sir, I can't really discuss the circumstances of the
investigation."

"Understood."

They ended the call. Corvath thought about what he'd learned so far. Colonel Welsh had given a much clearer picture of who John Channing was. And none of it led to any doubts that Channing, and possibly his father, might well be behind one of the worst terrorist attacks on US soil in history.

But where was he now? Corvath picked up the phone and dialed the Montgomery Chase apartments in North Charleston.

Corvath introduced himself and asked to speak with the leasing manager. A moment later, a woman answered the phone.

"Hello. My name is Detective Sergeant Jimmy Ray Corvath. I'd like to ask you a few questions, if you have a few moments."

"Sure," the woman replied.

"I'm doing a routine background check on a Mr. John Channing, who applied for a lease at your complex last month."

"Yes, I know Mr. Channing. He's renting apartment 4162. Nice man."

"Any problems with Mr. Channing? Pays his rent on time?"

"No, sir, no problems. Is there something I should be concerned about?"

"No… just a routine check, employment related. I appreciate your time."

"No problem," she said.

He had Channing's location. Time to find out what John Channing was up to.

⌘

The Montgomery Chase apartments made up a small complex on the north side of Charleston. Built in the nineties, it had nine buildings built in three groups, with a leasing office and swimming pool in the center. Nothing unusual about it.

Corvath's only concern was being noticed. People paid attention when someone sat for hours in a vehicle in an apartment complex. Little he could do about it, but at least he found a spot shaded by trees about 100 yards from the entrance to Channing's building. A quick phone call, pretending to be a wrong number, established that Channing was home. Forty-five minutes later, Channing exited the building and climbed into a decrepit '98 Pontiac Firebird.

Corvath followed him out, making a mental note to himself to get a GPS attached to Channing's car. In the meantime, he'd just have to be cautious.

Channing drove about twenty minutes into downtown, stopping at a convenience store along the way. Once they entered the heavier traffic downtown, Corvath closed up the distance between them a little, worried about losing his quarry.

He needn't have worried. Channing pulled into a parking lot. Corvath followed, parking his truck several vehicles down. He watched as Channing paid the attendant, then went across the street into a location that immediately alarmed Corvath. Harry's Hog House—the same restaurant where he had briefed Hatfield and Valerie Murphy on the case just a few days ago.

Corvath didn't believe in coincidences. Hatfield had picked the location of their meeting a few days before. Harry's was just a couple of blocks from the headquarters of the Military and Law Enforcement Department.

Corvath needed to know who was inside. But he had to do it without being recognized himself. If Hatfield was in there, the game would be up immediately. Damn!

He took out his cell phone and dialed Ambrose Hall.

Ambrose answered immediately.

Corvath didn't beat around the bush. "John Channing is meeting someone at Harry's Hog House. If it's Hatfield, they'll spot me immediately. I need to get someone else in there, ASAP."

"That's perfect, Detective, I've been craving take-out anyway. Ten minutes—I'll send one of the detectives from Charleston PD. Call me if the situation changes."

"You got it," Corvath answered. He disconnected and continued watching.

Less than ten minutes later, a younger man in a suit and tie entered the building. It took him less than five minutes to exit the building, carrying his takeout order. Corvath waited anxiously for a phone call.

The phone rang a few minutes later; it was an unfamiliar number.

"Corvath."

"Detective Sergeant Corvath? This is Detective Harliss, I'm Charleston PD, detailed to the special prosecutor's office. Mr. Hall sent me to check out your suspect and the person he's meeting with."

"Yeah, go ahead."

"Okay, I made your suspect, John Channing. He's in the back booth, meeting with two men. Mismatched pair. White male, about forty, balding, blue eyes, glasses, in a grey suit and tie. The other is a little younger, white male, mid-thirties, jeans and black T-shirt. Well built, looks like he spends a lot of time in the gym."

"All right. Ditch your takeout order somewhere; I want you to hang around in case they split up. If they get into a vehicle, I want the license plates, understand?"

"You got it."

"Stay out of sight. I'll call you when they exit."

Corvath waited impatiently. At least it wasn't Hatfield in there. That would have been truly disappointing. But he couldn't rule it out.

Corvath's phone rang again. Faith. He answered it, keeping an eye on the front door of the restaurant. "Hey, babe, what's up?"

"I'm just checking in, Billy. Is there...? I'm just worried. About the other night."

Corvath sighed. "I know, hun. But I'm working a different case now; they pulled me off it after DHS's little stunt."

"I know. I'm just... I'm scared, Billy."

"Hun, don't be." Corvath paused a moment. He didn't like to lie to Faith. But he didn't want her terrified DHS was going to cart him off, either. "I've dropped that case entirely. They've got me tailing some former marine now, totally unrelated."

"You'll be home for dinner?"

"I don't know. I'm on a stakeout right now. I'll call."

"I love you," she said.

"I love you, babe. Try not to worry."

Corvath saw another man walking toward the restaurant. He quickly ducked down out of sight. It was JD Roberts. Holy shit.

"I gotta go right now, hun."

He hung up the phone, knowing that now she was going to worry even more.

Corvath suddenly realized he might be on the verge of blowing the biggest conspiracy case of the century. The Reverend Roland Channing, a respected—if somewhat kooky—evangelist, establishing his own brand of neo-theocracy by infiltrating the government with his disciples. JD Roberts, who grew up right across the river from Channing, and was now a high-level official with the Department of Homeland Security. John Channing, briefly the chief suspect in the second worst terrorist attack ever to take place in the United States. Until DHS turned the investigation away.

If he was right, this was beyond terrifying. Roberts was in a position to arrest virtually anyone with impunity. A few years ago, during President Obama's administration, congress had granted DHS and the military the right to indefinitely detain American citizens. No charges, no Miranda rights, no habeaus corpus. No constitutional rights at all as soon as DHS labeled someone as a terrorist. Which meant that anyone who challenged Roberts was extremely vulnerable. Who else was tied in with this? Other government officials? Members of Congress? Higher-level officials in DHS or other agencies?

There was no way to know. Corvath knew this much: it was too big for him. He'd follow the evidence where it led him, but the danger was real: if he found out too much, he was likely to find himself held indefinitely. And he had a wife and kid to worry about.

Ten minutes later, John Channing left the building and walked across the street to the parking lot. Corvath waited. He would follow Channing's trail later by getting a tracking device put on his car. Right now, his bigger interest was who the two unknown men were.

The other two men came out a moment later, accompanied by Roberts. Roberts immediately turned to his left and walked away from the restaurant. The man in the suit turned to the right. Corvath dialed Detective Harliss.

"You take the suit. Get his license plates, or track where he goes as far as you can without being made. Do not let yourself be identified. I got the guy in the T-shirt."

"Got it," Harliss said.

Corvath hung up without another word.

The man in the T-shirt got into a big brown Ford F-150 pickup—well used and splashed with mud—in the parking lot Corvath was in. He was as Harliss had described him: big, muscular, with bulging biceps that strained his T-shirt. Short, military-style haircut. There was a military parking sticker in the window of his truck. Corvath couldn't see it well enough to tell whether the sticker was current. He took a quick snapshot of the license plate with his phone.

He pulled out of the parking lot behind the Ford. It led him to the left, and after two quick turns got onto the on-ramp for I-64 East/I-77 South. Traffic was heavy this time of day, so Corvath kept back several car lengths. This was going to be a problem if they ended up on an isolated road, but he was okay for now. The driver staying just at the speed limit, even though other cars were passing him.

The Ford exited at the Marmet/Chesapeake exit for West Virginia 94, just south of Charleston. The highway here was bounded by dense trees on both sides. At the bottom of the ramp, the truck took a right turn, and the road immediately narrowed to a two-lane blacktop. Corvath fell further and further back as the truck continued down the road. For minutes at a time he let the truck fall out of sight entirely.

He drove for nearly forty minutes, and started to get worried as the road wound deeper into the mountains. Then, Route 94 simply dead-ended into the Coal River Road at Racine. Damn it! Which way had the Ford gone?

Corvath barely knew this part of the state. Along the coal river were miles and miles of old coal camps and tiny towns nestled into the hollows. Corvath had some distant cousins who lived somewhere around here, in Logan County, but he'd rarely been in the area.

There wasn't much to Racine that he could see, just a few buildings. Corvath shrugged. He had to make a decision. He turned left, to the south, which would lead to Sylvester, Whitesville, Pettus and beyond.

Five minutes later he came around a corner and had to slow to a stop. A US Army patrol was blocking the road.

A soldier in full combat gear, with an apparently loaded M16 rifle, approached him.

"License and registration, sir?"

Wow. Corvath reached in his pocket and handed over a folder containing his badge as well as his ID as a detective with the State Bureau of Investigation.

"Soldier, I'm Detective Sergeant Corvath, State Bureau of Investigation. Has a brown Ford F-150 passed through here in the last few minutes?"

The soldier looked at the ID in confusion, then shouted. "Hey, LT? This one's a detective, he's asking me questions."

A young lieutenant, who had been standing at a parked Humvee, walked over.

"Afternoon, sir," the lieutenant said, taking the credentials from the soldier and looking them over.

"Lieutenant, I'm trailing a suspect. Did a brown Ford F-150 pass through here in the past few minutes?"

The lieutenant nodded. "Yes."

"And you got the driver's ID?"

"Yes, sir, but I don't think I can release that—"

"Never mind that. Who's your commanding officer? I'll go through channels later, right now I need to keep following him."

"Captain Wellstone, sir. Bravo Company, First of the Fifteenth Infantry. Let me get a scan of your ID, and you'll be on your way, Detective. You're about three or four minutes behind the truck."

Corvath waited impatiently while they took a digital scan of his ID, then finally got on his way.

Unfortunately, by that time he'd lost the truck.

SEVENTEEN

R EPRESENTATIVE Gil Barnhart, the chair of the committee, leaned forward and spoke into the microphone. "Ms. Murphy, first of all I'd like to thank you for appearing before us today."

She muttered an incoherent thanks, and the speaker went on.

"As I'm sure you are aware, significant questions have been raised in the media and by my peers here in the Legislature regarding... well, regarding where your loyalties lie. Your father was commander of the West Virginia National Guard during our brief war for independence, and was executed for treason. But if you are confirmed as Secretary, you will be in charge of the police and military forces of this state. Would you care to enlighten us as to your position on these matters?"

Valerie listened carefully as Barnhart phrased his tortuous, barbed question. There was no right answer, not when responding to a legislature that had voted near enough unanimously to commit suicide just a few months before.

The hearing room was crowded, with a surprising number of journalists and photographers for a state-level confirmation hearing. It seemed as if most of the spectators were holding their breath after the question.

She leaned toward the microphone, and, finding that her hands were shaking following the representative's attack, laid them flat and firm on the table. She cleared her throat.

"Representative Barnhart, I appreciate the question, and it is an important one. Let me preface this by making one thing very clear. My father was an honorable man, and I loved him with all my heart. I believe his execution, which happened with unprecedented speed and lack of judicial process, was a… a travesty of justice. That said, he raised me to have my own mind, my own opinions, my own beliefs."

Barnhart nodded as she spoke. The other representatives on the panel seemed to relax a little. Had they been afraid she would break down? Or rant against her father? She didn't know.

She took another breath and continued. "This is a complex issue, and I'll try to thread my way through it as clearly as I can. First of all, I want to make clear that I firmly believe that the federal government continues to head in the wrong direction with regards to civil liberties and the Constitution. The Department of Homeland Security in particular has too much power over the lives of all Americans, and the appalling tragedies and deaths we faced in West Virginia last year due to abuses of that power are tragic beyond belief.

"That said, I opposed the independence referendum, and did everything in my power to prevent it from coming to war. I believed, than and now, that the best way to solve these problems is through the democratic process.

"Now, with regards to the very real needs of the State of West Virginia: As Secretary of Law Enforcement and Military Affairs, my primary concerns will be with public safety and law enforcement. That means, among other things, doing my best to stop this growing insurgency in its tracks. Because while I am sympathetic to the belief that the federal government is out of control, I firmly oppose the methods of terrorists and insurgents who would kill from ambush, attack civilians and take West Virginia down a bloody road that will result in far more harm than we have already experienced."

The panel didn't look happy, but she didn't know enough about the different members to even guess where their political leanings lay. She looked from one to the next, trying to gauge the effect of her words.

Wade Davis leaned over and whispered, "Perfect opening, Valerie. Relax, you'll be fine."

Next up was Mary Pearson, the democratic representative representing Charleston.

"Ms. Murphy, since the end of the war, we've had virtually no police presence in Charleston at all. The city is bankrupt and can't pay the police, and as I understand it, your agency has furloughed nearly eighty-percent of the state patrol. What are your plans to address this situation?"

Valerie nodded. It was a question she'd prepared for. "Representative Pearson, this is the number one challenge facing the department. We've already begun three key initiatives to address the problem. First, I've opened negotiations with the federal Justice and Homeland Security departments seeking emergency funding to get the police back on the street. Second, using the limited resources we have, we're organizing community watches in every jurisdiction in the state. Finally, we've received approval to re-activate the state National Guard under federal authority. One brigade of the guard will be seconded to the Governor to provide emergency response in the worst hit communities."

A murmur rose amongst spectators and journalists. No announcement had been made yet about the re-activation of the guard, nor the promised presidential pardons for former rebels who served two years on active duty without incident.

Barnhart leaned forward and spoke into the microphone. "Ms. Murphy, I'd now like to move to my biggest concern regarding your nomination. Would you care to comment on the story reported today in the Charleston Gazette regarding your videotaped sexual escapades?"

Valerie froze. What in God's name was he talking about? She felt a bead of sweat form on her forehead, and nervously wiped it away.

"Ms. Murphy, please answer the question."

Valerie cleared her throat, then spoke into the microphone. "I'm not aware of the story, nor of any… videos involving me in such situations. I'm afraid I can't answer your question because I don't know anything about it."

Barnhart gave an indulgent smile. "Ms. Murphy, you are aware that you are under oath?"

Valerie sat up straight. "Of course I am. And the answer to your question, Mr. Chairman, is that I've not seen the story and cannot comment on it without knowing the contents."

"Well, then, Ms. Murphy. We will take a five-minute recess so you can familiarize yourself with the specifics."

Immediately reporters rushed her and began shouting questions. She shoved her way past them with the assistance of Henry, and he led her to an office down the hall.

Immediately she pulled out her tablet and searched for the article.

Valerie's blood froze at the headline: "Secretary-Elect Murphy Accused of Using Official Vehicle for Sex Meeting."

Underneath, a grainy screenshot from what looked like a webcam. It was most definitely her, with David Brown. She blinked, trying to push back involuntary tears.

Where the hell had this video come from? She knew the room intimately; it was David's apartment in New York. But they had never made videos. Or… to be more accurate, she'd never made any. Had David made them? How often had his laptop sat there, open and turned on, facing the bed, when she'd been visiting? Why in God's name would he do such a thing without her consent? Or worse, allow it to be published?

She forced back rage, swallowing the emotion into her churning stomach, and forced herself to read the article.

It was simple and brief. An anonymous source—someone in the department of course—had told the Gazette that she'd used an official car to meet with David for dinner last week. The article didn't mention the restaurant or that she'd left to return to work. Rather, it left open the worst possible interpretation, identifying David as her some-time lover from New York.

The video itself had been posted anonymously to over twenty forums on the Internet during the last twelve hours, and the same caller who had alerted the media to her dinner had also clued them in to the video, which had already gone viral.

Valerie had to force back vomit.

Without thinking, she hit the speed-dial for his cell.

Two rings, then he answered. "Hey, Val, what's up? Have you reconsidered coming to New York?"

"You son of a bitch! How could you?"

There was stunned silence at the other end. After nearly fifteen seconds, he replied evenly, "Valerie, what's wrong? How could I do what?"

"Videos? You made videos of us together without telling me? Or asking me?"

"Valerie…" he said, almost sounding as if he was choking. "I don't… I don't know what…"

She interrupted. "Don't bother to lie to me about it, David. They're all over the goddamn Internet and the newspapers. Why don't you go Google yourself and find out all about it?"

She hung up the phone and turned the ringer off. Then she closed her eyes, breathed, and very slowly counted to what felt like twenty-thousand.

Opening her eyes, she looked at Henry. "All right, I'm ready."

Looking sympathetic, Henry led her back to the hearing room.

సౌ

The morning after he lost the trail of the Ford F-150 and its driver, a quick check of the DMV returned the identity of the driver: Lucas Thompson of Pettus, West Virginia. An unemployed coal miner, he'd worked for the Eagle Mine in Whitesville until its closure five years before. He'd served a four-your hitch in the Army and was still on the active Reserve list.

As far as Corvath could find, Thompson sat out the West Virginia war, but he might have served in the irregulars: records of who had signed up for irregular forces were few and far between. No criminal record, just a couple of speeding tickets. According to his social security record, he'd not worked since leaving the Army. His current address was his childhood home in Pettus.

Nothing to do but follow the trail. Corvath set out that morning for Pettus and found the house an hour and a half later. South of Whitesville, the house was worn down, with clapboards faded to grey. The F-150 was parked in front. Corvath drove on past, then pulled off on the edge of the woods two hundreds yards beyond the driveway. The house remained just within view, and with his binoculars he could just make out the truck through the trees.

He didn't wait long. Thompson came out of the house thirty minutes later, started the truck, and headed north, back toward Charleston.

Thank God he had filled up the tank this morning.

Corvath followed as Thompson drove back into Charleston, exiting the highway toward downtown. He finally pulled to a stop at a crowded intersection near the capitol building. The traffic light was out, and cars were taking turns going through the intersection, with frequent associated honking and yelling among drivers.

Corvath parked and got out. Thompson looked much the same today: still in a black T-shirt and jeans, with the addition of a loose Army fatigue jacket, zipped up halfway. It was too warm for it. He walked into one of the few still-open diners. Corvath stopped to buy a newspaper and followed him in, taking a seat at the counter.

Thompson took a seat in a booth in the back, across from an unfamiliar man. This one was older, in a loose hunting outfit and full beard.

Corvath didn't have anything resembling probable cause to take any action yet. He satdrinking his coffee and pretending to look at the paper while he kept an eye on the two jokers.

The diner sat at the corner of one of the most snarled intersections near downtown. The traffic signal had been blinking yellow for two weeks, and traffic here was at a continuous crawl.

The two men spoke quietly, and Corvath couldn't make out a word.

The older of the two men periodically looked toward the intersection with unusual interest. Something just wasn't right. Corvath considered calling in to the office for backup, but decided to wait.

Thompson jerked nervously when his phone rang. He answered it, muttered a few words, then hung up and said something to his pal. The two men stood; the older man threw a bill on the table and they quickly made their way to the door.

Corvath folded his paper, put a five on the counter and stood, too. He took his time, trying to look casual, stepping out the door about sixty seconds behind the two men.

Standing in the sunlight, Corvath had a much better look at them. The taller man was built like a panther: very lean, but his muscular build was apparent even under baggy hunting clothes. Ruddy skin made it clear he'd spent a lifetime outdoors.

Thompson was shorter, stout, with an angry squint and a nearly flattened pug nose that looked as if it had once had a violent encounter with someone's fist.

Both of them stopped at the curb, looking up the street at the very slow moving traffic. Then the short one pointed at a car: a dark grey Lincoln Town Car stuck about ten cars back from the blinking light.

Pug nose darted between two of the slow moving cars and began walking up the yellow line toward the Lincoln. The tall one stayed on the sidewalk parallel to his partner. Both men reached under their jackets.

Oh crap. Backup would have been nice.

⋘

Valerie Murphy swiped to the next page of the article, not really seeing the words. The latest media assassination—this time in the New York Times—was both appallingly inaccurate and hopelessly biased. The article was little more than the prurient and disgusting blog entries all over the web, all celebrating the fact that yet another political operative had been caught out in a sex scandal.

"Critics have suggested that in accepting the post, Ms. Murphy is disloyal to her father, Brigadier General Kenneth Murphy, executed last month for treason."

Her stomach hurt like hell.

She frowned and leaned forward to speak to her driver, Henry.

"How much longer does this traffic go on?"

Henry looked over his shoulder at her. "Don't worry, Ms. Murphy, it's only another block or so before this clears up. We'll get you back to the office shortly."

His voice was quiet. He couldn't help but be aware of how she'd been ambushed, her deepest personal life spread all over the internet as cheap porn.

She glanced back down at her handheld, switching to email. Out of the corner of her eye, she saw a man standing in the median, face focused, searching. Then he began moving quickly up the median toward the car, and reached inside his coat. She froze in fear.

"Son of a bitch!" Henry fumbled to release his seatbelt, reaching for his pistol at the same time.

The first shot came from an unexpected direction: another, bearded man on the sidewalk, pistol raised at her through the window, flew forward suddenly and hit the windshield.

Valerie let out a scream and ducked behind the seat as she heard the glass shatter into a million pieces and another shot was fired.

∞

The older perp was down hard. Corvath had taken a clean shot while was aiming at the woman in the back of the car, catching him in the lower back. He wouldn't be getting back up any time soon.

He turned quickly to Thompson. Too slow. Bad guy number two heard the shot and saw his partner go flying in time to turn on Corvath. For just a millisecond or so he met Thompson's eyes as he tried to bring his piece to bear. Too slow. Too slow.

Thompson let off a shot and Corvath felt a locomotive hit him. He fell to the ground with a grunt, just in time to see the driver of the car fire a shot through the window, taking out Thompson.

Christ, that hurt.

The driver got out of the car, rushing forward with his pistol to check both bad guys. Then he looked at Corvath and his eyes widened. Corvath recognized him: a member of the state's finest, Dennis Henry. Oh, no, he thought. Henry was security detail for Secretary Murphy. She must be in the car.

Coughing up blood, Corvath said, "Henry. Hey, bud, what's going on, man?"

Henry rushed forward. "Corvath... Shit, what are you doing here?"

"Bleeding. Isn't it obvious?"

"Yeah... Stand by, man, we'll get you some help. I gotta check on Secretary Murphy. Hold on, man."

Corvath grabbed Henry's hand. "Dennis... Call Faith. My wife. She's gonna freak."

The pain in his gut washed over him, and he said, "Oh, Christ."

His vision faded to white.

EIGHTEEN

THE sun was setting outside the Oval Office when President William Price stood as his visitors entered. Washington, DC's sky was lit in an array of oranges and reds as the sun went down, somehow putting Price in a mood of … what? Melancholy? Inevitability? The subject of the meeting lent itself to deep soul searching, even though Price knew he wasn't an introspective man.

First to enter was Doctor Carl Metzenberger, the National Security Advisor, flanked by Frank Rich, the Secretary of Homeland Security. Representing Congress—because such was a necessity for this meeting—was Senator Duane Townsend of Oklahoma and Representative Mark Skaggs of Kentucky. They were the chairs of the Homeland Security Committees of their respective houses.

"Have a seat, gentlemen," Price said. They took their seats, the congressional representatives across from Metzenberger and Rich.

"It's your meeting, Metzenberger. You may begin."

Metzenberger looked at Skaggs and Townsend and said, "I must advise you that everything you hear in this meeting is classified Top Secret. The President insisted that representation of both houses of Congress be present when this decision was finalized, and as the respective chairs of the Homeland Security Committees, with secret clearances, I'm sure you both understand the potentially severe consequences of intended or unintended release of state secrets."

Both men nodded, obviously intrigued. It was Price's experience that members of Congress loved being let in on secrets. More than likely they wouldn't care for this one.

"Well, then, we shall begin. The President, using his authority as the Executive of the United States, has both the legal authority and obligation to take action against enemy combatants who are waging war upon the United States. On multiple occasions since September 2001, successive presidents have ordered the targeted killing of such enemy combatants, both on and off the battlefield. On two of those occasions, such targeted killings were aimed at American citizens who had declared war on their own country."

The President winced internally, though he knew his face was unreadable. He had lost a great deal of sleep over one such decision—to order the assassination of an American affiliated with an extremist Muslim terrorist group. This, though, was on a worse order of magnitude.

"As you know, the Department of Homeland Security has conducted an extensive and wide-ranging investigation into the terrorist attacks of last year in Arlington, Virginia, and Charleston, West Virginia. That investigation has been headed by JD Roberts, the Special Agent in Charge of the Charleston Field Office of the Department of Homeland Security. I believe he has testified in front of both of your committees?"

Both representatives nodded.

"Based on that investigation, DHS has compiled a list of fourteen men and two women who we believe are primarily responsible for those terrorist attacks, as well as ongoing attacks against US forces operating in West Virginia and the surrounding states. They are insurgents, waging a war against their own country. They are terrorists."

Metzenberger paused, appearing to wait for a reaction.

Senator Townsend cleared his throat, then said, "Are we permitted to see this list?"

Metzenberger nodded, then handed over a sheet of paper to Townsend. "The list itself is classified Top Secret, so you may review it here, but may not take it from this room."

Townsend looked the list over very slowly, then passed it to Skaggs. Skaggs looked at it, then passed it back to Metzenberger.

Metzenberger continued. "It is the unanimous recommendation of the National Security Council that in order to quell hostilities against our nation, that these fourteen men and women be declared enemy combatants, and that they be found and killed as expeditiously as possible. I have here an order for the President's signature designating them as such."

Townsend coughed and cleared his throat. "What—what evidence do we have against them?"

Frank Rich leaned forward and spoke. "Senator, I've reviewed the evidence, and the case as a whole. It is both thorough, and without any reasonable doubt. If we bring any of these people into court, we'll convict them, without question."

"Then... why are we not attempting to capture them, and bring them into court?"

"I can answer that," Skaggs said. "Because they will provide a cause... martyrs even... for their compatriots. You saw the names on the list, Senator. Bring these people to trial and its going to cost us hundreds, or even thousands, more deaths. Do you want that on your head? I know I don't. I support the President one hundred percent on this."

Townsend nodded, looking somewhat queasy. Price could understand that; he felt queasy himself. He found himself intrigued, and a little disturbed, by Skaggs's eagerness.

"Mister President, here is the order." Metzenberger placed the executive order, classified Top Secret, in front of President Price.

The President sighed, then took a deep breath. He looked at the other men in the room, then said, sounding weary, "For the safety of my country, this is something I must do." The words sounded false even to himself.

He leaned forward slightly, took a pen out of his coat pocket, and signed a death warrant for sixteen American citizens.

NINETEEN

New York Times, April 16
PRESIDENT AUTHORIZES USE OF ARMED DRONES IN WEST VIRGINIA
By Marcus Jennsen
Washington, DC – President Price authorized the arming of unmanned drones in West Virginia Wednesday, targeting a group of what senior administration officials are calling "high-value insurgent targets." Acknowledging publicly for the first time that continuing violence in West Virginia amounts to an insurgency, the White House has compiled a list of individuals believed to be leadership of the rebels.

D ANIEL Anderson sat in the passenger seat of the SUV as it pulled up to the front of the Charleston Area Medical Center. A large red brick structure devoid of architectural features, the building sat slightly back from the street. They had already reviewed blueprints of the hospital, and it looked to be a straightforward matter to get in and out.

"Ready?" asked Collins Moore, the driver and team leader. Anderson had worked for Collins at the Oakland field office of DHS for the last two years.

"Yeah," Anderson said. He looked over his shoulder at Roberto Hernandez in the back seat. "You ready, man?"

Hernandez muttered assent, but misgivings were on his face.

"What is it?" Moore asked.

Hernandez shrugged. "Nothing, boss."

"You're not letting it rattle you that the target's an American, are you? He's still a fucking terrorist. And we've still got orders."

"Yeah, I know. Just never thought I'd be doing this in an American city."

Moore shrugged. "If it was Baghdad, you'd have no problem. And most of those guys couldn't touch anyone in America in a million years. This one, though—you read the mission orders. He's leaking info to insurgents, getting American soldiers killed."

Hernandez muttered a curse. "All right," he said. "Let's do it."

Anderson stepped out of the vehicle. He had to admit, Hernandez was right. The whole mission was unusual. They'd been flown in from DHS's field office in Oakland, California overnight, then briefed. Their mission was to get in, take out the target, then get out on an immediate charter flight back to the West Coast. It seemed like a lot of money and resources—the local field office could have just arrested the man. The only answer was, they didn't want anyone to know what DHS was up to. Which made sense: even though they were doing the right thing—protecting their country—the liberals would have a field day with this one.

Whatever.

He and Hernandez walked side-by-side into the hospital. The emergency room was to the right, intensive care straight ahead. The target was currently stable but unconscious. At the intersection, they split up. Hernandez's job was to plant several small explosives. Not enough to do any damage or hurt anyone, but plenty to pull security and any cops away from the intensive care unit.

Anderson continued forward. In his cheap, off-the-rack blue suit, he could be anyone, visiting anyone. When he reached the intensive care waiting area, he walked past the reception desk as if he belonged there. In the waiting area, a woman he recognized from the dossier sat, flanked by what were certainly three cops, though none of them were in uniform. Family friends, most likely. Hernandez's diversion should pull them to the other side of the hospital in short order.

Four doors down on the right. The door had a window in it, so visitors could see in. The target lay there, nearly buried in the various medical equipment he'd been hooked up to. He was probably a goner anyway, with that nasty gunshot, but the President wanted to be sure. And you didn't disobey orders from the President.

Anderson raised his hand to his ear and pressed the button on the tiny radio transceiver. "Ready," he said.

Fifteen seconds later, a loud cracking sounded across the hall, then another, almost like gunshots. Anderson's eyes darted to the waiting area at the end of the hall. All three of the cops stood, looked at each other, then moved out.

Time. Anderson opened the door to the intensive care room.

Detective Sergeant Billy Ray Corvath lay unconscious, his breathing assisted by a respirator. He'd never know what hit him until he got to Hell with the rest of the terrorists. Expressionless, Anderson took his silenced pistol out of his jacket and fired two shots. Corvath's head was pulped.

Time to move. The life-support equipment would start sounding alarms within seconds. Anderson quickly wiped the pistol down and lay it on the bed. He backed out of the room and walked down the hall, in the opposite direction of the waiting room. He took an immediate right turn, then exited the intensive care unit through a pair of double doors just as a couple of nurses went running past him, back toward Corvath's room. As the door closed, he heard a scream.

The key now was to stay calm and act normal. He turned another corner. Through the glass doors ahead, he saw Hernandez exit the building and walk toward the sidewalk. Anderson followed him out as four cops came running through the doors. They never looked in his direction. He got into the SUV, idling at the corner.

Moore put the vehicle in gear and pulled out into traffic.

"Success?" he asked once they were moving.

"Yeah, target's eliminated," said Anderson.

"All right. Let's get you to the airport."

"Fine," Anderson replied. "Pull into a Starbucks on the way, okay? I need a cup."

"Sure."

TWENTY

Reuters, April 17
HIGH-COURT UPHOLDS MASS EXPULSIONS IN ARI-ZONA
The Supreme Court upheld a critical part of Arizona's crackdown on illegal immigration on Monday in a case involving the accidental deportation of a US citizen during last year's roundup and detainment operation, which saw more than twenty-four thousand illegal immigrants detained by Immigration and Customs Enforcement.

R EBECCA Mays sat up instantly when the phone rang, dropping the ebook reader on the floor at the foot of her bed. Her room, tucked in the corner of her parent's house on the edge of Whitesville, was neatly organized, with most things tucked into place and her bed made. A neat pile of school notebooks rested on her desk, the wall above it dominated by a huge poster of Irina Dvorovenko of the American Ballet Theatre during a performance of Romeo and Juliet.

The house phone hadn't rung since January: lines had been down across the state, and if her father hadn't bought one of those expensive satellite phones they'd have been cut off from the world.

She jumped to her feet, ran to her compact desk and grabbed the telephone.

"Hello?"

"Zoe? It's Joe."

"Uh—this is Rebecca, not my Mom."

"Well, I'll be damned. Little Rebecca. You don't sound so little anymore."

Rebecca smiled. "Uncle Joe, you know I turned eighteen in January."

"Well, darling, knowing and believing are two different things. How are you? School going okay?"

Rebecca laughed. "Have you been sleeping under a rock? School's been closed for months! They're saying we might be going back in a couple more weeks, but I don't know. I'm afraid I'm never going to graduate, now."

"Don't worry, kid, you'll be fine. Where's your Dad?"

"Dad? I don't know. He had to meet some guys from the Army a while ago."

Inspiration hit her. If she took a message to her father while he was meeting with the Army, maybe that guy, Corporal Turville, would be there. Before the thought was complete, she'd already spoken.

"If you want, I can walk a message to him. They're staying right across from the drugstore, in that abandoned house."

"Right," Joe said. "Mrs. Wilson's old place. She was our high school English teacher. Evil bitch. Oops—don't tell your Dad I said that. Why is your dad meeting with the Army?"

She giggled. Uncle Joe had always been a little funny, though he'd been pretty grim since his wife had died last year. It was nice to hear him sounding like himself.

"I don't know. Mayor stuff, I guess. Anyway, they brought in a whole bunch of guys, they got a roadblock, and guys downtown, and up at the dam. I guess Dad's got to work out some stuff with them."

"That's weird," Uncle Joe said, his voice sounding odd. "Why is the Army in Whitesville?"

"Didn't you know? They're all over: in Madison, too, all over the county. They're supposed to be helping us get things back up and running. Couldn't be quick enough for me."

Uncle Joe was silent for a long time at the other end. She could hear him breathing.

"Rebecca, do me a favor?"

"Sure thing."

"Don't worry about running any message to your Dad, I can call him later. Just... stay away from those Army guys, okay?"

Oh, for God's sake. She scrunched her forehead. "How come?"

"Look, I just got a bad feeling, okay? Lot a people have been hurt in the last year around here, and having the Army around may not be such a good thing. Beside, you know I used to be in the Army. I can tell you from experience, kiddo, they only think about one thing. and it sure as hell ain't polishin' their boots."

She blushed and giggled again. "Uncle Joe... last time I saw you, you told me that's all any guy thinks about."

"Well, yeah, that's true. But with the Army it's worse. Anyway, that don't matter. You just stay away from them, you hear?"

She rolled her eyes. "You may know a lot, but you don't know everything. Besides, I have to at least be nice: one of those guys saved my life last week."

"What are you talking about?"

His tone was urgent, unusually so.

She answered in a half-whine, feeling defensive. "Some lunatics were shooting into downtown. Didn't you hear about the helicopters that got shot down? You have been living under a rock. I got stuck in the middle of all that."

Uncle Joe didn't answer right away, but she could hear him breathing over the phone. Then, abruptly, he said, "All right. I'll talk to your dad about it. But you be careful, young lady."

Then he hung up, without even a goodbye.

Well, that was just weird.

Should she go down there anyway? If her dad was talking with the lieutenant, he might not thank her for interrupting.

But Corporal Turville might be there, and she wanted to talk to him. Oh God, she didn't even know anything about him at all, and she had no reason at all to think he was interested. If Dana was here, she'd tell Rebecca she was nuts.

She looked in the mirror. Her eyes focused in on the hideous mole below her left eye, then her flat-as-a-board chest, and sighed in frustration. Who was she kidding, anyway? Her nose was too big, she was shaped almost exactly like a number-two pencil, and with the schools closed, she wasn't even going to graduate high school.

She lay back down on her bed and stared at the ceiling. Damn it. She squeezed her hands into fists, remembering how much she had struggled with her ballet, how hard she had worked to learn the difficult—and sometimes dangerous—routines in cheerleading.

She wasn't ugly, she wasn't stupid, and damned if she was going to let her crazy uncle tell her what to do. Besides: she was intrigued by Jim Turville. Her first sight of him the other day, she and Dana had been walking along the sidewalk, freezing cold, when the helicopters approached. He'd been standing with the other soldiers, and when the shots were fired he'd reacted instantly, running to her and Dana and pulling them out of the line of fire.

It wasn't just that he was cute, which he was. His confidence, his willingness to risk himself to help her. His voice, which had sent chills up her spine.

She wanted to get to know him, and nothing her Uncle said was going to change that.

She stood up and headed for the front door, then immediately deflated on opening the door. A red truck was pulling into the driveway. Damn it! Her ex, Jesse Turner. Riding shotgun was her best friend, Dana Wilder. Dana's long blonde hair was in disarray from riding with the windows down, and she had a big grin on her face. Music blasted out the open windows as Jesse pulled the truck to a stop in the driveway.

The music cut off as Jesse cut the ignition. Dana shouted, "Hey, there, girl!"

Jesse at least had the sense to look a little abashed as they both got out of the truck. Rebecca had told him not long after Christmas not to come around anymore. He'd have some kind of excuse now; probably Dana had asked for a ride. And Dana knew better.

"Hey," Jesse said, not looking her in the eye.

"Hey," Rebecca responded.

Dana frowned, looking back and forth between the two of them. Then she burst out, "Oh, come on! I'm so tired of not being able to hang out with both of my friends at the same time. Can't you two just move on?"

Rebecca replied, a sharp tone in her voice. "I moved on a long time ago, Dana."

Jesse shrugged, then said in a monotone, "Friends? I'll leave you alone on the other stuff. Promise."

Rebecca looked at him, trying to gauge his sincerity. Then she sighed. It was true, she was tired of being stuck at the house, with schools and half of everything else closed, and tired of all the awkward moments with her friends.

"Sure," she finally responded. "Friends."

"Awesome," Dana said. "So you won't be upset if Jesse dates someone else?"

"Hardly," Rebecca replied.

"I ain't dating no one," he said, sounding defensive.

"You should," Rebecca replied. She bit her tongue before adding her thoughts: the sooner he started going out with some other girl, the sooner he'd forget her.

He shrugged again. As articulate as always.

"We're going into town," Dana said. "I'm so bored, I wish they'd open the school again. Want to come?"

"Sure," Rebecca said. "Let's go."

Moments later the three of them were in the cab of Jesse's truck as he hurtled down the narrow roads toward downtown Whitesville. Dana was singing along with the music, and Rebecca stared out at the trees. Spring was coming, thank God.

Moments later they pulled into downtown, and Jesse pulled the truck to a stop in front of the drugstore. There was nothing to do there, either, but at least they'd be doing nothing together. Besides, they might run into other friends.

Rebecca got out of the truck and followed the other two toward the entrance to the drugstore. Then she looked down the street.

The Army had set up their camp in the abandoned old house set fifty yards back from the road. A new, twenty-foot chain link fence surrounded the grounds. A Humvee with a mounted machine gun blocked the gate. And sitting on a lawn chair behind the fence was Jim Turville.

Rebecca swallowed, her throat tight. She felt stiff and awkward as hell.

"Hey," she said, her voice vague. Jesse and Dana stopped. "I'll be back in a few minutes."

Dana raised her eyebrows in surprise as Rebecca walked away.

&

Joe Blankenship hung up the phone, disturbed. Of course, he'd expected the Army to put troops in Whitesville and the rest of Boone County. That was standard practice. He hadn't thought it would happen this quickly, nor had he thought through the implications of how it might impact Mandy's family, still living in their hometown.

Joe was beginning to be troubled by his partnership with Roland Channing. True, Channing had resources Joe hadn't even imagined having access to. He had connections in government, money, access to weapons and people. At the same time, he was beginning to wonder if Channing had any conscience at all. He seemed to believe any methods were justified to accomplish their mutual goals.

If they even shared the same goals. Blankenship wasn't sure about that any more, and it troubled him. Especially because it appeared that Channing had decided Whitesville was to be Ground Zero.

Though he hadn't lived there for nearly twenty years, Joe knew Whitesville intimately. It was where he'd grown up, found his first love, and had his heart broken and then repaired by the same woman. He still remembered the day he'd realized he was falling in love with Mandy Mays as if it were only yesterday. They'd been sitting at lunch when the ground rumbled and shook at quarter-past twelve, silencing the sixty-odd ninth and tenth graders in the Clear Fork High School cafeteria.

The three teachers in the room stood as the shaking came to a stop. Ms. Pine, the music teacher, looked frightened as she whispered to one of the other teachers. A mousy woman, her expressions and gestures always seemed half-finished. Right now she looked frightened: her husband worked in the Eagle Mine.

Joe Blankenship leaned across the table toward his best friend, Bob Mays. "Something just let loose in the mine. Holy shit."

"Nah," Bob said. "Could have been anything. A big truck, maybe." Bob was light to Joe's dark: blonde hair clipped close to his scalp, blue eyes. Joe looked much like his father: swarthy with a strong hint of Native American blood in his bone structure.

Mandy, Bob's little sister, said in a quiet voice, "I hope so." She seemed into shrink in her seat next to Joe. Though a year younger than Bob and Joe, she was in the same grade: she'd skipped second grade.

Their hopes were dashed almost instantly by the sound of the alarm, mounted at the top of the coal tipple, just a quarter mile from the high school.

Mandy grabbed Joe's arm. "I knew it," she said. "I hate that mine."

"I'm sure everyone's okay, Mandy," Bob said. He rolled his eyes at Joe, as if to say, Sisters! He looked at his watch. "Bell's going to ring in a minute."

"Yeah," Joe said. He turned to Mandy. "Meet me after school? I'll walk over to the mine with you, so we can check together that everything's okay."

She nodded, her eyes round with anxiety. Bob scoffed. "You know, Joe, if you weren't my best friend, I'd kick your ass for chasing after my sister."

That brought a rise from Mandy. "Shut your mouth, Bob Mays. You ain't got no say in who chases after me."

Joe grinned as she leaned against him. Mandy was a smart girl, and knew what she wanted. Sometimes just holding her felt like grabbing hold of a piece of heaven. He wanted to hold on for dear life.

"Well, you just watch out, little sister. Joe may seem like a nice guy, but he's got a funny turn to him. Just wait, you'll see."

Joe gave his best friend the finger, then stood up when the bell rang. He looked around to see if any teachers were watching, then gave her a kiss on the lips.

"Don't worry, Mandy. Everything's fine, you'll see. Meet you after school."

Forty-five minutes later, Joe frowned and creased his eyebrows as he stared down at the almost blank page in front of him. Mrs. Wilson, his English teacher, was a goddamn sadist. Day after day, they wrote five-effing-paragraph essays. Day after day, Joe wrestled with the damn things. And day after day, his grade point average dropped.

It had been a little better lately, because Mandy had started helping him in English. Well, his grades weren't any better, but at least he enjoyed studying. Somehow he didn't think Mrs. Wilson thought of English quite the way he did. If she knew, the old woman would be scandalized. She'd been his father's English teacher in 1975, practically before history started.

When the loudspeaker let out a loud feedback whine, his pencil snapped in his hand.

"Mrs. Wilson? Can you please send Bob Mays to the office for early release, please?"

"Oh, shit," Joe muttered. Bob and Mandy's dad worked in the mine, side by side with Joe's father. If something had happened at the mine, it had probably happened to both of them.

"Joe Blankenship! How dare you say that filthy word in my class?"

Joe shrunk into his seat. "Sorry, ma'am. It just slipped out of me."

"Well, it looks like a trip to see Mr. Bateman just slipped into you. Bob, you go ahead to the office, and take your things."

"Yes'm," Bob answered, his voice shaking. Joe met Bob's eyes as the other boy struggled to stuff his books into his backpack.

Mrs. Wilson began writing on a familiar report slip. Joe had made more than one visit to the assistant principal in the last three months. She was interrupted by another loud screech from the loudspeaker, followed by the voice of the school secretary.

"Mrs. Wilson, please also send Joe Blankenship to the office please, for early release."

Joe's heart sank. It couldn't be nothing but an accident at the mine. Oh, son of a bitch. He stood, shaking, and stuffed his books into the bag. His dad worked on the continuous miner, a massive machine that ripped into the coal seam, tearing out hundreds of tons of coal each day. Had something happened with the machine? Or had the ceiling collapsed? God, let it not be that. Joe and his dad didn't exactly get along, but that wasn't the same thing as wanting to see him hurt—or worse.

"Come on," Joe said to Bob, and they both hefted their bags and walked toward the door. Joe didn't bother to wait for permission from Mrs. Wilson.

Mandy was already in the dark, wood-paneled office when they arrived. She stood against the wall, shaking. Mark Radley, the union supervisor from the mine, stood with Mr. Bateman, the assistant principal.

Joe and Bob stood to either side of Mandy, and Joe put his arm around her. That earned a frown from Mr. Bateman, but right now Joe didn't give a shit.

"Kids," said Radley, "I'm sorry to bring you bad news. There's been a collapse down in the mine."

Mandy burst into tears, and Joe pulled her a little closer.

"Your dads was repairin' the continuous miner when the ceiling cut loose."

"Are they okay?" Bob asked.

"Well, they're both still down there, and they're alive. We don't know if they're hurt, or how bad; all I know is they're working to get 'em out right now. They're both still talking, so they can't be hurt too bad. Your moms are already there, and asked me to pick y'all up."

Joe nodded. "Okay. Let's go."

Twelve hours later, the three teenagers were still waiting. Joe sat on the ground, leaning against the base of a tree. Mandy lay with her head in his lap, and a few feet away, Bob sat with his legs crossed, slowly tearing the bark off of a twig.

Twenty feet away, their mothers sat in chairs inside the wood-frame office near the top of the mine-shaft. Rescuers were down there desperately trying to clear the tons of rubble in order to bring the two men back to the surface. All they knew was that both of them were still alive—Zachary Mays had his legs trapped under the rock, and Warren Blankenship lay next to him, his arm trapped.

Joe hadn't said so, but he had a feeling Mandy and Bob's dad wasn't going to live. Or if he did, he wasn't going to be worth much. No way the doctors were going to be able to repair that kind of damage— and that was if they could prevent another collapse. They'd sat through several rumbles in the last twelve hours, and every moment counted now.

Bob cursed and threw his twig away. "You ever wonder if we're going to be in the same way in ten or twenty years?"

"What do you mean?" Joe asked.

"You know what I mean. Are we going to be down there in that damn mine? Working? I always tell myself I'm going to find something else. Make Whitesville a place where you can live without having to go down in the damn mine. Or maybe I'll just go somewhere a thousand miles away."

"Zoe wouldn't like that," Joe said.

"Yeah, that shows how much you know," Bob said. "Latest is she wants to go to California and be an actress. 'Course, Zoe changes her mind about once a week about what she wants to do with her life."

Joe shook his head and shrugged. "More power to her. I don't know, I always figured I'd end up in the mine. I'm not exactly likely to get a scholarship or nothin', and it's for sure my Dad can't afford to pay for college."

He didn't say the obvious: there were no guarantees either of their fathers would even survive the night.

Mandy turned toward him at his comments and slapped him lightly on the shoulder.

"Don't you say that," she said, her voice firm. "Don't you ever say you're going to work in that mine."

"Why the hell not?" Joe replied, his voice wounded.

"'Cause I ain't marrying no damn miner. I'm not sittin' outside that office waiting to find out if my husband is going to live or die. That. Is. Not. Going. To. Happen."

She punctuated each word with a finger jabbed into his shoulder.

"Who said anything about gettin' married?" Joe cried.

She stood up, tears in her eyes. "Joe Blankenship, sometimes you are just as dumb as my brother."

She stormed off to the office and slammed the door when she went inside.

Joe and Bob stared at each other.

"Well, dummy," Bob said. "Maybe she's right."

They didn't talk again until they heard the sound of the shaft elevator. The men were being brought up alive.

Joe wished to God that had been their fairy tale ending: everybody lived happily ever after. But of course, it didn't. Bob was mayor in Whitesville now, with Zoe making herself busy as a housewife. Mandy had been killed by the feds, and nothing would ever be the same. All he could do now was try to shine some light for the next generation: for Rebecca and the other kids coming up now. Maybe they could grow up in a truly free country. He'd long ago learned that he couldn't protect anyone. He'd promised Mandy he'd protect her, over and over again. He'd made a lot of promises.

But in the end, he'd failed her.

Almost two years after the mine accident, he'd been awakened in the middle of the night.

He'd been sprawled on the old, tattered couch in the living room, watching an old black-and-white horror flick. Elvira, Mistress of the Dark, had just cut into the film to make fun of the bad acting. Joe was half-laughing when the loud ringing startled him. He reached over and picked up the old rotary phone. His eyes glanced to the digital flip-clock radio on the stand next to his parents' bedroom. The plastic tabs, long since yellowed from age and cigarette smoke, had just flipped to 2:05 AM.

"Hello?"

"Joe? It's Mandy." Fear raced through him at the sound of her distraught voice.

"Mandy, what's wrong?"

"It's my Dad. Can you... Can you come get me? I'm .... Please?"

"Where are you?"

She sniffed, loud. "Downtown, in front of the drug store." Her voice broke into a tremor, and she whispered, "Please hurry? It's cold out here."

"I'm on my way."

Joe stood, then stopped. His father, wearing a dirty t-shirt and boxer shorts, stood in the doorway to his bedroom, looking out at Joe.

"What's going on, Joe? Where you headed?"

Joe tensed and looked reflexively at the floor, then back at his dad. "Picking up Mandy. I think her dad's on a rampage again. She called me from downtown, asked me to come get her."

The older man nodded his head slowly. "You best get going then. Car keys are on the kitchen table."

Joe let out a sigh of relief, then whispered, "Thanks, Dad."

Outside was silent and extremely cold, the woods crowding in close to the house, a narrow stretch of stars clear in the sky between the hills. Joe's breath steamed as he got into the truck and started it. The venerable engine coughed to life on the third try, and he backed away from the decrepit frame house and steered out onto the empty road. The truck cab still hadn't warmed much when he reached downtown five minutes later.

Mandy was hard to miss, standing in the icy cold in front of the drug store in an old pair of sweats and a giant Tweety Bird T-shirt. What the hell had her old man done?

He pulled to a stop, leaned across the seat and opened the door. "Hey, get in."

She stepped up into the cab, and he took off his down coat and passed it to her. "Truck's not warmed up yet; put this on."

Trembling, teeth chattering, she nodded gratefully.

"Let's get back to the house and get you something warm to drink."

She folded her arms across her chest and pulled her knees up close.

Joe had long since learned that Mandy would talk when she was ready and not a moment before. Right now, his priority was to get her indoors next to a space heater with a hot cup of tea. All the same, he felt the stirrings of rage at the crippled bastard who had fathered her. Zack Mays might have been a good miner, and a good friend to Joe's dad, but he was also an out-and-out son of a bitch, especially when he was drinking the hard stuff. Usually the first week or so of each month, right after his disability check came.

This being the third day of February, the sinewy old sot was due for a brawl.

Back at the house, Mandy sat on the couch in front of the electric space heater, wrapped in a blanket. Joe poured steaming water into a large mug, then dropped in a tea bag and two spoons of sugar. He carried the cup into the other room and handed it to her. She took it, looking grateful, and cupped the mug between her hands.

Joe sat down across from her and held his hands out toward the space heater.

"You want to talk about it?" he asked.

She didn't answer right away. Her face showed lines of strain and her eyes still reflected fear. Mandy didn't scare easily.

They both looked up at the sound of Joe's dad clearing his throat from the cracked bedroom door. He pointed toward the small pile of blankets and pillows resting on the floor at the end of the threadbare couch. "Joe, you can sleep on the couch, and let Mandy have your room."

His shook his head in regret, frowned, then said gruffly to Mandy, "I know your Daddy's gone off the deep end a few times since he got hurt. You're welcome to stay here as long as you need to. You're family, far as I'm concerned, understand?"

Mandy's eyes watered, and she whispered, "Thank you, Mr. Blankenship."

"Here, now, none of that eye waterin' silliness. I'm off to bed. Joe, you take good care of her, understand?"

"Yes, sir," Joe responded.

The old man looked between them, then firmly closed the door.

Mandy took a sip of her tea. "Sometimes I think I'm going to hell. Because I wish my dad was dead, and I had yours," she whispered.

Joe responded quickly. "Wishes ain't acts, Mandy. You can't help what you feel, and God knows your dad's not been right since the accident."

She shook her head. "He wasn't right before the accident. It's just now he's got an excuse to be a complete bastard."

Joe shrugged.

She whispered, "He came at me with a knife, Joe."

He sat up straight. "He did what?"

She closed her eyes. "I think he was hallucinating. He kept shouting about Mom and the devil and... I don't know. Bob heard the screaming and came running, grabbed the knife from him. He pushed him over out of the wheelchair." She opened her eyes and the tears ran freely down her face. "My dad's a... a monster, Joe. I think he would have hurt me if Bob hadn't stopped him. I just... just ran. I didn't know what else to do."

Joe reached out and took her hand. She was shaking.

She hiccoughed, then almost whispered, "Thank you for coming to get me, Joe."

Joe squeezed her hand gently, looking into her eyes, and said, "I'd come get you anywhere, Mandy. No matter where you were. No matter what. I'll keep you safe."

Hours later, his eyes popped open at the sound of something heavy hammering against the front door. The house wasn't much to speak of: cheap framing and clapboard siding that had seen its best days well before Franklin Roosevelt beat Herbert Hoover in the Presidential race. The entire edifice shook from the hammering on the door.

Joe shot off the couch and opened the door. "What the hell?"

Zack Mays jerked the shotgun he'd hammered against the door back to his lap, then brought it up and pointed it at Joe.

"Where is she, boy?" he thundered.

The twin barrels of the shotgun were so big Joe couldn't see anything else at all.

"Mr. Mays... uh..."

"Don't mess with me or I'll turn your hide into a god damn rug! Where is she?"

Mandy's father's eyes were wide and bloodshot. His words were heavily slurred, and not just from drink: the right side of his face seemed to have collapsed in on itself, as if all the muscles on that side had let go. Heavy jowls on that side hung down, and a small spot of drool collected on his chin.

Despite the thumping of his heart, Joe realized the man cradled the shotgun on his left side. His right arm hung loose against the armrest of his wheelchair. Zack Mays had suffered a stroke, and recently. Did he even realize it? They'd known for a while he wasn't in his right mind, but Joe couldn't help but wonder if he had a mind left at all—and if not, what that meant for Joe, standing at the wrong end of a loaded a shotgun.

At that moment, he heard both bedroom doors in the house open nearly simultaneously behind him. Without turning, he called out, "Mandy, Dad, stay back!"

Mays's eyes narrowed. "I told you not to fuck with me, boy. Send her out here now."

Joe took a deep breath, and spoke slow and clearly. "Mr. Mays, let's calm down. Mandy's perfectly safe, and we don't want any accidents."

"Yer goddamn right, boy. You think I don't know what you're up to, dragging my daughter out in the middle of the night? I ought to blow your goddamn no-good head off right here and now."

Joe swallowed. "Sir, with all due respect, until you sober up, Mandy's staying right where she is. I won't have her hurt." He tensed as he spoke. Heavy footsteps were approaching behind him: his father. He needed to calm this situation down before Mays did something crazy.

A beat-up, rusted pickup pulled up behind Mays's van. Bob shot out of the cab. "Dad! Put the shotgun down!"

"Shut up, Bobby! This is between me and the boy, here."

Joe's dad appeared beside him, gently pushing Joe to the side.

"Zack, you're not gonna hurt a kid, now, are you?"

"Your boy picked up my daughter in the middle of the night! What the hell you think I'm gonna do?"

"Now, let's chill out just a little, Zack. Mandy was out in the cold without even a coat to keep her warm. And Joe here slept on the couch—gave Mandy his room, so she'd be warm and safe. You got nothing to worry about."

The shotgun started to waver, then lowered just a little bit. Joe didn't hesitate. He jumped forward and grabbed it, raising the barrel into the air, then yanked it savagely away from Mandy's father. Zack Mays let out a string of curses, then an animal cry as the bones in his trigger finger snapped.

Joe stepped back quickly as his dad went to Mays and grabbed his shoulders. He opened the stock and cleared the loaded rounds, dumping them to the ground.

Mandy burst out the front door, wearing a baggy pair of Joe's jeans and a T-shirt that nearly hung to her knees. She kneeled beside her father, who was howling in pain.

"Daddy? Are you all right?" Her voice was frantic.

Mays lashed out viciously with his unharmed fist, hitting her in the face with the sound of crunching bone. She fell back to the ground with a cry.

Joe shoved the wheelchair-bound man backward, then crouched above Mandy as Zack Mays let loose a string of expletives. Joe gently lifted her as she held a hand against her face. Blood was pouring from her nose.

Bobby cut off the cursing from his father. "You vicious old shit! What the hell did you do that for?"

By this time the neighbors were watching from their front porches, and Joe heard the sound of an approaching siren.

Joe's dad said, "Bobby, keep your dad over there and shut him up. Joe? Get Mandy some ice for that face. What a cluster-fuck." He shook his head.

"Come on inside, Mandy," Joe said quietly.

The pair went back into the house just as a sheriff's deputy turned the corner onto the street. Joe's dad and Bob could deal with them for now.

That row ended up being the last straw. County services were called in, took a good look at the situation, and promptly placed Bob and Mandy in a foster home. Zack Mays spent some time in jail, which didn't do him any harm, and probably did Mandy a world of good.

It wasn't fair. It wasn't fair that someone so kind and sweet and good had been killed, but no one had been punished. It wasn't fair that she was gone. It wasn't fair that he had to go on living without her.

TWENTY-ONE

Washington Post, April 20
**SKAGGS CALLS FOR AUSTERITY MEASURES AFTER
UNEMPLOYMENT REACHES NEW HIGH**
Washington, DC – Rep. Mark Skaggs (R-KY) called for increased austerity measures after yesterday's labor department reports showed unemployment at an all-time high of 22 percent. "The time has come to rein in government waste and let our economy free," Skaggs said in a prepared statement.

THREE days after they'd arrived in Whitesville, Jim Turville was already as bored as he could be. As the quick reaction force, Sergeant Nguyen's squad pretty much had nothing to do but sit around. Two guys maintained security on the vehicles, always manning the machine guns. Otherwise, after the first day, spent frantically filling sandbags to place around the perimeter of the camp, the rest of them had spent their time doing just about nothing.

Right now, he was sitting in a lawn chair next to one of the Humvees, cleaning and oiling his M16A4 rifle. Unusually, the weapons they carried now had never seen service—they'd come straight from the factory.

Other than cleaning weapons, they played cards. They played video games. They dealt with Corporal Meigs's increasingly hostile moods. And then more nothing.

Of course, the thought of Corporal Meigs made Turville smile for a change. Yesterday, Turville's fire team had crushed Meigs's at Hearts. Turville had never been so happy in his life.

But now he had to correct that, because walking toward him was the most beautiful thing he'd ever seen. She'd just stepped out an old red truck, along with Tall Girl and some guy. Turville continued cleaning his weapon, but kept his eyes on her.

Now Short Girl was approaching as her friends stood watching. The guy looked as if he was about to throw a massive sulk. Short Girl, though... Jim almost slapped himself. Dude, her name is Rebecca.

She wore a pair of faded blue jeans that hugged her hips, and calf-high boots that looked well-used. A burgundy turtleneck sweater hugged her upper body, accentuating her breasts and slim waist.

Turville reminded himself that he didn't want to piss off the Lieutenant, and by extension, the Mayor of this town. He'd had a crappy last year, but things were off to a better start so far this year.

"Hi," she said, stopping just outside the fence. She crossed her feet, resting her weight on one foot while the other pointed at the ground, and folded her arms across her chest. Her left hand absently rubbed her right arm.

"Hi," he replied self-consciously. His eyes explored her face. There was a tiny mole under her right eye the color of a penny, which accentuated smooth, almost translucent skin. Her eyelashes were long and drew attention to large brown eyes.

"I hope I didn't embarrass you the other day. I just never got a chance to say thank you." She spoke with a slight back-country accent with rich, warm tones.

"No problem," he said. "Give me just a second here." It took longer than a second, but considerably less than thirty for him to slap the parts of his rifle back into position. His practice reassembling rifles in the dark during basic training had finally proven useful. He slung it over his shoulder, stood, and walked over to the gate opening.

"I'm Jim," he said, holding out his right hand.

She shook. "Rebecca."

"So what can I do for you, Rebecca?"

She smiled, and he felt short of breath.

"Well, I sort of was looking for my Dad— I think he's with your Lieutenant. But I also wanted to talk to you."

Oh, shit, Turville thought. He didn't need to get in trouble for messing with some high school girl. But God, was she pretty. He could have spent an hour just staring at her.

"Well," he heard himself say, "The LT and your Dad took a drive up to the top of the dam. They'll be back in a bit. Why don't we take a walk while we wait?"

Open mouth, insert entire combat boot, Jim. What the hell are you thinking?

"Okay," she said, shoving her hands in her pockets.

He looked up at PFC Leo where he was manning the machine gun in the Humvee.

"Yo, Leo," he called.

"Yep," Leo answered, his expression just short of a leer.

"I'm taking a walk down the street. Yell if we get a call."

"Okay, man."

He turned back to Rebecca. "I've got to stay close. We're the quick reaction force this week, so if anything happens, I got to move in about three seconds."

She shrugged. "Okay."

A truck roared past, shaking the ground as they turned toward the street. They crossed in silence.

He pointed toward the drug store. "Your friends?" he asked.

"Dana and Jesse. She's my best friend."

Interesting that she didn't say who the guy was.

"So what's your story, Rebecca?" he asked, feeling awkward as hell.

She shrugged. "Not much of one. I'm supposed to be graduating high school in a few months, but school's been closed since January."

"Your Dad said you were going off to college next year?"

"Yeah," she replied. "At least I hope so. I got an early acceptance to Marshall, but I don't know what's going to happen with the schools. Who knows? Things have been crazy."

"Yeah," he said. "Crazy I understand."

"What about you?" she said.

"What you see. Joined the Army last year, expecting to be sent off to the Middle East, and instead they sent me to war practically around the corner."

She laughed. "Where are you from?"

"Falls Church, Virginia."

"Well, that's not too far."

"Feels like a million miles sometimes."

"Well, we are pretty much in the middle of nowhere. If you wanted to find an exciting spot, Whitesville probably isn't it."

"Exciting enough for me," he said. "I don't like having people shoot at me. Which reminds me: I know you got your truck back, but are they doing anything about the damage?"

She smiled. "Yes, my Dad said the Army was paying for everything. It's in the body shop now."

"Oh, good. I was a little worried. I didn't want to return your kindness with a bunch of bullet holes in your truck."

She laughed. "That wouldn't be that unusual around here. Trucks with bullet holes, I mean."

"Huh?"

"Well, we've got our share of hunters. My Dad goes shooting sometimes with Uncle Joe, and then we're stuck eating venison for days. Seriously. Ewww."

They walked the length of Boone Street, Whitesville's main corridor. Black marks from the fire still darkened the street.

"How long do you think you're going to be here?" she asked.

"Don't know," he replied. "They're telling us quite a while. Army's worried that folks are pissed off about losing the war. They want us all over the place, as kind of a local police force."

"That's probably a good thing," she said. "You heard the sheriff got murdered last week?"

"Yeah, I heard about it. Not much left in the way of local cops, are there?"

She shook her head. "No. My Dad says it's not a huge deal—there's not much crime around here. Mostly drunks beating up on their wives. It's almost like a ghost town anyway—not too many people left, especially since they started scraping off the top of the mountains around here."

"We drove past one of those on the way down here," he said. "Looks like the surface of the moon."

"It does."

Turville stopped walking. They were two blocks from the Humvees now, almost out of sight around the curve.

"This is as far as I can go," he said.

She turned toward him and tilted her head to the left. "Do you like being in the Army?"

"I don't know. Sometimes I do, sometimes I don't. I've had some bad moments in the last year. Then I got shot in January and spent three months in the hospital. Just got out three weeks ago."

"Really?" she said, eyes wide.

"Yeah... I kinda of forgot to duck, you know?"

She giggled. "Not funny."

"Then why are you laughing?"

That made her laugh harder.

As they turned back toward the Humvees, Turville's tension increased, but he forced out the question.

"I have to ask you something. I'd like to invite you to dinner or a movie sometime, but are you, like, old enough? Am I going to have your Dad coming after me with a shotgun or something? 'Cause, you know, I don't need that kind of trouble."

She giggled again, harder this time. "Somehow I don't see my Dad coming after you with anything but flowers. He can't seem to talk about anything but you lately. And yes, I'm old enough to go to dinner. If you ask nicely."

He stumbled, and his heart beat harder. "Okay. Well, the rest of this week pretty much sucks, and you'd have to do the driving, but can I take you out to dinner?"

"Yes, you can take me to dinner. Or even come out to our place. It'd thrill my Dad."

"I bet your Mom would love it too. I'll have her chasing me with a pitchfork, huh?"

She frowned. "Maybe I was wrong about you after all. You be nice. My uncle told me to stay away from you guys, that everyone in the Army has only one thing on their minds."

He shrugged. "Well, that's true enough."

She laughed.

Looking up toward the dam, he saw a Humvee making it's way down the face, turning around one of the tight switchbacks.

He pointed toward it. "That'll be the LT and your father. We should head back."

They slowly turned back toward the tiny house, keeping the conversation inconsequential. Turville racked his brain, trying to both keep the conversation light, but interesting. She was incredibly cute, but he had serious doubts whether this was a good idea. On the other hand, it had been a long time since he'd dated a girl and she seemed interested.

As they reached the gate, he said, "I know you gave me your number before, but I passed it on to the LT when he turned your truck over, so can I get it again?"

They exchanged contact information, and he keyed hers into his phone. Moments later, the Humvee rolled up. Lieutenant Blake and Bob Mays got out of the vehicle.

"Rebecca," Mays said. "Corporal Turville."

Turville nodded at the Mayor.

Before Turville could say a word, Rebecca said, "Dad, I hope I wasn't too forward, but I've invited Corporal Turville to dinner with us. Is that okay?"

Mays raised his eyebrows, then looked at Lieutenant Blake. "Lieutenant, I'd be delighted to host the corporal, if that's all right with the Army."

Blake looked as if someone had forced him to swallow an uncomfortably large pill, but he nodded. "Of course, Mayor. Timing may be a bit awkward to work out, given Corporal Turville's duties, but we'll work something out."

On top of the other Humvee, Santiago was manning the machine gun. He waited until Turville caught his eye, then gave Turville a lewd wink. Turville frowned at Santiago, annoyed, and looked away.

The mayor and the lieutenant shook hands, then parted. Rebecca followed her father to his car, then she walked back across the street and entered the drugstore, leaving Lieutenant Blake and Turville standing next to the Humvees.

Blake gave Turville an unforgiving eye.

"Corporal, I don't even want to know what you are getting yourself into here. But be pretty goddamn careful."

Turville swallowed and said, "Yes, sir."

☙

Two hours later, Turville was busy googling Rebecca Mays on his phone. Signals had been spotty since they'd arrived, but tonight he had four bars. Tillman and Nowell were manning the machine guns on the Humvees, and Santiago was playing solitaire. Sergeant Nguyen had taken Meigs's fire team on a patrol through the town.

Turville found Rebecca's Facebook page and friended her. Aside from that, there wasn't much of her on the internet, though there were a few articles in the Charleston papers that mentioned her in connection with a ballet troupe.

"You're looking very quiet," Santiago said.

Turville shrugged.

"Is she eighteen?" Santiago asked.

Turville rolled his eyes and set the phone down. "Yeah, she's eighteen."

Santiago grinned. "Cradle-robber."

"Dickhead," Turville responded.

"You should get her to introduce her tall blonde friend to Nowell."

"Jesus, Santiago, I just met the girl, okay? We're going to have dinner, that's all."

Santiago's grin grew. "Trust me, Turville, if there's anything I know, it's how women work. I was just going to have dinner with Claudja, and the next thing I knew, I had two children running around. Make sure you have good protection for dinner."

"Oh, fuck off, Santiago."

"The minute I get home to my wife," Santiago said.

"Incoming," they heard on the radio. The voice was casual. "Looks like Nguyen and alpha team."

Santiago and Turville stood and quickly got into combat gear, then went outside and crouched next to the Humvees. This was standard operating procedure even when known friendlies approached. With just one fire team in the house, things could get ugly quick if they were attacked. There simply weren't enough soldiers to go around given the scope of their mission.

Sergeant Nguyen got out of the first Humvee. He was followed by Meigs in the second, as well as the remainder of the
squad.

"Anything to report, Turville?" Nguyen asked.

"Negative, Sergeant. It's been quiet."

"You and Santiago are taking watch at midnight; have you
had any sack time?"

"Yeah, Sarge. We're good to go."

Nguyen led the others into the house. Turville checked in
with Tillman and Nowell, then headed inside, too. He settled
in on the ratty couch and went back to Facebook. Rebecca had
accepted his friend request. He grinned.

Seconds later he noticed Meigs standing over him. Turville
looked up, and said, "What's up, Meigs?"

"What's this about you and some girl in town?"

"Nothing. Just dinner with her family."

"She's a civilian, Turville. Why don't you just shoot her
now, get it over with?"

Turville felt a surge of rage. "Shut the fuck up, Meigs."

"Oh, crap," said Leo, sitting in the corner. "Time for the
big-dick contest."

"Think I should warn her, Turville? Think she knows you
shot a black kid and got away with it?"

Turville felt his face get hot. He stood up, eye-to-eye with
Meigs

"Back the fuck off, Meigs!"

Meigs tilted his head. "Why, you cracker motherfucker?
You gonna shoot me, too?"

Santiago stepped in. "Take it easy, guys. We're supposed to
be fighting the enemy, not each other."

Leo, sitting with his head in his hands, said, "Meigs, leave
him alone. That's all over with."

"Yeah, motherfucker," Meigs replied. "It's over for the kid he shot."

Santiago stepped between them, hands in the air, facing Meigs. "Meigs, let's cool it down. We don't need a fight in here."

Nguyen's booming voice chimed in, as he entered the room. "Who is fighting? There better not be any fighting, or you guys will be digging latrine pits and filling them in for the next week!"

Nguyen looked back and forth between Meigs and Turville. Meigs backed off fractionally, and Turville took the opportunity to walk away. As he did so, he thought he could feel Meigs's eyes boring holes in his back.

TWENTY-TWO

Science News, April 22
MAYER CORP DENIES RESPONSIBILITY FOR PET DEATHS
In the opening arguments of a case thousands of former pet owners are watching, Mayer Corporation attorneys argued that the company is not responsible for the sudden deaths of an estimated 22,000 pets last fall. The company argued that the lawsuit should target their supplier, Tigris Industries, which produced the genetically modified grain used as filler in Mayer's popular dog food brands. Investigation into the deaths of the pets indicated that the deaths were caused by outgassing of cyanide from the modified grains. Mayer Corp. filed for Chapter 13 bankruptcy protection three months after the pet deaths were first reported.

VALERIE Murphy stood on the edge of the plaza in downtown Charleston, overlooking the river. Even though the kiosks and other small businesses that used to operate here were all closed, families still gathered near the river, and people were sitting on benches placed throughout the plaza.

Dennis Henry stood a few feet behind her, scanning the crowd, his jacket open. Whatever discomfort she may have felt about his constant presence was gone. It was difficult to forget that when two men bent on murdering her opened fire, Henry had calmly and without hesitation dispatched one of them, saving her life.

She turned to him and smiled. "If I haven't said so already, thank you for the other day."

He shrugged. "That's my job, ma'am."

She heard approaching footsteps. Ambrose Hall was walking across the plaza. His blue double-breasted suit and elegant tie looked out of place. He smiled as he approached.

"Valerie," he said.

"Thank for meeting me here, Ambrose."

"Of course. It's a beautiful day out here, it's good to get out of the office."

"It's also private."

He was expressionless. "Let's have a seat then. Is General Murphy going to make it?"

She replied, "He should be here in a few minutes."

They walked over to an unoccupied bench and sat next to each other. A few minutes later they were joined by Tom Murphy, who was trailed by his aide-de-camp. Murphy gave Valerie a one-armed-hug, then shook hands with Ambrose. Henry backed a few feet away, watching the plaza and everyone in it.

"Anything further on Detective Corvath?" Ambrose asked.

She shook her head. "Nothing useful. I've had detectives combing over the surveillance video from the hospital, but hundreds of people came and went during the two hours before and after he was killed. They're out questioning potential suspects, but not getting anywhere."

"And the weapon?"

"Reported stolen here in Charleston two years ago. No ballistics match with anything—it doesn't look like it's been used in any other crime. And the shooter wiped it down before leaving it. No fingerprints."

Ambrose sighed. "I've reviewed his case notes, but there isn't anything from the last 24 hours he was working the case. All we know is he'd been tracking John Channing, and that led him to follow Lucas Thompson from Pettus, down in Boone County. Thompson is one of the shooters who attempted to kill you. But he's a blank. He doesn't even have a home phone. Almost no known associations, no friends, not married. He's been living down there alone since he got out of the Army."

Valerie leaned forward and said, "I want the two of you to hear me out for just a moment. This isn't even a theory yet, just speculation. Some very far out speculation."

Ambrose said, "I'm listening."

General Murphy nodded.

"Do you think there is any possibility that Corvath was killed by DHS?"

Ambrose frowned. "Why?"

She shook her head. "I'm just thinking through the possibilities. Think about it for a second: we already know JD Roberts showed up at Corvath's house and threatened him with detention if he continued investigating the case. Roberts was in charge of DHS task force on the Arlington bombing, and killed the investigation into Roland Channing. We don't have any connection between Roberts and Channing other than geographical, and that's tenuous. But if Roberts is playing straight, what possible reason would he have to halt an investigation?"

"You're suggesting that Roland Channing is somehow responsible for the Arlington bombing," Ambrose said.

Valerie nodded. "If you take that as a starting point, there might be some sense to what we are seeing. Let's say, just for a minute, that somehow Roberts is connected to Roland Channing. He gets put in charge of the investigation into the bombing, and deliberately steers it away from John Channing toward Muslims. There's plenty of people who would believe the bombing was conducted by Islamic terrorists. So attention goes in a different direction entirely. Meanwhile, because of the attack, DHS gets all kinds of new powers. So far, they're the only ones who have benefited from the bombing. No one ever claimed responsibility for it."

"You know that's essentially the argument Dale Whitt made last year. Before he was assassinated," Ambrose said.

She nodded.

"What about Hamilton Biomedical?" Ambrose asked.

Valerie frowned, then said, "It would fit if Channing is planning some kind of bioterror attack."

"He would have to be insane."

"No…" she said, "just a fanatic. Channing believes that the government should be dominated by Christians, by Old Testament law, effectively. Read through his past statements. He's said publicly, for years, that the United States is doomed because secular law trumps religious law. He's spent years educating and grooming hundreds of people. Working them into positions within the government. So… what happens if there is a major crisis—a pandemic. Hundreds of thousands of people sick, dying and afraid?"

"DHS steps in."

"Exactly. DHS steps in and effectively takes over, backed by the Army."

"What about the President? Congress?"

"After what we saw last year, can you see President Price interfering?"

Ambrose shook his head. "No. I think in the end, he'd be supportive of it. He's said it all along: the United States is a Christian nation, and always has been."

"Yeah. And look at his candidacy. In the primaries, the mainstream evangelicals ignored him in favor of one of his opponents. But he did have the backing of the hard-right evangelicals. The ones who believe in Old Testament law. He was backed by the kind of people who believe that women should be submissive to their husbands and that homosexuals are an abomination."

Tom Murphy shook his head. "Valerie, you're painting with way too broad a brush. Yeah, I agree there are some nuts out there, but you can't suggest that just because someone is a believer, they would support that kind of terrorism."

"I'm not suggesting that," she replied, defensively. "But you can't deny the connection is there. These people are operating with a different moral code: it's not terrorism if it is sanctioned by God."

Murphy's lips thinned, his face tense. "You sound like a teenager, Valerie. The politics of Christians are as varied as anyone else. I'm a believer. So was your father, though he was a lot more passive about it."

Valerie looked at Tom skeptically.

"My father?"

"We were both raised Catholic, Valerie, and the last thing he did before he died was go to confession."

She had to bite back a bitter reply, then realized her eyes were watering. She struggled for a moment to lock away the emotion, then said, "So you don't think there is any connection?"

"Oh, I think it's entirely possible. I just don't want you to fall into the trap of lumping all believers in the same pot. It may be politically incorrect for me to say it, but the fact is, I believe the salvation of our souls is far more important than all this political crap. And yes, you'd probably be uncomfortable to know that I share a lot of beliefs with John Channing. But that doesn't mean I'd ever support terrorism. And a link between Channing and JD Roberts is a long way from suggesting that DHS would actively aid and abet a bioterror attack."

"But don't you see? It doesn't have to be DHS as a whole. Just a few well-placed people."

Ambrose nodded unhappily. "If she's right, General, we can expect that whatever was stolen from Hamilton Biomedical is going to end up being used."

"Yes," Valerie said. "And then… God only knows what will happen."

They were silent for a few minutes. Valerie's mind was racing through the implications. This was worse than anything she'd considered until now. Much more dangerous.

Finally Murphy said, "I'm willing to agree this is plausible. Muslims don't hold any monopoly over terrorism. And while I may be sympathetic to Channing's beliefs, I'll never agree with those kinds of methods. So the question is, what do we do?"

She slowly shook her head. "I'm at a loss. How do we fight something like this?"

Ambrose sighed. "I don't know. DHS holds all the cards. If it's true, we're up against something bigger than we've ever dealt with before."

"I'm going to ask Roberts to lunch, I think."

"You're going to what?" Ambrose's voice rose at the end of the sentence.

"Don't worry, I'm not going to make any accusations. Or even any reference to this. I want to know more about him."

"What possible pretext will you use?"

She shrugged. "Interagency cooperation? In theory, we're all supposed to be on the same side."

Ambrose shook his head. "That's a bad idea, Valerie."

"I don't think so. I want to know what makes JD Roberts tick. In the meantime, we quietly keep digging."

"How?"

"Follow up on the leads we have. Especially, I want to know what else Roland Channing has his hands in. Who else in the government is he connected to? What's his angle? And especially whether his little cult an isolated phenomena, or a representation of something much larger. Look, if Roland Channing is gunning to build some kind of theocracy, we need to know how much support he has. We need to know if there's any risk of him succeeding. Because that would mean the end of the country my father believed in. Do you understand?"

Ambrose said, "Of course I do. I certainly don't want to live in Roland Channing's America."

"Then we need to do something about it."

Murphy nodded slowly. "In the meantime, I'm going to direct my planners to start looking at the possibility of some kind of epidemic, and build contingency plans to contain it."

TWENTY-THREE

New York Times, April 25
**FOURTEEN DEATHS REPORTED IN INSURGENT AT-
TACK**
By Marcus Jennsen
Washington, DC – Military officials confirmed the deaths of 11
civilians and three military doctors in Morgantown, West Virgin-
ia, where insurgents bombed an Army clinic providing medical
care to civilians.

R EBECCA Mays was at school the day the war arrived at
Highview. It was the first day back after the holidays.
Snow was still heavy on the ground, and with the ex-
ception of some of the men from the town—and a few boys from
their senior class—away with the National Guard, neither she
nor her friends had paid much attention to it. It was politics and
posturing in Charleston and Washington and most of it didn't
make much of a difference to them.

Then on the morning of January 2, a series of loud explosions rocked the hollow, and the lights went out.

Toby Robertson let out a howl when the classroom went
dark, and Ms. Robertson—his mother, and their US History
teacher—sent him to the office with a detention slip.

Dana, sitting in the desk next to Rebecca, leaned toward
her and whispered, "Are you and Jesse coming to Hannah's
party Saturday?"

Rebecca spoke without thinking. "Why me and Jesse? Why
not just me?"

Dana raised her eyebrows. She hunched over, closer to Rebecca.

"What? Trouble between you and Jesse?"

Rebecca rolled her eyes.

"I'll tell you later," she whispered.

She refused to answer any more questions, trying to pay attention to taking notes. She was tired of being Rebecca and Jesse, Jesse and Rebecca. They'd been dating for two months, and everyone in the school treated them as a single entity.

When Jesse asked her out the first time in November, she'd been flattered. He was popular and good looking. But their relationship had palled within a couple of weeks. Jesse's idea of fun was to get sick drunk with his buddies, and that wasn't Rebecca's cup of tea. Two parties—two weekends in a row—carrying him to his truck and driving him home was just stupid.

On a Saturday in mid-January, she sat down with him at the McDonalds in Racine and broke the news.

He didn't take it well.

"I never knew you were such a fucking tease, Becca," he lashed out, red-faced and angry.

She sat back. She'd never realized he was such an asshole. It hit her that Jesse wasn't reacting this way because he loved her. It was because one of his possessions had acted up on him. She wasn't his partner; she was his toy.

Rebecca leaned across the table, her palms flat on the surface.

"Don't be a jerk, Jesse. You have no call to talk to me like that."

He muttered a curse. "You didn't have any problem dating me before. What is it. you got some other guy waiting in the wings? Who is he? I'll kill him."

She shook her head.

"No, Jesse. There's no one else. Can't you just accept that this isn't working? Can't you just accept that we... we don't have anything in common? At all?"

"What are you talking about? Of course we do!"

"No," she said, her tone final, "we don't. And I'm not going to argue about it. I want us to part as friends, Jesse, like we've always been. Okay?"

He shifted in his seat. His forehead was creased in the middle, whether from anger, stress or just lack of understanding, she didn't know.

"I don't think I can go back to being friends."

She closed her eyes. "I was afraid of that. But that's the way it has to be," she said quietly.

He stood up as if to walk away, then abruptly sat down again.

"You don't like me."

She leaned back, rolling her eyes impatiently. "Oh, for God's sake, Jesse!" She knew she was being unkind, knew she was going too far, but she was too angry to stop. "Don't be so goddamn needy! It's not like we've got rings on our fingers, okay? We've only been dating a few weeks!"

"That's how it is, huh? You had some fun and that's that?"

"Actually, I didn't have that much fun."

"Well fuck you, Miss Priss Bitch. Fuck you, and fuck your friendship."

He stood up, truly enraged now, and headed out of the restaurant. At the door, he came to a stop, apparently realizing he'd driven them there and she'd have no way home if he left. He looked back at her for just a second, then turned away. He got into his pickup, slammed the door.

It roared to life, and Jesse sped out of her life, leaving scorched tire marks in the McDonalds parking lot.

She knew she should feel something. Upset? Distress? All she felt was relief. She relaxed over a book for half an hour, then called Dana and asked for a ride home.

Jesse had been her first and only boyfriend. At the rate she was going, he'd be the last, too. What was she thinking, going to dinner with Jim? He was a soldier. Either he was humoring her, or he just wanted to get into her pants. What did she know about him? Basically nothing

Not to mention that whether she liked it or not, there was a war going on. The explosions in January hadn't really touched Whitesville, but the attack and downing of the helicopters, followed by the arrival of Jim and his platoon, signaled a change.

She didn't know whether it meant a good change or not. She didn't know where it was going to lead.

&

The razor didn't actually shake in Jim Turville's hands as he carefully. Nonetheless, he paused, took a steadying breath, then quickly finished. He packed away his shaving kit, placed a soft-cap on his head instead of the more familiar helmet, and headed to the front door of the house.

Outside, the crickets and other insects made a roar, the sound resembling a jungle. Turville approached the Humvee where Lieutenant Blake stood next to Sergeant Nguyen. Their eyes darted to Turville when he came into view.

Blake was frowning; Nguyen was staring resignedly into the distance.

"Corporal Turville," the Lieutenant said.

Turville straightened his posture.

"Sir?"

"For the record, your sergeant disapproves of this little outing. I'm pretty close to that, myself, but I recognize the fact that some good might come of it. You are on notice: don't fuck up our relationship with the locals. Am I clear?"

Turville swallowed.

"Yes, sir."

Blake frowned. "I'm not sure you get the seriousness of this, Corporal, so I'm gonna be as blunt and crass as I feel necessary. We're fighting what looks to be the beginnings of a full-fledged insurgency here. You know what's going on in your little corner of the world, but you may not realize that the attacks aren't just taking place here. We had half a dozen MPs killed in Morgantown this week, too. We depend on the good will of the locals. Especially the local government. Especially the mayor."

Each time he said "especially," the Lieutenant moved a little closer, poking Turville in the chest, hard.

"In short, everything we're doing is at risk of being completely and absolutely fucked if you decide to try to stick your dick into things. Or more explicitly, into anybody. Am I crystal clear, Corporal?"

"Yes, sir."

The Lieutenant and Sergeant Nguyen looked at each other, then back at him, as if to gauge the sincerity of his response.

Turville cleared his throat. What exactly did all this mean? We don't approve, but we're going to let you go ahead anyway. We think you're going to fuck it up, but we're officially disclaiming responsibility. Was this their way of placing blame on him? It sounded a little too much like, "We're going to send you into a fucked up, violent, seething, angry neighborhood that's armed to the teeth, but oh, by the way, you can't protect yourself, and if you do, we're going to blame you for whatever happens."

He was a little too familiar with that kind of buck-passing.

"Sir, may I ask a question?"

Blake eyed him. "Go ahead, Corporal."

"If you are so strongly opposed to it, why are you giving the okay? Why not just restrict me to the barracks?"

Nguyen snorted and shook his head as if in disbelief.

Blake's face flared with anger. "Because, Corporal, I was overruled. When the CO found out that the invitation came from the mayor, he told me I'd better roll out the red carpet for you. Clear?"

"Yes, sir. My apologies, sir. It wasn't my intent to put you in a difficult situation."

Blake's face tightened in anger. "You, Corporal, are the one in a difficult situation. I'm sure it will all be fine, provided you can maintain the presence of mind to keep your fingers — and your dick — out of places they shouldn't be. Am I clear?"

Turville took a breath to calm himself before responding. "Yes, sir."

"Dismissed, Turville."

He resisted the urge to salute the Lieutenant, which would have been a beacon to any watching insurgents. Instead, he muttered, "Thank you, sir," and walked as far away as he could get and still be within the bounds of their little outpost.

It was getting dark out, and the insects were even louder now than before, if that were possible. Few electric lights came on in the town as the sun went down: perhaps a few with generators and access to diesel fuel. For the remainder, a window or two was visible in the distance, with the telltale signs of natural lighting: flickering, yellow and brown shades.

As he looked toward the ridge, a pair of headlights pierced the darkness. That would be her, he hoped. Few enough people went out after dark these days, and when they did, typically they hurried home.

The headlights slowed to a stop. That would be the tactical control point, or roadblock, at the north edge of town. Two minutes later, the lights started moving again, and Turville heard the radio in the Humvee crackle. A disembodied voice crackled out of the vehicle. "Blue four, this is gate post. Turville's girlfriend is approaching, over."

Sergeant Nguyen, the Lieutenant and Turville all muttered curses simultaneously, though Turville felt certain his reasons were different from theirs.

He straightened his posture unconsciously, and tugged the uniform blouse into a reasonably straight position. He rubbed his hands across his clean shaven chin and watched the lights approach.

She pulled to a stop and opened the door of her pickup, slid out of the driver's seat. She wore a white dress embroidered with red flowers, snug around the neck and waist, and matching dark red pumps. Turville caught his breath at the sight of her in the light. She was stunning. He approached, and was annoyed to find Lieutenant Blake right beside him.

She smiled and said, "I'll have him back by midnight."

Lieutenant Blake sputtered just a moment, and Turville stifled a laugh. She looked at him, eyes bright, and said, "You ready?"

"Let's do it," he replied.

Rebecca blushed furiously, and for a moment Turville was merely puzzled. But the Lieutenant's face had also turned bright red—with anger—and Turville stammered, "I uh... not... um... 'it,'—I mean, let's go?"

By that point he was so flustered he couldn't think of what to say. She burst into laughter.

"Come on," she said, then got into the truck.

They rode in an uncomfortable silence until she had driven past the roadblock, going north. The forest swallowed the road, and she slowed down, taking the broad switchbacks slowly. "You look beautiful in that dress," he said.

She blushed, and smiled. "Why, thank you, Jim."

Abruptly she slowed the vehicle, then said, "I want to show you something."

Seconds later, she expertly turned off onto an unmarked road into the woods, then began climbing a steep road with tighter switchbacks up the ridge line. Every time she turned, he swayed a little in his seat. He felt naked without his rifle.

Turville was startled when, five minutes later, the sun shone through the trees. He'd forgotten how early the sun fell below the ridgelines, darkening the hollow. She slowed, then came to a stop at an overlook on top of the ridge. To the west, near the horizon, the sun cast deep orange hues across the sky and through the trees. Behind and below them, the valley was shaded in complete darkness.

She turned the ignition off, then slipped out of the vehicle.

Turville opened his door and got out.

She smiled. "I come up here sometimes to watch the sun set."

A concrete picnic table sat next to a stone wall which paralleled the dropoff over the ridge. She sat on the table, smoothed her dress over her lap. Feeling tense, he sat down next to her. He looked out at the setting sun, then back at her. Her back was straight, hands folded in her lap as she looked off toward the sunset. Looking at her now, he realized her nail polish was the same color as the red flowers on her dress. A tiny spot of mascara had smeared on her upper eyelid, but if anything, it made him more aware of just how pretty she was.

"You're nervous," he said.

She giggled. "A little."

"It's okay, so am I. I ... something about you..."

She turned toward him, looking up into his eyes. "You don't seem like the nervous type."

"What you see is a carefully cultivated appearance of competence and skill. Inside I'm ... scared as hell I'm going to screw this up."

She swayed, leaned against him, then jerked back a little too quickly.

"Tell me about yourself," she said. "I don't know anything about you at all."

As the sun slowly set, he told her about growing up in Virginia, his father, and the bitterness in his home after his dad came back from Iraq. The nights of drunken rage, and nights when his dad sat staring at the television, there but not there, unable to break free of his self-imposed isolation and anger.

"Are you ever afraid that you'll end up like that if you stay in the Army?"

He sighed. "Sometimes, yeah. I mean... I can understand it. I've not been in the Army long, but I've seen some screwed up... I've... It's not easy to talk about it."

He felt her touch his shoulder, very softly. It lasted just a second, but the faint touch was intense.

"It's okay. You don't have to," she said.

"You might be better off finding someone more like you to hang out with."

She laughed, a low sexy sound in the back of her throat. "That's a bigger challenge than it might seem. Most of the guys I go to school with don't have any ambition beyond watching Monday night football."

He stared out at the rapidly darkening sky. "I'm no prize, Rebecca. Just a guy trying to get through life."

"Maybe. We're still getting to know each other. But here's what I know about you: you believe in something. Every day you get up and put your own life on the line to help other people. When that mess started downtown, you didn't duck or hide. Your first response was to find the nearest person in danger and protect them. That's... remarkable."

He looked at the ground. "Don't think that's all there is to it."

"What do you mean?"

Turville sighed. "You're right, I did. But... I've also done some dumb things. Do you remember when Dale Whitt was assassinated last fall? And the Army was sent into Charleston, and that kid got killed?"

"Yeah," she said.

"I was the guy who killed him. I wasn't... I didn't follow orders properly. I got scared, and when that kid came running out of the alley I thought he had a gun. And I shot him."

Her eyes widened in shock for a moment. Then she tilted her head and looked at him closely. Turville saw that her eyes begin to water. "Jim... I'm so sorry."

He continued talking. "It's not something I can ever take back. Or change. Whatever else happens, for the rest of my life I know I ended that kid's opportunities to have a life—to have a dream. I took him away from his family, and then walked away, scott free."

"That makes you a human who makes mistakes. Nothing else."

Her closeness was intoxicating. It was baffling that she could look at him, after he'd exposed the worst thing he'd ever done, and have her accept it. He stared at her, desperately wanting to kiss her, and said, "Deadly mistakes."

She smiled back. "I'm not used to talking this openly with anyone."

He looked into her eyes and smiled. He didn't want to break the mood. But he didn't want to scare her away either. Turville bit his lip, then released it and spoke.

"They'll be expecting us soon."

She sighed. "Yes."

They stood together and walked to the truck. He ached to take her hand.

Rebecca turned the key, and a low whine came from the engine. The starter engaged, but not enough to catch.

"Oh, hell," she said. "Battery's low. I should have thought; this has happened a couple times recently. I think my alternator's going out."

He laughed.

She turned toward him, her face incredulous. "What?" With a little more distance between them, it seemed like she'd regained her equilibrium, her confidence. He chuckled again.

"Are you sure you didn't plan it? Get me into an isolated spot in the mountains, and oops, the battery is conveniently dead? Now we're stuck together."

Her mouth twisted wryly, and she lightly slapped him on the shoulder. "Don't get so excited. In fact, get out and push. If we can get it rolling down the hill, I can pop the clutch and get the truck started."

Turville howled with laughter and opened the door. She put the truck in first gear, depressed the clutch, and turned the key. He leaned hard against the doorframe, and the truck began to inch forward. A little further, and the truck silently began to pick up speed and roll forward on the slope. A few steps further, and Turville jumped back in the cab and slammed the door shut.

Rebecca had a look of intense concentration on her face. The truck moved a little faster. When it hit around ten miles per hour, she took her foot off the clutch.

The truck shuddered, almost stalled, then the engine caught. She switched on the headlights, and Turville caught his breath at the sight of the man standing in the road. She screamed and slammed on the brakes. The engine coughed once and died.

The man in the road was gaunt, his black hair long and on the edge of unkempt. A bristly beard grew in all directions.

Rebecca put her hand flat against her chest, took a deep breath. She leaned her head out the window. "Oh my God— Uncle Joe?"

Turville blinked in surprise.

Rebecca jumped out of the cab, ran forward and said, "What are you doing here? I almost ran you over! You scared the hell out of me."

Turville got out and followed her more slowly. The man hugged Rebecca, but his attention was on Turville. His gaze scanned the uniform and combat boots, then met Turville's eyes. Turville shivered. There was no warmth in that stare.

The man broke off the hug. "I was just headed to your place. Sometimes when I'm in town, I like to come out here and watch the sun set. I wasn't expecting to find you here."

Her eyes flashed toward Turville, and she held her hand out. Turville took it, but he somehow felt that was a mistake in front of this man.

"Uncle Joe, I'd like you to meet Corporal Jim Turville. He's the man who saved my life."

Turville said, "It's nice to meet you, sir."

The man looked at him and spoke in a cold tone. "Joe Blankenship."

Blankenship scanned the uniform again. "No mistaking what you do for a living. What M-O-S?" He was referring to Turville's military occupational specialty.

"Infantry, sir."

Blankenship grunted. Turville couldn't make out the message behind it for sure, but it felt like contempt.

The three stood in an awkward silence broken only by the sounds of the night: an owl in the distance, crickets, frogs, who knew what else.

Rebecca pulled Turville a little closer, then said, "We're headed back to the house right now. Can you follow us, Uncle Joe? I'm having some trouble with the truck."

Blankenship stared at her for a moment, no expression on his face. Then his eyes darted to Turville again, then back to his niece.

"Yes. We should move out."

A few moments later they were moving again. Turville sat in the truck with Rebecca, with Joe Blankenship following behind them in his own truck, a much older pickup covered in mud and dirt.

As she drove, Turville said, "Your uncle... I don't think he cared much for me."

She frowned. "He did seem odd, didn't he? I've hardly seen him in the last year, just once or twice. Ever since my aunt died last year, he hasn't been quite right."

Turville asked, "How did she die?"

Rebecca sighed. "She was killed when DHS raided the factory where she worked."

"Oh God, that's awful," Turville replied.

He started to ask her if she thought Blankenship was involved with the insurgents, but stopped himself and made a conscious effort to change the subject.

∽

Rebecca's house was impressive. Not large, but tastefully decorated. Little details caught his eyes: the color of a bowl on the table filled with fruit matched the table cloth. Expensive, understated furniture. Books on the shelves, and framed family photos throughout. Turville had grown up in a house always on the edge of chaos: rarely clean, never fully decorated, always on the verge of a blowup between Mom and Dad. He felt peaceful here. Rebecca and her mother were hand drying the dishes, but they'd insisted Turville sit and not help.

"Jim, would you like to see some pictures of Rebecca growing up?" asked Rebecca's mother as she finished drying the last plate.

"No, he wouldn't," Rebecca replied at the same time Turville said, "I'd love to, Mrs. Mays."

Rebecca rolled her eyes.

"Call me Zoe, please," said Rebecca's mother. "Bob's mother was Mrs. Mays."

For a moment after she said the words, her face clouded as if she was lost in a none-too pleasant memory. With a visible effort, she shook her head slightly and returned to the present.

Turville smiled, trying to reassure her. "Zoe, then. Yes, I'd love to see them."

Rebecca dried the last dish with a towel, set it in the rack next to the sink, then stuck her tongue out at Turville and crossed her eyes. Turville laughed, then stood and followed Zoe into the living room.

Zoe took a thick album off the shelf, sat down on the couch, and patted the seat next to her.

Turville sat down next to her, and she opened the album and began flipping through the pages.

"Here we are," she said, pointing to a photo of a tiny girl— no more than a toddler. In the photo Rebecca wore a pink ballet outfit with a flower.

"Rebecca's always been a fantastic dancer."

Standing behind the couch with her arms crossed over her chest, Rebecca said, "Oh God, mother, must you always embarrass me?"

Zoe turned and smiled at her daughter. "Why be embarrassed, darling? It's true."

Rebecca flushed.

Zoe flipped through the pages. Rebecca at school, at museums. Rebecca at six in a group of photos of the family together in Washington, DC.

Rebecca on stage, at sixteen. Her head up, a smile on her face, she wore a white dress with bare shoulders, lace cuffs on her arms and a tiara: her left leg and arm extended behind her back and her right arm extended forward.

Turville caught his breath. "That's beautiful."

Rebecca almost choked behind him, but Zoe said, "Yes, it was. Rebecca's in the River City Youth Ballet; last year she was the Snow Queen."

Turville looked up at Rebecca and winked, then leaned close to Zoe. "Any chance you could email me a copy of that?"

Zoe's smile grew. "I'd be happy to, Jim."

Rebecca shook her head. "Oh, God. I should have known you two would hit it off."

The next page showed a photo of the entire family: Bob and Zoe sat next to another couple; Rebecca was seated on the ground in front of them. The resemblance between Bob and his sister Mandy was obvious. Joe Blankenship looked different in the photo than the man Turville had met this evening: young and happy, with his arm curled protectively around his wife.

Turville glanced at the closed door of the study, where both men had gone as soon as dinner was finished. He touched the photo.

"That's Joe's wife? The one who died last year?"

Zoe nodded, her face sad. "Yes. Mandy was a wonderful, generous-hearted woman, and a good Christian. Joe's heart broke when she was killed."

Unexpectedly, Rebecca leaned forward and put her arms around Turville's shoulders.

Zoe looked at them, a thoughtful look on her face, but said nothing more. A moment later, the study door opened. The two men came out of the study, both looking unhappy. Blankenship went to the front door, putting on his jacket as he walked. Turville caught a glimpse of the tattoo on his bicep as he put on the coat. "De Oppresso Liber," it read, and displayed a knife and a green beret below the motto. Special Forces.

Blankenship opened the front door, walked out without a word, and shut the door behind him forcefully.

Bob turned toward them, and his eyes fell on Rebecca, her arms around Turville.

He frowned. "I think it's probably time for Jim to get back to the Army, isn't it?"

Turville checked his watch. Eleven-thirty. "Yeah," he said, "I'm afraid so."

Rebecca stood, leaving him feeling bereft as her arms left his shoulders.

"Is Uncle Joe leaving? Without even saying goodbye?"

She sounded disappointed.

Mays frowned. "Sorry, Berry, your uncle had some business to take care of. He promised to visit again soon."

His tone seemed off. Turville tried to ignore it: he didn't know the man, after all.

The four of them stood, and Rebecca said, "Mind if I take him back in your car? The truck's acting up."

"Sure, honey," Zoe said. "Let me get you the keys."

Turville walked around the couch to stand next to Rebecca. She reached for his hand and took it. Mays's eyes dropped to their hands, and Turville couldn't help but notice the lack of warmth in them. It was a marked change from before the meal, when all of them but Joe had been laughing and talking animatedly. What had Joe said to her father that brought about the abrupt change?

Zoe hugged Turville as they left, and Mays shook his hand.

In the car, Rebecca said, "Well that was just uber-weird. You'd think it was my dad hitting menopause instead of mom."

Turville laughed. "I suspect he just isn't comfortable with some soldier hanging around his daughter."

She touched his shoulder. "You're not just some soldier, Jim."

They drove in a comfortable silence back to town, and through the roadblock. She pulled the truck over a block short of their destination.

"Jim... I had a nice time with you. Despite the fact that you got along with my mother."

Turville smiled, reached out with his left hand and lightly touched her neck. "I did, too."

She leaned close, and in the pit of his gut, he was terrified. He looked into her eyes. Should he kiss her? Would she freak? Would she think he was pushing too quickly?

The internal debate was brought to a close in an instant. She kissed him, a slow, gentle and almost chaste kiss.

As they parted, he could still feel her lips on his. She met his eyes and whispered, "Call me."

He smiled, then said, "I'll be thinking of you."

She smiled, and he slid out of the car and gently closed the door behind him. He walked toward the Humvee, light headed with happiness.

∾

Jim Turville leaned back in his bunk, smiling. As promised, Zoe Mays had emailed him the Snow Queen photo, along with three or four others. He stared at them, entranced. Santiago, sitting across the room, gave him an odd smile.

PFC Nowell said, "So what's the word, Turville? How'd it go?"

Turville looked up at Nowell. "I'm in love, Nowell."

Nowell laughed. "In lust, more like. Wish I could find myself an eighteen-year-old cheerleader."

Santiago leaned across his bunk and slapped the top of Nowell's head. "Shut up, man. Can't you see the man is happy? There's nothing more important than love."

"No one falls in love that fast, Santiago."

Santiago laughed. "You know nothing, country boy. I fell in love with my wife thirty seconds after she fed me dinner the first time."

Nowell chuckled, then said. "I bet she showed him some skin, that's why he's so happy."

Santiago frowned. "If you ever spoke of my wife that way, I'd break your fingers off one by one and feed them to the pigs. Or worse, the Air Force."

Turville smiled. "Don't sweat it, Santiago. He's an idiot. I'm going to marry Rebecca."

Santiago raised his eyebrows. "You've asked her?"

Turville shook his head. "Not yet. But I know it. Just as much as I know you'll eventually bring your wife to the States, have twenty kids and live happily ever after."

Nowell burst into laughter. "Oh-ho, now we're getting into fairy tales. Y'all is a couple of girls, you know that?"

Turville smiled, then flipped back to the photo of Rebecca in the white dress. He turned the phone around, held it toward Nowell. "Look at her. Have you ever seen anyone so beautiful in your life?"

Nowell looked at the photo. "Ballet dancer, is she?"

Turville nodded.

Nowell smirked. "Bet she's flexible as all hell."

"Motherfucker," Turville responded. "That's enough out of you."

"Cierra la boca!" Santiago muttered. "Nowell, I will personally take you outside and teach you more civilized manners if you don't apologize to the corporal right now."

Nowell chucked. "Yeah, yeah, whatever. Sorry, Turville. I didn't mean to hurt your delicate feelings."

Turville turned away in disgust, picked his phone back up, then browsed to her Facebook page. Before he could stop himself, he texted, "Rebecca, thank you for a wonderful evening."

Thirty seconds later he had her response.

"It was fun!!!!!"

The multiple exclamation points were followed by hearts and other random characters.

He smiled and put the phone down.

TWENTY-FOUR

Washington Post, April 30
DRONE ATTACK KILLS 3 INSURGENTS
Washington, DC – An unmanned drone killed 3 insurgents Wednesday, according to Pentagon officials speaking on conditions of anonymity. The attack took place in Walkersville, West Virginia.

FIGHTING not to roll his eyes, JD Roberts deleted the email from his boss, Jo Ann Tamburinno, the Director of Federal Protective Services in Washington. Tamburinno had only the vaguest understanding of the situation in West Virginia, or in America for that matter. A political appointee,

Tamburinno was a retired Coast Guard Rear Admiral who had spent most of the last ten years working for BoozAllen Hamilton, one of the many "Beltway Bandit"firms circling Washington like vultures.

Not long after the cease-fire in January, President Price had canned the previous director, as well as most of the leadership of the Charleston field office. At the time, Roberts had been head of the interagency task force investigating the Arlington bombing.

Accepting the job of Special Agent in Charge here was a no-brainer. Roberts wanted to be where the action was.

A popup on his screen reminded him it was time for the weekly recap meeting. He locked his computer and stood, put on his jacket, and left the office.

Lorena Wilson, his administrative assistant, looked up as he came out.

"I'm headed over to the recap meeting."

"Fun, fun," she said.

He grimaced. "It's a necessary evil. Hey, I forgot to ask you—how is Chloe doing?"

She smiled. Her teenaged daughter had been down with the flu for several days. "Better, boss, thanks for asking."

The phone rang, and she answered it. As he was turning to leave, she said, "JD, you might want to take this one. It's Valerie Murphy from the state law enforcement department."

He frowned. He certainly hadn't been expecting a call from Valerie Murphy. "Yeah, I've got a few minutes."

He walked back into his office and picked up the phone.

"JD Roberts speaking," he answered briskly.

"Mr. Roberts, it's Valerie Murphy."

"What can I do for you..." he asked, with a deliberate pause before he finished, "Miss Secretary?"

"I'm calling on sort of a peace mission. We didn't get off to a good start, and the fact is, we ought to be working together, not at cross-purposes. I'd like to invite you to lunch."

Weird, he thought. Murphy was in some ways a pretty typical political appointee: not even remotely qualified for her job. Plus her father was a traitor, and she'd been under a cloud herself. On the other hand, she had a point: his life would be a lot easier if he could get cooperation from the state agencies.

"All right, Miss Secretary. Where and when?"

"Tidewater Grill? It's convenient to both our offices. To-morrow at noon?"

He took a breath. "All right. I'll be there."

Roberts hung up the phone and stared at it for a few moments. He didn't trust Murphy's sudden friendliness. On the other hand, the old dictum to keep your friends close and your enemies closer, held true. That was probably exactly what she had in mind. The more he knew about her intentions, the better. The fact was, Roberts was playing an extraordinarily dangerous game. One misstep, and all his work on behalf of his country could go to Hell in a hand basket.

ଏ

Nearly the first words out of Roberts's mouth threw Valerie off balance.

"You were impressive at your confirmation hearing. It must have been quite a shock to learn about those ... videos."

Valerie flushed. It hadn't been nearly long enough to get used to the idea that David, her former fiancé, had filmed them secretly while they were making love in his New York apartment. For the first time since his death, she was grateful Ken Murphy was no longer alive.

She hadn't spoken with David since the day of the hearing, and likely would never speak with him again, if she could help it. Federal agents had been to visit her, however, from the FBI and the Securities and Exchange Commission. Along with the pornographic videos—which had been spread all over the internet—David's computer had contained the details of the blind trusts David managed for several leading federal officials. As a result, the possibility that his computer had been hacked and its private contents released became a matter of concern. To date nothing had been publicly disclosed, but it was still a possibility. And of course, it was typical that the visiting agents continued to return to the details of the original disclosure from David's computer: the videos he'd made of the two of them without her knowledge or consent.

"Yes, it was," she responded. Typical, she thought, that he would bring that up. She wondered how many years it would be before those videos weren't the first thing a man thought of when meeting her. She wondered if Roberts had seen them. It was disturbing. She felt violated, knowing that in his mind he might be picturing the grainy webcam videos of her in the nude with her former lover.

Roberts's expression looked as if he'd bitten into something unusually bitter. He said, "Honestly, I'm surprised you haven't filed suit against your ex."

She shrugged and glanced around the room for a minute. Not happy to be discussing this topic, especially in a crowded restaurant, she responded, "There's a strong possibility criminal charges may be filed against him, though from what I understand it's unclear if what he did was against the law. I'm not interested in revenge. In any event, to be honest, this is a dead issue. What I wanted to meet about was to discuss ways we could work together."

"Of course," he said. "Sorry—I didn't mean to bring up what must be a difficult subject for you."

She felt a flash of irritation. Of course he meant to bring it up. He was trying to make her uncomfortable, off balance. He was playing power games. Before thinking it through, she decided to hit back.

"So, I understand you were on the investigative team for the Arlington bombing last year."

He narrowed his eyes. "Yes, that's correct. I transferred here in January, after my predecessor, um... retired."

"That must have been a difficult investigation."

"It was, though I can't discuss it much; most of it is classified."

She waved a hand in acknowledgement. "Of course. I imagine you had to do a lot of difficult juggling between different jurisdictions and agencies, though. Which is some of what we're dealing with now."

He said, reluctantly, "Yes, that's true. DHS was in charge of the investigation overall, but a number of other agencies were involved."

"Did you have problems with any other agencies? I can't imagine the FBI was happy with you being in charge."

"What are you implying, Secretary Murphy?"

She raised her eyebrows. "Oh, nothing at all... I just know from my years on the hill that turf battles come up a lot. For instance, if the FBI was following one set of leads, and DHS was going somewhere else... I imagine that would lead to some tension."

"None at all," he said flatly.

She smiled. "That's fantastic. It's exactly the kind of cooperation we need here."

"Well... that would be the case if your agency wasn't riddled with leaks and insurgent sympathizers. It puts you in a... difficult position."

She nodded. "We're working on that, of course. It takes time."

"I'm sure it does." His tone was dry.

"The kind of cooperation I'm looking for is primarily contingency planning. During our first meeting, you seemed hostile to working together. Obviously I'm concerned about the possibility of an outbreak of some kind. We still don't know what was stolen, but even in the absence of that knowledge, there are steps we can take to ensure there's a viable response in place."

He frowned. "Won't be necessary. We've completed our investigation, and final inventories were conducted. Nothing was stolen."

She raised her eyebrows. "Nothing at all?"

"Well... no biological samples, I should say. Data was stolen... Disks. We've concluded it was industrial espionage, not terrorists."

"I see. Well, that's good news."

"Yes, it certainly is."

"It makes me wonder, then, why Billy Ray Corvath was murdered."

His response was tepid. "I thought he was shot when the insurgents attempted to kill you."

"He was recovering nicely from the gunshot wound. But someone went into the hospital and killed him with a silenced pistol."

"That's unfortunate."

Unfortunate. Wow. Roberts was ... scary. She probed a little more directly. "It looks rather bad, doesn't it—considering that three days before he was killed, you threatened to make him disappear if he continued pursuing the investigation into Clifford Wells's death."

Roberts narrowed his eyes. "It may look bad, but it's coincidence. Corvath was a cop, and the fact that he was in intensive care was public knowledge. I'm sure there's plenty of criminals who wanted to see him dead."

Valerie tensed. Her mind flashed to Corvath, lying in the street bleeding after saving her life, then lifeless in his hospital room bed two days later, a bullet through his skull. If she hadn't been convinced before, now she was sure Roberts had something to do with Corvath's death.

"You know what's interesting, Roberts? Maybe you can give me your take on this, since you worked on the Arlington bombing investigation. See, the day before he tried to kill me, and shot Corvath, Lucas Thompson met some people for lunch here in Charleston. At Harry's Hog House. I'm sure you know the place. Anyway, he met with John Channing and... some other guy."

Roberts's eyes widened almost imperceptibly. He sat up straight.

She smiled, then said. "Channing was briefly the prime suspect in the Arlington bombing, wasn't he? And here's the crazy thing: Clifford Wells dated a woman named Margaret Rutledge. She's an employee at Hamilton Biomedical, and grew up in the same town as Channing. In fact, Channing's father, Roland Channing, paid her tuition for college."

"Small world," he muttered.

"It is," she said, her smile fixed in place like plaster. She looked him in the eyes. "Very small. Crazy coincidence isn't it, that they all live right across the river from where you grew up?"

Roberts blinked rapidly, leaned forward, then said, "Almost as crazy as putting the daughter of an executed traitor in charge of ending a rebellion started by her father."

She sat up straight, then said, "Mr. Roberts, is something bothering you? Your eye is twitching. Do you need some water?"

"The only thing bothering me is that I'd hate to see something terrible happen to a young woman who is clearly in way over her head. These are dangerous times, you know."

"Especially," she responded, "For people playing both sides."

"Murphy, you want to be careful what you're getting into, and what you are implying. Don't think it's too late to make you disappear, just like your father or Corvath."

He stood abruptly and threw a twenty on the table. "So much for interagency cooperation," he said, and walked out of the restaurant.

Valerie sighed, sagging into her seat. Oh, Christ. What the hell had she done now?

TWENTY-FIVE

San Francisco Indie Reader, May 3
POLICE KILL 3 IN ATTACK ON OAKLAND PROTEST
Police opened fire on the Oakland protest encampment yesterday, killing 3 people and sending 14 to the hospital, in what was described as an operation to quell "rioting and civil disorder."

JIM Turville didn't realize his hands were shaking until he tried to hit her number on the speed dial and dialed his mother instead. He hit cancel before it could connect, then dialed Rebecca. Three rings later—an eternity—she picked up.

"Jim!"

"Hey…" His mouth dried up. She was going to think he was a stalker or something. It had only been a week since their first date. They'd emailed back and forth constantly since then. Jokes. Stories about their past, their friends, their lives. She was far more focused than he was, and he was shocked to learn that she practiced her dance upwards of four hours per day.

"I'm so glad you called," she said. "What's going on?"

He took a deep breath and spit it out. "Listen, I got a seventy-two hour pass. What are you doing? Want to get together?"

"Oh my God," she said. "I'd love to, but I've got to go to Charleston for a rehearsal…"

"Really? What for?"

"Oh, it's um, Sleeping Beauty. I'm, um… I've got a part in it."

"Oh, wow," he said. "What if…" He trailed off.

"You could come if you want, but bring something to read—you'll be bored. But," she said, sounding unsure of herself. "We could… grab some dinner after?"

Turville smiled. "That sounds great."

"You said you've got three days?"

"Yeah… The other guys are headed to the base camp outside Charleston. But I don't have to go there, so long as I stay in touch with my sergeant."

"Well… I could ask my Dad if you could crash on our couch. We could… we could spend the weekend together?"

"I'd love that."

"I'll call you right back."

§

Three hours later, Turville was sitting on the floor in the back corner of the large rehearsal space of the River City Youth Ballet. A fiftyish woman with steel grey hair tied in a severe bun—introduced only as Miss Williams—gave him a severe, disapproving look when he'd arrived with Rebecca.

He pretended to surf the web on his phone. But the fact was, he couldn't take his eyes off of Rebecca.

He wasn't the only one. She stood out like a swan in the center of a crowd of pigeons. The dancers ranged in age from twelve to eighteen. Rebecca was clearly the star of the company, and she'd been cast in the lead role. She was intensely focused as the instructor shouted instructions, sweat occasionally rolling down her face as they repeatedly practiced difficult moves.

If Turville hadn't already been half in love, all it would have taken was the two hours spent watching her in rehearsal. He'd never imagined such intense focus on perfection. When she danced, it was like she'd left this world entirely: her entire focus was inward, eyes unfocused, the lines of her body concentrated: perfect, unadulterated grace.

Despite Rebecca's amazing performance, Miss Williams was shockingly critical. She sounded like one of his drill sergeants at Fort Benning.

At one point she pointed directly at him, and said to Rebecca, "Miss Mays, if you are unable to stay focused on this rehearsal, your soldier boyfriend will have to leave. In fact, if he keeps distracting you, I will personally dump him into the river. Or have him assassinated. We have a performance in three weeks, and you had better get yourself focused, young lady. I will not have the antics of some overgrown boy scout disrupt my rehearsal. Am I making myself absolutely crystal clear?"

Rebecca blushed bright red and whispered, "Yes, ma'am."

Turville looked at the floor and tried to make himself invisible. But he kept his eyes on her, fascinated by the way her neck and ears had turned bright red.

After the rehearsal, she quickly changed and met him in the lobby, wearing a comfortable sun dress. Without thinking, he took her hand.

Both of them stopped. He smirked, and then she grinned at him. Then, slowly, they walked out of the building holding hands.

In the cab of her pickup, she said, "Well?"

Turville swallowed. "Well, what?"

She looked at him. "Were you bored?"

He shook his head and grinned. "No, I was terrified. Now that I've got something to live for, I don't want to find myself in the bottom of a river with cement boots."

She giggled, then stopped short. "Now that you've got something to live for?" She whispered the words.

"Well," he said. Idiot, he thought. Why did you say that? "I mean… well yeah, um…." He trailed off, then spoke again, "You're a pretty incredible girl."

She blushed again, which made Turville unreasonably happy, then squirmed in her seat a little. "You're not so bad yourself, soldier. Why don't you take me to dinner?"

Half an hour later, still holding hands, they walked into a steakhouse south of Charleston. The restaurant was understated, inside a decaying building with a gravel parking lot. Music played on an ancient jukebox in the corner.

The hostess, a teenager with buck teeth, led them to a table on one side of the room and gave them menus.

"Bill will be your server tonight; he'll be right with you."

They sat down at the table, and he found himself staring at her again. Her face flushed and she looked down, then back up and met his eyes. The silence stretched for a moment.

"Can I ask you a question?" Turville asked.

"Sure."

"You were amazing in there. Why are you planning to go to school in Charleston?"

She smiled, looked down at the table. Then she shrugged. "Honestly... I was accepted to the American Academy of Ballet. It's all I've ever wanted to do. But... well... money. My parents do all right, but they can't afford to drop two hundred thousand dollars on college."

Turville leaned back. "Oh, man, that sucks."

Crazy thoughts were running through his head. Thoughts like, if they were married, he could transfer his GI Bill benefits to her, and she'd be able to go to college, no question. He mentally shook his head: they'd only known each other a couple of weeks. That was insanely premature. But after watching her dance? Thinking about her made him light headed.

She nodded. "I've applied for financial aid, but I just don't know yet. And well... Why get my hopes up? They'll probably just offer loans. Then I'd end up with tons of debt and no way to pay it back."

"That's depressing."

Face glum, she said, "Yeah. I mean... I don't talk about this much, because most of my friends don't get it. But ... there's nothing else I want in life. I started taking ballet when I was five, and I just... it's who I am."

"I'd do anything to have that kind of passion about something."

"What do you mean?"

Turville shrugged. "I did all right in high school, but there wasn't any ambition or passion. I didn't know what I wanted to do with my life. Enlisting in the Army... it gave me four more years to think about it and figure it out. At least when I do decide, college will be mostly paid for."

Joking, she said, "I guess I could always do that. Join the Army. I've had enough recruiters after me, but I never considered it. Even to pay for school."

"Not many opportunities for dance in the Army. I wouldn't suggest it." Turville was surprised both by how quickly he'd responded, and how vehemently. The thought of her in the Army, her creativity being squashed by the regimen, disturbed it.

"I guess not," she said.

He leaned forward, struggling to figure out how to say it without sounding... offensive? Condescending? Whatever.

"Look... Rebecca... I hope you'll do whatever it takes to keep that... that passion. Whatever it takes. Loving something that much is worth more than anything I've ever seen."

She blinked, looking at him, seemingly overwhelmed. "I...."

"Don't say anything," he said. "You don't need to."

She hesitated, then replied, "I wouldn't know what to say."

Heart pounding, he plunged forward. "Did you know taking me with you today would make me fall for you?"

Her eyes widened, pupils dilated. "No," she whispered, "But maybe I was hoping."

Neither of them noticed the waiter when he appeared beside them, until he cleared his throat.

"Hi," he said. "I'm Bill, I'll be your server this evening. Can I start you with something to drink?"

"Sweet iced tea," she said, not taking her eyes from Turville.

Turville broke eye contact, looked up at the waiter. "I'll have the same." His voice felt dry and scratchy.

"Sweet iced tea for both of you." The waiter hesitated a moment, then said, "You National Guard?"

Turville glanced down at his uniform, then said, "No, active Army."

"Oh," the waiter said, looking… disappointed? Angry? Odd, Turville, thought. The waiter stalked away.

Turville looked back at Rebecca. "I shouldn't have said that," he said. "It's too soon."

She blinked her eyes, her face unreadable. Then she said, "It's okay."

Turville grinned. "Just okay? That's what you say about stale pizza."

Rebecca raised her eyebrows. "You rate somewhere above that, I think."

"But not much?"

"Stop digging for compliments."

"I can't help it. I love to hear your voice. Especially when it's saying nice things about me."

She burst into laughter.

"You are so cheesy!"

He reached out tentatively, and took her hand. They held hands across the table, looking into each other's eyes for what felt to Turville like forever, until the waiter reappeared and spilled iced tea into Turville's lap without warning.

Turville jumped to his feet, dazed, then grabbed a napkin off the table and tried to clean his uniform. It was soaked through.

"Oh… I'm ever so sorry," the waiter said, his voice just slightly sarcastic.

Rebecca gasped, and Turville looked at the waiter, shocked.

The waiter gave a tiny smile. "Let me clean that up for you."

He threw another napkin on the table and walked away.

Seconds later, the waiter was intercepted by an older man, most certainly the manager. Turville gave up on his uniform. He tried to clean the table, but the napkins were soaked, too.

"Why did he do that?" Rebecca said. She sounded as if she was going to cry.

Turville shook his head, bewildered.

"Excuse me," the manager said. "I'm Roy Sharp... I'm gonna apologize for what Bill over there did, it was uncalled for."

Turville said, "Um... I think maybe we should have a different server."

"Actually... I think I need to ask you to leave."

"What?" Rebecca said, her voice high-pitched. "Why?"

Sharp looked uncomfortable. "Your boyfriend there. Bill's dad—my brother—is a prisoner of war. And we lost more than a few people from this town in the war."

Turville looked at the floor. "I'm sorry."

Rebecca wasn't nearly as conciliatory. Her tone sharp, she said, "And that's our fault? He didn't ask to come to West Virginia. And in case you hadn't noticed, the war is over!"

Sharp frowned. "Maybe, maybe not. But your soldier boy here needs to leave now."

"And what if we don't?"

"Rebecca," Turville said, his voice calm. "Let's just go."

Angry, she replied, "You're going to let them treat you like this?"

He shook his head. "It doesn't matter," he said quietly. "It's not worth the fight. Let's go."

She pointed at Sharp. "I hope you're proud of yourself. You shit." Then she grabbed her purse and stalked out of the restaurant.

Turville scrambled after her, stunned by the strength of her reaction. But the more he thought about it, the more it made him smile.

❧

Rebecca didn't know why she'd responded the way she had. Or maybe she did. Jim was ... amazing, and kind, and brave. And... hot. She flushed, feeling horribly superficial. Jim was terribly wounded. It had broken her heart when he'd told her he'd accidentally killed Logan Jefferson last fall. She couldn't imagine the kind of emotions he must be struggling with, the weight of responsibility. It was horrible, but it was an accident. Being the man he was, though, he didn't dodge responsibility.

No one had a right to make him feel unworthy. Nobody.

Her left fist was clenched around the wheel, turning her knuckles white, when she started the truck. It coughed a few times, then started.

Turville reached out and touched her shoulder.

"It's not that big a deal," he murmured.

"It is!" she responded. "He had no right."

Turville shrugged. "War affects a lot of people in all kind of different ways. If it was my brother being held prisoner, I don't know that I'd look at it any differently."

She looked over at him. "You're too good, Jim."

He gave a small smile, as if she'd given him a gift. For about the fiftieth time that day, she felt like she was on the verge of tears. Happy, joyous tears. What the hell was wrong with her?

Did you know taking me with you today would make me fall for you?

Yes, he'd truly said those words.

Oh. My. God. She was feeling overwhelmed. This was so unlike anything she'd experienced before. Dating Jesse had mostly been an annoyance, more than anything else. Something she felt like she had to do. But the more time she spent with Jim, the more she wanted.

They drove in silence for a few minutes, content to be next to each other. Every few minutes, she would steal a glance at him as he sat on the passenger side. The lower half of his normally clean shaven face had given in to a slight shadow. He had a small dimple in his chin that made her lightheaded sometimes. Once, when she glanced over, he looked over and met her eyes.

"Careful," he said. "Eyes on the road."

She felt her face flush as she fixed her eyes back on the dark road. "Then stop distracting me."

Turville chuckled quietly, a low, delicious growl that sent a tingle down the base of her spine.

"If you could be anywhere in the world right now, where would it be?" he asked quietly.

She frowned and thought for a moment. "I'd be... in New York City."

"Why New York?"

She shrugged. "It's alive. Alive in a way this place isn't. Or wasn't. I don't know. What about you?"

He laughed again. "I'd be wherever you are."

She twisted her lips, half in exasperation. "You set me up for that."

"I did." He looked smug.

"What happens when you leave the Army? Or do you plan on staying?"

"I don't know. College, maybe. I'm trying to picture spending my entire life being sent off to different wars. And... that doesn't work for me. I'll do my four years and be done. Sometimes I think I want to do something entirely different. Something where I'm helping people, you know? A doctor maybe. But medical school? I was lucky to make it through middle school. But I could be an EMT, or a fireman."

Hesitantly, she said, "Isn't your Dad a fireman?"

He nodded, silently. After a long pause, he said, "When I was younger... before he went to Iraq... Dad was my hero. He saved lives, you know? I still have a picture of him from... I guess the late nineties. It was in the newspaper. Coming out of a burning house, carrying a baby. He'd saved a little girl's life. I'm not half the man he was before the war."

"Don't sell yourself short, Jim. You're just about the bravest person I've ever known."

He shrugged. "I admire that kind of courage. But it doesn't come naturally. Truth is, I'm kind of a fuck-up. I do get it right sometimes, but mostly by accident, and mostly in spite of being terrified. You can't imagine what it's like in combat. Knowing that any second, the next bullet might take you down. Knowing that it's random— there's nothing you can do to stop it, prevent it, other than hunker down and pray."

"Do you believe in God?" she asked.

"I don't know..."

"My mom and dad do. We go to church every Sunday. But sometimes... I don't know. It seems to me that God wouldn't have let Aunt Mandy die the way she did. Or let the war happen the way it did."

"Maybe you're right. But sometimes it's not God who screwed up, but ... us. People like us. Me. God didn't make the war happen last year... That was people, very stubborn people who wanted what they wanted and didn't count the cost."

They fell into silence as she drove back home. Her thoughts wandered back to the helicopters being shot down over Whitesville; the sheriff murdered in his home; her Aunt Mandy being killed. It made it that much more tragic and preventable that a mere political disagreement that had resulted in those deaths. But then... the waiter at the restaurant, and his brother, a prisoner... on the one hand, they were pawns in the greater political picture. But it was individual actions, including refusing to serve Jim because of his uniform, that made it so much worse. As if the war could end up consuming everything she loved and cared about if they let it.

Twenty minutes later, she pulled up to her house. Rebecca unlocked the door and let them in quietly. It was late, but her parents were up: her mother was reading a book, and her father was working in his office. This was unusual: normally at this time of night, they'd be in their room already, reading and ready for bed.

Zoe stood and walked over to Rebecca, then kissed her on the cheek.

"Practice went well? Did you two have a good time?"

Rebecca struggled to answer for a few seconds, still angry about what happened at dinner. Finally she just said, "Yes, Mom."

A few seconds later, her dad came out of the office. He glowered just a little at Turville.

"We've made up the couch for you to sleep on, Jim. Um..." he shuffled his feet awkwardly, then blurted, "No sneaking upstairs to Rebecca's room. We're happy to have you stay, but you understand..."

"Dad!" Rebecca interjected, blushing bright red.

"Of course, Mr. Mays," Turville said. "I'd never do anything... anything to hurt Rebecca."

Bob smiled, then said, "Well, all right then. I'm off to bed."

The next two days were the happiest Rebecca could remember in a long time. In the morning, they had breakfast, then drove up into the hills and hiked to the top. There, they spread out a blanket and had a picnic. They talked about their lives, about their hopes and dreams. More and more, she began to imagine those dreams involving Jim. His grin was infectious, especially when he made one of his off-beat and sometimes goofy jokes. Most of all though, there wasn't a hint of selfishness in him.

It was as if there were no war. No tension with her friends, Jesse's friends. Just the two of them, laughing until she nearly cried. Finally, on the evening of the third day, she slowly drove him back to the base camp in Whitesville. At the gate, he held her in his arms, heedless of the glances from the other soldiers who stood guard. She felt warm and safe, the brush of his stubble against her face stirring warmth straight through her body.

With a last kiss, he said goodbye, turned, and walked back through the gate.

❧

Turville's mind was still outside holding Rebecca when he walked into the base camp. When he walked into the house, he barely noticed the guys from his fire team in the front room, shouting over a game of hearts.

Sergeant Nguyen was sitting in the small room that served as his shared office with the Lieutenant.

"I'm back, Sarge," Turville said.

Nguyen looked up from the report he was studying. He peered at Turville. "Corporal. Welcome back. Is there anything I'm going to need to worry about from the last couple days?"

Turville shook his head. "No, Sarge."

Nguyen frowned. "Then why the hell do you look so happy?" He held the frown for a few more seconds, then gave up and grinned. "Third platoon is going back out shortly. Make sure your fire team gets plenty of sack time; we'll be covering the dam for the next week, starting at 0700."

Turville said, "Roger, Sarge."

Nguyen waved a dismissal, and Turville turned back down the hall toward the front room again. He was trying to memorize the taste and smell and feel of her lips as they brushed against his. Unfortunately, as he entered the front door, he heard Corporal Meigs's raised voice.

"What the fuck is wrong with you, Santiago? Your uniform looks like shit."

Turville heard a low, murmured response from Santiago.

"Stand at attention, soldier," Meigs replied.

Turville walked into the room. Meigs was standing about two inches from Santiago, tension filling his posture. The rest of the fire team was watching from the table where they had been playing hearts.

Turville approached Meigs and Santiago. "Corporal Meigs, if you've got a problem with Santiago's uniform—or anything else—you need to come to me with it."

Meigs spun and faced Turville, hostility written on his face.

"Turdville," he said. "Your soldier looks like crap. Is this the standards you're holding up? Oh—that's right, you're not holding up any standards. You're off screwing with some civilian girl while the rest of us spend our pass at Camp Wingham." In a sarcastic voice, he said, "Did you have a nice vacation?"

Turville narrowed his eyes. "Yeah, I did, Meigs. Why don't you run along, so I can talk with my team."

Meigs stepped closer to Turville. His eyes were narrowed, his whole body tense. Turville could see the muscle in his neck twitching. Jesus, Meigs was angry. What the hell was his issue?

"Turville, you don't tell me what to do. Understand? Just because you got yourself shot in January doesn't mean you deserve all kinds of special treatment."

"I didn't ask for any special treatment, Meigs. I asked you to leave my guys the fuck alone, understand? You're not their fire team leader. I am."

"Maybe you should learn to do your job then, Turville. Your fire team is just like you: shit."

"Meigs, back off!"

Meigs reached out and shoved Turville. Turville stumbled back, then grabbed Meigs by the forearm to regain his balance.

Meigs's face twisted in anger and he jerked his arm back. "Dirty motherfucker, keep your hands to yourself. Isn't your teenage slut enough for you?"

Turville didn't think. As the words left Meigs's mouth he balled up his fist and threw a punch. His aim was off, barely brushing Meigs's instead of squarely hitting Meigs's face.

Meigs attacked in a rush, throwing three punches in succession. One of them connected solidly with Turville's nose. Shouting rose in the room; the other guys grabbed both of them, with Santiago and Nowell holding Meigs back.

Suddenly Sergeant Nguyen was between them, filling the room. In a voice that could probably be heard all the way at Rebecca's house five miles away, he shouted, "What the fuck is going on here?"

Turville sagged. Putting his hand to his face, he felt blood trickling out of his nose.

"Meigs! Turville! In my office, now! Move!"

Turville moved automatically, without thought. Back in Nguyen's office, he stood at attention in front of the desk. Meigs did the same, two feet to Turville's left.

They waited. Several minutes passed. Turville could hear Nguyen and the other men from the fire team drifting from the front room. He couldn't make out their words.

Ten excruciatingly long minutes passed by before Nguyen finally entered the office. He stalked into the room, his face tense and angry, then stood behind the desk and stared at them without a word. Turville kept his eyes on the wall above Nguyen's shoulder.

"You two have been at each other's throat for a year now," Nguyen began in a low voice. "This comes to a stop today. It's damaging our unit cohesion, and sets an unprofessional example for your subordinates. I'm of half a mind to bust both of your asses back to private and put someone else in charge of your fire teams. We're supposed to be fighting the enemy, not each other. Explain yourselves. Meigs first."

Meigs spoke, his voice still angry.

"Sergeant Nguyen, Turville intervened when I was disciplining a soldier for lax uniform standards. He's a crappy leader, sergeant: he wants to be friends with his fire team. He doesn't enforce standards. And then he threw the first punch."

"Turville?" Nguyen said.

"Sergeant, Meigs continually harasses my guys. When I came in he was being abusive to Santiago, and yeah, I intervened. Then he started throwing out insults. He shoved me and called Rebecca a slut."

Nguyen frowned. He took a deep breath. "You're both a couple of children. So I'm going to treat you like the children you are. I'm changing up the schedule. Turville, your team stays here. You and Meigs will guard the dam, together, just the two of you, for the next forty-eight hours. And if I hear one whisper of another fight, I'll have both of you busted back to private. Am I absolutely fucking clear?"

Turville frowned. The dam required at least two guards at all times. Neither of them would be able to sleep. "Yes, sergeant."

Meigs nodded. "Yes, sergeant."

"Then get your asses out of my office. Go relieve the men on the dam. I'll see you in two days."

TWENTY-SIX

New York Times, MAY 3
KENTUCKY CHURCH IMPLICATED IN INSURGENT ACTIVITY
By Marcus Jennsen
Frankfort, KY – Kentucky Attorney General Morris Rosenthal announced the results of a wide-ranging inquiry into the activities of a remote Baptist Church in Emerson, Kentucky today. The state filed charges this morning against Lucas Guthrie, pastor of the church, in a sealed indictment. In a prepared statement, Rosenthal said that Guthrie is accused of shipping hundreds of weapons, and tens of thousands of dollars, to insurgent sympathizers in West Virginia. Guthrie was reported missing four days before the charges were filed, prompting speculation that he may have already been taken into custody by the Department of Homeland Security. DHS officials have refused to comment on the case.

T HE phone interrupted Bob Mays's concentration. He sighed, set the impossible town budget to the side, and picked up the phone.

"Bob Mays speaking."

"Bob, it's Joe."

He leaned back at the sound of his best friend and brother-in-law's voice. "Hey! When are you coming back into town?"

"Soon," Joe answered. "Very soon. I probably won't be around much though. I've got a lot going on right now."

Bob nodded, then said quietly, "You're always welcome here, you know that."

Joe grunted. After a couple of seconds he said, "Listen, Bob, I want to talk to you about something."

"Sure."

"A little bird told me that Rebecca's soldier stayed at your house all weekend."

Bob frowned. "He did."

"Why?"

"He's a nice young man. I like him, Zoe likes him. And well… he and Rebecca get on well. Very well."

There was a pregnant silence, then Joe spoke in a sharp tone. "Bob, listen to me. You don't want to do that again. You don't want to have him around."

"Why not?"

"In case you missed it down there in Whitesville, there's a war going on."

Mays's memory flashed to the scene downtown a few weeks before: the wrecked, burned-out helicopters on the middle of River Street. The bullet holes in his daughter's truck.

"I'm aware of that."

"You're putting your family in danger. You're putting Rebecca in danger."

Bob shook his head. Joe's tone of voice had a chill in it that he'd never heard. They'd been friends for nearly three decades, brothers-in-law for two. Joe had never sounded like this. Was he directly involved in the insurgency? And if so, what did that mean for Bob and his family?

"I don't see it," Bob said, shaking his head, trying to ignore the questions racing through his mind.

"Bob, you've been my best friend since we were kids. I need you to listen to me here. You need to keep your daughter away from that soldier. You need to stop cooperating with the Army. You need to distance yourself from the feds. And quickly."

Mays struggled to come up with an answer and failed. But he didn't need to.

"Don't forget what happened to Sheriff Hughes."

Tension moved down Bob's back, his neck muscles tightening in fear. "He was murdered."

"He was a collaborator."

Mays felt his pulse quickening. Jesus. Joe was with the insurgents. And he'd just threatened Bob. He closed his eyes, feeling something akin to physical pain.

"What exactly are you trying to say?"

"What I'm saying is, I'm doing the best I can to protect you and your family. But you seem to be dead set on throwing that protection away."

"Joe, are you—how involved are you with this?"

He didn't expect an answer, so he wasn't surprised when he didn't get one.

"Don't ask me questions. You need to do what you have to do to protect your family. Understand me?"

Mays didn't have a chance to answer; Joe hung up with a click.

In a daze, Mays set the phone back into its cradle. He wiped his hand across his face and realized he was soaked with sweat. He thought back to Joe's visit a couple of weeks before. Joe had asked Bob to get him the surviving blueprints from Eagle Mine from the town offices. He'd refused to discuss why, and Bob chose not to question it at the time. But now he had the answer. The insurgents—Joe—they were using Eagle Mine as a base. That was the only answer. And Bob had unknowingly helped them.

❧

It had probably been twenty years since he and Joe had been in a real argument.

The four of them—Bob and Zoe, Joe and Mandy—had gone to a performance of a play by some god-awful amateur playwright at the Charleston Players. A double date in the city was awesome. But he had the feeling that just like him, Joe would have been happier with a football game and beer.

As always, Joe made the best of it. He was utterly devoted to Mandy. If she'd insisted on him wearing a chicken costume and standing beside the road, Joe would have gone for it. Wearing a jacket and tie for a play and a fancy restaurant? No problem.

Bob still didn't know what got into him that night.

Joe had come back from the bathroom, leaned over to Mandy and whispered, unfortunately loud enough for all of them to hear, "Have I told you tonight that you're the most beautiful woman I've ever seen in my life?"

Mandy's face flushed red, and her smile grew as her eyelids fluttered.

"No," she whispered, "but don't let that stop you."

Joe whispered something else, and her lips parted, moist. Her eyes darted to the table, and she curled against him.

Resentment flashed through Bob. It had been two years since they'd been placed in their foster home, and since that time, Joe and Mandy had become increasingly close. But he'd run into Dad three days ago. He chose this moment to mention it.

"Mandy, did I tell you I saw Dad the other day?"

She immediately tensed, and put her palms flat on the table. "No," she said coolly. "Where? Did you talk with him?"

"Downtown; he was coming out of the pharmacy. He 'bout blew a gasket when he found out about your early acceptance."

Prim now, her back straight, Mandy replied, "Why? He's off the hook for tuition; why should he care when and where I go to college?"

Joe took Mandy's left hand protectively in his right. The movement irritated Bobby. Joe was his best friend. Mandy was his sister. But sometimes he felt like it was the two of them against him.

Bobby shrugged. "Dad, you know? I don't think he approves of either one of us going to college."

"Fuck him. I don't need his approval."

Zoe gasped at her uncharacteristic language. "Mandy!"

Joe's eyes widened, and Bobby winced. His sister didn't use that kind of language.

"Forget about him," Joe said. "I'm proud of you, Mandy. Amazed."

"Well, she's a mental giant, especially next to you, bud."

Joe shrugged. "True enough, though I was smart enough to fall in love with her."

Mandy smiled at him and squeezed his hand. Bobby stuck a finger down his throat and pretended to gag. Zoe slapped his shoulder.

"Seriously, though," Bobby said, "Dad's… a mess."

"Oh for God's sake, Bobby," Mandy blurted out. "He's been a mess for years. What's new about this conversation? Does he have to ruin our night out, just like he ruined everything else in our lives?"

Bobby's lips tightened, anger rushing through him. Yes, Dad was a complete shit. But he was their dad, and now they didn't even have that.

"He didn't ruin everything, and he is our dad. I don't understand why you aren't the least bit concerned about him."

"That's because you didn't have to spend three years keeping him from raping you, Bobby."

Half the restaurant went silent at Mandy's response. She looked around, horrified that she'd spoken so loudly, then whispered tensely, "Now can we please change the subject?"

Bobby felt his face go red. He knew he shouldn't push, but he found himself plunging ahead anyway, wanting to infuriate her.

"How can you say that Mandy?" he said loudly. "He never once put his hands on you. He's our father."

Zoe leaned close to Bobby, whispering urgently. "Bobby, will you drop it? You're upsetting her!"

"No!" Bobby replied to Zoe. "It's time I said it. It's her fault we've been stuck in a foster home the last two years."

Mandy gasped. "How can you say that?"

The hostess, a pencil-thin twenty-something woman in black pants and tight jacket appeared the table. "Excuse me. Would you all mind keeping it down? You're disturbing our other guests."

Bobby gave the hostess a nasty look, then muttered under his breath, "You know it's true. Dad was crazy, but manageable. Then you had to ruin everything. Look at him now: he's like a hobo—drunk all the time, living off his disability. You should have some feeling for your family."

Joe leaned forward. "Bud, you may be my best friend, but it's time to shut your mouth." His voice was low. "No one has a right to talk to Mandy that way."

Bobby said, "You stay out of this, Joe. This is between me and my sister."

Joe didn't pause or give any warning. With a straight, short thrust he clipped Bobby on the chin and knocked him out of his chair. Bobby's vision went white, and he found himself on his ass on the floor a moment later, Joe standing over him. Someone in the restaurant screamed.

A moment later, the restaurant's manager was there, a big-boned, red-haired man. "That's it. Get out now, or I call the cops."

"'S'all right," Joe responded. "I lost my appetite anyways. Let's go, Mandy."

Zoe kneeled beside Bobby. "Come on, Bobby, let's go."

Joe faced Bobby outside. His hands were still clenched into fists. "Are you finished, damn it?"

Mandy took Joe's arm. "Calm down, Joe," she whispered.

Bobby cupped his chin where it was bleeding and said, "Yeah." He sighed, shame flooding through him. Sometimes nothing made sense anymore. They'd both been happier since moving to their foster home. But damn it, he missed both of his parents. He looked at his sister. "I'm sorry, sis. I shouldn't have said that."

Mandy burst into tears. "You're sorry! Do you have any idea what a nightmare it was for me after Mom left? Every time Dad got drunk, I had to keep my door locked! I never knew when he was going to come around, trying to paw at me. He wasn't just drunk, he was wrong! Every night since then I've thanked God we don't live with him anymore. You want me to have sympathy for him? No, thank you. Maybe one day I can learn to forgive him, but don't you ever tell me it's my fault. I was twelve years old when he started! Twelve!"

She turned and hugged Joe, burying her face against his chest. Big shuddering sobs shook her whole body. Joe put his arms around her waist and held her tight.

"Oh, shit," Bobby said. He sat down on the curb, still cradling his chin. "I'm sorry. I'm so sorry." He looked up at Mandy, his stomach turning, his limbs heavy with shame. "Mandy, forgive me. It's not you, never was. Sometimes I'm just... so angry."

Mandy broke away from Joe and sat down on the curb next to him, then put a hand on his shoulder.

"I don't blame you, Bobby. I'm angry, too. It's not you, and it's not me, and it's not even Dad, I think. I'm sure he wasn't always that way. It's the town we live in, and the mine, and the accident, and everything. It made him crazy and... mad as hell. You protected me from him, and don't think I don't know that."

Joe kept his mouth shut but joined the party, sitting down next to Mandy. Zoe sat on the other side of Bobby and took his hand. He was the asshole of the night, so the girls gave him all the sympathy and attention.

Mandy smiled. "Do you remember before Mom left, when he used to come home from the mine with roses every Tuesday? There he would be, covered head to toe in black dust, but holding that red bouquet?"

"Yeah," Bobby said. He took a breath, then added, "Sometimes I could kill her for leaving."

Mandy's smile turned bitter. "Me, too. Not for leaving, I understand that perfectly. But for leaving us with him. I never understood why she didn't take us."

Silence settled over the foursome. Then Bobby looked over at Joe. "No hard feelings, Joe? I'm not sore, I deserved it."

"Yep, you did," Joe answered. "No hard feelings, bud, you're still my best friend even if you are a blockhead sometimes."

Bobby chuckled. "Someday we'll look back on tonight and laugh."

"Well," Zoe responded, "I won't be laughing if I don't get something to eat before the play."

Mandy nodded. "Me, neither."

"Well, since the fancy French restaurant we couldn't afford is out... how about pizza?" Joe stood, then took Mandy's arm and helped her up.

TWENTY-SEVEN

Boston Herald, MAY 4
RIZZO CALLS FOR MASSACHUSETTS SECESSION
By Francis Esposito
Boston Mayor Thomas Rizzo called for Massachusetts to secede from the United States in comments made at a fundraising dinner last week, according to anonymous sources who attended the dinner. Claiming that the comments were "off the cuff," the Mayor's office went on to point out that in the last four years, taxpayers in Massachusetts paid $4 in federal taxes for every federal dollar that came into the state. In an official statement, the Mayor's spokesman said, "Regardless of Mayor Rizzo's unofficial comments at a private dinner, the fact remains that Massachusetts taxpayers continue to subsidize southern and western states, which benefit the most from federal spending."

R EBECCA Mays got out of the pickup, then reached across the seat and took out the covered dish. Carrying the dish in both hands, she approached the Humvee where Specialist Leo manned the machine gun.

"Hello there," she said. She looked up at him and gave a big smile, showing a lot of teeth.

Leo was nonplussed, but responded relatively quickly. "Hello, ma'am. What can I do for you?"

"I brought some brownies for you guys. Is Jim around?"

Leo eyed the dish. "Turville? He's um, on a special assignment, won't be back until Wednesday. Let me get the LT— he'll have to clear you in."

On an assignment until Wednesday? Jim hadn't said anything about that. And she hadn't heard from him since she'd dropped him off last night. Why had she come down here? It was crazy and stalkerish— she'd just dropped him off twelve hours before, and here she was with brownies. He was going to think she was clingy. Why hadn't he called?

Leo spoke into the microphone attached to his helmet, and two minutes later Lieutenant Blake came out the front door of the dilapidated house. "Hello, Miss Mays. Um... if you're looking for Corporal Turville, he's tied up; won't be back for a couple of days."

She smiled, trying to hide her disappointment. "It's okay, Lieutenant; I just wanted to bring some goodies down for your platoon. You guys are far from home, I figured it would be the least I could do."

"Well," he said, eyes shifting from her to the dish, to Leo, then back. "Come on in, then. And thank you."

She followed the lieutenant into the house.

Inside, Turville's fire team was gathered in the main room around a folding card table, a game of spades in progress. The men looked up as she entered behind the Lieutenant, then all of them came to their feet. Rebecca felt flooded with doubts. She shouldn't have come here like this... especially with Jim gone somewhere else. What would they think? She wanted the guys in Jim's platoon to like her, but what would it look like, her coming alone like this? Her eyes darted to the floor.

Blake said, "Gentlemen, this is Ms. Rebecca Mays, the mayor's daughter. She, um, brought you guys some snacks."

One of the men--tall, olive skinned, with dark hair--stepped forward and held out a hand. "Private First Class Jesús Santiago, at your service."

He took her hand in his and bowed over it, gently kissing her hand. It was charming and... and weird. She giggled, and Lieutenant Blake cleared his throat.

"Lay off, Santiago," Blake said.

Rebecca was blushing as another man, a blonde, red-faced soldier came forward. "Ma'am, I'm Phil Nowell, from De Queen, Arkansas. You could say I'm Corporal Turville's, uh, right-hand man."

The youngest soldier, a lanky black man with the single stripe of a private said, "I'm Karim Tilman. And don't listen to nothing Nowell says, he's 'de queen' of BS."

Santiago burst into laughter and gave Tilman a high-five.

"Well," she said, trying to recover the confidence she'd felt when leaving the house. "It's nice to meet you guys. Jim's told me a lot about you... I just wanted to bring you a snack or something. To say thank you for being here."

Santiago swept a chair back from the card table and gestured toward it with his arm. "Have a seat, Madam."

She giggled and sat down, then unwrapped the plate, loaded with fresh, warm brownies. "Please—help yourselves."

Blake shook his head, then said, "I'll be in my office. Ms. Mays, you're welcome to stay a little while, though these delinquents have to go back on duty at the roadblock in about an hour."

Rebecca smiled, then said, "Thank you, Lieutenant. Please help yourself to a brownie before you go?"

He hesitated just a moment, then said, "Thank you, I believe I will."

After the Lieutenant stepped out of the room, Santiago shuffled the cards, then dealt Rebecca in as if she'd been there all along.

The game proceeded quickly after Santiago explained the rules. A few at a time, the other soldiers in the platoon came and grabbed brownies, thanking her politely and leaving.

"Pardon me saying so, Rebecca, but Turville is a lucky guy," Nowell said.

She blushed. She felt like she was the lucky one. "Thank you; I appreciate that. Though to tell the truth... he's lucky to have you guys. It's a... it's a relief to know that if he's in danger, he'll have you guys with him. I mean... we've only been out a few times, you know? But he depends on you guys every day."

Santiago leaned forward and said, "I don't wish to disagree with such a beautiful young lady, but we're the lucky ones in that case. Corporal Turville doesn't know it, but he's a natural soldier."

"What do you mean?" she asked.

Nowell said, "Well... he's a total fuck-up in garrison. But crazy brave under fire. Has he told you he earned the bronze star for valor?"

She shook her head. "What's that?"

Nowell met her eyes. "It means... well, it means he's a hero. During the invasion he ran out into a field being raked by machine-gun fire to save his platoon sergeant's life."

She blinked, and tried to imagine it, but couldn't.

"Is that when he was injured?" she asked.

Santiago nodded. "It is. And of course, you know he did it again, to pull you out of the line of fire when the bastards attacked us here last month."

She opened her mouth to speak, then closed it and shook her head. She couldn't get her mind around the idea. But the more she thought about it, the more... well... fuzzy she felt. Because there was one thing she was pretty sure she knew about Jim Turville. That he was in love with her.

And he was in a damn dangerous profession. For the first time since they met, it struck her just how dangerous. She put her arms around her chest as if to contain the emotion that made her eyes water.

She whispered, "You guys will help keep him safe, won't you?"

೧

"Becca? Aren't you going to be late for rehearsal?"

Zoe called the words upstairs as Rebecca ran up them. Her daughter had just rolled up in her pickup, ran into the house and stomped upstairs.

"I'm getting ready now!" Rebecca shouted from her room. "Truck wouldn't start again—I had to get a jumpstart. I think my alternator is nearly shot."

Zoe looked out at the old truck, then called upstairs. "I'll drive you."

Rebecca stuck her head out of her room, still getting dressed. "Thanks, Mom."

Zoe smiled. Given that Rebecca was still very much a teenager, sometimes her responses were barely human. It was nice to get a genuine thanks. She grabbed her purse, threw her book inside, and went looking for the car keys.

In the car, they headed out of town toward Charleston. It would be tight, but they should just be able to make it, if traffic wasn't too backed up at the roadblock.

Just north of town, Zoe breathed a sigh of relief at the roadblock. Only two cars ahead of them. Two soldiers stood on either side of a four-door sedan, one talking to the driver. Another soldier manned a machine gun on a Humvee overlooking the road.

The sedan moved forward, and the pickup truck ahead of them moved into place. It sported a white decal in the rear window depicting a pole dancer. Classy.

The soldier on the left, a tall Latino man, spoke with the driver for a few moments, then used a hand-held device to scan a picture of his driver's license. After only a moment, the soldier handed the license back, and the truck moved forward.

Zoe felt a wave of apprehension as the soldier waved her forward. She didn't know why—she wasn't doing anything wrong. And her husband was the mayor, after all. But something about having fully armed soldiers stopping every vehicle set her on edge.

She pulled to a stop and the soldier bent over to look in. He smiled widely and said, "Hello, Miss Rebecca. And you must be Mrs. Mays."

Zoe's eyes widened, then she looked back and forth between Rebecca and the soldier.

"I am," she finally stammed. "Zoe Mays. Rebecca's mom."

"Jesús Santiago, ma'am, at your service. Now and forever. Miss Rebecca's brownies have earned the lifelong servitude of all of us."

Rebecca giggled, and Santiago grinned at her. "Please forgive me, ma'am," he said to Zoe, "but I'm afraid I have to scan your driver's license."

"Of course," she said. She took the license out of her purse and handed it over.

He took a few seconds scanning the license, then returned it and said, "All done. You have a wonderful afternoon. And Miss Rebecca... can I convince you to send me your recipe for the brownies? I have to send it to my wife, in hopes she'll make them for me."

Rebecca laughed. "Sure thing, Santiago. See you later."

He waved them on. Zoe smiled, bemused. "You certainly are friendly with the soldiers."

Rebecca shrugged. "Santiago is in Jim's squad. He's a nice guy… He's trying to get his American citizenship, so he can bring his wife and kids here."

Zoe raised her eyebrows. "Really? Where's he from?"

"Honduras."

"I didn't realize you knew them all so well."

Rebecca shrugged. "Not so much. I stopped by earlier to take brownies to Jim and his squad, and ended up staying and playing hearts for a while with them."

A tug of anxiety ran through Zoe. She took a calming breath, and reminded herself that Rebecca was eighteen years old and was probably smarter than either of her parents had been at that age.

"You just be careful. I'm not sure how comfortable I am with you hanging out with a bunch of soldiers."

"Oh, Mom, don't worry. They're a good bunch. And they're extremely protective of me. And Jim, for that matter."

Zoe glanced at Rebecca.

"About Jim…."

Rebecca looked at her.

"Yes?"

"You care about him."

Rebecca's entire face and even her ears flushed red. She nodded quickly.

"How serious is this?"

Rebecca whispered, "It's pretty serious."

Zoe sighed. "You haven't known him that long."

"Long enough, Mom. He's … he's a good man. He is. My only worry is…" She cut herself off.

"Your only worry is… what?"

Rebecca sighed.

Zoe watched, fascinated, as her daughter's eyes welled with tears.

"What is it, hon?"

Rebecca shrugged violently, then said, "I worry about him getting hurt. He's a soldier. He's already been shot once."

Zoe took a deep breath and let it out.

"I can understand that. Your grandfather—Bob's dad—he was a fighter pilot. And he got hurt, badly, before he ended up coming back to Whitesville and working in the mine. Honestly, it destroyed his life. That kept your uncle and aunt apart for years."

"What do you mean?"

Zoe frowned. "Mandy was terrified of getting tied down here in Whitesville—always afraid of Joe getting hurt in the mine. She used to say there was no way in hell she'd ever marry a coal miner."

"But she changed her mind."

Zoe nodded. "She did. It was right before you were born, when the terrorists attacked the World Trade Center. She lost her best friend in the attack. I guess she realized that anyone could be in danger, any time, and that she couldn't cut herself off from life because of that fear."

Rebecca nodded. "Was that after he was in the Army?"

"Oh, no. He enlisted not long after September 11. Went to Iraq and Afghanistan several times."

"Wow, I … I didn't realize all that. How did she deal with it?"

Zoe said, "She prayed. She helped take care of you, especially when you were younger. She got a job and lived her life, and waited for him to come home."

Rebecca sniffled. "I understand why Uncle Joe is so… angry. Losing her tore out his heart."

"Yes... I don't think any of us ever imagined losing her the way we did. Your Dad doesn't show it much, not like Uncle Joe, but losing his sister... it broke him in some ways. They were very close."

Rebecca sounded like she was going to cry when she spoke again. "Mom?"

"Yes, Zoe?"

"I think... I think I love him."

Zoe sighed. It was too soon. Rebecca was too young. But she knew what she had felt at that age.

"All I can tell you, Becca, is take your time. Find your heart, and follow it. I'll be with you whatever happens."

TWENTY-EIGHT

Press Release
May 4; Contact: CDC, Division of Media Relations, 404-555-2712
CDC Reports Increase in prevalence and morbidity from Methicillin-resistant Staphlococcus aureus (CA-MRSA)
The Price administration announced this morning the allocation of $1 billion in emergency funding allocated to the detection and early prevention of methicillin-resistant Staphlococcus aureus (CA-MRSA). The emergency funding is in response to the most recent statistics on CA-MRSA, which showed a more than 250% increase in prevalence of infection among young people since 2016. Deaths from the infection, popularly known as "flesh-eating bacteria," reached 56,000 in the United States last year.

AMBROSE Hall glanced a moment at the framed photograph on his desk. It was old, very old in fact. In the picture, he was fourteen years old, looking uncomfortable in a suit and tie, standing in between his mother and older brother.

He closed his eyes. He'd made one more attempt to talk to his mother. Suggested that they go together to visit Ernest's grave.

She'd been unwilling. She went to visit Ernest every week, she said, had gone every Wednesday morning since his funeral in 1994. But she wouldn't budge on her Christian principles. Her younger son lived a life of sin and until he sought Jesus and redemption and renounced his life of sodomy, she would have nothing to do with him.

It was a train-wreck, slowly unfolding, and there was nothing he could do to stop it. She just went on and on. As far as she was concerned, her only son had died in 1994.

Ambrose finally, slowly, hung up the phone, and decided to make no further attempts to contact her.

Interesting. He would have thought, at near enough to fifty years old, that his mother had lost the power to break his heart again. But he was wrong.

Ambrose would be happy to leave West Virginia and his past behind. Again.

Later that afternoon, Valerie showed up in his office, with no warning. They took a walk outside the building, escorted by her guard.

"I may have screwed up," she said.

Then she went on to describe her lunch with JD Roberts.

"You're certain?" he asked, "He threatened you?"

"He told me it wasn't too late to make me disappear, just like Corvath or my dad."

Ambrose sighed. She was in a precarious position. The evidence of Roberts's involvement in any of this was circumstantial, and in order to make what appeared to be a conspiracy theory stick, they were going to need a lot more than circumstantial evidence. She needed insurance, and she needed it quick.

"All right, a couple things you need to do right away."

"I'm listening," she said.

"First, you need to document everything. Your meeting with Roberts. His threats. The evidence about Channing and his son, the case notes Corvath kept before he moved over to my office. Everything. You get one copy, and copies need to go to people you trust."

"That would be you and Al Clark."

"No one else?"

"Not really. Certainly no one else in West Virginia."

"I know a couple of journalists who might be interested."

She took a deep breath. "Do you think we're ready for that?"

"I don't see much choice. But it can't be just anyone. It's got to be someone with impeccable credentials, who is willing to buck the system and raise some hell if necessary."

She bit her lower lip.

"Second thing," he said. "You need to beef up your security. Two guards, around the clock. You need the best possible security system you can get in your apartment. And send your nephew back to Georgia; having him stay with you is an accident waiting to happen."

"He'll be going back in four more weeks anyway."

"Good enough, I guess. In the meantime, we need to make sure you're as protected as possible. We can't prevent anyone from coming after you, but at least it will force them out into the open. If you're isolated or alone, they could just have you killed and make it look like a robbery, or suicide. Force them out into the open, and they'll have to come up with some other way, like manufacturing charges of some kind."

"When Corvath was threatened by Roberts, and went back home, he found his home computer had been… compromised," she said quietly. "He said it was riddled with child porn."

Ambrose nodded. "That would be a very effective way to shut someone up. Arresting him for having child porn would have made anything he said suspect. Where else are you vulnerable?"

"What do you mean?"

"What I mean is, do you have other areas where… secrets exist? Any questionable stock trades? Secret bank accounts? Lovers on the side? Anything they can use to preemptively attack you?"

"Other than David's secret porn tapes, I can't think of anything. And that came as a complete shock to me—I had no idea they existed. Maybe my finances, they aren't that great."

"That doesn't stop them from manufacturing something, but it's a start. How vulnerable are your computers? At work? At home?"

She shrugged. "I'm no computer security expert. But I have low-tech security: I leave my computer turned off and unplugged when I'm not using it."

"We need to find an expert."

"Bobby can probably handle that."

"Your nephew? He's a kid."

"He knows computers inside and out."

"Valerie, I don't think you're taking this seriously. You need a professional."

"All right. I'll make some calls."

Ambrose sighed, stopped walking and faced her. "Valerie… Is your passport up to date?"

She shook her head. "No, it expired a couple years ago, why?"

He looked her in the eye. "You may want to consider some emergency contingency plans."

"Like what?"

"Like having your passport up to date. And a few thousand dollars in cash set to the side somewhere. A place to run."

"Jesus, Ambrose," she muttered. Despite everything she'd seen, she still had difficulty putting the risks in personal terms.

"I'm not kidding Valerie. It might already be too late, but just in case. It would be better to be in exile than dead."

"I wouldn't know where to go. Nor could I get my hands on that kind of money."

"Start working on it. Didn't your Dad leave you anything? How bad are your finances?"

She shrugged, then shook her head. "His life insurance didn't pay out, because… because he was executed. I've got the house up for sale, but it isn't moving. Umm… about sixty thousand in student loans."

Ambrose stared at her in shock. He'd had no idea that her financial situation had become so grave. "Do what you can."

They parted ways, and Ambrose returned to his office, wracking his brain and finding no solutions.

On his return to the office, he found a man in civilian clothes sitting in the reception area. He looked military, though. Late twenties, dark, low-cropped hair, blue jeans and a white button-down shirt.

He looked over at his administrative assistant. "Hey, Molly, I'm back. Any messages?"

Her eyes darted to the waiting man with an odd, guarded expression. "No messages. That's Matt Floyd… here to see Detective Corvath."

Ambrose raised his eyebrows. She obviously had chosen not to tell the visitor about Corvath's death.

"Oh?" He turned toward the man. "Mr. Floyd?" he said as he approached. "I'm Ambrose Hall—the special prosecutor. I understand you are here to see Detective Corvath?"

Floyd stood. He licked his lips, then rubbed his hands on his jeans. "Yes, sir."

"Perhaps I can help you? I'm afraid Detective Corvath is... dead."

Floyd's eyes widened. "What happened?"

He was setting off all the alarms in Ambrose's head. "He was... killed. Shot to death, I'm afraid. Was he... a friend? I'm sorry to give you bad news."

Floyd shook his head, almost violently.

"I didn't know him. I should go."

Ambrose reached out and gently touched Floyd's arm. "Sir... if it helps, I'm familiar in detail with the cases Corvath was working. If you've got something you need to discuss..."

"All right." His voice cracked a little.

"Come on back to my office, then."

Floyd looked extremely nervous as Ambrose led him back to the office. Ambrose wracked his brain for the name. He'd come across it in Corvath's files, somewhere. The man was obviously extremely rattled. Whatever the problem was, it was serious. Or at least, he thought so.

Then it came to him. The head of security at Hamilton Biomedical was an Army captain named Matthew Floyd.

Stepping into the office, Ambrose said, "Why don't you have a seat. Would you like some coffee, or a cold drink?"

Floyd sat stiffly. "Um... Coke, please, if you have any."

Ambrose pressed the intercom on his phone. He looked up at Floyd and smiled, then intentionally said something that he knew would likely throw Floyd even more off balance.

"Molly? Can you bring me a tomato juice? And a coke for Captain Floyd."

At the words "Captain Floyd," Floyd jerked up straight.

"You know who I am?"

"Corvath's case notes. He told me he'd been trying to get a meeting with a Captain Matt Floyd at Hamilton Biomedical. I presume that would be you?"

Floyd nodded. "Yes, sir."

"I'm going to reassure you here and now that anything you tell me here is confidential, and won't be shared beyond these walls, without your okay. I want you to relax a little bit, and tell me why you're here, Captain."

Floyd took a deep breath, then said, "Bear with me. To be perfectly honest with you, I never imagined doing this... going outside of channels like this."

Ambrose nodded tensely.

There was a knock on the door.

"Come in," Ambrose said.

Molly appeared, gave them their drinks, and stepped out, closing the door quietly.

"Detective Corvath left a message for me at home a few weeks ago. He had attempted to see me at Hamilton, but couldn't clear the front gate. As it turned out, I wasn't even there that day, but had I been, the result wouldn't have been any different. In any event, I saw it in the duty officer's log, and didn't think much of it until I found the message on my home answering machine. He said he was looking into Cliff Wells's death... that he didn't believe it was suicide, and might be connected to the break-in."

Ambrose nodded.

"Under normal circumstances, I would not be bringing this to you. I'm an officer in the United States Army, you understand. It's not how we do things."

"I understand," Ambrose replied.

"In any event, part of my job as head of security was to conduct the investigation into the break-in, as well as work with the investigators into Cliff's death. Cliff was a decent guy—very into his computer stuff. He was a professional. There was no sign of depression, none of the warning signs of suicide. The one thing that struck me as off during the investigation was the conclusion regarding his relationship with Maggie Rutledge. You know who she is?"

"I do—she was the last person who saw him before he died, that we know of. They went out on a date."

"That's right. The thing is, she told the investigators that they had only been out once—that she didn't know him well at all."

"That's right."

"That's not true, though."

Ambrose leaned forward in his seat. "Oh, really?"

"Cliff had been working with us for three months. And he and Maggie met the very first day he was there. They ate lunch together pretty much every day. You can go back through our front desk logs and there it is. Every day they signed out together, came back together. Even if they didn't go off site, they would eat in his office. It was a known thing in the office—a budding romance.

"Problem is, the logs disappeared. So did the computerized logs, which—if you could look at them—would have shown them using their pass cards to get in and out of the building together. The logs are gone, the backups were erased. Everything. I even pulled the offsite backups, and there's nothing there. Three months of video of the front entrance, gone. I was very thorough. But none of this made it into the final report of his death."

Ambrose sat perfectly still, running this through his mind. "Who has that kind of access?" he asked.

"No one." Floyd stared back at him, his face looking haunted.

"Someone obviously does."

Floyd shook his head. "No. See, the Army detailed my company for security. We're assigned there for a year, and we'll be replaced in June. But the jurisdiction for the facility falls under the Department of Homeland Security. We're just detailed temporarily."

"I see. So... DHS is responsible for security. And the backups. Is this under Washington, or the local field office?"

"Local. JD Roberts is in charge."

Ambrose felt a chill. "Who signed off on the final report?"

"Roberts, again."

"What brought you to me, then?"

"The discrepancies in this report, as well as the final one, on the break-in investigation. When I saw the final report on the break-in, I knew I had to do something. So I contacted my Army superior. I reported what I'd found, and my concerns. And I was given very clear orders."

"What were they?"

"To back off. I was ordered to drop the subject permanently, and informed that my Army career would likely be over if I didn't."

Ambrose closed his eyes, rubbed the bridge of his nose between his thumb and forefinger. "I see. That's serious. Can you tell me about the report on the break-in?"

"Yes. That's the biggest part of this. The final report states flat out that no biological samples were stolen. And that's not true."

Ambrose sat up straight. He looked at Floyd. "What was stolen, Captain Floyd?"

"Eight vials of bird-flu virus. It was genetically modified as part of a research project to identify what mutations could make it easily transmissible among mammals."

"Bird flu. Tell me more."

"Okay, let me clarify. H5N1 is the virus strain we're talking about. It is extremely rare in humans—you usually get it from direct contact with infected poultry. It's also extremely dangerous. The death rate in infected humans is something like sixty percent. Anyway, about ten years ago some researchers discovered ways to induce mutations which make it easily transmissible in mammals."

"Good lord, why?" Ambrose said.

"They were attempting to model the sort of mutations would cause it to spread in the wild and cause a pandemic."

"I see. And the result?"

Floyd said, "They were successful. The strain that was stolen from Hamilton was the modified strain. If released, it could be devastating."

"But the investigation report said nothing was stolen. Why?"

"I don't know," Floyd said, frustrated. "I wrote the first draft of the report, then sent it up to DHS. Once out of my hands, DHS officials take it from there. But yesterday, during my final walk through of the building, I saw that Dr. Seeger, the director of the facility, had left a copy of it sitting out on his desk. It's classified material, and shouldn't have been left out, so I took it to return it to the classified materials safe. And I happened to glance down and notice that, first of all, the report was a lot thinner than it should have been, and second, that the executive summary had been dramatically shortened. Basically, my conclusions on the investigation were gutted, as was all of the evidence related to the break-in."

"Jesus H. Christ."

"Yes, exactly." Floyd hunched over. "Look, I could lose my commission for this, or go to jail. But people's lives are on the line."

He reached in his pocket and pulled out two folded, stapled reports. "This is the copy of the report I submitted. The second one is the one that went to Washington."

Ambrose took them. "I promised you confidentiality. But now I'm going to ask you for permission to get this to the people who need it."

"Who do you have in mind?"

"General Murphy for sure, and the Governor. Possibly the press."

Floyd looked at him closely, then said, "Do what you need to do."

TWENTY-NINE

"Good news," Bob Mays said, as he set his coffee cup next to the sink.

Sitting at the kitchen table, Rebecca looked up from her e-reader expectantly.

"School's opening back up on Monday."

She jumped out of her seat. "Really?"

He nodded, smiling. "Yes."

"I never thought I'd say this, but that's great! I've been going crazy stuck in the house."

He grunted. "Your mother and I have been going crazy with you stuck in the house."

Rebecca crossed her arms over her chest and barely stopped herself from sticking her tongue out. "I've got to get my stuff together. Can I go buy a couple new outfits?"

"Whoa! It's not like the first day of school!"

"Well, it's almost like that."

He smiled. "All right. But keep it appropriate."

"Seriously, Dad? Did you wake up with a different daughter?"

"All right. I've got to get to work. What are you up to today?"

"I'm going to go to Charleston with Dana—shopping." She felt a grin lighting her face. "Thigh-high leather boots, maybe? Mesh? No, fishnet stockings! I'll probably get my navel pierced, and…"

He threw his hands up in surrender, laughing. "All right, all right, I get it! I'll see you tonight, kiddo."

The minute he left the house, she raced upstairs and called Dana.

"Did you hear? School's open Monday!"

"Oh my God, Becca, do you know what time it is? Why are you calling so early?"

Rebecca looked out the window. It was broad daylight. The clock on her desk said 10 am.

∽

Turville checked his watch as the Humvees pulled to a stop beside the road. It was 10 am.

"What's the deal, boss-man?" Nowell asked Turville. "Why we stopping?"

Turville shrugged. "I don't know."

He opened the door of the Humvee and stood, craning his neck to look ahead down the road. The three Humvees ahead of them were stopped, too. Something was in the road in front of them. It looked like a large carcass… a cow?

"Jesus," he muttered. "There's a dead cow in the road."

"I don't think we're in Kansas anymore," Nowell replied, a smirk on his face.

At the front of the column, Lieutenant Blake was talking on the radio, pacing in a circle. Turville wondered what was he doing. Calling animal control? Asking for permission to drag the dead cow out of the road? This was bizarre.

Blake called something Turville couldn't hear to the second Humvee, and one of the soldiers from Meigs's fire team jumped out and ran up to him.

∽

Dana said, "I think your boyfriend is at the bottom of the hill. I can see their trucks in the road."

Rebecca smiled. "Are you serious? What are they doing?"

"I don't know, just standing around. So what happened last weekend? You never told me any details! Not fair."

"Well… he came with me to rehearsal, slept on the couch here, and we just… we spent the weekend together."

"Mmmm, sounds like fun. Did you sleep with him?"

"God, Dana—no!"

"Why not?"

Rebecca felt her face flush, and said very quietly, "I think I'm in love with him, Dana."

∽

It happened so quickly Turville wouldn't have seen it if hadn't already been looking at the lieutenant's Humvee. One moment, Private Grant was manning the machine gun in the cupola of the first Humvee, scanning the woods on the steep, wooded hill above them to the left of the road. The next, he was gone, a splash of blood splattering across the roof.

The sound of the shot came half a second after Grant disappeared.

"Take cover!" Turville shouted to his fire team. "Sniper!"

His fire team scattered, hunkering down in the woods around the Humvee.

They heard another shot a few seconds later.

Turville scanned the woods, his heart pounding. He counted heads quickly. His fire team was intact. Where the hell were the shots coming from?

છ૭

"Oh, my God. Something's going on," Dana said. "I just heard shots."

"What?"

"The soldiers are spread out all over the road, and someone's shooting—I think one of them is hurt."

Rebecca's heart pounded. One of the soldiers was hurt?

Over the phone line she heard the crack of a rifle, then the rattle of a machine gun. Dana whimpered.

"Oh, shit, Dana. You need to get somewhere safe now! Go to your basement!"

છ૭

"Stay down!" Turville shouted. "We need to find the shooter!"

He scanned the treeline. Nothing. Nearly a minute had passed since the last shot. The woods were quiet. Way too quiet. He could hear the wind rustling the leaves, and in the distance, the quiet rippling of water from the river. High above them up the ridge, a house was nestled in the trees, barely visible through the woods.

At the lieutenant's Humvee, the platoon's medic was leaning agaіnt the tires; apparently efforts to save Grant's life proved useless. The lieutenant was leaning against the side of the Humvee, talking on the radio, reporting their situation.

Turville continued to search the woods, questions racing through his mind. Was the sniper still out there or had he escaped? There was no way to know. Fear made his stomach turn. They didn't even know where the shot had come from.

"Shit," he muttered.

They heard the crack of another shot, and this time the crunch of metal as a bullet punched into the driver's side of the lieutenant's Humvee. That at least gave them a direction: the sniper was somewhere in the woods above them, near the house up the hill.

"Flush him out!" the lieutenant called. "Machine guns, sweep the hill, recon by fire."

Turville called out. "Santiago, Nowell. Sweep the hill!"

Santiago and Nowell burst into motion, planting the bipod mounted squad automatic weapon on the hood of their Humvee. Nowell swept the machine gun across the hill above them, sending tracers flying up into the woods. Not fifteen seconds later, he let out a cry and ducked down.

"I'm hit!" He slumped behind the Humvee, and Santiago took over the machine gun.

Turville crawled to Nowell and examined the wound. The sleeve was torn open, blood pouring down his arm. The sniper had mostly missed: a narrow furrow tore along the skin of Nowell's upper arm a quarter-inch deep.

"You'll be fine, Nowell, it's not bad."

"Shit," Nowell said. "It doesn't feel fine."

Santiago fired the machine gun again. Spent brass ejecting from the machine gun fell all over Nowell and Turville.

"Jesus, Santiago!" Nowell shouted. "Can't you do that somewhere else?"

Turville burst into laughter even as he bandaged the injury. "Shut up, Nowell."

He was crazy: some asshole was shooting at them, and he was laughing. What the fuck was wrong with him?

Someone shouted, "The LT's hit! Fuck!"

Turville glanced to his right. The lieutenant was down, hard, blood spreading all over the front of his uniform.

Sergeant Nguyen shouted, "Everybody get down! Fast movers on the way!"

Santiago fired another long burst from the machine gun, then ducked down behind the Humvee next to Turville and Nowell.

∞

Tears were running down Rebecca's face. On the other end of the line, Dana was whimpering in fear.

"They're shooting at the house!" she shouted.

"Get to the basement!" Rebecca replied. "Go!"

"I'm afraid!" Dana cried out.

Rebecca cringed as she heard more shots over the phone line, then the sound of shattering glass.

∞

The jets came in fast and low, the sound of the turbines so loud they drowned out the machine-gun fire. Two jets overflew them once, then looped around and headed back toward them, hugging the ridgeline. Turville squeezed his eyes shut and felt his body leave the ground, then slam back into it as his vision went white.

The explosion was so loud he felt it in his body rather than heard it as twin thousand-pound explosives annihilated the hill above them, shredding trees and vaporizing the house.

Santiago said something, but Turville couldn't hear it over the ringing in his ears. Both of them looked, wide eyed, at the devastation uphill from them. Hundreds of trees were flattened; smoke and flame was everywhere. The house was gone—a blackened crater nearly a hundred yards wide all that remained.

❧

The line went dead without warning.

"Dana? Dana!"

Fifteen seconds after the line went dead, the house shook with a sudden blow that cracked one of the windows and sent her Dad's coffee cup off the counter, where it shattered on the floor.

Rebecca held the phone away from her face and redialed Dana. Straight to voicemail.

She closed her eyes, trying to quell the sudden panic than ran through her. Dialed again: voicemail again.

Not even realizing she was crying, she tried Jim and got his voicemail. She had to see what had happened, she had to know if Dana was okay.

Jesse! Even though she hadn't called him since before they broke up in January, she hit his number.

It rang twice, then he picked it up.

"Hey," he said.

"Jesse, something's happened! I was on the phone with Dana and she... she was scared, there was shooting, and then she was cut off and there was this, this earthquake, and—"

"Holy shit," he said. "I felt it; I thought they dropped a nuke! You were on the phone with her?"

"She won't answer! I'm afraid, Jesse! She might be hurt!"

"I'm three minutes away."

Rebecca stuffed her feet in a pair of ballet slippers without even bothering to change out of her flannel pajamas. She ran out to the front porch, and waited, bouncing on the balls of her feet. She dialed Dana three more times while she waited. No answer.

Jesse's truck tore into their driveway, leaving streaks of rubber at the turn. She ran to the truck and got in the second he'd stopped.

"Dana's house," she said.

Jesse threw the truck into reverse, backed out, then took off, the acceleration pushing Rebecca back into the seat.

"What happened?" he asked as he turned left onto the road that would take them to the top of the ridge.

"We were just talking, and she said the soldiers had stopped off the road below her house. Then there was shooting—a lot of it. I could hear it, her windows were breaking. Then she got cut off, and... Jesse, I felt my whole house shake."

Jesse muttered, "Everyone within twenty miles must have felt it. Almost there. Rebecca... she'll be okay."

At the top of the ridge road, he turned right, headed toward Dana's house. Thirty seconds later, he screeched to a stop.

The trees were flattened for a third of a mile, most of them smoking.

"Oh my God," Rebecca whispered. "Where... where is her house?"

"Holy fuck," Jesse said. He put the truck in park and got out.

Rebecca's eyes started to pick out details. The house had been... somewhere in the middle of a hundred-foot wide crater. Debris was everywhere... wood, crazy chunks of drywall, half a toilet leaning against a tree. She stumbled, looked down, and found herself staring at a strappy, glossy red, closed-toe sandal. Dana's mother's.

She was breathing too fast, light headed. Jesse screamed Dana's name, but Rebecca already knew that was pointless.

Dana had been in the center of this explosion.

Dana was gone.

Rebecca sobbed, tears and snot running down her face. She stumbled toward the remains of the house.

At the bottom of the hill, she saw a line of soldiers, rifles at the ready, beginning to move up toward them. Jim would be with them, but she didn't care. She shook her head, trying to wrap her mind around what had happened. Jim and his platoon had killed her best friend.

How could she love someone who had killed her oldest friend in the world?

She glanced at Jesse. His face filled with rage when he saw the soldiers.

"Motherfuckers!" he screamed.

He turned on Rebecca and grabbed her upper arm, hard. "That's your new fucking boyfriend! How do you like that shit, Becca? He killed her!"

Rebecca struggled to pull away from Jesse, her vision blurred by tears. He was hurting her, his fingers digging into her upper arm painfully.

"Stop it!" she shouted.

Her vision went white when he slapped her hard, across the face. She fell to the ground.

Jesse pointed at her.

"You're a fucking cunt, Rebecca! A traitor! That was your best friend! What the fuck are you gonna do now? Run off to your killer of a boyfriend? You gonna go fuck him?"

Jesse was shouting so loud he didn't hear the car arriving, nor did he see Bob Mays come up behind him.

Rebecca gasped as her dad grabbed Jesse's right arm and twisted it up behind his back, doubling Jesse over. Bob Mays's expression was murder, eyes narrowed and teeth clamped together. Jesse struggled to rise, and Mays clouted him on the side of the head and twisted the arm again, tighter.

Jesse let out a cry of pain.

"You ever touch my daughter again, you fuck, and I'll kill you. Understand?"

He shoved Jesse to the ground, then kicked him hard in the side.

"Stay away from her!" he shouted.

Jesse backed away on his butt, moving crabwise. Rage and grief warred across his features, and he finally said, "She's a fucking whore. I'll gladly stay away from her!"

He got up and ran to his truck, then sped off.

Rebecca folded in on herself, arms across her chest, knees pulled up, sobbing uncontrollably. A few feet in front of her, she could see a miniature rose-patterned lampshade, scorched on one side. It had been in Dana's bedroom since they were six years old.

She wanted Jesse to go away. She wanted her father to go away. She wanted the pain to go away.

∽

Bob Mays was silent on the drive back to their house. Rebecca stayed curled up in the passenger seat, staring out the window, her face vacant, eyes glazed. During the short drive, he glanced over at her several times, but there was no change. She was in shock, he thought. An angry red handprint marred the left side of her face.

Zoe's car was parked in front of the house when they pulled up. Thank God she'd gotten his message. Mays considered himself a competent man, a good father. But this... he had no idea to handle a daughter who had just lost her best friend, probably due to the actions of her boyfriend, then assaulted by an ex-boyfriend. What do you say? What do you do to help?

He put the car in park and said quietly, "Let's go inside, Becca."

She said nothing, just opened the door and stumbled out of the car. Rage building, Mays thought about John and Linda Wilder. They'd likely both been at work when the bombs destroyed their home and killed their daughter. Did they even know yet what had happened? Something else he would have to deal with, and quickly.

He got out of the car and followed Rebecca into the house. Zoe was sitting on the couch when they entered. Her arms were crossed over her chest, worry on her face. She looked up, saw her daughter, and froze. Her eyes darted to Mays, and he could see the question and fear behind her eyes.

Zoe held out her arms to Rebecca, but Rebecca shied away.

"Honey, tell me... what happened?"

Rebecca shook her head. "I ... I need to go lay down." Her voice broke as she spoke, and she immediately ran up the stairs. Mays and Zoe watched her. By the time she reached her room and slammed the door, she was wailing.

Mays closed his eyes and took a deep breath, trying to stay calm. Teeth clenched, he said, "I don't know any details yet... but John and Linda's house was destroyed by a bomb."

"Oh, my God," Zoe said. "How... why?"

Mays shook his head. "The Army was there. I've no idea what happened. But... Dana was home when it happened, I think she was on the phone with Becca, because when I got there, Becca was there with Jesse freaking out, and he had just hit her."

Zoe closed her eyes. "Oh, my God. You're saying the Army did it?"

"I'm going down there right now to talk to Lieutenant Blake and find out what happened."

Zoe shook her head. "What is she going to do about Jim? Was he there?"

"I've no idea, Zoe."

Zoe's face was bleak. "She loves him."

"Nobody falls in love that quickly. And at that age, she doesn't know what she wants out of life. She's too young."

"We did," she replied.

"What?

"We fell in love that quickly. And you knew exactly what you wanted out of life. Why are you underestimating your daughter?"

"I don't want her to make mistakes she can't recover from."

"And what mistakes did you make, Bob, that you regret so much?"

He frowned, closed his eyes. "Zoe, calm down. I've got things to do, and you have a daughter to care for."

Anger in her face, she said, "Go, then. Take care of your... your mayor stuff. I'll stay here and try to pick up the pieces of our daughter!"

THIRTY

THE patrol returned to base almost immediately. Turville sat in the passenger seat of the Humvee, staring out at trees as Santiago drove. His mind a thousand miles away, he barely noticed when they came to a stop.

The silence in the vehicle was unbearable.

"Everybody out," he said.

The rest of the platoon filed out of their vehicles, dirty and dispirited. Lieutenant Blake had been medevacked from the field, as had Private Grant, though it was too late for him. Nowell's injury didn't rate a medevac, though it would a Purple Heart.

Meigs dropped his rucksack and web gear in the middle of the floor. His back slumped, he walked straight to the wall, leaned his head against it for a second, then reared back and punched the wall, hard. With a grunt, he did it again, then again, indenting the drywall, tearing cracks in the wall.

"Fuck! Fuck! Fuck!" he screamed.

Turville stared at Meigs in shock. He was a jerk, but almost always in control. And Grant had been one of his guys.

Turville approached Meigs, put his hands on his shoulders and gripped them hard. Meigs spun around, rage on his face.

They looked at each other for a moment, than Turville said, "I'm sorry about Grant, man."

Meigs's face twitched violently.

"Motherfucker was eighteen. He's got a six-month-old daughter. Joined the Army so he could give her some kind of life, you know?"

Turville replied in a low tone, "There's nothing you could have done."

Meigs stared at him, his eyebrows pulled down, forehead wrinkled, nostrils flared. Then the anger seemed to deflate, and he curled in on himself, shoulders slumping.

"Thanks," he muttered, then pushed away.

Turville turned back to his fire team. Nowell and Santiago were staring at him, dumbfounded. Tilman was busy untying his boots.

"You guys okay?"

"Yeah," Nowell muttered. "Just wondering if we got the fucker that killed Grant."

Tilman said, "Did you see that house? It fucking evaporated. Nobody lived through that."

Nowell shrugged. "We don't know the shooter was in the house."

"Who gives a fuck?" Tilman replied. "If he wasn't, well, whoever was in there probably knew about it. Let him on their land. If you help the fucking insurgents, you might as well be one."

Turville quietly said, "I hope you're right. I'd hate it if it was civilians in there."

"Fuck them," Tilman said. He stared at Turville in defiance.

Turville stared back, then shrugged and turned away. He was too tired to argue the point. Instead, he stumbled into the room he shared with the rest of the fire team, dropped his gear, and slumped onto the stiff army cot.

A moment later he dug into his duffel bag and pulled out his phone. He hit the power button and waited impatiently for it to boot up.

No messages, no texts.

He dialed Rebecca. It rang twice, then went to voicemail. He furrowed his eyebrows. She must have looked at it and hit Ignore.

Turville sighed. He needed to talk. He dialed again, and this time it did go straight to voicemail.

Was Rebecca okay? Why wouldn't she answer?

A few moments later, he got his answer. Her text message said, Don't call me. I don't want to hear from you ever again.

Turville squeezed his eyes shut in shock. What the fuck?

He lay back on the cot, staring at the ceiling, confused and afraid. What the hell happened? Was it something to do with the firefight? Who lived in that house?

He stared at the message, then angrily texted back, I can't do that. I love you. Please answer the phone.

She didn't respond.

Tilman sat on the cot across from him, cleaning his rifle, looking angry.

Santiago was smearing antibiotic ointment over the furrow on Nowell's shoulder. "You're lucky to be alive, Nowell. You should count your blessings."

Nowell chuckled. "Oh, trust me, Santiago, I am. I get a Purple Heart for this—I'll be a hero now. I bet I'll be able to pick up girls just like Turville."

"Shut the fuck up, Nowell," Turville muttered.

The room went silent, Nowell and Santiago staring at Turville in shock. Turville stood up and walked out of the room. He carried his rifle into the main sitting room, disassembled it and began cleaning it.

Ten minutes later, he looked up when Sergeant Nguyen left his office, walked into the living room and opened the front door. He froze, his heart pounding, when he saw the Mayor with Specialist Leo, his heart pounding.

Nguyen said, "Come on in to my office, Mr. Mayor."

"Where's Blake?" Mays said.

"Wounded. I don't think it's serious, but he was medevacked out. I'm running the platoon until he gets back."

"Jesus," Mays said. "I need to know what the hell happened today."

Nguyen shrugged. "Sniper, caught us out in the open. One of our guys was killed, and two wounded."

"So you responded by dropping a bomb on a civilian house?"

Turville's eyes were fixed on Bob Mays. Mays was clenching his fists, face red, eyes bulging in anger

Nguyen shook his head. "We didn't have any choice, Mayor; the fire was coming from up there. The sniper, whoever the hell it was, was holing up in that house or right next to it."

"Bullshit," Mays said. "There was a seventee- year-old girl in that house. Her parents are at work, and I have to go tell them now that their daughter is dead."

Nguyen grimaced and stared up at the ceiling for a moment, his expression unreadable. "I'm sorry, Mr. Mayor. But we didn't have any choice."

Turville felt a sinking feeling. Rebecca's best friend Dana lived up in that direction somewhere.

"What, do you just shoot randomly?" Mays shouted. "You didn't have any choice? You get shot at, and you just kill everybody in sight? Is that it?"

Turville knew he shouldn't interrupt, but he couldn't stop himself. "Who was it?"

"Stay out of it, Corporal!" Nguyen shouted.

Mays answered, "It was Dana Wilder. Rebecca's best friend."

"Oh, God," Turville said.

"Mr. Mayor, I understand why you are upset... but sometimes accidents happen. I'll call in to our Company Commander; I'm sure he'll arrange for—for compensation... of some kind." Nguyen stumbled over his words, his expression shifting from concern to horror, and it was obvious he was both out of his depth and fully aware of how inadequate his response was.

Mays's face went slack.

"Compensation? Are you insane? What possible compensation could there be for the loss of your child?"

Turville felt sick, hollow. No wonder Rebecca wouldn't take his call. She'd never talk with him again. He felt his eyes water and angrily wiped them. He quickly put his rifle back together, stood and slung it over his shoulder.

"Mr. Mays...."

"Turville!" Nguyen said, a warning in his voice.

Ignoring the sergeant, Turville said, "Please... please tell Rebecca I'm sorry. And I understand."

Mays stared at Turville. He blinked hard, his expression shifting to disgust. Then he turned and stormed out of the house.

ᛈ

The knock on the door came again, but Rebecca ignored it, curling up under her blanket and covering her head with a pillow.

"Rebecca? It's time to wake up."

She didn't respond. She felt numb, knowing that the only thing holding her together was thinking about nothing at all. If she could just hold on to that emptiness, she might make it through. Somehow.

The door opened. She sensed her mother moving into the room, then felt her sit on the mattress. Zoe Mays sighed, then rubbed Rebecca's shoulder through the blanket.

"Rebecca," her mother said. Her voice was low and soothing. "I know you're devastated. I... I can't even imagine what you are going through right now. But don't you think it will be a little easier if you get up?"

Rebecca gritted her teeth. "I'm not getting up, Mom. Please. I just... I can't. Not today."

"You'll have to face it eventually, hon."

"Don't you think I know that, Mom? And no matter what I do, when I go, Dana will be gone. And Jim will have killed her."

Saying the words just made it hurt more. Her voice broke, and she whispered, "Mom, just please... please go away. I'm begging you."

Zoe sighed, and Rebecca felt her mom's hand leave her shoulder. For a moment she thought her mother was going to leave, but then she did something unexpected.

Curling up on the bed behind Rebecca and put her arms around her. "It's all right, hon. I'll be right here."

Rebecca couldn't remember the last time her mother had hugged her that way. That was all it took for her to break down again.

She moaned, grief pouring out of her—so much that she thought it would never stop. They stayed that way until she finally fell into a numb, exhausted sleep.

య

When Rebecca woke up, her mother was gone. She slowly opened her eyes, stretched and rolled over. A glance at the clock showed her it was almost 2:30. So much for the first day back at school.

She sat up slowly, then rested her head in her hands. Severe headache coming on. Coffee first thing.

She stood and glanced at herself in the mirror. She was a wreck: her hair looked like she'd been electrocuted, and dark bags showed under her eyes. She was still wearing the same filthy pajamas that she'd run out of the house in yesterday.

She heard voices downstairs, one her mother's, one a man's. She tilted her head, listening, then realized it was Reverend Franks, their pastor. Oh, joy.

She didn't want to see Reverend Franks. But she knew her mother would force her to sit with them, so she wasn't going downstairs like this. She chose an old sundress from her closet, then stepped across the hall to the bathroom to shower and brush her teeth.

Twenty minutes later, feeling physically refreshed, if not emotionally, she descended the stairs.

Her mom sat at the coffee table with Reverend Franks, both of them drinking coffee. Franks stood when Rebecca came down the stairs.

"Hello, Reverend."

"Hello, Rebecca. Your mother and I are talking; would you like to join us?"

Well, that was inevitable, she supposed.

"Yes, sir. Let me just get a cup of coffee; I'll be right in."

Five minutes later she sat in the chair across the coffee table from her mom and the preacher. She sipped her coffee, hoping the headache would ease a little.

There was an awkward silence until Franks said, "We've had a terrible tragedy here, haven't we? How are you holding up, Rebecca?"

Rebecca shrugged. She didn't know how to answer the question.

Franks raised an eyebrow. "Your mother tells me you didn't want to go in to school today."

Rebecca exhaled, and said, in a sharper tone than she intended, "Would you? My best friend was killed yesterday. How am I supposed to feel?"

Franks leaned back, resting his hands across a generous belly.

"We all deal with grief a little differently. Loss. Grief. Anger. Whatever you are feeling is okay, Rebecca."

"Well, thank you for your permission."

"Rebecca," her mother remonstrated.

Franks held up a hand toward her mother. "It's all right, Zoe. I understand a little of what your daughter is going through."

Rebecca seemed to have completely lost her filter. She spoke before thinking. "You do?"

"I do. Can I tell you a little about my own experience of grief?"

Rebecca nodded, jerkily.

"My brother. He was a sheriff's deputy. We grew up not too far from here, in Lorrie's Hollow, back when people still lived there. Our father drank himself to death when we were kids, and we spent much of our lives in foster homes... Not too differently than your father. Anyway, my big brother joined the sheriff's department. I was... on the other end of the law. Always in trouble. Drinking and worse. He did his best to keep me out of trouble, but, well... trouble followed me."

"What happened to him?"

Franks looked down at the table. "In 1994 the department raided a meth lab. He was shot to death. The thing was... I knew the guys who did it. Not well, but I'd bought from them before. In some ways, I felt responsible for his death."

Rebecca blinked back tears.

"What I realized then, Rebecca, was that… I couldn't go back and change anything. I couldn't bring my brother or my parents back. I couldn't turn back the clock and be a better brother. I couldn't take back the drugs I'd done, or the times I'd gotten in trouble, or the many things I did that broke his heart before he died. All I could do was go forward. And that meant I had to make it matter. I had to make his death—and his life—mean something. If there was nothing else I could do, I could make my life a monument for my brother. Does that make sense?"

She nodded, slowly.

"So… I moved forward. Even though I felt like I was dead inside, I took steps forward every day. Every day I pretended I was alive—for my brother. And eventually… eventually the healing came. A long time after that, I came into the ministry."

"Dana was killed by the soldiers. By the Army."

"Your mother tells me… she tells me that you love one of the soldiers."

Rebecca shot a hard look at her mother, then closed her eyes. Tears began rolling silently down her face again.

"Yes. I think. I don't know. I told him… I told him not to call me any more."

"Oh, honey," Zoe said, her voice sad.

"I don't know how to deal with this, Mom. I don't know what I'm supposed to think, or feel." Her voice dropped to a whisper. She didn't want to keep talking, but didn't know how to stop. "I feel like I'm being torn in two. How am I supposed to forgive this? I don't see how I can ever look at him again."

Frank looked at her, compassion on his face. "I can't tell you the answer, Rebecca, nor can your mother. We can support you, and love you, but in the end, you'll have to make your decisions. You'll have to think over it, pray over it. Eventually you'll be given the right answer."

Rebecca didn't want to tell him that she didn't pray any more. She didn't even believe any more. She looked at Reverend Franks and realized that he could probably see that. He probably saw right through her. He probably knew the rage she was feeling, and the guilt. Because wouldn't loving Jim be a betrayal of her best friend? It would be as if she was saying it was okay, as if she didn't care about Dana, as if the things Jesse had said about her were true—she was a traitor.

"Thank you, Reverend Franks. I... I don't know what to think or feel right now, okay? It's going to take some time."

"Of course, dear."

She looked at her mom. "I'm going to go back to my room, okay, Mom? I'll go to school tomorrow, I promise."

Her mom looked like she was going to break down in tears. Rebecca turned away. She didn't have room to deal with her mother's issues right now.

THIRTY-ONE

THE day of the funeral dawned with a cloudy, hazy sky. Turville and Nowell, on watch together, watched as the sky changed from black to a deep blue, then lighter. Tinges of brown shot through the sky.

Turville was exhausted. He'd been awakened halfway through the night, stifling a scream. He'd dreamed of a girl, sixteen years old. It was the girl who had been killed in the

Arlington bombing a year before. Her body had been on the ground near where the platoon had offloaded at Crystal City, her legs blown off, the ground soaked with blood. In the dream, he'd gone to cover her body, and the girl's face had morphed into Rebecca's.

Turville closed his eyes. Remembering the dream was almost as disturbing as experiencing it the first time had been. He bit back a sudden urge to vomit.

"It's gonna be a scorcher today," Nowell said.

"Yep."

"You heard from her?" Nowell asked.

Turville shook his head.

Nowell said, uncharacteristically, "Sorry, man. Sucks."

"Yeah," Turville replied. "It does."

"For what it's worth," Nowell said, "I know I can be an ass sometimes about stuff. But... I'm sorry. I know you had a thing for her."

Turville looked over at Nowell. "You're all right man. No matter what everybody else says about you."

Nowell let out a laugh that was almost a bark.

After a few minutes, he said in a pensive tone, "I'm a little worried about today."

"Yeah," Turville responded. "I think we all are. But Reverend Franks and the Mayor... they're both pretty levelheaded. I don't expect things to get ugly."

"They already are," Nowell responded, nodding toward the new sign at the door of the pharmacy across the street. The same pharmacy where they had taken refuge the first time they were in Whitesville. Hand lettered, it said, "NO SOLDIERS OR DOGS ALLOWED." It went up the day after Dana Wilder was killed.

Nowell continued. "Every time I think of that day, all I can think is: what if it was my daughter?"

Turville looked at Nowell, surprised. "Yeah, I know. Me too."

"Hard to blame them for being fucking pissed," Nowell replied. "I wish there was something we could do."

Turville nodded, looking across the street. The sign wasn't the only evidence of the town's rage. Someone had spray painted across the front of one of the vacant storefronts, "GO HOME MURDERERS."

On foot patrols around town, people who had welcomed them only weeks before stared at the soldiers sullenly. Kids had even gotten in the act: an eleven-year-old had thrown dog crap at the Humvee yesterday, splattering Leo in the face.

Some of the guys were furious. They were here to protect these people. They'd come here to help, and lost one of their own in an ambush from hiding. No one in the town gave a shit about Grant's death. Instead, they were treating the rest of them like they were dirt.

But the platoon was split: half of them in a rage at the townspeople who seemed to be siding with the insurgents, the other half freaked out that they'd killed a civilian girl. Turville, with the dubious distinction of being the only soldier in the platoon who'd accidentally killed a civilian before, was lost, stuck in the middle. Horrified that Dana had been killed, he also knew that it was inevitable. If the insurgents kept fighting, more civilians would die. And things would only get worse.

If this kept up, this deployment was going to be long as hell.

☙

Rebecca looked in the mirror, a frown on her face. She'd finished applying her mascara and other makeup, but she wasn't happy. She still looked as if she'd been deathly ill, and the severe black dress didn't help matters.

Who cares, she thought. There was no one to care how she looked anyway. There was surely no way around the fact that today was going to be miserable.

She was going to Dana's funeral.

It didn't seem real. How was it possible that her best friend since the third grade was dead—blasted into nothingness? The Wilders had opted for cremation; there wasn't enough of her left to warrant a coffin, anyway.

Rebecca grimaced, angry with herself for the crazy thoughts going through her head. The gulf of emptiness she'd felt had been replaced with anger. Anger at the Army for killing Dana. Anger with Dana for not running to the basement, though she supposed it wouldn't have done any good anyway. Anger at Jim. Anger at whoever the hell the insurgents were, for bringing the war to Whitesville in the first place. And, anger at herself, for loving Jim—for having doubts and second thoughts about breaking off with him. It had been six days since they'd spoken—six days that she'd been ignoring his texts and Facebook messages, six days that her heart had been slowly breaking.

On Tuesday, she'd gone back to school. It was surreal. There was Dana's absence of course, but on top of that was the crazy outpouring of grief from the student body, including people who barely knew Dana. Everywhere she went girls were crying, and guys were wearing black armbands. She didn't know what that was about, until someone told her that Jesse had organized it. The armbands were supposed to show solidarity with both Dana and the rebellion. As if Dana had cared about the rebels and the fighting one way or another.

Few of the students would speak to her. Again thanks to Jesse, who had wasted no time spreading the rumor that Rebecca's boyfriend had killed Dana.

There they were grieving, throwing fits, crying in the hall-way, leaving flowers at Dana's locker, all the while shunning and isolating Dana's best friend.

They could all go to hell as far as Rebecca was concerned.

She stared in the mirror and saw nothing there but exhaustion.

Finally, she squared her shoulders and walked downstairs. No point in any further delay. Her parents would be ready soon enough, and they would go to the funeral. The wake afterward would be hosted by her parents since the Wilders no longer had a home. Life would go on, and she had no clue what that meant.

ↄↄ

At 0900 hours, Lieutenant Blake, who had been released back to duty the day before, gathered the platoon in a loose formation at the gate. Nowell and Turville were still on guard at the Humvee, but Blake positioned the formation close enough they could hear.

"All right, here's the deal," Blake said. His voice was subdued, exhaustion clear on his face. "The Wilder funeral is going to be held right at the corner this morning. I'm sure you're all aware of the tensions in town since then."

The master of understatement, Turville thought.

"I want everyone on alert, but we're to maintain an extremely low profile. No change in guard positions at the gate, but everyone else is to be in full up gear and ready to go if anything happens. Turville's fire team will stay in place on guard. And I want to make one thing clear: if something happens, no one takes any action without my go-ahead. Am I clear? Even if you get shot at. You take cover, and wait for orders. There's going to be a shitload of pissed-off people at this funeral. We're not going to make it worse."

Turville listened, and for once found himself agreeing one hundred percent with the Lieutenant. He just hoped to God nothing happened.

Rebecca would be at the funeral.

He closed his eyes. He wanted to see her, more than anything else in the world. But he was afraid. She hated him now, and with good reason.

જી

The church parking lot was full, and cars were pulled up to the curb, lining the road in both directions for two hundred yards, except a small gap in front of the army barracks. Bob Mays started muttering as soon as he realized they were going to have to walk in.

"I'm supposed to be speaking," he said, "They should have saved a parking space."

Zoe patted his hand, her voice a little condescending as she said, "I'm sure they've got a lot on their minds, Bob," then she went back to doing her makeup in the vanity mirror.

Rebecca ignored them, her eyes riveted on the Humvee parked in front of the army barracks. Jim was manning the machine gun on the roof of the Humvee. She could feel his eyes following them as they drove by, then turned around and drove back out to find a parking spot. It felt like she was under a searchlight, she couldn't escape. Worse, they'd be walking back that way. For the thousandth time that day, she wanted to cry.

Zoe met her eyes in the vanity mirror. "You hanging in there, Becca?"

Rebecca nodded, afraid to speak out loud. How was she supposed to answer that? How was she supposed to get through this morning in one piece? She wanted to ask if they could go around the back alleys of River Street to get to the church. She wanted to go home. She wanted to scream. She wanted to go to Turville and hit him in the face. She wanted Turville to hold her. She wanted to hear his voice telling her that everything would be okay.

～

Jim Turville watched as the Mays's turned their car around and drove two hundred yards down the street looking for a parking spot. They finally stopped just on the edge of downtown, in front of the Whitesville Motel, a two-story, ramshackle structure that looked as if it had been built during a much more prosperous time in this tiny town.

In the distance, they got out of the vehicle, all of them dressed predictably in black. Rebecca wore a severe black dress, her hair tied back in a bun. They started walking toward the church—toward him. He tried to take his eyes off of her, but couldn't. As she got closer, he could see she was almost clumped over, shoulders hunched forward, her head down, grief overpowering her. Dark circles under her eyes showed she hadn't been sleeping.

More than anything else in the world, Turville wanted to abandon his position and go to her. He wanted to say he was sorry. He wanted to take her in his arms and tell her that she was his world, that he loved her—that he'd do anything in the world to protect her and make her happy.

But she didn't want him. She didn't want to hear from him, she didn't want to see him. She carefully kept her eyes averted, looking everywhere but directly at him. She was breaking his heart.

❧

The walk took forever, as if they were walking five miles in front of Jim, instead of two hundred yards. She struggled to keep her eyes away from him, knowing that his were following her every step. She couldn't breathe.

Rebecca was shaking when they finally entered the church. Tears started to flow again, unbidden.

The church was packed more tightly than she'd ever seen it. Whitesville had barely four hundred residents, and it looked like every single one of them was jammed into the room. They were crowded into the pews, standing and packed into the aisles on both sides and behind them. The heat was suffocating. Someone near her had powerful body odor, and she found herself gulping air through her mouth. Way at the front of the room, she could see the Wilders. Mrs. Wilder was crying, her face buried in her husband's shoulder.

Many of the men she saw, especially the younger ones, wore black armbands.

Oh, God. They were turning Dana into some kind of martyr for the war. They were turning her friend into something she wasn't.

Rebecca found herself shaking with anger. They were using her. They didn't care about Dana. They cared about their stupid politics and their stupid war. They were going to use Dana's death to create a hundred more tragedies, a hundred more deaths, a hundred more widows and grieving mothers. They were wrong. And she had no idea what to do about it.

The crowd stirred, then silenced as Reverend Franks took to the pulpit.

Franks, who usually wore pale blue or grey suits, was today in unrelieved black, as was virtually everyone in and around the pews. His face looked strained, washed out, with deep hollows for eyes and thinning hair that was unusually windblown. It looked as if he'd spent precious little time sleeping in the last five days, which might well be the case.

Rebecca found herself unconsciously holding her breath, nervous and afraid. She'd seen the tension in town, the graffiti across from the barracks. She'd seen the whispers of young men wearing black armbands.

It wouldn't take much to set the town on a path of vengeance.

And with that realization, something else washed over her. She thought about Jesús Santiago, and his wife and children. Rebecca felt warmed by her newfound friendship with him, and was a little in awe of his determination to provide a new home for his family. She thought about Phil Nowell, the smart-ass country boy from Arkansas, who had promised her they'd do all they could to keep Jim safe. She thought about Karim Tilman, and the dream he'd described of going home to Detroit to work on building a better community. Above all, she thought about Jim, who had saved her life, who had opened up to her, who had shown her courage and vulnerability.

Dana was dead, yes, but she couldn't blame them. She couldn't hate them. And no matter how hard she tried, she was never going to stop loving Jim Turville. In just a few short weeks, he had become her life.

She would grieve for Dana. But she wouldn't let Dana's death be a cause for more hate.

The question now, though—would he ever forgive her, after she'd unceremoniously dumped him via text message, likely at the time when he needed her the most?

A wave of whispers swept across the church as Franks began to speak. Rebecca listened with half an ear. Platitudes, she thought. God's ways are mysterious. Come to a place of stillness with your grief. Celebrate Dana's life. Blah. Blah. Blah.

If it had been up to her, the memorial service would be held at Dana's favorite place: Forever 21 at the Charleston Mall. Dana would have spent her last dime there if she'd known she was going to die. After the service, they'd move across the mall to the diner and force everyone to suffer through double-chocolate fudge shakes while listening to bad fifties rock.

Her fantasy of Dana's ideal funeral was interrupted though, when Franks shifted to a new topic, one that was far less welcome. Muttering began in the audience. It started out quietly among just a few people, but quickly grew in volume as the townspeople listened to the direction from their pastor.

"Even as we deal with our grief, however, we must address our response to this tragedy. Many of you, whom I've spoken with in recent days, have called for vengeance, and justice. And let there be no doubt that there is no justice in the offer of cash compensation to the Wilders, who cannot be bought off for the loss of their beloved daughter with thirty pieces of silver. But let me remind you of the words of our Lord Jesus Christ, who tells us, 'Dear friends, never take revenge. Leave that to the righteous anger of God. For the Scriptures say, I will take revenge. I will pay them back, says the Lord.' Let me remind you that, though our hearts cry out in anguish at the loss of our loved one, further conflict will not bring her back."

As Franks spoke, Rebecca looked around the room. Expressions in the congregation ranged from bafflement to outrage. Her eyes met Jesse's across the room: Jesse wore a black armband like most of the high school senior boys. He gave her a look of disgust and looked away.

Near the front, her Uncle Joe had ceased any pretense of courtesy; he was whispering urgently into a cell phone. Murmurs rose across the room as Franks continued.

"Jesus's words echoed those of the prophets who came before him. Leviticus commands us, 'Do not seek revenge or bear a grudge against one of your people, but love your neighbor as yourself. I am the Lord.' And so, I implore you, as Jesus himself did: do not take it upon yourself to seek vengeance upon the soldiers who brought this harm onto our community. It is ours to live as our Lord did: to love our enemy, to learn to forgive. To do unto others as we would have done unto ourselves. Let us pray."

Even as he said the words, Rebecca knew he'd lost the room. She tilted her head, but watched. Few of the men in the room bowed their heads as Franks began to speak the words of his prayer.

"Dear Lord, today we beseech you to help heal the hearts of the Wilder family, who have lost such an important loved one in this terribly tragedy. We ask you to lighten their load, to bring the love of your Son, the Lord Jesus Christ, into the hearts of all the men and women of Whitesville who have suffered this grievous loss. We pray to you on behalf of the soldiers, who know not what they have done...."

"No!" The interruption was a tortured cry from John Wilder.

Franks stopped his prayer at the cry, looked up, and met Wilder's eyes. He continued, "Lord, we pray to you to bring the joy of your light back into the lives of John and Linda Wilder—"

"Stop!" Wilder cried out. "I'll not pray for the bastards who took my daughter!"

An angry rumble rippled through the crowd, and Rebecca shrank against her mother.

"It's their fault!" Wilder cried out. "They didn't have to drop a fucking bomb on my home! They didn't have to—to—they ...." He broke down into sobs, a terrible, animal sound as he pulled his wife Linda into an embrace and hid his face from the congregation.

A familiar voice—her Uncle's—carried clear across the entire congregation, "I'm not listening to any more of this pacifist bullshit."

Uncle Joe got up, and under the eyes of the entire congregation, walked out. He slammed the front door of the sanctuary behind him.

The sound of the door seemed like a signal to the rest of the congregation. Many men stood. Arguments broke out between husbands and wives, fathers and daughters, and as the clamor rose, no one but Rebecca noticed Reverend Franks sink first to his knees, then prostrate at the altar.

ဢ

"They're coming out," Turville said into his radio. "Everyone stay alert."

The first person out the door was Rebecca's uncle, Joe Blankenship. He was talking into a cell phone. He was moving quickly as he spoke on the phone, and nearly stumbled on the curb. he walked purposefully to an ancient pickup and drove away at the head of the crowd. Turville tensed. Blankenship was usually deliberate and precise. Something was wrong.

He was followed by ten, then twenty people, mostly young men wearing black armbands. He and the other soldiers had seen them around town all week, primarily on the arms of boys glaring at the troops.

He looked up at Nowell, who was now crouched in the turret ring of the Humvee. The first group of men—many of them teenagers—approached the barracks.

Turville keyed his radio. "Everybody stay calm—weapons on safe. You heard the lieutenant—no confrontation."

As the group neared, Turville realized how young many of them were. Mostly high school. He recognized Jesse Turner, Rebecca's ex, among them.

Keeping his weapon lowered took all the restraint he had. The gate was closed and locked, he reminded himself. They weren't coming over a fifteen-foot fence and the gate was closed and padlocked.

"Time to go, lover-boy." called out Jesse. "Time for you all to find somewhere else to go. Get out of our town!"

"Get the hell out!" shouted one of the others. About ten of them took it up as a chant, shouting, "Get the hell out!" over and over.

Turville kept his face impassive even as he listened with one ear to the lieutenant's frantic reports over the radio. It wasn't time to panic yet. These kids were hotheads, but they weren't suicidal. Nor were they the enemy. Turville reminded himself that if the shoe were on the other foot, he'd probably respond much the same way.

Then his eyes fixed on the church door. Rebecca and her family were coming out. Her eyes were red. But she looked at him and held his eyes. Then she mouthed two words that pierced his heart and almost made him cry, too.

The words she mouthed were, "I'm sorry."

A rush of hope and fear and love, all muddled together, ran through Turville as his eyes followed her.

Rebecca and her mother were jostled aside by more of the crowd emerging from the church. There were at least fifty, maybe seventy-five people in the street. Bob Mays trotted across the street and began remonstrating with the teenagers, telling them to move on.

Turville froze at the sound of the high-powered rifle shot. Behind him, Nowell let out a cry of pain, then screamed, "Fuuuuckkk! Not again!"

Turville glanced back. Nowell was holding his right hand, which was dripping—no, pouring—blood.

The radio exploded to life, shouts of "Take cover! Sniper!" in his ear.

There were screams in the street and the crowd scattered. Another shot rang out, this time hitting a civilian, a woman in a black dress who hit the ground like a hundred-pound sack.

Jesus! They were shooting at the civilians too! His eyes involuntarily jerked to Zoe and Rebecca, standing frozen in the middle of the street.

"Run!" he screamed at them. "They're trying to start a massacre! Get under cover!"

He fumbled with the padlock on the gate, then shouted over the radio, "LT, they're shooting at the civilians!"

Blake instantly gave orders to protect the civilians. First Squad, including Turville's and Meig's fire teams, would get the crowd under cover. Second Squad was to redeploy two hundred yards north, then attempt to find and engage the snipers.

Another civilian—a ten-year-old girl—was shot, her body thrown against the fence. The girl's mother screamed and caught her daughter before she hit the ground.

Turville got the gate open and the platoon deployed immediately. Turville ran to the center of the crowd, where Rebecca and Zoe Mays were, shouting "Get under cover! Go! They're shooting civilians!"

A bullet passed his head so close he felt it. He flinched involuntarily even as he grabbed Rebecca's arm and nearly threw her underneath a Nissan SUV. Then he grabbed Zoe Mays and an old man, shouting at them to take cover behind a vehicle.

That done, Turville gaped at the chaos in the street. Nowell was still crouched in the Humvee, wrapping a gauze bandage around his hand. Two men stood in the open near the gate, shouting at Tilman.

Turville heard a loud crack, and his vision went black for a moment. He stumbled forward, then looked behind him. Jesse Turner stood behind him holding a scrap two-by-four, rage on his face.

He raised the scrap again, and Turville reversed his rifle and slammed the stock directly in his face, knocking him flat. He wouldn't be getting up any time soon.

He scanned the scene again. Lieutenant Blake was out of the barracks now, crouching behind a car next to Bob Mays.

The rattle of multiple machine guns sounded to the north. Second Squad had identified the sniper positions and engaged them. For now, at this end, the fight was over.

But four civilians lay dead in the street, and near them, where he'd been shoving three children underneath a car, was Corporal Meigs. Turville stumbled to Meigs and fell to his knees, his stomach turning. A bullet had hit Meigs just beneath the visor of his helmet on the left side of his face. He'd never had a chance: the entire right side of his head was an exit wound.

Turville looked under the car. The terrified children were huddled under the car, crying. They were not going anywhere.

"Lieutenant, Meigs is KIA. Three kids under the vehicle here."

Blake nodded and spoke into his radio. The shooting was still going on, somewhere up the ridge line, but it seemed like the snipers were plenty busy now. Turville stumbled back across the street. Jesse Turner was still unconscious next to the Nissan SUV, his nose a red pulp. Fuck him. Turville crouched, looked underneath the SUV.

Three pairs of eyes looked out at him, one of them on the face of the woman he loved.

"Everybody okay?" he asked.

"Yes," Rebecca replied, her voice rough.

"Okay. Hang loose for now, there's probably more help on the way. All right? Stay safe."

Nguyen's voice boomed. "First squad, fall in on me! Now!"

Turville gave a last glance to Rebecca.

"I love you," he whispered, then ran to his squad leader.

❧

Rebecca stared out at the carnage, shock and terror warring in her mind. But her heart was fixed on one thing: For the second time since they'd met, Jim Turville had risked his life to protect her.

"Rebecca," her mother said.

"Yes, Mom?"

"I see now. Why you love him."

Rebecca nodded, then burst into tears. All she could see was Jim out there, getting shot at while helping other people get to safety. He never took a second to protect himself. He never paused, never ducked behind cover, never did anything but invite the snipers to kill him while he was making sure everyone else was safe.

He was crazy. He was looking for redemption for killing Logan Jefferson, and he wouldn't stop until it killed him. And the worst part was, she loved him so much, she was going to end up losing him.

She looked at her mother and tried to stop up the unending steam of tears rolling from her eyes.

"Do you see why I'm so scared?"

THIRTY-TWO

"That's two times, now. You're having more close calls than I want to think about," said Specialist Morgan, the platoon's medic, as he finished rewrapping Nowell's dressings.

Nowell shrugged and gave a lopsided grin.

"Two Purple Hearts," he said. "I am so getting laid when this is all over."

Santiago burst into laughter.

Turville leaned close and looked at the dressings, then said in a low voice, "You sure he shouldn't be evacuated?"

Morgan nodded. "Yeah, I'm sure. Nowell's one lucky bastard. Barely grazed the back of his hand. No bones broken, no serious tissue damage. Gonna hurt like a son of a bitch, though. Keep taking the painkillers, Nowell."

Nowell said, "Can I get some unlicensed painkillers? Little bit of Jack Daniels ought to do the job."

"Don't think so," Morgan replied. "Actually, if you drink while taking this stuff, it might kill you."

"Holy shit," Nowell said. "You suck, Morgan."

Morgan rolled his eyes, then stood, "See you guys later. I gotta head out to the TCP; Leo got a nasty knock on the head earlier."

Turville said, "Is he taking over the fire team?"

"Yeah, that's what I hear. That's fucked about Meigs."

Turville grunted. "Yeah."

He couldn't get his mind around Meigs's death. They'd finally established a truce while on dam guard duty together. Might even have ended up as friends, or at least respectful of each other. No more.

"Turville!"

The shout came from Sergeant Nguyen, out in the common room.

"On the way, Sarge."

Turville stood and walked into the main room.

Rebecca was standing in the doorway.

Turville felt his breath shorten and a sudden anxious pain in his chest. They hadn't spoken in a week, other than those few short, hasty words a little while ago. She looked hesitant, anxious, her hands wringing each other.

Nguyen looked back and forth between the two of them. "You got thirty minutes, Turville. Stay inside the fence line. Some of the locals are pretty fucking pissed at this point."

"Roger, Sarge," Turville responded, his voice low.

He approached Rebecca, feeling like he was underwater.

"Outside?" she asked, quietly.

He nodded, afraid to speak. They walked out to the side of the building together. Turville led her away from the one working streetlight. A couple of old milk crates sat against the building here, out of sight of the street. He set them three feet apart, then sat down on one. She sat across from him.

"I've missed you," he said.

Damn it, Jim. Just shut up. Let her say her piece, whatever it is.

"I... I came to apologize," she said.

He closed his eyes. "You don't have anything to apologize for, Rebecca. I don't blame you at all for reacting the way you did."

"Maybe I blame myself," she said.

"I don't understand."

"I didn't give you a chance. I don't even know what happened out there, and I didn't give you a chance to even say anything."

He shrugged. "You would have, eventually."

"Are you trying to get yourself killed?"

"What?" He was incredulous, both at the sudden subject change, and at the words.

"Today… you never… never did anything to protect yourself. It was all about everyone else— me, my mom, the other people out there. You could have been shot."

"Meigs was shot. And killed."

"Oh, God," she said. "I'm so sorry."

"Some of your neighbors, too."

She nodded. "I know," she said, her voice breaking.

"Rebecca… I just… that's my job, okay? How would I forgive myself if someone innocent died because of… well… Jesus, you know what happened last fall."

"Getting yourself killed now won't bring Logan Jefferson back to life."

God damn it! He blinked and looked away from her. "I know that, Rebecca. But I can't stop doing what I'm supposed to do. It's not like a job you can just walk away from, you know? I'm a soldier. At least for now."

"I know," she whispered. "And I'm so afraid for you. I'm so afraid I'm going to lose you."

He took a deep breath. She was afraid she was going to lose him? She'd broken up with him! It didn't make any sense.

He looked into her eyes. She looked scared. He was terrified he was going to say the wrong thing. But more than anything else in the world, he wanted to reach out and touch her. He'd missed her so much.

He took a deep breath. "You broke up with me," he said very slowly. "You said you didn't want to hear from me ever again."

"I was wrong."

"I can't promise you that nothing will ever happen to me. You know how things are. And they aren't getting better any time soon."

She sniffled, then said, "I'm so tired of crying."

Turville had to blink; seeing her in pain made him want to scream. His own eyes watered as he spoke again.

"I can't promise to stop that, either. I might end up being sent to some country halfway across the world. I might end up crippled or dead. I… I might end up breaking your heart."

She looked him in the eye, eyebrows raised anxiously, then reached out to touch his hands.

"So what can you promise?" she whispered.

He felt himself tense up, afraid to say it, afraid not to say it. Finally he opened his mouth. "I can promise to love you. As long as you'll have me."

A tear rolled down her face. "I love you, Jim."

He reached for her, done thinking and talking. Holding her in his arms, he looked her in the eyes. "I don't want to lose you again, Rebecca. It felt like… it felt like there was no point in living."

He leaned close and kissed the tear track that had run down her face.

She sucked in a breath, then turned her face toward his and their lips met.

༄

Rebecca Mays took the steps up to her front porch at a slow, dreamy pace, a tiny smile on her face. At the top, she turned around, looked back up the valley. She swayed a little put her hands up across her chest to grip the opposite arm, as if by doing so she could contain the warmth that flooded through her.

"Good night, Jim."

Dana was still dead, and that hurt worse than anything she'd ever felt in her life. Except one thing. Losing Dana and Jim at the same time.

When she opened the door and walked inside, she couldn't stop smiling. She closed the door, stood en pointe, and spun. The second time around, she saw her parents sitting separately in the living room, and she stopped, her face flushed.

Zoe Mays gave Rebecca a smile. "I take it that... things went well?"

Rebecca wrapped her arms around herself again and bounced on her feet a little. She nodded, a quick bounce.

Bob Mays frowned, his face tense.

Rebecca swooped into the room and sat down on the cushioned chair next to her mother.

Zoe gave her husband an odd look, then took her hand and said, "I'm very happy for you, Rebecca." She leaned toward her daughter, than said in a stage whisper, "Okay, tell me everything."

Rebecca giggled. "Mom, I ..."

Her father interrupted them. "I don't think you should see him anymore, Rebecca."

Rebecca gasped, looked across at her father. "What?"

Bob looked uncomfortable, his face tight. "You heard me, Rebecca. I don't want you to see Corporal Turville anymore."

Before Rebecca could answer, Zoe turned to her husband and said in a low, tense voice, "And when were you planning to share this with me, Bob?"

He looked at the floor. "We need to stop this before it becomes too serious."

Zoe replied, "It's a little late for that."

Rebecca looked at her father. She could feel heat on her face. "Daddy, why?"

Her father struggled to answer. "I don't trust him. He's dangerous. And you saw what happened this morning."

Rebecca felt her eyes watering and she struggled to hold them back. "You can't do this. Not now," she whispered.

Bob stood up and said, "I'm afraid I can. I forbid you to see him anymore, Rebecca. Don't cross me on this."

Zoe gasped. "She just reconciled with him, Bob!"

Rebecca stood, fists clenched at her side, and faced her father. "Give me a reason! A real one!"

Bob confronted her directly, ignoring the shocked look on his wife's face. "I've given you all the reason you need. I'm your father, and I forbid you from seeing that man. Now go to your room!"

She lost control of her tears. They streamed down her face in a flood, threatening to drown her. She could feel her face contort as she stood facing him, fists clenched at her sides.

"Why? Dad, why? Do you hate me? You don't want me to be happy?"

Bob took a step back, looking confused. "Of course I do, Rebecca."

Zoe stood. "You've got a strange way of showing it. I want no more discussion of this now. Rebecca, your father and I need to talk."

"No!" Bob shouted. "There's nothing to discuss. She's not seeing him again!"

At that moment, Rebecca hated her father. Hated him for taking away her warm, lovely feelings and replacing them with desolation with an unreasoning shout.

"You can't stop me. I'm eighteen years old. I'll date whoever I want."

"Not as long as you live under my roof!"

"There's plenty of other places to live!" she said, finally raising her voice.

"Stop it! Both of you, stop it!" Zoe shouted.

Rebecca stared at her parents, her heart broken, then turned and ran upstairs. She wasn't going to convince her father of anything. If she wanted to solve this problem, she was going to have to do it on her own. She slammed and locked her door, then threw herself on her bed and finally broke down and wept.

THIRTY-THREE

REBECCA Mays stared at the ceiling in her room. It was washed with color from the sunrise: deep purples and blues. Outside, she could hear the sounds of morning: birds chirping their morning songs as if there wasn't a thing in the world to worry about.

Rebecca felt drained. She'd cried herself to sleep, again, ignoring her parents when they'd come upstairs and knocked on the locked door, covering her head with a pillow and shutting out the world. Now she was just raw, exhausted. It seemed as if she'd shed more tears in the last week than in her entire life previously.

A car door shut outside, and she heard the sound of her father's car starting, then driving away.

She rolled onto her side and stared away from the steadily brightening window. She hugged her arms tight around her chest, but found that she was all out of tears. Closing her eyes, she pictured Jim and tried to picture her father's stupid ultimatum just vanishing. But the longer she lay there, the less she could ignore the fact that it wasn't just heartbreak she was feeling. It was anger. Anger that her father had practically tripped over himself encouraging her relationship with Jim, then reversed himself with no warning. And even more, anger that he'd refused to give her any kind of explanation.

Had Uncle Joe said something to him? What did he know, or think he knew? Was it all about the shooting yesterday?

For the first time in her life, Rebecca began to wonder if her father was just a coward.

She sighed. It didn't matter what her father thought. What mattered was simple: What was she going to do about it?

At that thought, she dragged herself out of bed and made her way to the shower. She wasn't going to accomplish much of anything lying in bed crying about it.

She showered, then dressed. Instead of the relaxed sweats she might have worn around the house, she took exceptional care with her hair and put on a conservative dress with low-heeled pumps. She had a pretty clear idea where she was going, but it didn't hurt to make the right impression. Her bag was already packed with several changes of clothes, her ebook reader, and some other essentials.

Downstairs, she set her bag at the front door, then walked into the kitchen.

Her mother looked up from her book and raised her eyebrows. "You look nice this morning."

"Thank you," Rebecca said, her expression guarded.

"Are you feeling better?" her mother's voice was cautious.

Rebecca met her mother's eyes, then went to the coffee pot and poured herself a cup. Did she honestly think it was that simple? Cry, go to sleep, make it all better?

"I'm not a child, Mother, and this isn't a scraped knee."

Zoe Mays gave her a wry smile. "I know you aren't, Rebecca."

"It seems Dad hasn't figured that out, though."

"Rebecca..."

"Seriously, Mom. Tell me the truth. Is there anything even slightly reasonable about Dad's actions? Am I missing some piece of the picture that will make it all make sense?"

Zoe sat, her face tight, unable to answer.

Rebecca let the silence stretch a few seconds, then said, "You know I'm right; you know he's being unreasonable, but you're going to take his side, as always. Tell me I'm wrong."

A flash of irritation crossed Zoe's face. "Well, since you're so smart and experienced, it sounds like you've got it all sorted out."

Rebecca sighed. "Mom, don't be upset. I know this isn't your fault. I'm just..." She trailed off, unable to demonstrate the longing, sadness and anger that roiled in her guts.

Zoe looked at the floor, then spoke, her tone miserable.

"I'll speak with your father about it when he gets home."

Rebecca nearly whispered, "Thank you, Mom."

She stood and walked to the front door, opened it and looked back, then picked up her bag. Quietly, but just loud enough for her mother to hear, she said, "I'll be back to pick up the rest of my things later."

She closed the door behind her and got into the truck in a hurry. Please God, she thought. Let it actually start this time. She turned the ignition and closed her eyes in relief when the engine turned over. She put the truck in gear and drove away just as her mother came running out of the house.

⁂

The house had been abandoned many years before, given over to the woods of an equally abandoned hollow where the coalmine had long since been tapped out. It was just over the border in Kentucky.

It was already dark when Joe Blankenship pulled his truck to a stop in front of the house. Two other vehicles were there. Joe got out of the car slowly, knowing that he was probably being watched. He scanned the area, then slowly approached the house.

The voice he was expecting spoke. "Hands up."

Joe stopped and raised his hands in the air.

"I'm expected," he said. "Joe Blankenship."

He heard footsteps behind him, then a young man in his twenties appeared, holding a rifle. The man took a picture out and compared it to Joe's face. Then he nodded. "Go on in. Reverend Channing is expecting you."

Joe nodded. He walked to the front door, stepping up the three wooden steps to the small front porch. The wood of the steps was spongy, almost fully rotted through. He walked carefully to the door, knocked once and opened it.

Inside, Reverend Channing was standing, talking with a tall man in a suit and tie. Joe felt a twinge of distaste. Channing had put him on edge, especially with the increasing toll on civilians in the fighting. And the suit? Probably a fed, or worse. The room they stood in was a dump: an old rotting couch, a few chairs, and an ancient RCA television with a busted picture tube. This place hadn't been occupied in many years.

Channing smiled. "Joe, it's a pleasure to see you."

Joe grunted. "We need to talk."

"Of course, of course. I got your message. You seemed upset."

Joe's eyes darted to the man in the suit, then raised his eyebrows.

Channing smiled. "Joe, this is a good friend of our movement. Anything you can say to me, you can say to him. JD, this is Joe Blankenship. He's our tactical commander. Joe, this is JD Roberts. JD is... let's say he is well placed to assist us, and has before in many things."

Joe nodded. "All right, then. What the fuck happened in Whitesville?"

Channing winced. "Joe, I realize you aren't a believer, but it's not necessary for you to use that kind of language with me."

"They were shooting at the civilians. Killing townspeople. And it's not the first time. Bunch of innocent people were killed up in Morgantown this week, too. When did we become the bad guys?"

Channing frowned at Joe. "Joe. Listen to me. I understand your feelings, and I share them. But you need to look at the big picture."

"I am, Channing. The big picture is we're trying to get the damn feds out of West Virginia. How did this help that? It doesn't make any sense."

Channing turned to Roberts, and said, "JD, perhaps you can explain it."

Roberts snorted, then said, "The big picture isn't just West Virginia. The big picture is all of America."

Joe shook his head. "I don't get it."

"Sometimes you have to make hard decisions, Blankenship. Have a seat, and let me give you a picture of where we're headed. I've been wanting to meet you ever since you and Reverend Channing started to work together."

Roberts walked over to one of the dilapidated chairs and sat. He waited until Channing and Joe sat, then said, "Tell me a little about why you're involved in all this, Joe."

Joe shrugged. "The feds killed my wife. I'm in this because the government is fucking out of control."

"I happen to agree with you," Roberts said. "I'm focused on returning our nation to its roots. To the Constitution. We were once a Christian nation, but now we've become something else entirely. And as a result, we're failing. We're losing our way. We're giving in to terrorists, we don't have any morals, we … worship drug abusing celebrities and let people just suck off the government and not give anything back."

Did they just not get it? By killing innocents, they were no better than the enemy. They were no better than the feds. What did it matter if they won, if in the process they lost their way?

"What does that have to do with killing civilians?"

"This is a war, Joe, and it is a war I intend to win. I've seen your records, by the way. You were a counterinsurgency specialist. The first step in our success out there in the field is separating the people from the occupying troops. You make them terrified. You destroy the morale of the troops. The people won't accept a radical change until it is too painful for them to do otherwise. You know this. The only reason you're objecting is because it happens to be your hometown."

Joe shifted in his seat, unable to clearly articulate his objections. "It doesn't make it right."

Channing leaned forward and said, "Of course not. But they are martyrs for our cause. If we're going to return to being a Christian nation, we have to take the necessary steps to make it happen."

Joe closed his eyes. What he saw behind those eyes was the house the Army had destroyed. The dead teenage girl inside—his niece's best friend. He'd done to another family exactly what had been done to him: brought down the same grief and horror and bitterness. And there was nothing, absolutely nothing he could do to take it back.

"I'm not happy about this at all. Innocent people are getting killed, Channing. That's not what I signed up for."

Roberts said, "I may have something better you can sink your teeth in to."

Joe looked at him, one eyebrow raised.

"In twelve days, the Vice President will be in Charleston."

Joe sat up straight and listened as Roberts continued. And for the first time since the near massacre in Whitesville, he began to smile.

THIRTY-FOUR

KAREN Greenfield let out a low grunt as she eased the weights down. She could feel sweat running down the side of her face and between her thighs. Enough for today. She sat up, grabbed a towel and wiped the sweat off her face.

The room could charitably be called a gym. Four sets of weights, a climbing rope, other athletic equipment scattered here and there. Two clusters of prisoners, virtually all of them prior enlisted women, bunched in different corners.

Karen was one of the few officers in the facility. Well, former officers. She was the only member of the West Virginia National Guard who had ended up here following the end of the war. The men had largely gone to Leavenworth, but all women prisoners in the Department of Defense ended up here, at the US Navy Consolidated Brig in Miramar, California.

Ironic. Her first time in California, and after three months she'd still not seen the outside.

It could have been worse. She'd been convicted of treason and murder, in a separate trial from General Murphy, but on the same day. He'd gone on to his execution within a week. She still couldn't get her head around that. A gentler, more patriotic man she'd never known.

Enough dwelling on the past. Right now, she needed to get through the rest of the day. That would be challenge enough. She stood, walked across the room to the sink, then splashed cold water across her face and dried it. As she finished toweling off, Staff Sergeant Tamara Johnson stepped into the room. Johnson was one of the supervisors, and not a bad sort. She was an Army MP, and must have felt out of place serving in a naval installation.

"Greenfield," she called.

"Yes, Sergeant," Karen responded.

"Go get a shower. You've got an official visitor coming. Make it quick. I'll escort you."

Karen nodded. "Yes, Sergeant."

Karen followed the lanky sergeant to the showers, pondering this development. What official visitor? Whoever it was had some influence: they didn't make exceptions to visiting hours for anyone, from what she'd seen.

Five minutes later she'd finished her shower and was escorted to a meeting room where prisoners usually met with their attorneys.

Outside the door, Sergeant Johnson stopped and looked at her.

"Straighten your uniform blouse, Prisoner Greenfield."

"Yes, Sergeant."

"All right, Greenfield. You go in, stop at the position of attention three feet away from the table. You know the drill."

Karen nodded. "Yes, Sergeant."

Johnson knocked on the door, and a muffled voice inside said, "Enter." She opened it and waved Karen in.

Karen walked into the room, stopped three feet in front of the table, and practically shouted, "Prisoner Karen Greenfield, Number 454754, reporting as ordered, sir!"

She stood in a perfect position of attention, eyes straight ahead, looking at a point a foot above the man's head. She did not salute. Prisoners weren't entitled to the hand salute.

"Have a seat, Karen, and relax."

Involuntarily her eyes darted to the man's face, and she flushed with shame.

It was Cory Avedis—now a lieutenant colonel. They'd been close friends in college. Cory and her former fiance and lover, Mike Morris, had been roommates.

Blinking back the emotion, she stiffly took a seat across from him. She sat, back ramrod straight, and said nothing.

"Christ," he said, "I never in a million years imagined this moment."

Her eyes dropped to the floor. "Nor did I, Colonel."

"I mean it, Karen. Please relax. For the next little while, pretend I'm the guy you made fun of incessantly when we were college kids, all right? It'll make this easier on both of us."

"Yes, sir," she responded. "But you and I both know that we're not still in college. From the looks of it, you're a battalion commander now, and I'm a federal inmate."

He shook his head. "Still stiff-necked as always. Look, I'm here because I need your help."

Puzzled, she looked up at him. "My help? What could I possibly help you with?"

He slid a tablet across the table to her, turned it on. A photo of Joe Blankenship. Only he looked remarkably different than she remembered. Bearded, a lot older. Haunted.

"Recognize this man?"

"Yes, sir. That's Joe Blankenship. I worked with his wife at the Saturn Plant in Highview. He was a team leader in the irregulars during the war, and enlisted in the National Guard in December, if I remember correctly. Lots of military experience… Iraq, Afghanistan, at least."

Avedis nodded. "That's correct. He enlisted right after September 11, spent ten years in special operations. Counterinsurgency specialist... or he was. Got pretty fucked up during his last tour, took a swipe at a new lieutenant and got thrown out. As I understand it, he was owed some big favors... he got out with an honorable discharge by verbal order of the president."

"Bush?"

"Obama. This was in 2012. Which means Blankenship knew someone in the Pentagon who had enough weight to convince the President to intervene before he was court martialed."

Thoughtfully, she replied, "I didn't know any of that. Mandy... his wife... she worshipped the ground he walked on. Very devout woman... very kind."

"Know where we can find her?"

She looked puzzled. "You don't know?"

Avedis looked impatient. "Would I be asking you if I knew?"

"You can find her in Highview Cemetery. She was killed by agents of the Department of Homeland Security last May. During the raid on the Saturn plant."

Avedis looked stunned. "Holy shit. How did we miss that? Christ, now it all makes sense. And I bet DHS knew, and just didn't bother to tell us! Those sons of bitches!"

"Colonel, what's going on?"

"What's going on is this: on Friday, Joe Blankenship—or a friend of his, uploaded a video to YouTube, where he effectively declared war on the United States all by himself. An hour later, insurgents in West Virginia ambushed four separate Army units and tore them all to shit. They've assassinated several people who cooperated with the federal government, and tried to get more. Do you know Valerie Murphy? She was your General Murphy's daughter. Now she's secretary of Military Affairs and Law Enforcement. They tried to knock her off Friday, and nearly succeeded."

Karen stared at Avedis, stunned. "They tried to kill Valerie? But... Joe knows her. Not well, but still..."

Avedis shrugged. "Apparently now she's the enemy."

"What does this have to do with me?"

Avedis rolled his eyes. "Come on, Karen. You know these people, or at least some of them. You know their relationships, who knows who, who drinks with who. I need your help running them to ground. I need your help stopping this war."

She stared at him. "Aren't I just as suspect? If you listen to DHS, I was the instigator of the whole damned war."

"These people are killing civilians, Karen. They aren't patriots."

"And you think I am?"

He shrugged. "You never gave me any reason to think otherwise. Shootouts with DHS notwithstanding, I totally get why you did what you did. I disagree, strongly. But I get it. I can't see you sanctioning terrorism. You know they blew away a minister right in front of his congregation? Because he was preaching rapprochement with the feds?"

She shuddered. "Jesus."

"Yeah, exactly. Look... I'm going to lay it out plain and simple. I need your help. I want to spring you out of this place and bring you back with me to West Virginia."

"In what capacity?"

"You'll be a regular Army private, Karen. Detailed to military intelligence. You serve two years, and then you're home free. I've got authority to offer a presidential pardon to a limited number of former West Virginia National Guard officers and soldiers."

She gasped. A presidential pardon ... she'd be out of prison. She'd be free.

But at what cost? She'd been a traitor once already. Would this be even worse?

"I... I need to think about it."

He shook his head impatiently. "I don't have time for that. What the hell is there to think about? If you don't accept, you'll be here the rest of your life. In case you hadn't noticed, they aren't offering parole to people who commit treason. And besides, these people are killing civilians. "

She shot back, "Last I saw, so was DHS."

He nodded. "Look, I get that. And I can tell you, if nothing else, your little war raised one hell of a shockwave through Washington. But this is different, and you know it."

She sighed. He was right, of course. She couldn't support any kind of insurgency that targeted civilians, nor would Ken Murphy have ever approved of such a thing.

"All right, Colonel. I'm in."

☙

Karen Greenfield was stunned by the speed at which things moved. Within three hours of the completion of her meeting with Cory Avedis, her few things had been packed and she was in the prison headquarters office, signing enlistment papers. A former tank company commander and one of only half a dozen women officers in the combat arms of the US Army, she was now Private Greenfield, primary specialty Military Intelligence. That was a damn site better than being a prisoner

The papers were clear enough. Her enlistment was for two years, but could be extended for the convenience of the government, as always. If she completed her enlistment successfully, she'd receive a presidential pardon. If not... back to prison, for the rest of her life.

An official car and driver transported her and Lieutenant Colonel Avedis to the airbase, where they boarded a small turboprop bound for Charleston. As soon as the plane hit cruising altitude, Avedis passed her a tablet.

"Here's all we have on Blankenship and his confederates. Your first assignment is to fill in as many details as you can, starting with the fact that DHS killed his wife. They're holding out on us, and I don't like it."

"Yes, sir. May I ask a few questions? Not necessarily related to the case?"

Avedis looked at her, nodded quickly.

"When we get to West Virginia, where will I be assigned? What do the next few days look like?"

"For now, you'll be reporting to me, assigned to Headquarters company of my battalion. Later on, we'll—we'll figure out something."

"Okay," she said. "Where is your headquarters?"

"Morgantown. Used to be second brigade headquarters of the National Guard."

Karen swallowed. She'd spent what seemed like months in that building during the standoff between the federal government and the state. Right after her shootout with the DHS. Right after she saw Mike Morris for the first time in years.

Before she could stop herself, she asked the question. "Um... have you heard from Mike?"

Avedis glanced at her. "Morris?" He raised an eyebrow. "I didn't realize you guys were..."

"We sort of ran into each other in Charleston last fall."

He nodded. "I remember. There was some media, if I remember correctly? Yeah, he's been assigned to Third Infantry Division. They're deployed in Madison, Wisconsin right now. Riot duty."

She nodded. "Ugly duty," she said.

"Yeah... almost as ugly as West Virginia."

She looked out the window at the countryside flowing below them. It looked so peaceful from twenty-thousand feet...

hard to believe that country below them, so beautiful from so high up, was fracturing.

"If you want to send me back to prison, Colonel, I would understand. But I have to tell you, I have a lot of doubts about what we're going to be doing."

Avedis was silent for a while, then said quietly, "That's part of what made you such a good officer, Karen. Nothing is black and white. That's also why you can't go back."

She nodded without reply and began reading the files.

စာ

Rebecca Mays parked her truck facing downhill, just above the Highview Motel. If the battery was dead again when she came back, she'd be able to roll it down and pop the clutch to get going again, if she had to.

She got out of the truck and was struck again by how incongruous this beautiful late spring day was. The sky was perfectly clear, and she could hear birds singing in the woods. Her feet crunched in the gravel as she walked down the hill. It felt peaceful, but she was anything but peaceful. She was still seething with anger at her father, thoughts which kept circling over and over again to his angry ultimatum the night before.

Her father was a reasonable man. He always had been. Measured, calm, thoughtful. He'd always been the one to take the time to talk things out and come to a consensus.

That's why it made no sense at all, the way he had behaved the night before. After returning home from finally reconciling with Jim, he'd given a flat directive: she wasn't to see Jim anymore, under any circumstances.

Her father had also taught her that no situation couldn't be fixed. He'd taught her, verbally and by example, that she could overcome challenges of any kind. And that was why—faced with this challenge—she'd come up with her own solution. A solution that didn't involve her knuckling under to his stupid demands.

As she crossed the street toward the hotel, she glanced three blocks down, to the small Army compound. Two soldiers were on duty at the gate, perhaps looked like Santiago and Tilman. She waved, not knowing whether they would see her, and then walked up to the office of the ramshackle motel and rang the bell. A few moments later, her Aunt Leah entered the office from the adjoining room and smiled.

"Rebecca! Your mother told me you might end up dropping by!" Leah walked over and embraced her.

"She did?" Rebecca asked, stiffening. If her mother had called ahead, that meant she realized Rebecca was planning to leave home. What was she going to do now? She'd been sure Leah would take her in and maybe allow her to work at the motel in exchange for room and board.

Leah nodded. "Yes. Why don't you come tell me about it."

Rebecca took a deep breath, then nodded quickly. She followed Leah around the counter and into the back office. It was organized chaos: papers everywhere, the back wall stacked with linens, a profusion of coffee cups, stacked rolls of toilet tissue and paper towels, and other items.

Leah pulled out a chair for Rebecca next to a crowded desk, then turned her own chair to face her.

She sat down.

"Tell me the problem, dear," Leah said.

In halting words from the beginning, the words started to flow as she described her first meeting with Jim Turville, then their first dates, their emails back and forth, their phone calls. She talked about how he made her feel safe, how she laughed when she was with him. When she talked about her father's demand that she stop seeing Jim, her fists clenched at her sides.

"I'm not going back home," she said. "He told me as long as I lived under his roof, I couldn't see Jim. So that's that. I won't live under his roof."

Leah gave her a compassionate smile. "Are you sure running away is the right thing to do? It seems... drastic."

"I'm an adult, Leah. It's not running away at this point. It's solving a problem."

Leah nodded, but her expression was skeptical.

Rebecca hesitated, suddenly afraid Leah would say no, then plunged ahead. "I came to ask you for help. Or... more specifically, to ask for a job."

Leah raised her eyebrows.

"I'll do anything—clean the rooms, clean toilets, whatever you need. I'm good with tools, too. All I ask is room and board—you don't have to pay me if you don't want to."

Leah looked thoughtful. "It's true, I don't have a lot of money to pay you. But rooms I have, and all of them empty. I assume you'll need to work around your school hours."

Rebecca nodded, feeling a rush of relief. "Yes, ma'am... I usually get home around 3:30. I've got rehearsals two nights a week and on Saturday mornings, too. But if necessary, I can drop—"

"Don't even say it. You'll stay in your show, that's too important to drop. But yes, you can stay. And yes, I'll put you to work."

Rebecca closed her eyes, and said, "Thank you. Thank you so much."

"I have some ground rules, however."

"Okay."

"Your boyfriend can't stay in the room. Ever. I don't allow that sort of thing in my motel."

"Of course not."

"And you'll have to stay in school no matter what. I want you here in the office, finishing your homework, every night. Once that's done, you can do the work you'll have. It's not a lot—we've got few enough guests, except occasionally on the weekends. I don't even know why I keep this old place open."

Rebecca closed her eyes, flooded with relief. "Thank you."

"You might not thank me after a weekend of cleaning up this old place."

An hour later, she was settled in the room closest to the office. It was small, with a twin bed and a tiny desk. The threadbare carpet smelled of mildew, and the showerhead was rusty, with virtually no water pressure. As she arranged her toiletries in the bathroom, she thought it most closely resembled a gas station bathroom, except for the addition of the tiny shower.

But for now, it was hers.

Finally, she took out her phone and stared at it. Leah would have called her, but she owed it to her mother to tell her first hand. How do you call your mother and say you aren't coming home? How do you tell that person their husband's bullheaded decision had driven off your only daughter?

Her mother would be heartbroken, but her decision was made. She wasn't going back. Not until and unless her father saw reason.

Enough. She was spending too much time worrying about it without actually doing it. She dialed.

"Hello?"

"Mom? I'm calling... I'm calling to tell you that I'm going to work for Aunt Leah. At the motel."

She heard her mother exhale, as if she were expecting the call.

"Mom, I'm going to stay here. I'm not coming home."

She heard her mother sniffle, and realized that her mother had been crying. Before she could stop herself, tears ran down her face. Damn it! She hadn't intended to get emotional during this conversation.

Her mother replied, slowly. "I know, Rebecca. I had already called Leah and told her you'd probably show up there. I'm sorry."

"Mom, it's not because of you."

"I know that. I just... Rebecca, I don't know what to do here."

The words were like a blow, because her mother always knew what to do. Whether it was a scraped knee, an injured ankle from practice, a cutting blow from the other girls at school—her mother had always been there, always able to help. She always knew the words to make everything better.

But there wasn't any making this situation better.

She finally responded. "There isn't anything you can do, Mom. I'm sorry."

Her mom sighed at the other end of the line, then said, "You just be careful, young lady. We'll sort this out soon enough. Do what your Aunt Leah tells you, and call me tomorrow."

Rebecca sniffled, then said, "I will."

∾

"Okay," Turville said. "Let's start over."

Nowell rolled his eyes. "How many times are we going to do this?"

"As many as it takes to get it right, Nowell."

For the last two hours, they'd been going over parts of the "Common Tasks Manual," a set of basic tasks every soldier was supposed to know. It was boring, repetitive, and necessary. The current task was one of the most basic: evaluate a casualty.

"This is bullshit," Nowell said. "They're just trying to keep us busy."

Turville shrugged. "Whatever. For right now, it's our job. I know this is basic stuff, but seriously, you think you don't need to practice this?"

"Whatever. Let's get on with it."

"All right. Santiago, you're our casualty. Nowell, walk us through it."

Santiago grinned, then sprawled out on the floor.

Nowell approached Santiago. "All right, first step, approach the casualty, and kick him in the side."

"Nowell, shut the fuck up and get on with it," Tilman said, sounding angry. "You better take this shit seriously. It's not like we haven't had plenty of guys hurt lately."

"Yeah, I'm one of 'em, asshole."

"Guys," Turville said. "Chill."

Nowell sighed. "All right. I approach the casualty, get a first impression of his injuries. Check for responsiveness. Ask him if he is okay. Does he respond?"

"No," Turville replies.

"Okay. Tilt his head to open the airway. Check for breathing and chest injuries."

Turville nodded, then looked up at a yell from down the hall.

"Turville! Get your ass in here!" It was Sergeant Nguyen.

"Continue, Nowell. I'll be back."

Turville turned and walked down the hall, entering the small office. Inside, Blake sat behind the desk, scowling. Sergeant Nguyen stood to the side, his arms crossed over his chest. Blake looked exhausted, slumped in his chair. Though his injury the week before had been superficial, he still moved slowly, painfully.

"Yes, sir?" Turville said.

Both men stared at Turville for an uncomfortably long interval. Finally, Blake spoke.

"Turville, when was the last time you saw the mayor's daughter?"

"Last night, sir. After the funeral."

"You want to tell me what the fuck happened?"

What the hell? Turville was confused, and he blurted out an answer. "We talked, sir. That's it."

"Then why the hell did her father just show up here, all pissed off?"

"I have no idea, sir. We haven't had a chance to talk since."

"Turville," interjected Sergeant Nguyen. "You are in potentially deep shit here, now. We need to know what is going on."

"Sergeant, I have no clue. What did Mr. Mays say?"

"He said to keep you the hell away from his daughter. He was very clear, and very angry."

Turville stared at Sergeant Nguyen, his heart rate suddenly spiking. "That's it? No reason?"

Blake leaned forward. "Turville, he doesn't have to have a reason. But whatever the hell it is, he is pissed off. And a pissed-off mayor means a pissed-off platoon leader. You understand? What the hell did you do, feel her up or something?"

"No, sir!"

"Well, can you think of any reason at all that the mayor would come down here basically demanding your head?"

Turville shook his head. "No, sir. Unless..."

"What?"

Turville shrugged. "Sir, her uncle, Joe Blankenship. Used to be a Special Forces guy. He's... never liked me. Maybe it's something to do with him."

"Why do you think that?"

"He was here yesterday. First person out of the funeral. He was talking on the phone, and hauled ass right before the shooting started."

Blake and Nguyen looked at each other, and Blake muttered, "Holy shit." He began shuffling through some papers, then slid one across the table. "This Joe Blankenship?"

Turville looked down at the page. It was a terrible likeness—a grainy copy of a copy, but it was Blankenship.

"Yes sir, that's him."

"Son of a bitch," Blake muttered. He leaned forward.

"Turville, have you ever discussed tactical matters with Miss Mays? Patrols? Manning? Anything like that?"

"Of course not, sir. Not that she'd be interested, anyway. Why?"

Blake nearly yelled his response. "Because her uncle is suspected to be the head of the local insurgency, Turville!"

Turville's eyes widened. Holy shit. "Are you serious?"

"Do I look like I'm fucking joking, Turville? We've lost two soldiers this week, in case you missed it; not to mention that we killed a civilian teenager and pissed off everyone within ten thousand miles! I'm not in a joking fucking mood!"

"No, sir. I understand."

"How many times have you met this guy?"

"Just once, sir. The first time I went out with Rebecca."

"But you saw him yesterday. You're sure."

"Yes, sir. It was definitely him."

Blake closed his eyes, leaned back in his chair. Turville tried to remember whether he had ever said anything to Rebecca or her father that might have been operational information. Routes, movement, anything at all about their defenses, few as they were. He couldn't think of anything.

"All right," Blake said. "Here's the deal. Number one, you are to stay away from Rebecca Mays. You're confined to the barracks, except when out on patrol or other details. You're not to call her, or contact her in any other way."

"Sir," Turville began to protest. Not contact her in any way? They couldn't do that—he couldn't handle that.

"No arguments, Turville. I don't have time for this bullshit."

"Sir, with all due respect, you can confine me to the barracks, but telling me I can't talk to her on the phone? That's not right."

"I don't really give a shit, Turville. That's the way it is."

Turville shook his head. "Sir, I don't understand why, and I don't think it's right."

Nguyen exploded. "Corporal, we didn't ask your god damn opinion! You'll follow orders, you understand?"

"Since when does the Army tell people they can't contact their girlfriends?"

Blake said, "All the time, Corporal. And frankly, it's for your own safety. If her uncle really is heading up the local insurgency, has it occurred to you that he probably wants to see you dead?"

Turville didn't respond. He tried to breath, calm down. What was she going to think, if he just dropped out of sight—didn't speak with her or email her or contact her in any way?

No way.

THIRTY-FIVE

S WEET mother of all ironies, Karen thought, as the Humvee pulled up to the gate of the former brigade headquarters for Second Brigade of the West Virginia National Guard, just outside of Morgantown, West Virginia. Last fall, she'd been essentially confined here, effectively a fugitive from federal officials, protected by the National Guard.

The structure, though basically sound, had changed. First, of course, was the hand-painted sign on the front, labeling it the headquarters of the 352nd Military Intelligence Battalion. Fences, hastily repaired with sandbags and guarded by an infantry detachment, looked to have been destroyed, run over by armored vehicles. The building itself was scarred: a blue tarp had been secured to a large hole in the second floor, which must have been the entry point of a high explosive round from a tank or missile of some kind.

This was characteristic of what little she'd seen of West Virginia since her flight the day before. Arming her with orders and enlistment papers, Avedis had dumped her at division headquarters in Charleston, where she'd endured the initial in-processing while he went on ahead to his headquarters in Morgantown.

In-processing didn't have much in the way of surprises, except her repeated failure to salute passing lieutenants in the headquarters. That would take some getting used to, and twice she'd been stopped and reprimanded by young officers.

By the end of the day, she'd been issued uniforms, received a battery of shots, and given a billet in the transient enlisted women's barracks, where she spent an uncomfortable night trying to sleep while a young PFC in the next bunk over regaled her fellows with stories of her drinking escapades during her assignment in Germany.

This morning, she'd caught a ride with a courier heading to headquarters of the MI battalion. During the ride north from Charleston, she was sobered by the still very visible signs of the war. Several buildings in downtown Charleston were rubble. Even now—four months later—the drive north on the highway was littered with the occasional burnt-out tanks and armored vehicles, including an entire company's worth of Abrams tanks. She stared out the window as they passed. The tanks looked like they'd been hit by Hellfire missiles from an aviation unit: it was a graveyard of blacked vehicles, the rubber treads melted, barrels drooping.

Her own company had been destroyed in a similar fashion—her survival due to nothing more than pure dumb luck. When her tank was hit, she'd been standing on top of the back deck. The explosion threw her nearly a hundred feet into a snow bank.

The rest of the crew wasn't so lucky. Of the 72 men under her command, 19 were killed, thirty severely wounded, and twelve were missing by the final engagement west of Harpers Ferry. The survivors—injured, suffering from shock, exhaustion, and freezing cold—surrendered.

"You okay?" the driver asked her a few minutes after they'd passed the destroyed tank company.

That's when she realized she'd been gritting her teeth and clenching her fists. Sometimes her rage at the politicians who had refused to find a peaceful settlement last fall was too much to contain.

"Fine," she said, then continued looking out the window, ignoring him.

On her arrival at the headquarters, she was quickly ushered into the headquarters offices, which were as familiar to her as her own home. She waited several minutes before a harried soldier, a young Specialist barely out her teens, told her to have a seat and wait.

Nearly half an hour later, a very young-looking lieutenant limped into the room. Pale, with nasty looking burn scars on his neck, he walked slowly and deliberately, as if planning every step.

The Specialist, whose nametag read "Young," said, "Can I help you, sir?"

Karen's mouth curved into an involuntary, wry smile. Rank had its priveleges, and one of them was immediate service. A second lieutenant might be very low in the scheme of things, but was certainly a lot more important than a broken-down twenty-nine-year-old Army private previously convicted of treason.

"Lieutenant Calvin Stewart," the man said. "I'm reporting in to the battalion commander."

"This way, sir; he's expecting you," she said promptly.

He limped after her, into the office General Murphy had occupied last fall. Jesus, it was a small world. Her own office as assistant S3—Operations Officer—was three doors down. Leaning forward, she saw that office was now occupied by a florid-faced Army major, currently looking nonplussed as he read through a thick report.

After a ten-minute wait, Specialist Young stopped in front of her. "The Colonel will see you now," she said. "This way."

Karen stood and followed. Entering the office, she saluted and reported for duty, then waited.

"Have a seat, Private Greenfield," said Lieutenant Colonel Avedis.

"Thank you, sir," she said, uncomfortably. To her left sat the lieutenant. At first glance, notwithstanding the scars on his neck, she would have pegged his age at nineteen or twenty years old. But glancing down at his hand, she saw the class ring. West Point. That would make him at least 22. His face had an arrogant cast to it as he glanced over at her.

"Lieutenant Stewart, this is Private Greenfield. All right, the reason I called you in here together is that you are both new to the unit. We've got a fairly sensitive mission here, Lieutenant. To be blunt, I want to track down the details and whereabouts of Joe Blankenship, a man we believe to be one of the leaders of the insurgents operating in the state. So far we've come up with zip. Not just us—he's being hunted by the FBI, DHS—I don't know who all. Unfortunately, all my assets are tied up. But you've been assigned here, Stewart, and you don't have a job yet. So you get the job."

Stewart frowned. "Sir, um... with all due respect, I don't have much in the way of expertise in this sort of thing."

"That's fine. Think outside of the box. Also, that's where Private Greenfield comes in. I'm assigning her to you and this project. You'll operate out of the S2/S3 shop. She's intimately familiar with the locals, and knows Blankenship. You have at least a basic understanding of how an MI battalion is supposed to operate. Between the two of you, I want some results."

"Yes, sir," they both said.

Avedis looked at them both, as if carefully choosing his next words. He finally said, "Private, I want to make it clear to you. He's the boss of the operation. I presume I don't need to give you any instructions on the chain of command."

Wow, she thought. Her eyes darted to Lieutenant Stewart, who had raised his eyebrows at the extremely unusual comment. Privates didn't need to be told they were supposed to follow orders: that was the natural order of things.

"No, sir," she responded.

"That said," Avedis replied, turning to Stewart. "I want you to rely on Greenfield's expertise. Number one, she knows the locals. She lived here for many years, and worked with Blankenship's wife. Number two, prior to her current incarnation as a brand new Army private, she was an experienced and capable combat commander, one of the only women in the combat arms. If you have any doubts, let me explain that she wrote the operations plan for the defense of Harpers Ferry this January, then commanded one of the four tank companies that effected that defense."

Stewart's eyes widened.

Karen kept her eyes down. She didn't know what she thought of all this. Intimidating the hell out of a brand-new lieutenant on his first assignment didn't seem like a very effective command technique to her.

On the other hand, at least it was out in the open. She'd know soon enough whether or not Lieutenant Stewart was effectively able to work with someone he thought was a traitor. Whatever effect it had on him, she had no idea, because nothing but silence followed Avedis's statement.

Finally, Avedis said, "Thoughts? Greenfield? Where do you recommend starting?"

"Highview," she said. "I know some people there we should talk with right away."

"Lieutenant?"

Stewart shrugged. "I don't have enough facts to answer the question yet, sir. I'll defer to Greenfield's expertise for now."

"I have a question," she said.

Stewart quietly corrected her, "You have a question, sir."

She winced. "Sorry, sir."

"Go ahead," Avedis said.

"Before we go into the field, I'd like to assemble a list of people who knew Joe and Mandy. Anyone who might know where he is, or who had contact with him since the war, as well as the rest of his unit in the irregular forces. Is there a way we can run those names? Background checks, criminal records, credit reports?"

"Yes, of course. Work that out with Lieutenant Stewart. Now. This is delicate. You're obviously not eligible for any kind of security clearance. But you need to know a lot of this. Stewart, I'm going to depend on your judgment here. Get Private Greenfield the facts she needs, but maintain control. Clear?"

"Yes, sir."

"Any other questions?"

They spent a few minutes working through some logistics.

Finally, Avedis stood, and said, "I've got a meeting. Get to it."

☙

Come on, Bobby thought. Surely your password can't be that easy.

Damn. It was. All it took was a quick look through Asa Vance Hatfield's personnel file, and some guesswork, to determine that his password was his brother's middle name. Idiot. He made a mental note to remind Valerie that the IT department needed to join the twenty-first century and require actually secure passwords for the executives.

In the meantime, he had some digging to do. Logged in as Hatfield, he scanned through Hatfield's home and department directories on the network. Lots of interesting stuff: Budgets, personnel listings, case files. Stuff that would normally put him to sleep, of course, but it was different when digging through some place he wasn't supposed to be.

One file caught his eye almost immediately. Insurgent Case Files. He copied the entire directory to his laptop.

For the last week, Bobby had been manning a desk in the lobby of the Department of Law Enforcement and Military Affairs. His job was simple:… when people came in with tips about the insurgents, he was to take initial information, then pass it on to the right people. But who in their right mind would walk in here and report the insurgents if they wanted to stay alive?

It was make-work, something to keep him out of the way and busy. Out of the way he was, busy he was not.

All the same, he was grateful. The night he'd brought home that F on a world history test, his dad had clocked him, giving him a nasty black eye. It wasn't like he didn't know the answers, even with his eyes closed or half asleep.

Unfortunately, the night before the test, he'd been trying, without much success, to slip into the corporate network at Six Flags over at Georgia, so he could mail himself tickets. He'd been up all night.

He'd left all of the answers on the test blank, and wrote across the top in large block letters, "Q: What did the unemployed engineer say to the unemployed history major? A: Nothing. There's no such thing as an unemployed engineer."

After that, he'd gone to sleep at his desk.

Needless to say, Doctor Wilson hadn't appreciated the joke. A phone call home, some yelling, a punch in the face, and twelve hours later he was on the bus on the way to West Virginia in hopes of convincing his cousin to take him in. And now here he was, temporarily interning in this backward government department with a hopelessly insecure network. At least exploring the network provided plenty of diversion.

The best part was, two visiting agents from DHS, working on a joint investigation, had left their laptops connected to the network the day before. Bobby had managed to grab the entire contents of their hard drives, though he'd not had the time to go through them yet. With any luck, though, there would be enough information to penetrate DHS's network.

That, of course, was serious work—and dangerous. He'd go cautiously. Very cautiously. Those were people you didn't want to screw around with. It was one thing to wander into some company's computers, or a backwards state government. It was another thing entirely to break into a federal government system, especially one run by the Department of Homeland Security.

The elevator rang, and cousin Val stepped out, flanked by her constantly present bodyguard. With a few keystrokes, he closed everything.

She was carrying a big bag slung over her shoulder, stuffed with thick envelopes. It looked heavy. The bodyguard was carrying a gun, his hands free. So much for chivalry. But considering he'd saved her life, Bobby figured it was okay.

"Let's take a walk," she said.

Bobby raised his eyebrows. "A what?"

He wasn't being deliberately obtuse. This was just bizarre. Despite the fact that he was crashing on the couch in her apartment, and technically working for her, Bobby had seen very little of Valerie over the last few weeks. She was insanely busy with her job, and worked hours that would have made most grown men cry.

"A walk," she said. "It's something people do when they want to get somewhere on foot."

Bobby grinned.

"Sure," he replied.

He closed his laptop, stuffed it in his backpack, then stood, slinging the backpack over one shoulder.

He turned to Trooper Henry, the bodyguard, and said flippantly, "You stand on one side and I'll stand on the other. We can absorb bullets from both sides that way."

Henry narrowed his eyes, then swept them away dismissively.

Valerie sighed. "Your social skills haven't improved much, you know."

"Not funny?"

"Not really."

"I'll try harder."

"Please don't."

He sighed and fell in step behind her. They paused for a moment as Henry held up a hand, indicating they should stay in place. Henry stepped out the revolving door of the building, scanned the intersection in all four directions, then waved them on.

Trooper Henry led them a block down the street, left on a cross street, then paused at an intersection. Traffic was snarled here; the signal out, cars pushing their way into the intersection in a chaotic mess. Henry turned a full circle, eyes scanning everywhere, then nodded to Valerie.

"All right, we can talk here."

"Jesus, Valerie, what's going on? What's with all the cloak and dagger? We can't talk in your office?"

She looked at him, a frown pulling down the corners of her mouth. "I'm in a considerable amount of danger at the moment. Since you're staying with me, so are you."

"Wouldn't it be safer, then, to meet in your office? Isn't that why you've got the bodyguards all the time? To protect you from the insurgents?"

"Not that kind of danger," she said.

He waited for her to elaborate. She didn't. Finally, he said, "Come on, Val. Spill it."

"I can't talk about it in detail. But I've pissed off the wrong people. Not just insurgents, but the federal government. Bobby, I think it's time for you to go back home. Having you here is putting you in a lot of danger."

Oh, shit. He wasn't ready for that.

"Val, look, I've registered for summer school back home, so I can catch up with class, I guess. But I need more time. Things are bad at home right now."

"They may be bad," she said, sounding slightly condescending. "But not life threatening."

"You're exaggerating the problem."

"No, I'm not. In case you missed it, a couple guys tried to assassinate me last week. And one of the cops who stopped it, and got himself injured, ended up dead."

"What happened to him?"

"He was in the hospital, and someone snuck in and put a bullet in his head."

"Holy shit."

"Yeah. That's why I want you gone."

"Look," he said. "I can help you."

"No, you can't," she said impatiently.

Damn it. "Yes, I can. Don't ask me how, but I've cracked the network in your department. Which, by the way, has lousy security. I think I can find your traitor."

Her face went pale. "You did what? How?"

"It wasn't that hard," he said. "Plus, I was bored. I've been going through Hatfield's files, and—"

"Stop," she said, interrupting him. "I don't want to hear this. Whatever it is you are doing, you need to stop now."

Screw that. He blurted out, "You should look into Barry Rosenthal. I know he's not on your prime list of suspects, but there are good reasons to suspect him."

Henry looked at him, eyebrows raised.

She shook her head. "What are you talking about?"

"Rosenthal wrote several letters to the editor in support of independence back in November and December. The drafts are still on his computer. Okay, so a lot of people supported it. But he did more. I know he's in charge of personnel and all, but back in January, he pulled the files of just about everyone in the department. As best as I can tell, he was looking for people who had family detained after the war. Plus, he's a major financial fuck-up. He's screening calls from half-a-dozen creditors. And the last bit, and probably the most important? His eighteen-year-old son has been detained. He's National Guard."

"Oh my God. We hadn't even considered him."

Henry shook his head at Bobby, looking surprised at first, then thoughtful. "It's plausible, Miss Secretary."

Valerie tensed up, her eyebrows drawn in low, and crossed her arms over her chest. "It's more than plausible. Why the hell haven't our own investigators come up with this?"

"Rosenthal doesn't have direct access to the information that was leaked. That's why her was never considered a suspect." Bobby said. "But he has plenty of access to people who do. There are all kinds of possibilities here. That's why you need me to stick around."

She shook her head. "No. Bad idea. We've lost enough family. I can't... I can't be responsible for you getting hurt."

"Damn it, Val, I could get hurt anywhere! Just give me two weeks. Please... Two weeks, and I'll be a good boy and go home to my asshole of a dad. Please?"

She sighed. "All right. Two weeks, no more."

Yes! He grinned. "I'll get you all the information as I get it, and —"

"Stop," she said, interrupting his enthusiasm. "First, we can't talk about this anywhere in the headquarters building. Or in the apartment."

Huh. "You worried about bugs?"

"Yes," she acknowledged. "We'll have lunch in three days. Just go for a walk, and get hot dogs or something by the river."

He nodded. "All right."

"In the meantime, I've got a job for you."

"Excellent. More challenging than waiting for someone to come in and report insurgents?"

She smiled. "Slightly. I've put together some insurance. In case DHS tries to make me disappear. I need you to mail out these packages. I'll give you some cash for it. Send them over-night, with signed delivery. Three of them I want you to deliver by hand, to Governor Clark, Uncle Tommy, and Ambrose Hall. Everything is in the bag."

He nodded. "All right. Do I get to know what's inside?"

"No."

He'd find out anyway. It's not like her depressingly easy password, K3nny, hadn't been trivial to figure out.

"All right. Mail the packages. They're insurance."

"Yes. Then come straight back. I don't want you wandering the streets without protection."

"Val, I haven't pissed off both sides in a war, you know. Nobody's looking for me."

"Yes, well, that could change any time. You be careful, Bobby."

He nodded, thinking Valerie really needed a vacation. Or some Valium. Or both.

"I will," he said.

Thirty minutes later, he was sitting in the office supply store. There were six envelopes, all of them thick. The three for Uncle Tommy, Governor Clark, and Ambrose Hall had letters attached to the front with instructions to security guards to call her office when he arrived, and noting that the packages were to be hand delivered only. The other three were interesting. One was addressed to Marcus Jennsen, a reporter with the New York Times. The second to a reporter with Salon.com. The third, oddly enough, was to his mother.

He opened that one. Inside, a cover note from Valerie was taped to another envelope. The cover note read,

Dear Lisa. I'm sending this to you with the request that you hold on to it indefinitely. The possibility exists that I may be in some danger. In the event anything happens to me, please post the enclosed files on the Internet, in as public a forum as possible. It is critical that you do this anonymously. Bobby may be able to help you with that.

Love you very much. With any luck, we can get the whole family together for Christmas this year. I'll be thinking of you.

Your niece, Valerie.

Bobby rolled his eyes. Like his mother would have a clue how to post anything anonymously. She'd leave a trail of clues so clear the feds would lock her up forever. Bobby would take care of this one, as soon as he finished reading the contents of the package.

An hour later, he had finished reading the file and sat shaking with anger and disbelief. He'd read through the reports delivered by Captain Matt Floyd to Ambrose Hall, both the original report documenting the theft of the H5B1 samples as well as the official version. From there, he'd read the reports from Detective Sergeant Corvath's investigation into the death of Clifford Webb, the links between Roland Channing's Christian publishing empire and terrorism, and the further links between Channing and JD Roberts of the Department of Homeland Security.

This was some scary, scary stuff. And it all came back down to Roberts, Channing, and DHS. Including the Arlington bombing.

As he read, his mind kept returning to one fact. This was why his uncle Ken had died. This was the reason for the war. Because some assholes wanted to grab power any way they could.

Well, fuck them, he thought. Not while I live and breathe.

Hmm. Time to put his skills to some productive use.

കൗ

"All right, let's get started, gentleman."

The words, spoken quietly but with authority by Roland Channing, brought silence to the room.

Joe Blankenship took a seat next to Ethan Judson, his second in command. A friend for many years, they'd served together in Iraq, and later in the irregulars here in West Virginia. Ethan was slumped in his seat, looking relaxed and tired in his well-worn hiking boots and blue jeans. They sat in a large dining room with broad, highly polished plank flooring in a very large two-story house with an expansive portico and white columns, not far from Morgantown.

"For those of you who don't know each other, let me provide some introductions," Channing said. He was sitting at the head of the antique mahogany dining table. "I'm Roland Channing, bishop of the New World Pentecostal Church. This is my son, John. He's is a Marine Corps veteran who served in Fallujah."

John Channing sat across the table from his father. Muscular, his head nearly shaved, he held an air of coiled violence. The globe-and-anchor emblem of the Marine Corps covered part of his upper arm.

Channing pointed to the fat man across the table from Joe. "Nathan Wyatt, Deputy Sheriff in Taylor County. Wyatt led a team of irregulars in defense of Morgantown in January, and he's held his team together in the area. They've been responsible for some fairly spectacular actions since, including the firing of an Army ammo dump. Joe, that's where we got your surface-to-air missiles, by the way."

Joe nodded to Wyatt with grudging respect. The surface-to-air missiles had brought down two Blackhawk helicopters in Whitesville several weeks earlier.

Channing pointed to Joe. "Joe Blankenship. Special Forces vet, counterinsurgency specialist. Joe's sainted wife Mandy was killed by DHS last fall, and he led the irregulars in the defense of Harpers Ferry. They're located down in Boone County now. Beside him is his second in command, Ethan Judson."

John Channing yawned, stretching ostentatiously. Of all the men in the room, he was the one Joe watched the closest. Channing struck him as arrogant, something about his near constant smirk and physical presence told him this was a dangerous man, a man who was prepared to do whatever it took to get what he wanted.

"I'm bringing you all together now because it is time we took things to a new level."

Silence followed his pronouncement. Roland waited, looking at each of the men in the room before he spoke again.

"Since March, you all have been slowly escalating your individual wars against the feds. I believe it is time to bring our insurgency to a new level, both in West Virginia and outside of it. There are two things I intend to accomplish today. First, I want to pick an overall tactical commander. While I can bring leadership in the nature of godly things, I will be the first to admit I know nothing of war. Second, I would like to discuss strategy. We have some very real opportunities approaching, and we must grasp them."

Joe leaned forward. "Overall command? Are you sure that is workable? We're spread all over the place."

"Of course each of you will continue to have autonomy over your local areas. But we must follow an agreed-upon strategy."

Joe shrugged. "Who do you suggest?"

John leaned forward. "I'm volunteering for the job." His voice was deep, and grating.

"Why you?" Joe asked.

John shrugged. "I'm a former officer in the Marine Corps. I know leadership. I know insurgency. I know tactics. My team has the expertise and equipment to get the job done. We won't shirk over the little details, or hesitate to do... what is necessary."

Joe narrowed his eyes. Channing had to be referring to the incident at Dana Wilder's funeral in Highview, when Channing's allies had fired indiscriminately into a crowd of civilians. Unfortunately the tactic had worked. People in Highview were terrified. Terrified of the Army, terrified of the insurgents. They were staying low, cooperating with insurgent activity, and refusing to cooperate with the Army. Exactly what Channing had been trying to accomplish.

Wyatt leaned back in his chair, resting his hands on his considerable belly. Joe wondered how he could possibly have led a team of insurgents. From an armchair? He sure as hell wasn't out humping a pack in the woods with them.

Wyatt said, "Let's not forget, this isn't just about West Virginia. It's about taking our country back. I want it to be about God, and under Roland Channing's guidance. His son is the logical choice."

Joe looked back and forth between the other men. Was this worth the struggle? It wasn't as if he hadn't served under other men his entire military career. But something bothered him about both Roland and John Channing. They were turning this rebellion into some kind of holy crusade.

Would Mandy have approved? She was a believer, something Joe had never been. He'd come home from his second tour in Iraq when the change came. She'd come through the fear by turning to God, and he'd supported her. It hadn't bothered him when she'd insisted on going to church every Sunday, when she'd spent her evenings reading the bible instead of cheap novels like when they were growing up. If it held her together, and helped her stay happy, he supported it.

He could picture her now. She'd tell him it wasn't about who was in charge. It wasn't about people: it was about doing God's will, whatever that was. Both the Channings seemed to believe they knew. Joe didn't have a clue. But he did know starting an alliance with a power struggle wouldn't accomplish anything.

"Fine," he said. "I'm agreeable."

Channing smiled. "I'm so glad, Joe. I'm sure, with God's blessing, our venture will be successful."

"Amen," Wyatt said.

Whatever, Joe thought.

"John, will you share your plan with the others?" Roland said.

John stood. "Yes, sir."

He walked over to a map of West Virginia, heavily marked up. "As you all know, my father is working on several things at the national level. Among other things, we've effectively infiltrated a number of key agencies, including the Department of Homeland Security. Over the next few weeks, they'll be working to intercept the efforts of those who oppose us. One of our key goals is to get a supporter into the White House."

Joe sat back. They were thinking big.

"How do you intend to do that?"

"As you know, Vice President Hamilton will be in the state in less than a week and a half. He's slated to give some feel-good speeches alongside the government about how wonderful their counterinsurgency efforts are. I'm looking to accomplish two things in the next two weeks. First, we need a major victory under our belt. That's where you come in, Joe."

"Me?"

"Yes. Your mission will be simple, but very dangerous. I want you to eradicate the Army presence in Boone County."

"That's not as simple as you think. We can ambush their current forces, sure. But they'll send in more. A lot more."

"Exactly. What we want is a major escalation. Think Tet Offensive. They can outman us every day of the week. But we can embarrass them. Make them respond with overwhelming force. Make them bloody. What I want you to do is create a plan to crush the Army down there. Yes, they'll send reinforcements, but it will be a propaganda victory. Everything goes up on Youtube. Everything gets published. Make the people of America freak. I want one or more of those soldiers executed, publicly, posted on the internet. I'm going to ask Deputy Wyatt here to loan you some men to beef up your force. While you're doing that, you'll be distracting attention from the other prong of our plan."

"Which is?"

"Vice President Hamilton won't leave the state alive. When he's dead, with luck we'll get a supporter appointed by the President in his place."

Joe grimaced. "How the hell are you going to do that?"

Channing interjected, "Joe, please. Let us not blaspheme. I have good reason to believe we can sway the appointment of a new Vice President. And from there, who knows? President Price will almost certainly be re-elected next year, unless the Democrats manage to pull off a miracle. Then, four years later, our man will be the natural successor."

Joe grunted. "And my job is to get the ball rolling. Kick the Army out of Boone County."

"Don't kick them out, Joe. Kill them."

છ૭

The smell of bleach was starting to give Rebecca a headache. She leaned back on her heels. Time to take a break. For the last hour, she'd been scrubbing room 12, which had been vacant for a good year or more since the last guest. Leah didn't employ a housekeeper, and for whatever reason, she hadn't been in here in a long, long time. Rebecca'd had to replace the light bulbs before she could even get started. The linens were in terrible shape too—she'd replaced those right off. Then scrubbed. And scrubbed more. The bathroom was clean now, no question, but its appearance wasn't terribly improved.

Done for the night. There was no big press of guests, just the occasional weekend stay. She was going to suggest to Leah that they rotate guest rooms, however, so none of them had a chance to get this nasty. It was going to take forever to get rid of the small of mildew in here.

She sighed. It has been a very long day. For the second day in a row, her so-called friends had made sure there were no seats at the table for her. Walking away, she heard Rhonda Peterson mutter, "Whore." The other girls at the table tittered. Rebecca walked away, head high, back straight, desperately hiding how much she wanted to fall apart.

It was Jesse. He'd been spreading poison about her ever since Dana was killed. When she went back to her locker at the end of the day to get ready to go home, she'd opened it to the sound of giggling from some of the girls nearby. Two dozen condoms had been stuffed through the vent, and when a bunch of them fell out and spread all over the floor, the giggles had turned to outright laughter.

She'd attended three funerals in the last week. Even there, she was isolated, as if the entire town had separated from her unconsciously. No one spoke with her, no one offered a word of kindness. It felt as if she'd ceased to exist.

After school, she'd come home and completed her homework, which had been dramatically increased in the rush to complete senior year on time. A short dinner alone, then she'd gone straight to work changing linens and cleaning rooms.

She stood and stretched, her back aching, then loaded the cleaning supplies on the cart, stepped out of the room and locked it. Finally, at nearly 10 p.m., she was in her room, show-ered and in her pajamas.

She checked her phone. No phone calls, no text messages. She'd tried several times to get in touch with Jim to no avail.

She slipped her laptop out of its bag and checked her email, and there it was.

Rebecca,
Sorry I haven't been able to call or text. Your dad visited Lieuten-ant Blake. I don't know what he said, but I've been confined to bar-racks, and my phone was confiscated for the duration. I'm sending this email from Nowell's xbox.
You can text me through Santiago at 512-555-1212, or email me. Nowell and I will be on guard shift between 1 and 2 a.m. tonight. After that, I've no idea. We're slated to go back on patrol for a few days soon, not sure when.
I love you,
Jim

She smiled, then grabbed her phone and texted Santiago:

Tell you know who: 1 am. Thx.

છ્ડ

At exactly one in the morning, Rebecca got out of bed. She threw a coat on over her pajamas, slipped on her sandals and opened the door to her room, stepping onto the narrow balcony of the motel.

There was no light at all other than a flickering, dim fluo-rescent in the window of the drugstore. The silence was near enough to overpowering: no traffic, no people, nothing. She tried not to make any noise as she gently closed the door, then walked quickly down the stairs and across the parking lot.

It was only two blocks to the Army's rented home, a five-minute walk. But for the first time in her life in her hometown, she didn't feel safe.

Heart pounding, she slowly approached the army compound, knowing someone would be watching through night vision goggles. If it was Nowell and Jim, fine. But she didn't know for sure.

Almost there. As she reached the gate, she heard a whisper. "Over here."

It was Jim. He was twenty feet away, standing at the fence.

She ran to him, and linked hands with him through the wire of the fence, then leaned her head against it. He did the same. Their faces nearly touched, but not quite.

"How are you holding up?" he whispered.

"I'm... going through the motions," she replied.

"I'm so sorry about Dana, and the others."

She nodded. "I know," she responded, then in a low tone, really meaning it. "I know."

"Your dad came up here."

She nodded. "He's put down an ultimatum. I'm not allowed to see you, ever again."

"Whoa. I guess I shouldn't be surprised."

She looked at him, taking in his deep blue eyes. "I've left home," she told him.

"What? Why?"

"My dad. You. He can't just announce that he's cutting out my heart, Jim. And not even give a reason for it. I'm an adult."

"Where are you staying?"

"My aunt owns the motel. She gave me a job, and put me up."

He sighed. "You didn't have to do that for me."

She smiled. "I didn't do it for you, Jim. I did it for me."

He squeezed her hand gently through the fence, their fingers intertwined. "You know I love you, Short Girl."

"I love you, soldier boy."

"You should go home. The LT will have a fit if he catches me talking to you. But I promise you, we'll work this out, okay? You can contact me through Santiago, or email for longer stuff."

She smiled, then said, "I'll send balloons over the wire. Or homing pigeons."

"Nah, we'd probably shoot them down. Email's better."

She giggled. Trying not to mash noses against the chain link fence, they carefully kissed. She turned and walked back to the motel at a slow, dreamy pace. For the moment, she was happy and relieved. Tomorrow would be another day. In fact, she thought, she should just go see the Lieutenant. Her father might be the mayor, but she could be pretty damn persuasive herself.

With that thought, she returned to her room and fell into a deep, dreamless sleep.

THIRTY-SIX

B Y the time the sun came up, Karen had been driving east in a rented car for nearly two hours, while Lieutenant Stewart read through the files on Joe Blankenship. Starting out on I-68, she'd taken the exit for Berkeley Springs and cut across the state on State Route 9 to Charles Town. She wore worn jeans and a red-checked flannel shirt, both purchased from a thrift store the day before. The lieutenant was also in plain clothes. They'd quickly decided their mission would be better accomplished in civilian garb.

It would have been a few minutes quicker to go through Hagerstown, which Lieutenant Stewart had been quick to point out. She'd argued, persuasively, that the more he saw of the back roads and towns of the state, the more he'd understand what he was dealing with. The interstate could be anywhere in America, but on some of the twisting, curving roads in the mountains, there was nowhere else in the world you could be. She had other reasons, however, to take this route. Somewhere along this stretch of road was the place where her first and only combat command came to an end under a rain of hellfire missiles.

Much of the ride, there was little evidence of the war other than many, many closed businesses. But not long before Charles Town, she began to slow down, her eyes darting to the fields beside the road.

It wasn't long before Stewart noticed. "What's wrong?"

She took a deep breath, knowing they would be there in a matter of seconds. Just ahead, over the rise…

Eight blackened, burnt Abrams tanks, on the east side of the road.

She pulled over without a word and let out her breath in a slow exhale. She hadn't even realized she'd been holding it.

"Holy shit," Stewart muttered under his breath, looking at the tanks.

She turned off the ignition and opened the car door, getting out before he could ask, "Where are you going?"

Pretending she hadn't heard, she rapidly crossed the busy street, leaving the lieutenant to struggle with his files and papers in the passenger seat and follow her or not. The guard rails had been crushed when the tanks had crossed them five months before, and had never been repaired. Spread out in a herringbone pattern, they had been parked to cover all avenues of approach. Not that it had done any good against an air assault.

At the head of the column, on the right side, main gun depressed almost to the ground, turret turned over the side, was Bravo-66. The tank she had commanded for three years, in peace time and in war.

Most of the front of the tank and the turret was blackened from the fire, which must have raged for hours. The track was melted—snapped in two. Now, she could see clearly why she'd had the luck to survive. The missile had hit the right front slope, knocking off some of the right side road wheels and burrowing into the front armor. She'd been shielded from the worst of the blast by the turret itself. Just enough to throw her a hundred feet through the air into the snow, and put her in the hospital for nearly two months.

Breathing heavily, she climbed onto the front deck, ignoring the fact that her hands and clothes were instantly smeared with thick black soot. On top, she could see that the turret itself was heavily damaged. The blowout panels were gone, the ammunition compartment gaping open and black. Inside the turret was a jumble of blackened and melted equipment. No one had even bothered to secure the two M240B machine guns: both were so melted they were little more than scrap metal.

She was breathing heavily, her heartbeat through the roof. The smell was overpowering, even after all these months—the sharp pungency of cordite. She could almost hear the sound of the main gun going off, the ring of metal hitting metal as the spent rounds dropped into the basket. The whispering of Frank Haggett as he prayed and prayed right before the first shots were fired in Harpers Ferry.

She was jerked back to reality by a shout.

"What the hell are you doing, Private Greenfield?"

She looked down. Her hands and clothes were smeared black with soot and grease. Stewart's face was a bright shade of red and his eyes bulging a bit as he shouted.

She didn't know how to answer his question. Finally, she said, her voice calm, "I'm thinking about Frank Haggett."

Baffled, he said, "What? Who?"

"Frank was... seventeen. He enlisted in December, right before the war. Didn't even really go through training. He was just a kid."

She shook her head. "His granddad was killed along with General Murphy's wife about four years ago—a random robbery. Anyway, Frank wasn't really going anywhere in life. He dropped out of high school, was washing dishes at Sally's Diner when the state voted for independence. So he enlisted, went through a very short basic training, and ended up as my loader. He and Crump, the driver... both were just kids. They were fueling the tank when we got hit, and they burned to death."

She blinked her eyes, trying to drive back tears. "Sergeant Bowen at least probably died quickly. He was inside the turret loading main gun ammo. The explosion was... massive."

She looked down at Stewart. "Bowen's wife, Madison... cute little blonde thing. She was a waitress at Sally's Diner, and had helped Frank get a job there. That's how he ended up enlisting—he'd met Sergeant Bowen through her. She was six months pregnant when the shooting started. I've no idea what happened to her. I mean, I'm sure she's had the baby, but..." Her voice trailed off.

His face was rigid. "To be honest, Greenfield, though I'm sympathetic to the wife... It's hard for me to drum up much sympathy for a bunch of people who betrayed their country."

She shrugged and answered, her voice sounding tired. "I'm sure that's true, Lieutenant. That's not the point. I don't care whether you have sympathy for them. But if you're going to accomplish your mission, you're going to need to understand a little about them. You need to know a little about why Blankenship made the choices he did. Why I made the choices I did.

"The guys on my crew—in this tank company—were decimated. We were fighting a force a twenty times our size, with far superior weapons. We didn't have any air support or resupply; we were running out of ammo and fuel, and still managed to slow the Army down for three days as they rolled in.

"Blankenship ran a company of irregulars—snipers mostly. They were on foot, slogging through three feet of snow, fighting mechanized infantry. And if they're out there now, still fighting a guerrilla war? You can bet they won't be easy to trap or kill."

"I don't understand you," he said. His mouth was pinched tight, contemptuous. "You were a commissioned officer and betrayed your country. How the hell am I supposed to trust anything you say?"

She shrugged. "Honestly, sir, I don't care if you do or not. I made the decisions I did because they were the right thing to do."

"So why are you here now? Isn't this another betrayal? Do you just have no... no moral compass at all? You just switch sides at will?"

She rocked back, then began making her way off the turret. "Lieutenant, things are never that simple." She said with anger. "Let me ask you a question. As an officer, what would be your responsibility if you saw another agent of the federal government committing a crime? Let's say, for example, shooting into a crowd?"

"I'd intervene, of course."

"Yeah? What if they were rounding up innocent people? Tying them up in the street? Arresting children because they were in the wrong ethnic group?"

"You're full of shit, private."

"No, sir," she said, her voice icy cold. "That's exactly the situation I was in. I swore an oath to defend the Constitution, and never once did I waver from that oath, even when it put my life and freedom on the line! Don't you ever say that I'd just switch sides to whatever's convenient. If that was the case, I'd have resigned my commission and walked away last fall! Or turned a blind eye when it would have been convenient."

By the time she finished, she was standing directly in front of Stewart, her face red.

"Private, that is enough! You are way over the line."

"Fine, sir. Send me back to prison. The company's better there anyway."

"I'm calling Colonel Avedis as soon as we stop. This is ridiculous. I don't know why the hell they let you out of jail. I don't know why you're even here."

She shouted, "Because they're killing civilians! What we did—as misguided and doomed as it was—we were doing the right thing. Not attacking and killing civilians. I don't care what your political beliefs are; nothing justifies that. So yeah, I helped the wrong side. We did the best we could, and we lost. But if it continues as a private war, no one will be safe, and the feds will just use it as an excuse to become more oppressive than they already are."

He took a deep breath, then said in a calmer tone, "Okay. I can see that."

She exhaled, a little deflated. She'd been ready for further confrontation.

"Look," he said. "Maybe we need to... establish some ground rules. Before we go any further. I don't really understand where you are coming from, but— I'm not as dense as I look. Let's stop somewhere so you can clean up, and we'll get breakfast."

She nodded. "All right, sir.."

Back in the car, they were both silent. She merged back into traffic, heading into Charles Town. Once there, they'd head up US 340, back to Highview, where the events leading up to the war had started.

She saw a large gas station ahead on the right. "I'm going to pull in there and get cleaned up." After a pause, she said, "I apologize. For losing my temper."

"And the insubordination?"

"Yeah, sure, that too."

"All right. You're forgiven."

She gave a half smile. She couldn't help liking the kid, even if he was clueless.

Twenty minutes later, wearing a secondhand dress, hands and face clean, she pulled to a stop at a diner in Charles Town.

Inside, they took a booth in the back, sat down, and ordered.

"All right," Stewart said. "You say I need to understand. Tell me your story."

She looked at him doubtfully, then said, "All right."

She began with her life growing up in Kentucky, then going to Bowling Green University. "That's where I met Jim. Colonel Avedis, rather. He and my fiancé were roommates at the time."

"Your fiancé? I didn't realize you were married."

"I'm not. Mike and I broke up our senior year. He ended up going Infantry. For the record, it was his unit we fought in Harpers Ferry."

"Ouch," he said. "Nothing like an ex-girlfriend with a big gun."

She smirked. "You have no idea. Anyway, he's with 3rd ID now, on riot duty in Madison, Wisconsin. You have to understand... I was just at the end of my senior year of college when they announced a pilot program allowing women into the combat arms. I was in the first class through Armor Officer Basic.

There were only three of us in that class; a few more in Infantry and Artillery. This was a huge deal, and it only lasted a couple years before President Price issued an executive order putting a halt to it. I was grandfathered, so they didn't kick me out. What they did do was sideline me, as well as the others who went through training with me. Application for regular Army status was denied at the end of my first two-year commitment. I was a first lieutenant in Armor branch, and they didn't want women in Armor."

"So what did you do?"

"Started looking for work. My degree is in computer engineering. I got a few job offers, and I ended up taking the one at Saturn Microsystem in Highview."

"Why there? Kind of remote, isn't it?"

"Not as remote as where I grew up. But the reason I took the Saturn job is simple enough. My interview with Saturn was with the plant manager, Ken Murphy."

He raised his eyebrows. "That Ken Murphy?"

She nodded. "Yes. At the time, he was battalion commander for Second Battalion, 432 Armor. National Guard, based out of Highview. He said they were looking for a good company XO. I got the spot, and eventually made captain and got my own company."

He nodded. "Okay. So what happened? In the files, it said there was some kind of clash with DHS at the Saturn Plant?"

She nodded, and told him how the plant had been closed, the employees ended up taking the plant over, then the disastrous response from DHS, which had resulted in the deaths of David Firkus and Mandy Blankenship among others.

"You've got to understand, at this point no one was talking confrontation with the federal government. The attack on the plant? It was... shocking. The initial talk of secession was just a gesture. We were trying to make the point that the feds had gone too far. Hell, we had a family in Highview arrested—Arabs who ran a shop in town—all the men in the family were arrested after the Arlington bombing, and there was no reason given. But I don't think any of it would have gone as far as it did if it hadn't been for the bombing of the federal building in Charleston."

"Right. When the National Guard and DHS got into a shooting match."

"You know about it?"

"I was a little preoccupied at the time, but I read about it in the files on the way here. You were in command there."

She nodded. "That's right. And I made a judgment call that got one of my men killed, along with a DHS agent. That's when the standoff between West Virginia and the feds really started."

"So how does Joe Blankenship fit into all of this?"

She sat back. "Joe... okay, he's former Special Forces. Counterinsurgency specialist. Spent about four years in Iraq. He and his wife Mandy... They were utterly devoted to each other. They dated in high school, and got married while he was in the Army. She came to work for Saturn... I guess around 2006? During the worst of the fighting in Iraq, while he was over there.

"When he came home... well, Joe's a complex guy. Angry, intimidating. I don't know what happened in Iraq, but nothing good, that's for sure. She did her best to take care of him. He'd get work for a while in a coal mine somewhere, then get laid off or fired. I remember for a while he was doing day labor, then odd jobs around town. After she was killed though... it was as if he'd been lit on fire. He tied himself to Dale Whitt, the guy who started the independence movement, and ended up taking over after Whitt was killed."

"Okay. So we know why he's doing it."

"Revenge," she responded. "Anyway... in December the legislature passed a bill authorizing raising a force of fifty thousand volunteers. Irregular forces; they were to be given uniforms, but they pretty much provided their own weapons. The idea, stupid as it was, was to attach irregular units to each regular National Guard unit. Provide covering fire, ambush, support, whatever. Joe organized an irregular attachment that was assigned to us—about sixty men. They were stationed all along our line of retreat, as a harassment force. I lost track at that point... got blown up, then sent to prison. But my guess is, Joe and his guys never demobilized. After we lost the war, they melted off into the woods and started organizing an insurgent campaign."

He looked at her for a moment, his eyes penetrating. It made her uncomfortable, until she noticed a grudging respect growing in his eyes. "Okay, I get it, I think. I don't approve of what you did ... or agree. But I understand. So... where are we going now?"

"Well, there are a couple of people I want to see. Linda Judson used to work at Saturn; I knew her pretty well. Her brother Ethan was second in command of Joe's company, and they served in Iraq together. If he's still alive, she might know where to find him. Also, the guys Joe used to play poker with. It drove Mandy nuts. She was pretty vice-free, at least publicly. Didn't approve of drinking or gambling, and Joe loved to do both with these guys."

"You think they'll have any clue where he is?"

"No idea. But it can't hurt to find out. Also, we're going to check my house."

"Why?"

"Well... I've been in prison, okay? The house was probably foreclosed on two months ago. But if it hasn't been emptied, we might find some files there. I had a roster of Joe's unit, among other things. No idea if it's there or not, but it can't hurt to check. Not to mention... well, it was my house."

He nodded. "Okay. Your plan sounds good for now."

Karen felt a sudden sense of relief. Bargaining with a brand new lieutenant out of West Point hadn't been on her list of priorities in life a few months ago, but if that was what it took now, she could live with it. Now the question was: would her plan accomplish anything? She hoped they didn't arrive in Highview and find out it was a dead end.

❧

"God, Karen, it's good to see you. Sit down, please. And... I'm sorry, what was your friend's name again?"

Linda Judson was just on the other side of thirty-five. It had been well over a year since Karen had seen her, and she had changed: strain showed in new lines around her mouth and eyes that hadn't been evident a year ago. On the other hand, she'd lost a lot of weight, which had been a struggle for her for years.

Lieutenant Stewart smiled. "It's Calvin. Calvin Stewart."

"Calvin... I'm sorry, I'm terrible with names. Karen will tell you, it took me like a year before I stopped calling her Kate."

Karen laughed. "It's good to see you too, Linda. How have you been?"

"Oh, you know. Getting by. You can see I've managed to keep the house, thank God, since no one's going to buy it."

"What are you doing now?"

"Would you believe waiting tables? I got a gig at a steakhouse in Loudon County. It's a long as hell drive, but at least some of the bills are getting paid. What about you?"

Karen looked at Stewart, who had advised her to come up with some plausible lie. Problem was, there was no plausible lie. Her trial and subsequent conviction had been front-page news across the country.

She sighed. "I got an early release."

"Working for the feds now?" Linda asked. Her voice was cautious.

Karen nodded minutely. "The Army."

"So I guess you're here looking for Ethan. Look, there's not much I can tell you. I've only seen him once since January; he came around about two months ago."

Karen replied, "It's not really Ethan we're looking for, Linda. It's Joe Blankenship."

"Joe? Why?" Her expression was frozen, careful. They were friends, but Karen didn't think that extended to turning her brother in to the feds. She was going to have to be very persuasive.

"Well… Joe has gone public as a leader in the insurgency. We believe he's been involved in some very high profile attacks. Look, Linda, I know you don't want to get Ethan in trouble…"

"Oh, he's perfectly capable of that all on his own."

Karen smiled. "I'm sure he is. But the fact is, they're in a lot of danger. And so are people who aren't involved in this in any way—innocent people."

"Mmhmm… I'm sorry I can't help."

Karen looked at Lieutenant Stewart. "I think you should show her the photos from the funeral, Lieutenant."

Stewart raised his eyebrows. "All right."

He reached around the couch to the small bag he'd carried inside with him and took out a manila folder. He started laying out several photographs one by one, side by side.

"Ms. Judson, this picture is of Dana Wilder. About a week ago, she was accidentally killed in a firefight between insurgents and the US Army. Down in in Whitesville."

"I don't know what that has to do with me." She looked defensive.

Stewart ignored her and placed a second picture on the coffee table.

"This is Emily Barkes. She was twelve years old, her family residents of Whitesville. Here's why it has to do you with you, Ms. Judson. Three days ago, most of the town turned out for Dana Wilder's funeral. And in an attempt to provoke a—a massacre, I suppose... insurgents opened fire on both the troops nearby and the crowd exiting the funeral itself. Emily... the little girl... was shot to death by an insurgent sniper."

"Oh my God," Linda said. She looked carefully at the photo, and tears began to form in her eyes.

"Now, Ms. Judson... this photo was taken at the funeral. As you can see, in the picture is Joe Blankenship. He was the first person to leave the funeral, after shouting comments about revenge at the pastor during the service. He walked out, talking on a cell phone, and drove away. Moments later the insurgents opened fire. What I'm saying is, Joe caused this little girl's death. She was one of four who died at the funeral."

Linda looked away, then angrily wiped a tear from her eye in a quick, jerky motion. Finally she said, "You think Ethan is involved in this somehow."

"We don't know," Karen responded. "But we're certain Joe is. And you know why. Mandy."

Linda nodded, then sniffled. "Yes. Mandy. None of this would have happened if they hadn't attacked the plant—killed her and Dave."

She reached out and picked up the picture of the little girl.

"Mandy wanted kids so bad," she said, her voice very quiet. "She was getting fertility treatments, you know. Before the plant closed. She and Joe had been trying for several years. She always said she wanted to prove she could be a mom, that she could be the mom her own mother wasn't."

She paused, then muttered, "God, I need a cigarette. What the hell was I thinking, trying to quit?"

She stood, walked over to the kitchen counter, and retrieved a pack of cigarettes and matches from the drawer. Her hands were shaking so hard she had to try four times to light a match, then quickly puffed and gave a little cough. Karen darted a quick glance at Stewart. Were they getting to her?

"Joe came back here for Ethan the second week in January," Linda said finally, looking at the floor. "They've got some kind of base camp down in Boone County—I don't know exactly where. But from what Ethan told me, they've got sixty, maybe seventy guys down there. Bob Mays might know, but I doubt he'll talk."

"Bob Mays?" Stewart prompted.

Linda answered, "Joe's brother-in-law. He's the mayor or something down there."

Karen stood, struggling with her own feelings. She understood exactly why Joe was doing what he was doing. Everyone in Highview did. Part of her felt traitorous, doing this to her friends. She walked over to Linda and put a hand on her arm.

"I know this was hard," she said quietly, "but you're doing the right thing."

"Just please…" Linda pleaded, "please help my brother, okay? He's in too deep."

∾

"General Wells, thank you for meeting with us on such short notice," said Tom Murphy. "You remember my niece, Valerie Murphy? She's Secretary of Law Enforcement and Military Affairs in West Virginia."

"Yes, of course," Wells said. "Have a seat. I assumed from your phone call that this was urgent."

Valerie took a seat at the table across from Wells, and Murphy sat down next to her. They were sitting in a small conference room at the Northern Command headquarters at Peterson

Air Force Base. The flight to Colorado Springs had taken most of the day already, and when the meeting was finished, they'd be turning around and flying back to West Virginia immediately.

"It is urgent, General," she said. "You'll recall when we met a few weeks ago, the issue came up about a break-in at a biomedical research facility not far outside of Charleston?"

"Yes," Wells said.

"We're going way outside of normal channels, here," General Murphy said. "You'll understand why in a moment. First I need to go through a couple of details, if you'll bear with me."

"Fine, do it," Wells responded.

Murphy reached in his briefcase and handed across a thin sheaf of paper. "This is the report compiled by the Department of Homeland Security on their investigation into the break-in. Their conclusion was that nothing of serious import was stolen. You'll see in the executive summary that DHS concluded it was industrial espionage: they were looking for software."

Walls glanced at the report, then said, "I've read it already. I'm sure you're aware this is compartmentalized as secret, Murphy. I'm curious how you and Secretary Murphy obtained a copy."

"I'm getting to that, sir. But first, I need you to see this." He handed over another, thicker report. "General, this was the original report submitted by the investigating officer, Captain Matthew Floyd. Floyd is Army, and temporarily assigned to security at Hamilton Biomedical."

Wells furrowed his brows, and glanced at the report. "This I haven't seen. Summarize the difference, please."

"Sir," Valerie said, "Before the report was scrubbed by DHS, it said that the security breach included the theft of samples of a genetically modified strain of the H5N1 Avian Flu."

"Modified how?"

"To make it transmissible between mammals. This is re-search that's been going on a few years. They've been trying to identify ways in which the virus could mutate to become a pandemic. It appears that they were successful in getting it to pass between mammals through airborne transmission. The reports—both the original and the scrubbed version—were turned in to our special prosecutor by Captain Floyd. He was distressed by some of what he had learned, and felt that the information needed to get into the right hands."

Wells stared at the report, then muttered something.

Finally, he said, "Excuse me a moment," then stood up and opened the door. "Lieutenant Barker!" he shouted. "Get me the accident report you brought me yesterday morning. Captain Matthew Floyd!"

Valerie looked at her uncle, eyes wide. Accident report? He shrugged minutely, and they waited.

Three minutes later, Wells sat down across from them, a report in his hands.

He frowned, looking at the report. "It seems there may be more to this than we thought. Captain Floyd was involved in a single-car accident, driving from Charleston back to Hamilton Biomedical the day before yesterday. His car hit a bridge abutment and he was killed instantly."

Valerie leaned back in her chair. Floyd was dead? Was it really an accident? Her uncle's expression mirrored her own shocked one. "Oh, my God."

"Let me make sure I've got this straight," Wells said. "Captain Floyd shows up in your special prosecutor's office, claiming that this virus had been stolen. He submitted a report, and DHS scrubs it of any mention of the virus. Then he leaves, gets in his car, and is dead an hour later."

Valerie closed her eyes. "Sir, our chief investigator was murdered last week. He was shot during the assassination attempt on me, then someone walked into his hospital room and killed him with a silenced pistol."

Wells stared at the reports. "What do we know about this avian flu?"

"This particular strain is deadly," Murphy said. "In the wild, it's rare in people, because it can't be transmitted from person to person. People get it from coming into contact with infected poultry, mostly in Asia. The mortality rate is something like sixty percent of those who become ill."

"Then why the fuck is DHS trying to hide this?" Wells's face was flushed, eyes narrowed.

"General," Murphy said, "we have reason to believe that the Special Agent in Charge of DHS in West Virginia is somehow aligned with religious extremists. Valerie, please tell General Wells what you've found thus far."

Valerie took a deep breath, then outlined what they'd learned so far about the connections between JD Roberts and Roland Channing.

Wells stared at them as she spoke, his expression frozen. She couldn't read his face. She knew it sounded like a conspiracy theory, but too much was happening that didn't make sense here.

"It's tenuous, but your argument is strengthened significantly by the existence of this modified report," he said. "All right—you've done the right thing bringing this to me in person. I'll follow up from here. I'm taking this straight to the President. Murphy, I'll call you after I meet with the President, and let you know where we will head from here. In the meantime, what kind of contingency plans do you have? In the event terrorists release this stuff?"

"Within the limits of my manpower, we've developed plans to shut down the major roads in the state and institute quarantines," Murphy said. "We're setting up vaccination centers throughout the state, but that presupposes the existence of vaccine supplies, which we don't have at this time."

"I'll see what I can do to fix that."

"Thank you, General. In the absence of that vaccine, all we can hope to do is contain it. But I'm sure you're aware how difficult that will be in the event of an outbreak."

"Do what you can. I'll speak with you tomorrow."

∽

Ethan Judson looked over his shoulder at the car trailing them. "I know we gotta cooperate, Joe, but I'd love it if we could lose those nuts."

Joe looked in the rearview mirror at the smallish sedan matching their speed fifty yards back. "Yeah. Especially that freak Hoover." Tobias Hoover had a foot in two different camps: he was a member of Wyatt's irregulars, but was also a close confidante of Roland Channing. At their introduction, he'd told Joe that they were doing God's work and launched immediately into a sermon.

Ethan grunted, then lit a cigarette. He took a long drag from it, eyes focused on the glowing coal at the end, then exhaled, filling the cab with smoke.

"I know I'm not exactly planning on living forever, but do you have to fill up my car with that stink?" Joe asked.

Ethan shrugged. "Don't have to, but... yeah."

"Whatever."

"What's the plan, boss?"

"Don't call me that, asshole. And the plan is simple. We're gonna skullfuck those soldiers. Wipe them out, all at once."

"They've got machine guns. And air support."

"Yeah, but based on what I've seen, they don't have much brains. First problem, their lieutenant has his head stuck up his ass. Only three soldiers up on the dam? Less than a full squad guarding the house? They need three times as many soldiers to secure this area. Or more. You want to know the plan? We're gonna drop a missile right on that house. No screwing around, just kill everyone. Same time, we ambush their patrol. Box 'em in, then cut them down. No one left except the three chumps up on the dam. I'm thinking we'll send your nephew after them."

Ethan snorted. "My nephew's three years old."

Joe shrugged. "That's all it will take. Only reason I haven't done it before now is that they'll come down harder, and with more force, right away. Wasted effort. But if that diverts some forces from protecting the Vice President, I'm all for it."

Ethan glanced back over his shoulder again at the car following them. His eyes were narrowed, lips pursed in distaste.

"Joe, listen... I've got a lot of doubts about those guys, though."

Joe sighed. He had plenty of doubts, too. But they couldn't accomplish anything with fifty guys, no information, no resources. They needed Channing and Wyatt. "Yeah, so do I."

"Did you know about the snipers? At the funeral."

"Yeah. But they were supposed to be shooting at the soldiers. I never expected what happened."

Ethan shook his head. He gave Joe an almost pleading look. "Why are we still working with them?"

Joe shook his head. He shared Ethan's worries. But it wasn't that different than when he was in Iraq. In 2005 they'd fought the hell out of the tribes in the Sunni triangle. A year later, they were allies with the very same people. Sometimes you couldn't be too choosy about your friends. "What choice do we have? You know what they say: the enemy of my enemy is my friend. We need them. They've got resources and connections we don't have."

"They're fanatics. If they thought God told them to kill everyone, they'd do it."

The scary thing was: Ethan was right.

"Yeah. That's what scares me. It's why I've got to keep control of this thing."

"I think it's too late for that, Joe."

THIRTY-SEVEN

W HEN Valerie walked into Harry's Hog House, she wondered for the hundredth time how they managed to stay in business. Virtually every restaurant in Charleston was empty these days, and this one was no different. Far more people were crowded into the continually growing homeless camp around the capitol building than were out shopping and eating in restaurants.

Ambrose Hall was already sitting in one of the high-backed booths in the back of the room. She walked over, her heels clicking on the wood floor, then slipped into the booth. They greeted each other, then she placed her order.

Ambrose launched straight into business.

"All right. I've been investigating, and asking a lot of question. My method's been pretty simple: identify anyone with specific knowledge of troop movements or other information leaked. Cross-reference them to find out who had access to all of them. We're down to a very short list of suspects, Valerie."

Valerie nodded. "Any favorites?"

Ambrose nodded slowly, frowning. "You're not going to like this."

"I already don't like it," she replied. "What are we looking at?"

"Your number one suspects are Wade Davis and Asa Hatfield."

She shook her head, not entirely conscious of the movement. "Wade? I don't think so."

Ambrose sighed. "What's the first rule I taught you when you got to Washington?"

Valerie said, "Trust nobody. But I've broken that rule before, with you. With Al. My gut feeling tells me Wade is on the level. He's very loyal, and has been one of the only people in the entire department who has been in the least bit helpful."

"I think the solution to finding your leak is simple."

She raised her eyebrows, waiting for Ambrose to elaborate.

He nodded. "Over the next few days, you're going to give information to each of your suspects. It's going to be slightly different for each one. Lead a false trail, Valerie. One of them will follow it. Then you'll know."

Valerie sighed.

"All right," she said. "If that's what we have to do, we'll do it. And God help whoever it is."

"Indeed. How did the trip out west go?"

She shrugged. "I'm not sure, to be honest. Wells seemed generally outraged, and he says he's going to take the information directly to the President. But you know how things went with President Price last year. He'll do whatever is in his interest. I'm not confident his response will be helpful."

"Nor am I. On the other hand, the more highly placed people know what's going on, the safer you will be."

"Possibly. I'm not sure anything will make me safe. I didn't get a chance to tell you one thing. You remember Captain Floyd. After he left you, he was in an 'accident' on the way back to Hamilton Biomedical. Drove himself into a bridge abutment."

Ambrose closed his eyes, and Valerie continued.

"I had Hatfield check into the investigation. There's no evidence of... anything. He wasn't drunk. Streets weren't wet. There was no reason for the accident. And the scary part? No skid marks, except the last twenty feet. He was driving about seventy, and very suddenly, and for no apparent reason, swerved fifteen feet out of his lane."

"Someone ran him off the road."

She nodded. "Yes. That's the only real conclusion. But who the someone was, we'll never know."

"I think we already know."

"Yes. I think so."

Ambrose sighed. "Be careful, Valerie."

❧

Rebecca waved to Joel Leo as she drove away from the checkpoint, and within a minute she was driving down the two-lane highway toward Charleston. She had a little over an hour to get to dance practice, and was running late. Only three more weeks of rehearsals.

She was late because she'd been stopped by Jesse on her way out of school.

"Rebecca!" he'd called, just as she came out the doors.

She'd stopped, her stomach tensing, as he trotted up to her. The last time they'd spoken, he'd hit her. When he approached, she backed away a few inches.

His face fell when she did so.

"What do you want, Jesse?"

He stood there for a moment, looking confused, shoulders slumped. "I came over to apologize. Look... I shouldn't have lost my temper that day. It was the shock of... Dana... everything. It was just too much."

Thrown off, she struggled to find words that made sense. No one at school had spoken with her in days, except for a few nasty comments here and there. Suddenly being approached like this, with an apology, was confusing.

Finally she just said, "I miss her too, Jesse. She was my best friend."

"Yeah, I know."

"Then why have you been going around the school spreading rumors about me? Saying those horrible things? Half the school won't even talk to me."

He looked at the ground, his eyes shifting near their feet.

"I was wrong, okay? I was angry."

She took a deep breath, crossed her arms across her chest. He was angry. Angry enough to make her life miserable. "I don't think that's much of an excuse."

"Look, I want to make it up to you. Can I take you out to dinner?"

What? Was he serious? He'd been telling everyone who would listen that she'd been sleeping with Jim, and implied that she'd done so with some of the other soldiers. For a week, as she walked the halls of the school, she'd heard the whispers. Slut. Whore. Traitor. Bitch. And now he wanted to take her out to dinner?

Struggling to control her anger, she simply said, "I don't think that's a good idea."

"Why not?"

"For one thing, between work and rehearsals and school, I don't have time for you. And second, have you even thought for a second what it's been like to be me the last couple of weeks? You son of a bitch, I lost her, too! Maybe I needed a friend after all this! But everywhere I turn, all I hear is insults, and rumors. Rumors that you spread. If your goal was to ruin my life here, you've done a pretty damn good job of it."

"I told you I was sorry," he said, his voice sullen.

"That's not good enough. I wouldn't have dinner with you if my life depended on it."

He jerked as if she had hit him. What the hell? Did he think she would go out with him again? Fall into his arms? Was he that big of a fool?

She didn't realize she'd raised her voice until she saw Principal Higgens at the door of the school. He looked up, then began walking toward them.

Anger settled on Jesse's face, his features tightening, his little eyes squinting.

"I never knew you were such a bitch."

"Oh, go to hell, Jesse."

She turned to walk to her truck, and he grabbed her arm.

All she felt at his touch was rage. She swung around and screamed in his face, "Get your hands off of me!"

She jerked away from him, then turned to run for her truck.

Halfway there, she heard him shout, "Go fuck your soldier, Rebecca! And while you're at it, go fuck yourself!"

At her truck, she threw her bag across the cab, fighting tears back. Please God, let the truck start! She turned the keys, eyes closed, and breathed a sigh of relief when it caught and turned over.

As she pulled away, she saw Principal Higgens, remonstrating with Jesse. She hoped he got suspended.

Damn it! she thought as she drove away. She was struggling to keep from crying. Again. It felt as if her whole life was falling apart. Dana was dead. She couldn't go home. Her father wasn't even talking to her, and every time she spoke to her mother it was the same tired refrain: when are you coming home? Jesse had seen to it that school was miserable, and on top of that, she couldn't even see Jim, because her stupid father had seen to it that the Army wouldn't allow any contact between them.

God, she hated everyone right now.

She was still struggling to hold back tears when she pulled up to the checkpoint not far outside town. There were no cars waiting, so she rolled up.

Specialist Leo, now a fire team leader, approached her truck. She rolled down the window, and tried to compose her face.

"Miss Mays," he said. "You doing okay? You don't look so happy."

She forced a smile. "I'm okay, Joel, just having a rough day."

"Turville said you'd probably be coming through, headed to a rehearsal. He gave me this to pass to you."

He reached in his pocket and took out a small envelope.

She took it and whispered, "Thank you."

"You'll be coming back this way later?"

She nodded. "In about four hours."

He nodded. "We'll still be here. You be careful, okay?"

"I will."

He waved her on, and she drove a hundred yards, then pulled over and tore open the envelope, leaving the engine running.

The note inside was short, in atrocious handwriting.

> *Just wanted you to know I'm thinking about you, Short Girl. I'd do anything to be with you right now. Anything. I love you.*
> *Jim.*

She laughed, and started crying at the same time. Short Girl and Tall Girl. But now Tall Girl was gone. She put the truck in gear and pulled out, letting tears stream down her face.

Ten minutes later, she'd stopped crying. As she turned around a wide loop in the road, an unfamiliar pickup pulled out behind her. It sped up, then swung into the wrong lane, accelerating fast.

What the hell?

She took her foot off the gas, startled, then saw that it was her Uncle Joe driving the truck. He waved, then pointed ahead of them, to a pull-off beside the road. A moment later he pulled off onto the gravel. At this rate she was never going to get to practice. All the same, she parked the truck behind his. She turned the key, then stepped out.

She didn't want to see Joe.

That, of course, was the other rumor she'd heard. The one she'd avoided listening to, avoided learning anything about. But she hadn't been able to avoid it altogether. The rumor was too widespread: Joe Blankenship had declared war on the Army in a video on YouTube. Joe was behind the black armbands. Joe was behind the attacks on the soldiers.

She waited beside the door of her truck, examining his appearance as he approached. He was wearing camouflage hunting clothes with a pair of sturdy combat boots, covered by an old, worn army jacket that bore his name on an embroidered label. It looked as if he hadn't shaved in a couple of days, as his beard was well beyond five o'clock shadow, giving his face a stained, unkempt appearance.

"Rebecca," he said.

"Uncle Joe," she responded, her tone distant.

"Sorry if I scared you. I want to talk to you."

"So, how come you didn't just stop by? Why this scare-the-hell out of me routine?"

He grimaced. "I think you know why I can't just drop by. It wouldn't be a good idea for me to show up in town right now."

"So it's true? The kids at school are saying you're behind all the killing going on around here."

His eyes narrowed and his jaw set. "It's true I'm doing what I have to do to protect our people. I'm not behind the killing, I didn't ask the Army to come here."

"You protect them by killing people? Joe, they were shooting into the crowd the other day. A twelve-year-old girl was killed."

"That wasn't me."

She raised an eyebrow. If it wasn't him, who was it? "Why did you stop me?"

"I heard you moved out. Because your father refused to let you date one of the soldiers."

She nodded. "It's true."

His face shifted into an angry sneer. "Why, Rebecca? Does your family mean so little to you?"

"That's not it at all. Jim—I love him. My dad couldn't give me a single reason. Nothing. He just dropped it on me."

"He's concerned about you," Joe said. His eyes were darting around, as if he were nervous, watching or waiting for something. Maybe he was afraid the Army was going to drive by and arrest him. Maybe he was lying, and just couldn't look her in the eyes.

"And why should he be concerned about me, Joe? What possible risk could there be to me dating Jim?"

Joe shook his head. "I think you know the answer to that."

Her stomach started to turn. Joe didn't want to say it outright. But he was making a threat. "I see. Because there are people out there who want to hurt him. Is that it? Are you out there trying to kill the man I love?"

His jaw jutted out, face pinched. Stubborn, angry. "They shouldn't be here."

"They wouldn't have to be if it wasn't for you and the people you're running around with."

"Rebecca, I don't have time to debate this. You need to stay away from him. You need to stay away from all of the soldiers. Whether you like it or not, they're in a lot of danger. If you're hanging around with them, you are, too."

She was shaking. "Well, thanks to Dad, I can't see him any more. Jim's been confined; he's not even allowed to talk to me."

"Good."

"I'm done talking with you." She started to turn away, but he reached out and grabbed her arm.

"You're done when I say you're done, young lady."

She held still, looked slowly from his hand on her forearm up to his face. She refused to let him know how scared and angry she was. In a very quiet and calm voice, she said, "Get your hands off of me."

He dropped his arm. "Rebecca. Listen to me." His tone was urgent. "I shouldn't even be out here talking to you. Much less warning you. But you're family. You need to keep your distance from them. Things are changing and quickly. You know that."

"All I know is that you're threatening someone I love. You, of all people, should know better than that."

His eyes widened, and she knew that she'd hit home. She opened the door of the truck and got in. Slamming the door closed, she turned the ignition.

God damn it! The engine turned over once, twice, then died.

She rested her forehead on the steering wheel and hoped for nothing more than to slide into the earth and disappear.

Without another word, Joe got in his truck and turned it to face hers, then popped the hood on both vehicles. Even as he got out a set of jumper cables and connected the batteries, she found herself wishing that an army patrol would swing by and stop. He was family, yes. But it was starting to sink in: He was also a murderer.

Sixty seconds later, she had the engine cranked. He disconnected the batteries and dropped the hoods of both trucks, then walked over to her window.

He stood looking concerned, then said, "You really should get that fixed."

"I'll bear that in mind."

"Please, Rebecca. Listen to what I'm saying."

"No," she responded. "You listen to what I'm saying. Killing more people won't bring Mandy back. All it will do is make things worse. You know that. Uncle Joe... it's not too late to stop."

He frowned. "It was too late a long time ago."

She closed her eyes for ten seconds, opened them, then put the truck in reverse and backed away from him. He stood watching her as she pulled out onto the road and began driving away.

As she shifted into second she glanced up in the rearview mirror. He was still standing beside the road watching her, shrinking in the mirror as she drove away.

THIRTY-EIGHT

SUMMER 1998

MANDY Mays accepted her diploma from the Principal, and smiled so wide her cheeks hurt. Her eyes darted to the audience and met Joe's. She felt a shiver of pleasure go down her spine. Following her brother, who had received his diploma moments before, she returned to her seat.

A few minutes later, the last senior had received his diploma and the principal called the graduating seniors to stand, then dismissed them for the last time. Mandy immediately ran to Joe and hugged him. He leaned close and their lips touched in a chaste kiss that turned passionate. She felt the pressure of his lips, the very faint stubble, and a lightheadedness that could have swept her to the floor if her love hadn't been holding her up.

They parted a few inches, looking into each other's eyes. Joe's smile was as big as hers: his beautiful, strong smile that was enough to convince her that everything would always be all right as long as she was in his arms.

Then she heard her brother say, low, shocked, "Oh, my God."

Mandy's eyes darted to her brother, then followed his gaze to the woman approaching them. No. Not possible. No, no, no. Why now?

Mandy's ecstasy flip-flopped into a clenched stomach and tears came to her unwilling eyes.

"Mom?"

The woman, her face a haunting older mirror of Mandy's, stopped three feet away, a hesitant smile on her face.

"Mandy... Bobby. Oh my God, you're all grown up."

Bobby moved to hug his mother, and she wrapped her arms around her son.

Mandy grabbed Joe's hand, squeezing it for reassurance. Her mind was frozen in place. Her mother. After more than ten years, she just walked in out of the blue?

A rapid flash of thought and emotion passed through her. How many nights had she prayed for her mother to return? How many times had she begged God for her mommy to come home; how many times had she cried herself to sleep? What the hell was her mother thinking?

The words burst out of her mouth before she could stop herself. "What are you doing here? What do you want?" Mandy's tone of voice was cold.

"Oh, darling," her mother said. "How could I miss your graduation?"

"It shouldn't be that hard. You've missed everything else in our lives for ten years."

Her mother's eyes watered. "I didn't want to, Mandy. I've always loved you. I was hoping... I don't know what I was hoping for, really. I'm sorry."

She's sorry! Mandy's mind was still stuck. The nights as a nine-year-old girl when she'd wept for her Mommy. Until they'd been placed in their foster home, it had been her and her brother and their dad. What she remembered was missed school events, the shock and embarrassment of having to go to her friends's mothers for advice when she'd gotten her period. Then when the nightmares really started—when she had to lock her drunken father out of her room at night, barricading the door with a bureau because God only knew what he would do once he started drinking.

How many times had she begged God to bring her mother back? Well, now it was just too damned late.

Mandy's voice rose to a screech. "You're sorry! You run away for ten years, you disappear on us and leave us in the hands of your abusive pervert of a husband, and you're sorry? You expect me to forgive you? Go ask God for forgiveness, because you're not getting it from me."

Her shout brought a sudden, oppressive silence to the crowded gathering. The families of thirty graduating seniors stared in shock, then quickly began moving for the exits.

Mandy's mother's looked stunned.

"Oh, God, Mandy, I'm...."

"Shut up!" Mandy screamed. "How dare you?"

Joe quietly said, "Easy, hun, let's just go."

She yanked her hand out of Joe's and screamed at her mother, "Get out! This is my graduation and you're not welcome here. Get out!"

The older woman shook her head, and she backed out, weeping.

"I'm so sorry, Mandy."

"Go!" Mandy screamed. Then she collapsed into a chair and began to weep. Joe swept her into his arms, and whispered, "It's okay, babe. I'm here for you. I'll always be here for you."

Mandy felt her whole body shake and shudder, and she began to moan and weep.

"I hate her, Joe. I hate her. How could she do this to me? Why did she leave? Why!"

The image of her mother--face stricken, backing away toward the exit--flashed through Mandy's mind again. What had she done? After all these years of wishing her mother were there, she'd shut her out, thrown her away.

A fresh bout of tears burst forth, and she whispered, "I want my Mommy."

Joe just kept hugging her, knowing better than to question her contradictions.

She barely noticed as the people she loved gathered around her. They moved on to dinner and later back to her foster parents' home. Finally, Joe kissed her goodnight and she shuffled off to bed, still feeling numb. That was a dream, though, because for the first time in years, she cried herself to sleep: bitter tears of loss and rage.

෴

The morning after graduation, Mandy slowly forced herself out of bed and stumbled into the kitchen, still in her nightgown. Face still splotchy from crying, her hair in a mess, she poured herself a cup of coffee, mixed it generously with cream and sugar, then sat down at the table across from her foster-father.

Rich Ellison owned a car dealership just outside Charleston. Not necessarily the most sensitive of men, all the same he deferred to his wife on most, if not all, decisions affecting their life. One of those decisions, made not long after the then-young couple learned they could never have children of their own, had been to become a foster family for the county's Child and Family Protective Services. Mandy and Bob had lived in their home for several years now.

Ellison carefully folded his newspaper and set it on the paper. He looked across the table at Mandy.

"So," he began, "do you think you'll live?"

Mandy stared at him, stunned. Then she saw a corner of his mouth jerk upward in a quirky smile, and she couldn't help but laugh.

"Yes, I think so. I'm sorry I was such a nutcase last night."

His quirky half smile turned into a full grin. "Teenage girls are entitled to be nutcases every now and then. And you had ample reason, I'd say."

She cupped her hands around her coffee cup, took a sip. "Thank you for that."

He waved his hand. "There's nothing to thank me for."

She sighed. "Yes, there's plenty. You've been there for me and Bobby... through everything. That's far more than I can say about our parents, and you didn't have to do it."

He chuckled. "Sure, I did. My secret to living a happy marriage is simple, Mandy: do what the wife says. That said, you and your brother have done as much for us as we ever did for you. Having you in our lives has been a gift."

A gift her mother had walked away from.

"So..." he said slowly, "With your mother in town... what are you going to do?"

"Do?"

He nodded.

She frowned. Why the hell should she do anything? Her mother wasn't part of her life—never had been, never would be. Mandy thought she would be fine if she never saw that woman again.

"I don't really see any reason to do anything different."

He nodded, then said, "I see. I only ask because..."

She interrupted. "She doesn't deserve anything from me."

He raised his palm in the air. "It's not really about what she deserves. I happen to agree with you about that: what your mother deserves isn't at issue here. She gave up her right when she left. But I am concerned about what you deserve."

"I think what I deserve is for her to leave me the hell alone."

He nodded. "That's probably true. On the other hand, you might also deserve an explanation, and an apology. You deserve some closure. I don't know what her reasons were. In the end it doesn't really matter, because it won't change the fact that she left. She left when you were vulnerable and couldn't protect yourself. I think you deserve an opportunity to tell her that."

At the words, "She left when you were vulnerable," tears began coursing down Mandy's face. Sometimes she wondered if the hurt would ever go away.

She sniffled, then said, "It's hard for me to imagine an explanation that would be good enough."

He nodded. "I'm fairly sure there isn't one. You're going to find as an adult, Mandy, that very often things aren't good enough. But sometimes not good enough will be all you have. I'm going to leave it alone; you'll have to decide on your own what you want to do. I know it will be the right thing. But if you do decide you want to get in touch with her, here's the number."

He held out a sheet torn from the notepad on the refrigerator door, a small sheet of paper bordered by flowers and a cocker spaniel in the lower right hand corner. The details of a life she'd never imagined when she'd been a little girl living with her drunken father: taking the time and effort to find a notepad for the refrigerator that reflected some small bit of beauty. It was inconceivable.

Mandy took the sheet, folded it twice, then whispered, "Thank you."

Ellison stood, then said, "Whoops, look at the time. Gotta run, Mandy. Let me know what you decide, okay?"

❧

Mandy's quiet knock on the door of the motel room did nothing to express the extreme anxiety she felt; the pounding of her heart, the fear that dug deep in her gut and made her want to start crying before this even started.

The door opened, framing the five foot two, brown-haired woman who had abandoned her.

Elizabeth Stanton-Mays looked across the threshold at her eighteen-year-old daughter, fear reflected in her own face. She seemed to study Mandy for a moment, then said, her voice rough, "Mandy. Thank you so much for calling me. Please come in."

Mandy walked into the hotel room and glanced around. The Whitesville Motel wasn't exactly a five-star accommodation, but it was all the town boasted. Her mother's second story room was small, with a slightly slumped bed draped in a threadbare bedspread. A small table was shoved against the wall next to the window, overlooking Boone Street.

Her mother had set out cups of hot tea. Steam rose into the air in a lazy pattern that caught Mandy's eye.

"Please, dear, sit down."

Mandy sat down stiffly, on the edge of her seat.

Her mother sat down across from her, equally awkward, and said, "I'm grateful you called."

Considering how to respond, Mandy finally said, "I didn't do it for you. I'm here for me."

Her mother nodded. "In that case, tell me... How can I help?"

Mandy bit her lip, trying to force back the wave of emotions threatening to overwhelm her. "I want to understand... I want to understand why you left us."

Her mother's eyes watered, and she whispered, "I hurt you so much, didn't I?"

Oh, now she feels bad about it. A little late for that, isn't it, Mom?

"Just tell me the truth."

Her mother slumped in her seat. "I just couldn't take it any more," she whispered. "I'm so sorry."

"Couldn't take what?"

"Your father... this town... this life! I ... it was never what I wanted. I love you and your brother more than you can ever know. But it was killing me. Every day I was dying a little more, and I knew that if it went on much longer, I'd really die, at my own hands."

It was as if her mother had stabbed her through the heart. "Were we so horrible, then?"

"No!" her other cried. "It was never you! It was me."

Mandy leaned forward, unable to stop herself, and said viciously, "Make me understand. Make me understand why you left us all alone with him."

A tear ran down her mother's face.

"When I met your father I was at Juilliard, All my life I'd done nothing in the world but dance. It was my life... the life I'd worked and bled for, but it was ... so narrow. Then your father swept in to my life. He was... so amazing back then. Glamourous."

Mandy found that hard to imagine, but didn't interrupt.

"Your dad had served in Vietnam, and stayed in the Navy when the whole country scorned Vietnam vets. I was... very young... when this white-jacketed fighter pilot swept me off my feet. We got married. I thought my parents were going to go insane. I dropped out of Juilliard and followed him to San Diego."

Mandy stared at her mother, incredulous. Her father, a Navy fighter pilot in Vietnam? Her mother a dancer at Juilliard? What the hell was this?

"What happened?" she whispered.

Her mother grimaced. "Life happened. Your dad was in a bad accident. He had to eject from a crippled jet; it went down in the Mojave Desert. His parachute deployed, but he landed on bad rocks, cracked his skull. He was in a coma for weeks; we didn't know if he was going to live or die. Finally, the Navy medically retired him, and we came here... back to his childhood home.

Mandy struggled to assimilate this information. The father she knew was a coal miner, nothing more.

"So," her mother said, "We made the best of it. When he'd recovered enough to work, your dad went to the mines, and I taught dance at a studio in Charleston. But... you can't imagine what it was like. Your father was so bitter about losing his Navy career. He would fly into a rage at the drop of a hat. He drank... so much. When he was drunk he would..."

Her voice dropped to a whisper. "He'd hurt me." She buried her face in her hands.

Mandy stared at her mother. Now that was the father she knew. A cruel, uncompromising bastard.

But even so, he hadn't abandoned his children.

Mandy said, "So you just... left. Abandoned your children to the abusive drunk?"

Elizabeth's eyes widened. "No! I ... I didn't have any choice. I couldn't stay here...not in this horrible town, with him, with my whole life narrowed down to absolutely nothing. I couldn't be stuck here in Whitesville, West Virginia, with absolutely nothing in life to look forward to but another beating."

Nothing in life to look forward to, Mandy thought. That's what Bobby and I were to her. Nothing. Slowly, forcing the words out, she said, "So what did you do?"

"I... I went back to New York. I tried so hard to get back to my old life... to work on Broadway, or a ballet troupe. I auditioned everywhere. I tried to keep tabs on you and your brother, but from such a distance... it was too much."

Auditions and Broadway. Way more important than protecting your children. That made sense, if you were a heartless bitch.

"Did you get back to it?"

Her mother shook her head. "No," she whispered. "It was too late. I'd lost it. I never got a single part. I ended up waitressing. Finally, I realized I had to come back here... to you... before it was too late."

Forcing herself not to cry, Mandy said, "You missed that boat, mother. It was too late the first time your husband tried to rape me. It was too late when you walked out the door without considering how much you were hurting a nine-year-old girl. I don't want you in my life, mother. I don't ever want to see or speak to you again. Not today, not tomorrow, not ever. You can go to hell for all I care."

She stood up quickly, knocking the flimsy hotel chair over.

Her mother sobbed. "Mandy, please! It's not too late, I know it's not. I can... I promise... "

Mandy whispered, "I had enough of your promises when I was nine."

She turned her back, opened the hotel room door and walked out, letting the door slam shut behind her.

∽

Joe Blankenship awoke to faint tapping on his window. Disoriented, his eyes darted around the dark room before the quiet tapping came again. Fingernails clicking against glass.

He jerked to his feet, then untangled himself from his blanket and moved to the window without turning on the light.

Mandy was outside in the dark. What the hell? He felt for the lock on the window, sprung it, then slid the window up.

"Mandy? What are you doing?"

"Let me in," she replied.

He reached out, grabbed her hands and lifted her to the windowsill. As she climbed inside, he switched on the desk lamp.

Her face was blotched. She'd been crying.

"What's wrong, babe?"

She came into his arms, furiously kissing him. Then she whispered, "Make love to me, Joe. Please."

Joe didn't have to be asked twice.

Afterward, they lay entwined on the bed. Drowsy, he turned to kiss her, and was stunned to see a tear rolling down her face.

"Mandy, what's wrong? Talk to me."

She stared at him, her eyes wide and brimming with tears. Abruptly, she got out of the bed and began struggling into her clothes.

Desperation seeping into his voice, he called her name again.

Finished buttoning her sweater, she sat down in his desk chair and faced him.

"Joe, listen to me. I don't have the strength to say this more than once."

A leaden feeling in his stomach, he nodded. "I'm listening."

Her face twisted in grief, she said, "I can't do this. I can't do it to you. Or to me. Or to what we might have one day. If I stay here in Whitesville, I'll die. Or even worse... I'll be like my mother. I'll leave you and our children when they need me the most. I cannot do that. I can't be that person, waiting to find out every day if you'll live to make it out of the mine."

She sobbed, then said, "I'm leaving, Joe. Tonight. And I won't be back."

Joe was paralyzed. He tried to speak—opened his mouth even—then snapped it shut. He whispered, a choked, painful sound forced past his breaking heart, "Please, Mandy. I'll do anything."

She shook her head furiously. "It's not you, Joe. Don't you see it? I'm the one who is broken. I just... I don't have the strength to keep loving you. Please don't fight me on this. If you love me, please let me go. I'm begging you."

She couldn't be doing this. No, no, no, no. Mandy was his life. Who would he be without her? Just another kid bound for the coal mine. A nothing.

A horrid sound of grief escaped his throat.

"Mandy... I love you."

She leaned over and kissed him on the lips. She whispered, "And I love you. That's why I have to go."

Then she turned and slipped out the window and out of his life.

THIRTY-NINE

T H E Robert Byrd Federal Building in downtown Charleston was a shell: formerly a busy twelve-story office building, it had been one of the first casualties of the war, blown up by terrorists last fall in a late-night bombing.

The truck bomb had carved a hole in the front of the first three stories, and much of the front of the building had collapsed at the site. The only saving grace had been the timing: destroyed in the middle of the night, only half a dozen people had been killed.

Valerie had been in Washington at the time of the bombing, but she'd been past the site often since. In the months following the bombing, the violence and lack of funds in the state had prevented much in the way of recovery work. Barriers still blocked the surrounding streets preventing people from approaching the site, but the building itself still stood, half ruined, a testament to the inability of the government of West Virginia to do much of anything without resources or funds.

Henry brought the car to a stop in the square in front of the federal building, in one of the few areas clear of debris.

"Here, ma'am. There's the gentlemen from the secret service."

"Thanks, Henry," she said. He hopped out and opened the door. She got out of the vehicle.

Two men in typical Washington uniform approached, both wearing dark suits and ties. The first held out a hand.

"Secretary Murphy? I'm Gerald Collins, United States Secret Service. This is Noah Barker."

"Pleased to meet you, gentlemen."

They shook hands all around, and she said, "I'm in your hands, Mr. Collins. What exactly is the plan here?"

Collins and Barker looked briefly at each other, then Collins spoke.

"Ms. Murphy, as you know, we're the advance team for the Vice Presidential visit to Charleston. I want to make clear one thing up front: this is nothing personal, but we'll be handling one hundred percent of the Vice President's security for the visit. I'm sure you understand, given the instability of the situation here."

"Of course," she said, even though she couldn't help but find the lack of trust irritating.

"Vice President Hamilton will arrive via military transportation and brought to the site at nine a.m. next Thursday. The precise route to be taken will be secret. Once here, the Vice President will address a select group of guests. My understanding is that Governor Clark will be introducing him?"

She smiled wryly, then said, "I don't have confirmation on that. I think it's being worked out with the White House Chief of Staff."

She didn't say that her and Governer Clark's arrest the previous year had occurred in a television studio when Clark and Vice President Hamilton were both guests on the show. That would be … awkward.

Collins nodded, and she had the feeling he knew exactly what she was thinking.

"Well, once they get that sorted, we'll go on from there. I expect the address to be brief, no more than fifteen minutes. From there, the Vice President will leave before any of the guests. During his address, access to the site and the surrounding blocks will be restricted— no one enters or leaves. The US Army will handle the external security, and Secret Service at the site itself."

"That sounds reasonable." She was starting to wonder why she was here at all. "What can we do at our end?"

"We'd like your department to assist on two levels: first, security along the route to the site. The Vice President will have an extensive Secret Service escort, but we'd like an additional escort from the state patrol to block traffic and prevent civilians from entering the route. We'll provide three alternative routes we'd like you to be prepared to secure, and will finalize those when the Vice President arrives. Obviously we want those routes kept confidential except between you and your most trusted planners."

"That's no problem," she said.

"Second, we'd like you to pre-vet the guest list. Invitees will be coming from the governor's office, and as I indicated, we'll be running background checks on everyone. But in addition to that check, I'd like your department to review them for potential insurgent connections."

Valerie nodded. "There are two things you can help with on these," she told him.

He raised an eyebrow.

"First, you may not be aware of this, but West Virginia is a financial disaster. We've laid off most of the state patrol. I need some assistance with funding to get uniformed officers to assist with security."

Collins replied, "I understood that would be a problem. The director has allocated one million for this. Will that do the job?"

Valerie nodded, pleased. She'd been worried she'd be turned down flat. Which would have made it very difficult to get any cops at all into the street, since most of them had been laid off. "Yes, that will do it. Second... this is a bit delicate..."

"Go on?"

"You are probably aware that my department has... bluntly, we have some leaks. Some people whose loyalty is questionable. I'd like you to provide me with six alternative routes... three of which you definitely will not be using. I intend to give those three to my suspects. To see what they'll do with them."

Collins looked pleased. "To help you ferret out your leak."

"That's right."

"Done."

"It's a deal then, Mr. Collins."

☙

By the time Karen and Lieutenant Stewart arrived in Whitesville, it was late in the afternoon. The town, situated in a deep hollow, was already dim despite the still-bright sky, the sun already behind the ridgeline.

"The motel will be right up here," Karen said.

"We've got half an hour before we meet with Blake," Stewart said. "Let's get checked in."

She nodded. A few moments later, she saw the ramshackle Whitesville Motel. With its faded, peeling paint, it looked forlorn, almost abandoned.

She pulled to a stop in front of the tiny office and they got out of the rental car.

Stewart stepped out of the car, grabbed his bag and looked at the motel.

"What a dump," he muttered.

"Beats prison," Karen responded.

He chuckled.

They walked into the office. It was tiny and very crowded. Behind the counter sat a girl eighteen or so, with dark hair. Her eyebrows were scrunched together in a frown. She was chewing on a pencil, staring at a calculus textbook.

She looked up and said, "Hello."

"Hi," Stewart said. "We need to rent a couple rooms."

"Sure thing," she said. She picked up two cards from the desk and slid them across the counter.

"If I can get you to fill these out. I'll need a copy of your driver's licenses. Oh, and its cash only. Credit card machine is down."

"No problem," he said. "You guys got wireless here?"

She smirked. "Yes, but it's slow as molasses. I've been thinking about getting two cups and a string to connect to the phone company."

Stewart chuckled.

"Anyway, I'm Rebecca. I help out around here; if you need anything, lemme know. My Aunt Leah owns the place; she's usually around."

"You go to school around here?" Karen asked.

"Yes, ma'am. I graduate this year."

"Must have been a tough year, with all the fighting."

Rebecca's face clouded, and her eyes dropped to the floor. "Yeah, it has been."

Karen spoke in a very quiet tone, "Did you know Dana Wilder?"

She wasn't expecting the reaction she got. Rebecca's eyes suddenly watered, and she said, "Yeah, she was my best friend. And I don't really want to talk about it. Is there anything I can get you guys to help you get situated? There's a vending machine down at the end of the first floor. Oh, and the ice machine's out, but you can pick up ice at the drugstore, it's one block up the street."

Karen met Stewart's eyes, then said, "No, thanks, and I'm sorry for intruding."

"There is one thing," Stewart said. "What's the best way to get to the Army post?"

Visibly struggling to get her emotions under control, Rebecca said, "Go out the front door and turn left. It's about a hundred yards down on the left. You can't miss it. Okay... Miss Greenfield, you're in room 11, and Mr. Stewart, you're in 12. You're both on the second floor."

"Upstairs?" Stewart asked. Karen was surprised, too. Given that the place was empty, she'd been expecting to be put on the ground floor.

Rebecca nodded. "You really don't want a ground-floor room, trust me."

Karen raised an eyebrow, wondering what could be wrong with them, then shrugged. "Thanks so much."

The room was tiny, dark, and not well furnished. It did have a tiny desk, however, and was clean. She tossed her bag on the bed, then took out her Army-issue laptop and logged in.

No emails.

She thought for just a moment, tapping her fingertips on the table. Then she quickly pounded out an email.

> To: michael.g.morris@us.army.mil
> From: karen.r.greenfield@us.army.mil
> Subject: Contact number
> Dear Mike,
> I don't know whether you've received my earlier message, or even if you'd want to. But if you have, and you want to talk, I'm currently staying at the Whitesville Motel south of Charleston, West Virginia.
> Anyway, I expect to be here for a few days. If you want to talk, the number here is 304-555-2322. I'm in room 11.
> Karen

She looked at the message, almost deleted it, then hit Send.

A few minutes after they'd settled into their rooms, she met Stewart out front and they walked the two blocks up to the Army outpost. As they walked towards it, she paid close attention. Surrounded by sandbags and a high fence with barbed wire on top, it didn't look terribly safe. The gate was blocked by a Humvee, with two guards, and she supposed there were probably a couple of guards around back. All the same, the outpost was terribly vulnerable, sitting in the open at the bottom of a hollow with high ridges on both sides. It wouldn't take much to take the place out—a couple of high explosive rockets or mortars would do it.

"This doesn't look terribly safe," she said as they approached. "Almost like they've been hung out to dry."

Stewart nodded. "I'd hate to be stuck out here with just a platoon."

As they approached the gate, a soldier walked out and challenged them. Stocky, with rings of exhaustion under his eyes, his nametag read "Leo."

"Can I help you?" he asked.

They both handed over their Army IDs.

"Lieutenant Stewart and Private Greenfield. We're here to see Lieutenant Blake."

Leo raised his eyebrows, most likely at their civilian clothes. "Hold on a few; let me check with him."

He turned away and began speaking into a radio, but Karen was quick to note that the soldier in the turret of the Hummer never took his eyes off them. These guys were exhausted, and looked like they'd been through hell. Both were in full combat gear, and she noted that except when she and Lieutenant Stewart approached, neither of them emerged from cover. This might be a small town, but based on the behavior of the soldiers, it was clearly a war zone.

"All right, come on in, and quickly. We've been getting some sniper activity the last couple of days."

He led them to the house, opened the door and waved them in. Immediately inside was a small living room. Two soldiers were stretched out on ratty couches, both in dirty, torn uniforms.

"Wait here," Leo said. "The LT will be out in a few minutes; he said he's tied up on the radio with our company commander."

Valerie nodded. Leo's tone when he spoke of the company commander bordered on disrespectful. At first glance, morale here was a disaster.

They sat on the third couch. Neither of the resting soldiers stirred. One of them was staring at a portable DVD player, headphones on. The other's eyes were closed.

"They look strung out," Stewart said quietly. "This has got to be tough duty."

She nodded. "There was always some comfort in knowing that I was surrounded by fourteen hundred-ton tanks," she responded just as quietly. "Even though I lost most of my company in the war… it wasn't like being exposed at the end of the line like this."

They were quiet for a moment. Then Karen said, "So, what's your story, Lieutenant? You know all about me."

He didn't respond for almost a full minute, simply keeping his eyes on the wall. Just when she thought he wasn't going to say anything at all, he said, "West Point. Graduated last year, went through the basic officers leadership course at Fort Huachuca last summer, then ranger school."

He was quiet for about thirty seconds, then said, "We were out in the middle of fucking nowhere, in the mountains near Dahlonega, Georgia. You familiar with the area?"

She shook her head.

"Terrain's very similar to here. Woods go on forever, it's all vertical. Anyway, we were on a night training mission. The chopper went down, landed half in and half out of a tree. Two of the guys on the team were killed, along with the pilot. I broke my back and both legs, so I spent most of my first year in the Army in traction. They released me from the hospital about three weeks ago, so I went on leave, then got assigned here."

"Jesus," she responded.

"Yeah. It was something. Took them about two hours to get a medevac out there, because of the weather. I was just stuck in the back of the chopper, hanging sideways, in the worst pain I've ever been in my life. I thought for sure my Army career was over before it started."

"That must have sucked."

He nodded. "Could have been worse. My parents didn't have to go to my funeral. Three of the guys on the chopper— that's what happened."

She inhaled deeply through her nose. Up until now, she'd seen Stewart as little more than a kid. Now he seemed so much more grounded. "Yes. Sometimes I feel guilty," she said. "I got off kind of easy in the end. A few months in prison, and now all of the sudden I'm free. Everybody else on my crew died… A lot of the guys in my company died."

He looked at her closely. "Do you regret it? You could have walked away."

She stared back. Her whole life was regret now. "No. I don't regret it at all. As screwed up and tragic as it all was, I still believe I made the right decision."

He nodded, his eyes showing real understanding for the first time.

"Lieutenant Stewart?"

They looked up. Lieutenant Blake, in a badly frayed, dirty uniform, stood in the doorway. Karen was shocked. He looked like he could barely stand. There were dark circles under his eyes, and he could have used a shave two days ago.

"Come on back," Blake said.

They stood and followed him into a small room, jammed with a desk and chairs around it.

"You want a coke or anything?" Blake asked. "They're warm, but better than nothing."

"No, thank you," she said.

Stewart shook his head.

Blake fell into his chair as if he'd been dropped. He leaned back, blinked, then said, "So, I got a message from higher that you guys would be coming. You're from division intelligence? What can I do for you?"

As if to emphasize the difference between Blake and himself, Stewart sat ramrod straight in his chair. "We're looking for a man named Joe Blankenship. He's tied up in the leadership of the insurgency, and our investigation led us to Whitesville. It's our understanding that this is his hometown, and that his cell of insurgents may be operating out of the area."

Blake sighed. "Yeah. I know of him. He was last seen before the funeral disaster last week. You know about that? Running off, talking on his cell phone. If I had to guess, he was calling in the shooters as he ran away."

"We've read the reports," Stewart responded. "Any ideas where they're operating from?"

"If I had any, he'd be dead. I'm going to suggest a couple people to talk to, though, and one of them is right here. Hold on a sec."

He stood and half-staggered to the door. "Get Turville in here!"

"He just crashed, sir— he was on duty all night," someone shouted back.

"I don't give a shit. Get him!"

Blake returned to his chair and sat down. "Sorry about that. Okay… let me give you a quick brief while we wait on Sleeping Beauty. We've got a couple of big players here in town: Reverend Franks, who runs the local Baptist Church, and Bob Mays, the mayor. Franks is having some trouble right now. At the funeral he publicly called for rapprochement, to leave us alone and not seek revenge. All well and good, except just about everybody got up and walked out, led by our friend Blankenship. The next Sunday, about three people showed up in church. In short, popular sentiment is not on our side."

A young corporal—Karen would have guessed nineteen—appeared in the doorway. He looked deadly familiar. As he shouted, "Corporal Turville reporting as ordered, sir," she realized where.

Though she'd never met him, there had been plenty of media coverage of the investigation into his shooting of a civilian in Charleston last fall. That was while she'd been a fugitive, holed up in the National Guard headquarters in Morgantown. Mike Morris, her ex, had been Turville's company commander at the time. Like all the other soldiers she'd seen, he looked exhausted and dirty now.

"Come in, Corporal," Blake said. "This is Lieutenant Stewart and Private Greenfield from military intelligence. I'd like you to answer their questions."

"Yes, sir."

When he looked at her, Turville's eyes widened a little, and he gave her a speculative look. She guessed he recognized her as well.

Okay, so the other big player, Mayor Bob Mays, is Joe Blankenship's brother-in-law, something I just recently became aware of, thanks to Corporal Turville, here. Turville's the only one of us who has met Blankenship."

She leaned forward and asked, "How do you know him?"

Turville said, "My girlfriend, Rebecca. He's her uncle."

Karen and Lieutenant Stewart exchanged a wide-eyed look.

Blake clarified. "Turville was dating the mayor's daughter. He isn't any more."

Turville gave the lieutenant a very false smile. "Not by choice. Mine or hers. Sir."

"That's correct," Blake said. "After the mayor forbade her seeing him, she ran away—went to work at the motel. The mayor is severely pissed... at us. Which is not something we need right now."

"So... the Rebecca working at the Whitesville Motel? She's your girlfriend?" Karen asked.

"Yes," Turville replied.

"We met her when she checked in this afternoon."

Turville suddenly seemed to come alive. "How did she look? Is she okay?" he interrupted urgently.

Lieutenant Blake interrupted, his tone harsh. "They're the ones asking the questions, Corporal, not you. You just give them the information they need."

Karen chose to ignore the Lieutenant. "She looked okay," she said to Turville. "Not necessarily happy, but she was studying when we got there. Friendly girl."

"Do you think you could pass her a message?"

"Turville!" Blake intervened, on the edge of a shout.

"Oh, for Christ's sake, Lieutenant," Karen said.

Blake gave her a hard look. "Private Greenfield, I'll thank you to not get involved in this discussion."

Stewart leaned forward. "Enough," he said with authority, "First, I'm pretty sure division sent down orders we were to get full cooperation? Lieutenant Blake?"

Blake frowned. "Yes, they did."

"In that case, may we meet with Corporal Turville in private?"

"Fine," Blake said peevishly. He stood and said, "I need to go deal with some issues anyway. Take your time."

He walked out without waiting for their response. Karen stood and closed the door.

"Okay," she said. "Please tell us more."

Turville looked back and forth between her and the Lieutenant. "Can I ask you a question first?"

"Sure," Stewart said.

"You were Captain Morris's ex right?" he asked, looking at Karen. "The one who got into the shootout with DHS last year?"

She nodded. "That's right."

"Okay. Just making connections. I thought you looked familiar."

"It's all right. To be blunt, I was on the side of the rebellion. In fact, we were on opposite sides in the battle of Harpers Ferry. But I'm working with MI now, because I don't believe there's any honor in fighting from the dark or killing civilians. And that's what the insurgents are doing. That's what Blankenship is doing. If you know anything that might help us find him, we need to know."

Turville stared at her, stunned. "You were defending at Harpers Ferry?"

She nodded. "I was commander of the tank company there."

"Holy cow," he said, his voice quiet. "I don't know how I feel about being on the same planet as you, to be honest."

She shrugged. "I'm not going to lie to you, Corporal. I am who I am."

She thought it was more than interesting that Stewart was sitting back, letting her take the lead in this discussion.

"Okay... that's fair, I guess. I'll tell you what I know."

Haltingly, he described his initial meeting with Rebecca Mays during the ambush back in March. How they had met later, and went on a couple of dates, followed by a weekend spent at her house.

"The thing is," he said, "It was clear right up front that Joe didn't want me around. He looked at me like I was a... a bug. That he wanted to squash. And right after he and Rebecca's dad talked, her dad became noticeably cooler toward me. Not exactly hostile... just distant."

"When did that change?"

"Right after the funeral. He came up here the next day, talked to Lieutenant Blake. I don't know exactly what he said, but he told them to keep me away from her. And so the LT restricted me to the barracks—he even confiscated my phone." His contempt for his lieutenant was clear.

"Have you seen her since then?"

Turville looked back at her. "Do I have to answer that?"

She smiled, but laughed inwardly. She was starting to like Jim Turville. "You won't get in any trouble. Nothing you tell us will get back to Blake."

He took a deep breath, then let it out, staring off at the wall. "Yeah, I've seen her once. She came over the other night when I was on guard duty. Stood on the other side of the fence. We... we held hands through the fence."

"I'm sorry," she said quietly. A few years had gone by, but she still remembered what it felt like to be that age, to be crazy in love.

He shrugged. "To be honest with you, I love her. They can stop me from seeing her for now, but they can't change that."

"So... when was the last time you saw Blankenship?"

"At the funeral. He hightailed it out of there, and then the shooting started."

"Any ideas where he's based?"

Turville shook his head. "None. Probably out in the woods somewhere. You should see the guy, he's intimidating as hell.

Used to be Special Forces. He's probably out living in the woods eating snakes."

"Do you think the mayor would know?"

"Could be. But I wouldn't advise mentioning me to Mr. Mays, under any circumstances. I don't think I'm exactly his favorite person anymore."

"No," Karen replied. "Especially since she left home over you. She must really love you."

Turville smiled. "She's amazing."

Karen thought Rebecca was a lucky girl. Turville may have been a screw-up when he was in Mike's company, but it seemed to her that he'd done a lot of growing up.

"Okay, I think we're done here. Lieutenant Stewart, did you have any questions?"

Stewart shook his head. "You're free to go, Corporal. Get some sleep; you look like you could use it."

"Um… can I ask you a favor, if it's not too far out? Would you be willing to, um, deliver a message to Rebecca? Since you're staying where she's working?"

"I don't—" Lieutenant Stewart started to say.

Karen interrupted him. "I'd be happy to."

Stewart gave her an annoyed look, but didn't say anything. She reached in her bag and handed Turville a sheet of notebook paper and a pen. He quickly wrote only a few short lines while they waited.

He looked up, his face somber, and passed the paper and pen back to Karen.

"You understand we'll have to read it," Stewart said. "In case you're passing secrets to the insurgents."

"Yeah, sure, sir."

"You're free to go."

Turville left the room.

After a few seconds, Stewart said, "You don't have very much respect for rank and the chain of command, do you, Greenfield?"

She took a deep breath, then replied in a very calm voice, "I do, sir. But sometimes it's easy to forget that I'm no longer a tank company commander, or the acting operations officer for a combat brigade. Nowadays I'm merely a private, and I need to remember to defer to the judgment of green lieutenants who've had their commissions for just a few months."

Stewart winced at the kernel of truth to her words.

Finally he said, "I have no idea how you are going to make it two years without getting yourself thrown back in prison."

She sighed. "Believe me, lieutenant, neither do I."

&

Rebecca Mays stifled a yawn. Calculus and history done. English next, but she'd take a short break first. She stood and stretched, then opened her laptop and selected the music from Sleeping Beauty.

Not much room to practice in here, but she could do the basic moves. After just a few minutes she was lost in the music, eyes closed as she swept her arms up, her feet extended until she was standing on her toes. She was in that position when the bell over the door rang.

She dropped her arms and spun around as the couple who'd checked into the motel walked back into the office. Her face flushed. No doubt they'd seen her.

"Wow," said the redheaded woman, Karen Greenfield, she remembered. "You're a dancer?"

Rebecca nodded, still a little breathless. "Just practicing a bit."

"Can we talk for a moment?"

Rebecca tilted her head, suspicious. "About?"

"Well first, I've got to give you this."

Karen handed her a piece of folded paper. Rebecca unfolded it and instantly recognized the handwriting. It was from Jim!

> *Dear Rebecca,*
> *The woman who is bringing you this note is from the Army. She seems sincere, and it might be a good idea to help her.*
> *Anyway. The reason I'm writing:*
> *I just wanted to tell you that I worship the ground you walk on. If I have to wait a day, a week, a month, or a year, I'll be here for you. I know things are very difficult right now, with you living in the motel and in trouble with your parents. If you need to go home, I'll understand, and I'll wait patiently. I want you to be safe, and happy, and I'd do anything to make that happen.*
> *That's it. Don't worry about it if you don't hear from me for a few days. I'm probably going to be away and unable to get in touch.*
> *I love you with all my heart and please don't ever forget it.*
> *Jim*

Involuntarily, tears poured down Rebecca's face. Angry at her lack of self control, she balled her right hand in a fist and wiped her face with her sleeve. She took a couple of deep breaths to compose herself, then folded the note and stuck it in her pocket.

Looking back up at the woman, she said, "Jim says I should probably trust you. Who are you?"

The man stayed silent. The woman, Karen, said, "I'm Karen Greenfield. Both of us are from Army intelligence. We're looking for your uncle."

She took a deep breath, her memory flashing back to Joe, threatening her and Jim. Whether you like it or not, they're in a lot of danger. If you're hanging around with them, then you are too.

"Joe?"

"That's right."

"What will happen when you find him?"

"That depends on him, really. It's time to stop the killing."

Rebecca nodded. "I don't really know much."

"There may be things you know, but don't realize it. Details that are important in a wider context. When was the last time you saw him?"

She swallowed. What was the right thing to do? Joe was family. And she had no doubt that if cornered, he would fight. She hadn't believed the rumors that he was involved with the insurgents. Not until she'd talked with him, and he'd so casually threatened Jim. After that, she'd gone to YouTube and seen the video he'd recorded.

I'm fighting because the feds killed my wife, he said in the video. I'm fighting to free my country.

He was wrong. He couldn't free his country by killing people. And there was no question that Dana was dead because of him. Emily Barkes, that poor little girl, was dead because of Joe.

She met Karen's eyes. "I saw him yesterday."

Karen's eyes widened, and she and the man looked at each other. "Yesterday?" Karen prompted.

Rebecca nodded. "I was driving to Charleston for ballet practice. The show premiers in three weeks. I think he must have known I'd be going that way, because he was waiting for me, right beside the road about a mile after the checkpoint."

"What did he want?"

"He knew I'd left home because my dad won't let me date Jim. And... he basically threatened me. He said that things were changing... that Jim and his guys were in danger."

She took a deep breath, closed her eyes, then whispered, "He said that if I stayed around Jim, I'd be in danger too."

"That must have been upsetting."

Rebecca gave a humorless laugh. "Upsetting isn't the word for it."

"What was he driving? How was he dressed?"

"He was driving a really old pickup. Not his—I'd recognize it. I don't remember what kind. And... he was wearing camouflage. Army jacket, hunting clothes. Combat boots. He looked like he'd been rolling around on the ground somewhere."

"Did he give you any hint where he's staying or working?"

Rebecca shook her head. Was there anything he'd said? Anything at all? She couldn't think of any. "No, I don't think so."

Before she had a chance to think it through, she blurted, "My dad might know."

"The mayor," Karen said.

Rebecca nodded. "I mean... look, I don't want to get him into trouble. But he and Joe have been friends since they were little kids. I'm not saying he knows anything... but... maybe Joe said something?"

Karen nodded. "We were already planning to talk with him."

"He won't be happy."

"I understand. This is upsetting for everyone. But... you see why we have to find him, don't you?

Rebecca nodded. "I do. Because of Dana. And Emily. All of them."

Karen nodded. "Please let us know if you learn of anything, okay?"

"I will."

They left the office. Rebecca looked at the time. Ten pm. She could close up now. She didn't realize she was shaking until she stood up. She took out the note from Jim and read it again. She'd give anything to be in his arms right now.

∽

Outside of his room, Karen turned to Lieutenant Stewart.

"She seems sincere," he said.

"I agree. My gut feeling is she's telling the truth. But we can't take it as gospel."

He nodded. "She's got plenty of motive to help the insurgents."

"Yeah. Her best friend killed by soldiers is a big one. Blankenship is family. She might just be one hell of an actress, playing Turville to get information from him."

He sighed. "Unless Turville is helping her intentionally."

She shook her head. "No. I'd give money that's not the case."

"Why? It's plausible."

"Not if you know his history."

"What? Here, come in and sit down."

She nodded, and followed him into the room. It was a mirror of hers, but in worse condition. She sat on the one chair, and he sat on the end of the bed facing her.

She gave him the details. Last year, when Mike Morris's company was deployed in Charleston, they'd been sent out on a search-and-cordon mission following the assassination of Dale Whitt, the most prominent secession activist. Turville shot and killed a civilian teenager, mistaking a video camera for a gun.

"Understand, Turville never put up a real defense. He had good reason: the orders they'd been given were senseless. Plus, it was arguable that the deployment was violating Posse Comitatus. Morris kind of threw himself on the grenade—he walked into the Article 32 hearing and took responsibility for everything."

"What ended up happening?"

"Charges were dropped, and a few days later the war started. And... that's basically it. I don't buy that he'd be deliberately feeding information to the insurgents. Is she lying? Possible, but I doubt it. I think this one is what it appears."

Stewart nodded, his expression guarded. "All right. I'm inclined to agree."

Good, she thought. "So, what's the plan tomorrow?"

"Reverend Franks and the Mayor."

"Agreed."

Distantly, she heard the loud ring of a telephone. She tilted her head. "I think that's me. Gotta run."

He waved dismissively as she stood and ran out of the room and into her own. She picked up the heavy, old-fashioned phone mid-ring.

"Hello?"

"Karen?"

She breathed. Mike Morris.

"Hi, Mike."

He coughed, then said, "When I got your first email, I didn't know what to think. How are you out of prison? And on active duty? You're making my head spin."

She laughed. "It's kind of complicated."

"No kidding."

"Short version is... they're offering pardons to people who serve two years satisfactorily. Under certain circumstances."

"And... what are your circumstances?"

"I'm detailed military intelligence. Trying to help track down some of the insurgents who have been blowing stuff up and killing people down here. I actually ran into one of your old soldiers today... Corporal Jim Turville."

"Oh, wow... I didn't expect that. Where did you run into that fuck-up?"

She blinked. "I don't know that he's that bad. I think he's probably done some growing up since he was under your command."

"I should hope so. He made corporal?"

"Yes."

"What kind of trouble is he into now?"

She chuckled. "He and the mayor's daughter fell in love. Neither the mayor nor Turville's platoon leader are terribly happy about the situation. She's run away to work in a fleabag motel, and he's restricted to barracks."

Morris let out a loud, long laugh. "Oh, wow. Now that sounds like the Turville I know."

"I suppose," she said. "I like him. And her."

"What, you've met her, too?"

"Afraid so. She's a nice girl."

"Wow. Crazy world."

She took a deep breath. Something about his voice seemed different. More confident than she'd heard it in a long time. "How have you been, Mike?"

He didn't answer right away. "I'm... getting through each day as it comes."

"That bad?"

"It's pretty bad. To be honest, Karen, when this deployment is over, I'm resigning my commission."

Karen sat down suddenly. "You're doing what?"

"I'm done with this. Done. Quitting. If I manage to live through this deployment, the Army can kiss my ass."

She shook her head in shock. This didn't sound at all like Mike. "But... what are you going to do? I mean... the Army, it's been your life. Isn't that why Amy left you?"

His response was quiet. "That was part of it, sure. She never approved of me, nor did her son of a bitch of a father. But that's not what it's about."

"What, then?"

He was silent.

"Mike. It's me. You can talk to me. Of all people, I probably get whatever the hell it is you're going through."

He sighed. "Look, it's just… really bad here. Really bad. Unemployment just hit 24 percent this quarter. It's the highest since the Great Depression. People are literally starving in the streets. There's a huge homeless camp near the capitol building."

She said, "I saw something like that in Charleston, too."

"Yeah… I guess it's the same type of deal. People who lost their jobs, their homes. And not small numbers. Thousands. We escort in trucks of relief supplies sometimes, and there are riots. It's like something out of a third-world country. But this is Madison, Wisconsin. Seriously. We had to fire into a crowd with tear gas and rubber bullets last week. Killed a couple of people."

She closed her eyes, trying to imagine the scene. She couldn't. Even after all that had happened, she still couldn't accept the direction the country seemed to be headed in. She shook her head, feeling something close to grief. "I'm sorry, Mike."

"This isn't why I joined the Army. It's not in any way what I signed up for. And besides, my career's over. I'll never get another combat command."

"It can't be that bad, Mike."

"Oh, come on, Karen. You know the score as well as I do. I was almost court-martialed. I guarantee you I won't make the Major's list next month. And once I get passed over twice, that's it. I figure I'd better get out while the getting is good. Go back to school."

"What are you going to do?"

"Law school I think. Then get a job doing something meaningful. Go to work for the ACLU or something."

"Oh, wow. I never pegged you for a liberal."

"People change. I never pegged you for a revolutionary."

"True."

"What about you? What are your plans?"

She shrugged, even though he couldn't see her. Somehow this conversation wasn't going the way she'd expected. Mike wasn't what she'd expected. It had been several months since they'd spoken. A lot had happened to her in that time, but it sounded like a lot more had happened to him. "I don't know. I'm going to do the best I can to help run down the insurgents. These are some bad people, Mike. Really bad."

"I believe it."

"Once that's done... I'll go where they send me, serve out my two years."

"So you're really a private?"

"I am. I'll tell you what's crazy about that. Cory Avedis just got a merit promotion to Lieutenant Colonel. He's my battalion commander."

"Holy shit. Are you serious?"

"Yeah. You should give him a call."

He laughed. "Who, me? I'm just a broken-down infantry captain, Karen. He's a rising star."

"Well... I owe him. He flew out to California personally to spring me from the naval prison there."

Mike sighed. "I'm glad you're out."

"Yeah, me too," she said. He had no idea how glad she was to be out.

"Will you keep in touch?"

Of course she would keep in touch. But somehow, something in his voice made it seem he was saying it because he felt like he had to—not because he genuinely meant it.

"If you want me to."

"I do. Just know I'm not the same guy you knew. A lot's changed for me."

A lot had changed for everyone. She'd gotten people killed and gone to prison. Nothing was ever going to be the same again.

"Trust me, Mike. You're not the only one."

They sat in silence for a few moments. She found herself just listening to him breathe. Nothing about Mike had made sense in years. And now... she just didn't know. She didn't know what was going on with him, and she didn't know how she felt about him. Finally, she said, "Good night, Mike."

"Good night, Karen."

She gently set the phone down.

FORTY

B OB Mays sat across his desk from the two visitors, feeling very uncomfortable. They wore civilian clothes, but had shown army IDs when they arrived. This was unusual, and right now he just wasn't ready for any surprises.

"What can I do for you?" he asked.

The redheaded woman, who was lower in rank but acted like she was in charge, leaned forward.

"What do you know about the whereabouts of your brother-in-law? Joe Blankenship."

Bob tried to restrain himself from wincing. Damn it, he'd known that's what this was going to be about. He shook his head. "I haven't seen Joe in some time. Since before the war, actually. He lives up near Harpers Ferry, long way from here."

"Oh?" she asked. "Are you sure? He hasn't been by to visit? No phone calls? Nothing?"

Oh, Jesus. Why did I say that? He'd always been a terrible liar, and now the first thing out of his mouth was not only a transparent lie, but also one he could easily be caught out on.

Bob shook his head, and tried to restrain the shaking in his voice. "No, nothing."

She frowned, then opened a folder and slid a photograph across the desk.

"This photo was taken at Dana Wilder's funeral just a week ago. I'm under the impression that you attended the funeral with your family. Are you absolutely sure you're telling us the truth?"

Bob sighed. The photo showed Joe leaving the funeral, talking on a cell phone. The church was clearly visible behind him.

"I ..." He stopped. His voice was quavering, and that wouldn't do. He cleared his throat. "I forgot he attended the funeral. We didn't get a chance to talk because he left in such a hurry."

She rolled her eyes. "We have verified information that Joe Blankenship visited your house during the first week in April. Did you forget that as well? What did you talk about?"

Bob felt pain spreading in his chest. Jesus, that hurt. Anxiety attack. That's all it is. Anxiety. Not a heart attack.

He took a deep breath, then looked at them.

"I... why do you need to know?"

She smiled, then said, "I think you know the answer to that, Mayor. Joe Blankenship is part of the leadership of the insurgents. Among other things, he's responsible for the near massacre at the funeral in your town just a week ago. I understand that he's family. But you need to know that the consequences of protecting him could be serious. Very serious."

The man, Lieutenant Stewart, spoke for the first time. "Greenfield, we're wasting our time. We should just turn him over to DHS. They'll shake the information out of him."

She raised her eyebrows. "True. That would be a real shame though. He'd probably be held for a very long time. Possibly years."

Bob gasped involuntarily.

"Look," she said. "We don't really have time to get into a long pissing match with you, Mr. Mayor. Blankenship may be your brother-in-law, but he's also a murderer. He's killed people in your town. He's threatened your daughter, for Christ's sake."

"What?"

"Oh, you didn't know that? He ran her off the road the day before yesterday, just outside of town, and threatened her safety if she didn't break off her involvement with Corporal Turville. Is this the guy you want to protect?"

Oh, Jesus. Joe was serious. There was no way in hell he'd do that unless he meant it. He needed to get Rebecca home, and now. And make sure Joe knew that he wasn't going to cooperate with the Army any more. The Army hardly had anybody here—there was no way they were going to be able to protect his family.

"Listen," Bob said. "If I knew anything, I'd tell you. Yes, I saw Joe in April. He came here, and we talked for a while. He was trying to get me to support his little war, and I told him no. That's it. I have no idea where he is. And... to be honest... if he knew I was talking to you, I don't know what he'd do."

"What if we can arrange for protective custody? Somewhere out of state, for you and your family?"

"I don't know anything!" he shouted.

"Where is your wife, Mr. Mayor?"

"She went to see Rebecca. No school today, so she thought she could catch her at work. To try to convince her to come home."

"Would she know anything?"

Bob shook his head. "No. She doesn't really know about any of this—I haven't told her what's going on with Joe."

Stewart said, "I don't think you understand, Mr. Mayor. I get it—Blankenship may have threatened you. But I guarantee you, if you are harboring or protecting terrorists, then what he'll do to you isn't nearly as bad as what DHS will do. They'll just make you disappear. We can protect you, get you out of town. All you have to do is tell us where he's holed up."

Bob shook his head. He couldn't answer anything. He had to protect his family, and they were full of crap if they thought they could protect him from Joe and the people he was working with. "I have no idea. None."

Stewart handed him a business card. Bob looked at it. Calvin Stewart. Lieutenant, Military Intelligence.

"I want you to think about it, and I want you to call me. Understand? That's my cell phone. We're leaving for Charleston to meet with some people, but we'll be back by tomorrow night. We'll give you twenty-four hours. If we don't have answers by then, this is going to get very ugly."

Bob looked at them, and said, "I … I've got nothing to say to you."

His visitors stood and left. He sat at the desk, shaking.

∽

Rebecca was changing the sheets in room 11, earbuds in her ears, listening to one of her favorite bands, when the doorway darkened. She looked up, and was shocked to see her mother.

Startled, she stood, stopped her iPod, and took out the earbuds.

"Mom? Hey."

"Hey, Berry." Her mom's expression was sad.

"What's up, Mom?"

"Can we talk?"

Rebecca nodded. "Just give me a moment to finish up here."

She quickly finished tucking the sheet in, then threw the dirty linen into the bag on the back of her cart and rolled it out of the room.

She turned to lock it, then said, "I'm right down here."

She rolled the cart to a stop in front of her own room, then entered. "Can I get you some tea? Or make some coffee?"

"No, thank you."

Zoe sat down next to the tiny desk, and Rebecca walked into the bathroom and quickly washed her face and hands, then returned to the room and sat down on the edge of the bed, across from her mother.

"What's up, mom?"

Zoe looked around the room. "Did you know your grandmother stayed in this room once? She showed up out of nowhere for Mandy and your Dad's graduation."

Rebecca looked around. "No, I didn't know." She'd never met her.

Zoe shrugged. "It's just as well. I know forgiveness is a virtue, but Mandy could never bring herself to forgive her mother for leaving. You know she was a dancer? Just like you."

Rebecca blinked. What was with the sudden nostalgia? "No, Mom. I didn't know that."

"She went to Juilliard. She was in college when she met your grandpa."

She barely remembered her grandfather. Her father had taken her to meet him once, at the VA hospital in Charleston. She remembered him as a bent old man in a wheelchair with a harsh, grating voice. She might have been four or five years old at the time. He'd smelled funny, like old musty sheets that hadn't been washed in years. He'd died not long after the visit.

"Rebecca... I came by to ask you to come home."

Rebecca clenched her teeth. "Has Dad changed his mind?"

Zoe sighed. "I'm afraid not."

The why bother to ask? "Then I think you know the answer to that."

"Look, Rebecca… I know that right now Jim's not allowed to see you, anyway. Don't you think it would be better to come home, just for a little while? I'm certain we can convince your father to change his mind. Besides, it's only a few months before you leave for college anyway."

"I don't know how I'm possibly going to be able to afford college."

Zoe smiled, a conspiratorial smile Rebecca hadn't seen in a while. "We got your financial aid packet back from the Academy."

Rebecca suddenly held her breath.

"What did it say?"

"It's not quite a full ride. But close. It's close enough that we can afford to pay the rest."

"Oh, my God. Are you serious?" Her voice rose to a shriek at the last word.

"Yes!" Zoe nodded rapidly, tears in her eyes.

Rebecca jumped to her feet and hugged her mother.

"I didn't think… I never thought I'd be able to actually do it! Oh my God. I have to tell Jim! He'll be so excited!"

At those words, Zoe sat back, deflated. "You… you really love him, don't you? You're serious about this."

Rebecca sat back down and said, very quietly, "Listen to me, Mother. Have I ever, in my life, defied you or dad about anything? Ever?"

Zoe shook her head and sniffled.

"This matters to me. More than anything. More than going to the academy. More than my dance. More than my life.

Jim is my life now, and I'll do anything to get him back. As long as Dad stands in the way, I'm not coming home."

"No boy should mean more to you than your ambitions, your life."

Rebecca shook her head. "You don't understand. He's not like the guys around here... like Jesse, or whoever. He wants me to go to the Academy. He wants me to have the life I've always dreamed about. I'm sorry, Mom... I know this hurts you. But if you want it to change, Dad's going to have to be the one to change his mind. Because I won't."

A tear fell down Zoe's face. "I've never known your father to be so ... I don't even know the word."

"Unreasonable?"

Zoe gave a half-laugh, sounding very sad. "Something like that. Rebecca... I'm afraid. He knows something. I'm afraid something horrible is going to happen. Like the funeral, but worse."

"It's Uncle Joe," Rebecca responded.

"What?"

"He threatened me the other day."

"He did what?" Zoe sat up straight, her eyes narrowing, lips compressing into a thin line.

Rebecca sighed. "He told me... that things were changing. That the soldiers were in danger, and that if I stayed with Jim, I would be too."

"That son of a bitch!"

Rebecca didn't have a chance to respond, because her mother started talking again in a hurry.

"That's it, you're coming home."

"No."

"Rebecca, you aren't safe here!"

"I won't be safe there, either. And I'll sleep in a ditch before I go back home, as long as Dad keeps me from Jim. Don't you understand? Haven't you ever been in love?"

Zoe closed her eyes, putting her hand on her chest. "Oh, God. How did we get into this situation?"

The question didn't really need an answer.

"All right," Zoe said. "I'm going home to talk with your father. He will change his mind. You just… be careful. But I will have you home by the end of this weekend. I mean it, Rebecca."

"Mom… I love you."

"I love you, too, darling."

ᘓ

Bob Mays was still shaking in anger and fear following the visit from the Army when he heard a loud knock on his back door. He jerked up in his seat.

The knock turned into pounding.

He got up and quickly walked to the back door. Through the glass panes, he saw his brother-in-law.

Bob opened the door, and Joe walked in, shutting it behind him quickly.

"Jesus Christ, don't you know the Army was just here looking for you? What the hell is wrong with you?"

Joe gave him a contemptuous look, shaking his heard. "Shut up, Bob. I'm here for information."

"What information?"

"The Army is going to be leaving here. For good. But I need to know when their patrol comes back in tomorrow."

Confusion and anger flooded through him. "How the hell should I know that?"

"You'd better fucking find out. You've spent the last few months cheek to cheek with the Army. Brother-in-law or not, you're a collaborator. I want a goddamned answer, and I want it now."

Anxiety flooded through Bob, making his arms feel weak, and he had to speak through a lump in his throat as he said. "You threatened my daughter."

"What?" Blankenship demanded. He took a menacing step closer to Bob.

Bob found himself backing away half a step, even as he demanded, "Where the hell do you get off threatening Rebecca? She's eighteen years old, for God's sake!"

Blankenship's face turned red.

He grabbed Bob's shoulders and shouted, "She's fucking one of the soldiers, Bob! They're the people who killed your sister!"

Bob felt a mix of panic and rage. Rage that Joe would dare speak about Rebecca that way. And panic because of what the implications might mean for her, for his family.

"Joe... what is wrong with you? This is all going too far!"

"Bob, you don't understand anything," Blankenship said condescendingly. "This is bigger than me, bigger than you. I'm not going to be able to protect you any longer if you don't do something to protect yourself. Get your daughter home, and now. Keep her away from them. And no more cooperation with the Army! Do you understand me?"

"No! I don't understand you at all! Mandy would never, ever have supported any of this. She'd be horrified by what you're becoming, Joe."

"Don't you talk to me about my wife!" Joe shouted, his neck tighly corded, veins bulging on his forehed. Joe stepped back, then swung hard with his right fist.

Bob's vision went white when the fist connected, right in the eye. He fell back and hit the wall.

He slid down, slumped to the floor in shock. They'd been friends his entire life, and he didn't understand what was happening now. He didn't understand who Joe Blankenship had become. And the man in front of him right now terrified him.

"Listen to me," Joe said through clenched teeth. "I'll be calling you at midnight. And I expect an answer. I don't care what you have to do; I want to know when the patrol returns tomorrow. And I better get a fucking answer."

"I'll do my best," Bob whispered.

FORTY-ONE

T HE ambush would have been difficult to see or contain even for a full company or battalion. Over the course of the last three weeks, Blake's platoon had established a pattern, moving the roadblock to one of several intersections, but always returning to the intersection of Bridge Avenue and Boone Street: the best choke point for traffic coming into Whitesville from the north.

The final piece of the puzzle came into place last night: Bob's quavering voice. He'd arranged an urgent appointment as soon as the patrol returned at eleven am.

An overgrown wooded hillside with an extremely steep slope overshadowed the road on one side, overhanging rocks and dense shrubs crowding the ridge. Bridge Avenue crossed the river fifty yards away, leading to the trailer park.

Boone split here going into town, and over the course of the last three days, the insurgents had carefully set up a series of hunting blinds in the trees along a hundred yard stretch on the hillside. Two dour cinderblock buildings next to the motel at the intersection of Bridge and Boone provided cover for the remainder of the insurgents. Both buildings had been abandoned for five years or more, and the absolutely silent presence of twelve men in various hunting outfits had gone unnoticed.

Joe Blankenship knew they were well prepared, despite the fact they were facing two well-armed squads of riflemen in their armored Humvees. The soldiers had been up all night on a patrol ten miles east, searching out one of Blankenship's snipers, who had melted away into the forest. Two dump trucks stolen from Boone County's downsized public works department were ready to block the choke point, and sappers had already prepared to blow the bridge. The final lynchpins were the three wire-guided missiles, delivered by Channing's people last night.

When the soldiers returned to Whitesville, they were going to receive an unfortunate surprise. At the moment, Joe Blankenship sat isolated in a hunting blind at the top of the bluff. Radio and telephone silence was critical to the success of this mission, but the time alone wore on him, and raised doubts and misgivings he hardly knew how to deal with.

He closed his eyes, picturing Mandy. In his mind's eye she was still the young, achingly alive woman he'd fallen in love with as an adolescent. He could smell her perfume, picture the dimples at the corners of her smile, the tiny gold cross pendant she wore on a narrow gold chain, and above all the happiness in her eyes when they reunited after September 11th.

He'd been thinking all night about what Bob had said.

Mandy would never, ever have supported any of this. She'd be horrified by what you're becoming, Joe.

He'd hit Bob, hard. But...what would her response be to his current path? Was Bob right?

It troubled him that he didn't know. She would turn to the Bible for guidance, he knew that, but in truth, that was little help. The Bible might tell you to rise up and smack your oppressors or it might advise you to knuckle under, pay your taxes and turn the other cheek.

Blankenship had never been much for turning the other cheek. Or for the Bible, for that matter. But if Mandy still existed somewhere, if her soul was looking down at him now, he had doubts she would approve of his single-minded course. And it went against the grain to commit to a path she would disapprove of.

Doubts fled, though, at the sound of approaching vehicles echoing off the mountains. Approved or not, his course was set. Blankenship scanned the road below him. A flash of light from the abandoned cinderblock building told him the men there were ready. More flashes came from the trees.

Bob Mays had been correct about the time the soldiers would return to man the roadblock. Say what he might about his brother-in-law and best friend from childhood (sometimes the words "moral coward" and "collaborator" replaced those labels), Mays had come through with the information he needed.

Enough woolgathering. It was time.

ớ

Rebecca Mays was at that moment wrinkling her nose as she stripped the sheets of the room Lieutenant Stewart had vacated last night. Her mind kept running over her mother's visit, but turned up no solutions.

Increasingly she was realizing it wasn't even about Jim anymore. The longer she was away from home, the more it was about asserting her independence. Returning home would be giving in. Returning home would be acknowledging his right to interfere with her decisions regardless of her own needs, for any reason.

She had a lot of questions. After talking with her mother, it was beginning to sink in that there had to be a lot more to this than her father simply changing his mind about Jim. But what? Did he know something about what was going on with Joe? Did he know that Joe had threatened her?

After her mom left, Lieutenant Stewart and Karen Greenfield had returned long enough to pack their bags and check out. They'd left her a nice tip and said they'd be back in two days.

As she stuffed the filthy sheets into a cart, she heard the sound of two diesel engines cranking somewhere outside. Loud ones. It must be the two dump trucks, which had parked the night before at the warehouse next door. With any luck, it meant the county was getting sorted out and they'd have trash pickup again soon.

Then she heard the first gunshot.

ε⁄ɔ

Jim Turville was staring off into space as the Humvee approached Whitesville. The LT's Hummer was in the lead, followed by Turville's fire team, then Sergeant Nguyen and his driver, then Meigs's fire team, with Matt Leo now in charge of Rodriguez and two new replacements who had been in the field less than three days.

Turville felt a flash of anticipation, despite his exhaustion. He hadn't slept more than cat naps in almost three days as they rushed all over the place, chasing down snipers who disappeared into the woods as if they had never existed.

As the convoy came in view of the town, he sat up, more alert. She might be there now—might even be outside. The white building was ahead of them on the left, just beyond the abandoned warehouse. Two dump trucks with the county public works department logo on the side were pulling out into the road now.

He sat up straighter when he realized the trucks weren't moving onto the road. They were moving to block it.

Turville switched on his headset and began to shout just as a shot rang out.

The lead Humvee instantly swerved to the right and slammed into the rocky escarpment, crumpling the hood of the heavy armored vehicle.

Santiago didn't wait for orders. He wrenched the wheel to the left, plunging the Humvee to the left, off the road.

Sergeant Nguyen's driver was neither as quick nor as lucky. Perhaps distracted or confused by the sudden gunshots and Santiago's sudden turn to the left, the third Humvee in the convoy plowed without slowing into the side of the lead vehicle. Turville cried out as he saw the driver's side of Lieutenant Blake's vehicle crumpled by the impact.

"Out! Out!" shouted Turville.

The fire team leapt from the vehicles, facing the town. Tracers leapt from the grey cinderblock building directly next to the motel, and Turville shouted, "Suppress that fire!" even as he prayed the bullets wouldn't pass through the cinderblocks and into the motel beyond.

Nowell yanked the charging handle on his M240 machine gun, rested it on its tripod and began firing a stream of bullets into the warehouse.

Turville's vision went grey suddenly, as a crushing concussion hit him. A moment later it registered itself as sound and light. The bridge had been blown, blocking their escape in that direction. A huge plume of smoke rose into the sky.

Turville gasped for air, then looked around. He regretted it. It was bad. Really bad.

The first and third vehicles in the convoy were out of action. If Sergeant Nguyen and Lieutenant Blake weren't dead yet, they were certainly incapacitated by the crash. Turville's hummer had made it to the side of the road, and everyone was out, prone and unwounded as far as he could see.

Meigs's fire team—Turville's old team up until his injury in January—Turville averted his eyes. The inexperienced driver had stopped dead in the road. Literally. Matt Leo lay on the ground on his side, a small wound on one side of his face and a huge exit wound on the other. The Humvee itself was covered with a spray of blood and brain from Leo.

The new recruits were nowhere in sight. Turville couldn't tell if they were injured, dead, or simply bugged out.

Probably dead. There wasn't really anywhere to run.

Turville turned his attention back to the building. There was no fire coming from the river, but the bridge had been blown, which meant the enemy was likely on their left as well as ahead of them.

"Santiago! Nowell! Tilman!" Turville called. "Rest of the platoon is dead, I think. We need to get the fuck out of here, and report up to the company."

A burst of heavy machine gun fire arced down from the trees on the hill above them, stitching holes through their Humvee and tearing it to shreds.

"Holy shit!" Nowell exclaimed.

The sight decided Turville. He turned his attention back to the building ahead of them.

"They're up on the escarpment, guys. We gotta get the fuck out of here now. Follow me." He began to crawl backwards, and then stopped at the feel of a circle of cold metal against the back of his neck.

A calm voice said, "I wouldn't do that if I was you."

ↄ∕ↄ

By the time the second set of bullets rang out, Rebecca was dialing 911. She didn't think the county's emergency services normally responded to battles in the street, but for sure they would know how to reach the Army.

The phone rang and rang. No answer. What the hell? She hung up and dialed again. Busy.

She screamed as bullets suddenly tore through the paper-thin walls of the old motel, and dropped to the ground. Fragments of plaster and old wallpaper rained down on her, and she fought not to cry. Jim was out there in that!

She began crawling toward the door, then flattened herself to the floor beside the bed as a loud crash shook the entire building. The window shattered inward, fragments of flying glass punching holes through the drywall and missing her purely because she'd dropped behind the bed. Had someone dropped a nuke?

Thirty seconds later, the sound of firing stopped suddenly. Her ears rang, and she stayed huddled on the floor, covered in plaster, glass fragments and dust until she was sure the firing had stopped. Then she rose carfully to her knees and peered out the window frame.

To her left, the streets in the town were completely empty. Whoever might have been outside when the shooting started had taken shelter pretty quickly. The army barracks were... gone. Black clouds of roiling smoke rose from the blasted building, a Humvee turned on its side and torn almost in two.

Too her right, a dump truck blocked most of her view of the street. But she could see smoke rising from two Humvees. A man dressed in hunting garb, carrying a rifle, stood next to a Humvee, then carefully pointed his rifle into the air and fired four shots, one right after the other. Was he signaling someone?.

She gasped. To the right, on the river side of the road, a group of men had gathered in a circle. Four soldiers were on their knees in its center, hands behind their heads. She squinted, trying to see better, then screamed when she realized who they were.

Before she realized fully what she was doing, she was out the door and running up the street toward them.

∽

Blankenship was pleased. The ambush had gone smoother than he'd imagined it would. Who would have thought two entire vehicles of soldiers would take themselves out right in front of them by crashing into each other? Blankenship's team had suffered exactly one casualty: one of the men was shot through the leg by a random machine-gun bullet. That would hurt.

On their knees in front of him were the four survivors of the attack. A Latino PFC, Santiago. A large black private, bleeding from one arm, Tilman. A country white PFC whose nametag read Nowell. He'd been on the machine gun. And finally Corporal Jim Turville, the son of a bitch who'd been pawing at his niece.

Blankenship looked at Santiago. "Wilson, get the camera out. We'll get this up on YouTube tonight."

Wilson took out a digital mini-cam and trained it on the four soldiers.

Blankenship nudged the black PFC in the back.

"You got anything to say for yourself? You going to beg for forgiveness for fucking occupying our home and terrorizing our people?"

Tilman looked up at him, met his eyes.

"I got one thing to say. You're a fucking traitor."

Blankenship shook his head, then raised his forty-five to the side of Tilman's head and pulled the trigger.

The body hit the ground with a thud.

He raised the pistol again to the spic's head.

"You? Got anything to say, you fucking wetback?"

He heard a scream. A familiar scream.

He looked up and saw Rebecca running toward them, screaming, "No!"

One of the men raised a rifle.

"No! She's a civilian! Stop her."

Two of the men ran forward and grabbed the girl by the arms. He hated to do this in front of her, but had no choice.

❦

It was a nightmare. Even as she'd run forward, she'd been too late to stop them from... executing Tilman.

She screamed, and one of the men raised a rifle, pointing it at her. The leader stopped the man with the gun, but if Jim was going to be killed she didn't want to live, anyway. She continued running toward them until two of the men grabbed her roughly by the arms.

The hunters wore stocking caps, their faces hidden, but the voice that had said to Santiago, "Nothing to say?" was familiar.

"Stop it!" she screamed, as tears poured down her face.

The bullet rang out and Santiago fell to the ground, his hopes and dreams for his wife and children dead with him.

The voice. No. No. It couldn't be. It was.

"Uncle Joe! Stop it! Don't do it, please—I'm begging you!" At the shock of the sound of their leader's name, the two men who grasped her arms loosened their grips long enough for her to wrench herself forward. She stumbled, falling to the ground in front of her uncle.

"Please, don't do this!"

"Jesus Christ," Blankenship muttered. He pointed two the two remaining soldiers. "Get those two out of here, back to the rally point."

One of the men looked at Blankenship, and she could see the sudden distrust in his eyes.

"What about her? She knows who you are?"

Blankenship said, "I'll deal with her. You get the fuck out of here, back to the rally point like I said!"

She met Turville's eyes as they yanked him to his feet and began pulling him away.

"I love you, Jim!" she called after him.

He stopped and looked over his shoulder just for a second, then was pulled away into the trees.

Her uncle leaned over and said in a very calm, quiet tone of voice.

"You listen to me, Rebecca. Listen carefully."

She looked up at him. His eyes were wide open, the rest of his face shrouded behind the mask. "Rebecca, you do anything at all… and I mean anything, to betray me, and your boyfriend is dead. You hear me? Not just dead executed like this trash, but tortured dead. I love you, darling, but you fucked up getting involved in this. Now go home, and keep everything you've seen to yourself. Am I clear?"

She looked up at him, tears in her eyes.

"Who are you?"

He looked back. "I can't answer that."

Then he turned and walked away.

She leaned back on her haunches, eyes falling to the bodies of Rodriguez and Tilman. Rodriguez, who had dreamed of bringing his wife and child to live with him in America. Tears started to fall, and she was afraid she'd never be able to stop them.

FORTY-TWO

BOB Mays sat at the desk in his study, staring out the window. The sunshine outside had an ominous quality to it, underscoring his sense that something terrible was about to happen.

An hour ago he'd heard an enormous explosion, echoing between the mountains. No telling where it came from or what it was about. Sadly, such sounds had become commonplace of late. All he could do was wait. Phone lines were down again, so his best bet was to stay right here. If something was wrong, Lieutenant Blake would send a soldier out here to report.

He kept telling himself that, but it didn't relieve his creeping anxiety. Not after Joe's visit last night.

Zoe had come home in a rage. She'd told him that if he didn't allow their daughter to come home—if he didn't allow Rebecca to date that son of a bitch Turville—she would leave him and take his daughter.

"I don't know what the hell is wrong with you, Bob! I don't know if it's your damn pride, or if there's something you know you're not telling me, but this is it. I've catered to you in everything in our marriage, but I won't on this. I'm gone by tomorrow night unless you let her come home."

She'd stomped away and locked herself in their room, refusing to allow him in. He slept on the couch. Or rather, lay there unable to sleep, tossing and turning, praying the last year away. How had his life become such a nightmare?

On his desk was a photo of Zoe and Rebecca last year during their trip to Six Flags in Maryland. A happier time—a time when things made sense. A time before the short civil war closed the schools, wiped out half the electrical grid and made a disaster of his home and his life.

God damn Jim Blankenship and his demands! Mandy was his sister, but Joe seemed to think he was the only person on earth who grieved for her loss or knew what to do about it. Not in a million years would Mandy have supported Blankenship's bloody, chaotic response to her death.

What the hell could he do about it? Was he supposed to turn in his brother-in-law? He could hardly explain to Zoe why he'd made the decision he had, and without that explanation, all she could see was his cold, seemingly senseless refusal to allow Rebecca to see the man she'd fallen in love with.

Damn Jim Turville too. If he'd never come, none of this would be happening.

His first priority right now was to get Rebecca home. She might be eighteen and a senior in high school, but she sure as hell wasn't ready to be living on her own, working in some flea-bag motel. Especially not with a war going on.

He'd write a letter. Come up with some legitimate sounding reason he'd forbidden her to see Jim Turville. Ask for forgiveness? That hardly made sense, because he couldn't exactly change his position. Not with Joe Blankenship hovering in the background. Turville, and all his fellow soldiers, had been marked for death.

Bob grimaced. What the hell kind of time were they living in that he could know something like that and not take action?

He knew the answer. He was terrified. Blankenship's rebels could go anywhere they wanted; they moved freely through the mountains, lived in an abandoned coal mine, and the Army wasn't going to be able to stop them. Blankenship was former Army for god's sake, a counterinsurgency specialist. The soldiers he'd seen— kids like Lieutenant Blake and Jim Turville—were totally unprepared to deal with that.

Bob's first priority was protecting his family and his town. That didn't mean collaborating with Blankenship's rebels, but it did mean tolerating them. Because the alternative was unthinkable.

Bob took out a pen and paper and began to write.

"Dearest Rebecca," he wrote. His pen hovered over the paper. He didn't have the slightest clue what to write.

The sound of a car approaching interrupted his thoughts. Would it be one of the soldiers, or someone else? Perhaps someone from the town.

He stared at the blank page, simultaneously waiting for the bell to ring and debating how to open his letter.

He heard a car door slam, and went to the study door and opened it. At the same moment, the front door to the house opened.

Bob blinked and swayed on his feet, trying to make sense of what he saw. Rebecca stood in the doorway, wearing old blue jeans and a T-shirt. She was covered in dust from head to toe, and glitter in her hair looked like fragments of shattered glass. The entire front of her shirt and most of her jeans were spattered with blood.

Zoe came out of the kitchen at the same moment the front door opened. Her hand flew to her mouth, and she stifled a gasp.

Rebecca's eyes flickered to her mother, then returned to him. Her features set in a tight expression of rage he'd never seen on his daughter's face before, and she approached him rapidly, looked up at him and whispered, "Where the hell is Uncle Joe staying?"

Zoe's face went from confusion to utter shock.

Bob felt his heart race. "Rebecca..."

"Where is he?" she shouted. "This is your fault. You knew. You knew! This wasn't an accident. You knew he was an insurgent, and that's why you didn't want me dating Jim!"

Zoe, as always, interceded, her voice calm and condescending. "Rebecca... you don't know that for sure..."

She shoved her father, tears streaming down her face.

"Yes, I do! I watched Uncle Joe execute Santiago and another soldier! Santiago had a little girl, and a wife back home! He killed him in cold blood, and took Jim, and killed the rest of the platoon! He threatened me! God damn it, Dad! It's your fault—you let this go on! I want to know where he is!"

Mays put his hand to his chest, a sharp pain shooting up his right arm. "Rebecca, please..." he whispered.

She spoke, her voice fading to a whisper, looking at him with pure pity. "You're a coward, Dad. I never knew that. I never would have thought it."

Tears streamed down her face as she continued. "Well, now you have to make a choice. Either you tell me where they are hiding, so I can take that to the authorities, or I go to them anyway and turn you in. This is life and death, and I don't have time to screw around. Tell me now."

Bob Mays looked at his daughter, the pain in his chest growing worse by the second, and he collapsed to his knees.

"I'm so sorry, Rebecca," he whispered. "They're in the Eagle Mine. There's... there's old blueprints in the top left-hand drawer of my desk."

She didn't pause to even look at him, just marched into his office. Mays groaned, the pain in his chest growing worse, and Zoe rushed to him.

She whispered, "Is she…"

He nodded, then gasped out, "Chest… hospital… heart."

Their bloodstained daughter had already run out the front door, map in hand. She left the door standing open, the bright sunlight shining in the doorway like a bold-faced lie.

FORTY-THREE

A PRETTY girl with brown hair, her clothes covered in dirt and blood, walked into the lobby an hour before quitting time.

Bobby Wright wasn't exactly loitering. For most of the morning, he'd been waiting to do his assigned job, taking down the names and contact information of people who came into the headquarters to report information about the insurgents.

The thing was, there weren't that many people. Two, to be exact. Called in anonymously.

Bobby didn't mind. When he wasn't busy doing his mind-numbing official duties, he was busy using his handheld to find out the limits of what he could explore in the department network. Security conscious they might be here, but clearly the department had a shortage of computer experts. Within a day, he'd found his way into much of the network, and by the second day he'd identified the names of the short list of suspected leaks.

She'd done him a favor, so he fully intended to do her one.

He'd narrowed down his own list of suspects to three people: Asa Vance Hatfield, the belligerent director of operations and former acting secretary, who had nearly blown a gasket when he'd learned of Bobby's presence in the headquarters; Barry Rosenthal, the head of personnel, who also had what could charitably be called major financial difficulties, and Wade Davis, the smarmy chief of staff Valerie relied on way too much.

Bobby was leaning toward Rosenthal, mainly because of the disturbing information he'd found in Rosenthal's credit report. Money could be a powerful motivator, and Rosenthal was drowning in debt he couldn't pay.

When the girl came into the lobby, Bobby sat up straight. She was maybe five-feet two inches tall. Her blue jeans and a grey T-shirt had seen its better days before being doused in what appeared to be blood. Her face was covered in scratches, and her brown hair had been tied up in a pony tail, then apparently showered in drywall dust and glitter. Broken glass? Her lower legs and knees were muddy. In short, she was a mess.

She strode across the lobby with quick strides, her head high. She was on a mission.

Bobby stood and quickly moved to intercept her.

"Hi; can I help you?"

She looked at him, eyes wild. "I need to talk to someone. It's life and death. I know where the insurgents are hiding in Boone County."

She knows what?

He blinked. "I'm Bobby Wright. I'm an intern, special assistant to the secretary. My job's collecting reports about the insurgents. Come on over here, tell me more."

She looked impatient. "No offense, I don't want to talk to an intern. I need to talk to someone who can do something. This is urgent."

Well, that was typical. No one wanted to talk to a sixteen-year-old intern. "There's probably no one who can get you to the people who matter quicker. Come here—tell me what's going on."

She closed her eyes and muttered something, then followed him to the small desk in a temporary cube at the side of the lobby. He sat down at the desk, trying to look as professional as possible, and waved her to the chair across from him.

"Okay, let's start with your name."

"I'm Rebecca Mays. I live in Whitesville. Now listen. The Army was ambushed in Whitesville this morning. My boyfriend is one of the soldiers, and he was captured. Most of the rest were killed."

"Jesus," he muttered, grabbing a notebook out of his desk drawer and writing quickly. "And you say you know where the insurgents are hiding?"

"They're in the Eagle Mine. It was shut down, abandoned in 2006. I've got blueprints."

He looked at her, stunned. "You've got blueprints? Okay— how exactly do you know where they are hiding?"

Her eyes darted to the floor. Her expression reflected... What? Shame?

"My father was helping them," she whispered.

He nodded. "I see. All right, give me two minutes." He stood and left the cube, then speed-dialed his cousin from his cell phone.

It rang twice.

"This better be important," Valerie Murphy said.

"I got a live one, Val. You know anything about some soldiers ambushed in Boone County this morning?"

"Yes," she said, sounding impatient. "An Army platoon was wiped out down there. I'm kinda busy right now, Bobby"

He exhaled. "I've got a witness you need to meet alone, right now. Somewhere private."

☙

General Tom Murphy entered the small conference room at five minutes after five, with Lieutenant Aaron Thrasher right on his heels. The occupants jumped to attention.

"At ease," he said.

Murphy approached newly promoted Lieutenant Colonel Cory Avedis. "Thanks for getting here so quickly, Colonel."

"Of course, sir," Avedis said. "I was in Charleston anyway. Can you tell me what this is about?"

Murphy responded, his face grim. "If I had any idea, I would share it. Secretary Murphy called me saying it was urgent, that she couldn't discuss it on the telephone due to security concerns, and asked for a meeting with us as soon as possible. I've only got fifteen minutes; we've got some bad stuff going down all over. You know one of our patrols got hit in Boone? It's a real mess down there—at least ten KIA, plus some missing."

Avedis nodded. "We may have some leads on that, General."

Murphy raised his eyebrows. "Oh?"

Avedis waved forward the pair of soldiers who had been standing at attention in the back of the room. "Lieutenant Stewart, Private Greenfield, this is General Tom Murphy."

Lieutenant Stewart was in his very early twenties. Ring-knocker, but looked like he'd seen some action based on the nasty burn scar on his neck.

The attractive red-headed private came forward. She was several years too old to be a private.

"Lieutenant. Private Greenfield." Murphy said.

Greenfield spoke up. "Karen Greenfield, sir. Formerly Captain in the West Virginia National Guard. I had the honor of serving under your brother, and working with him at Saturn Microsystems for several years."

Murphy struggled to contain his reaction at her full name. Ken had talked about her often.

"I see. So, What can you two tell me?"

It said a lot, Murphy thought, that the lieutenant immediately deferred to the private.

Greenfield laid a set of folders on the table. "General, as you may know—"

She was interrupted by the entrance of Valerie Murphy and two teenagers, one of them a girl who looked as if she'd been showered with blood. Stewart and Greenfield jerked in shock when the girl walked into the room, then they looked at each other in surprise.

Murphy looked at his niece, then looked in shock at Bobby Wright. What the hell was he doing here? He knew Bobby was in town, staying with Valerie, but bringing him to an official meeting? He shot a quizzical look at Valerie.

"It's a long story, Uncle Tommy... uh, General. But thanks for meeting with us so quickly. This is time sensitive and to be perfectly honest, I didn't want anyone in my department to know about it."

Murphy looked at Valerie. As weird as this was, he knew she wouldn't waste his time, and the condition the girl was in made it clear something serious was happening. "All right, then. Everybody have a seat. Valerie, you start, since you called the meeting."

Valerie gestured to the young girl. "General, this is Rebecca Mays. She's the daughter of the mayor of Whitesville, and has been dating one of the soldiers there, a corporal named Jim Turville."

Avedis muttered, "Holy shit," and shot a wild look at Private Greenfield and Lieutenant Stewart. Murphy gave him a severe look, and he quieted.

"Please," Rebecca said, looking desperate. "You've got to help Jim, they're going to kill him."

Thrasher, sitting next to Murphy, slid a folder in front of him and pointed a finger at a list of soldiers involved in the ambush. CPL James Turville was listed as missing.

"Go ahead, Miss," Murphy said.

Rebecca quickly described her relationship with Joe Blankenship and with Jim Turville, then the ambush that morning. Despite the inexperience and age of the girl, not to mention the shock she'd been through, she gave solid details about the ambush.

"The last I saw of them, Jim was being thrown in the back of a pickup and they took off."

"Any guesses where they went?" Avedis asked.

The girl nodded. "My father...." Her eyes teared up, then she swallowed, jutted her chin out, and spoke again. "My father... he knew Uncle Joe was involved in this. And told me where they were hiding. It's in the old Eagle Mine just outside of town. They shut the mine down fifteen years ago. I've got a map."

She took out a crumpled, dirty set of pages and laid them on the table. Blueprints, with handwritten details that looked to have recently been added.

"Rebecca," Valerie said. "How did you get away?"

Rebecca said, "Uncle Joe shot Santiago and Tilman. That happened as I was running up. And I screamed his name. That's when he ordered the others to take Jim and Nowell. I think he was going to kill them before I got there. He threatened me, but let me go."

Murphy looked to the others, then said, "Okay. We're going to need some privacy for a few minutes. Valerie, you stay. Bobby... I'm not even going to ask what you're doing here, but can you please take Miss Mays outside the room and wait for us in the hall?"

Uncharacteristically, Bobby simply nodded and said, "Yes, sir."

Rebecca left first, and Valerie shook her head when she noticed Bobby looking at the girl's ass as he followed her.

With the teenagers gone, Murphy said, "Avedis, your assessment?"

Avedis looked at Private Greenfield.

"Sir, she is who she says she is. We met her several times when we were conducting our investigation in Whitesville. I was just about to brief you on that family when they arrived."

She slid a set of photos across the table. "This is Joe Blankenship. He is, as best we can tell, the primary leader of the insurgents."

Her finger drifted to the right, to a photo of a blonde woman in a plain dress. "Mandy Blankenship, nee Mays. His wife, and the first casualty in the raid on the Saturn plant last May."

She shook a little as she said it. "I knew Mandy well. She was a good and kindhearted woman, and ... well, it was tragic that she was killed."

The third photo was of a balding man in a suit. "Mayor Bob Mays of Whitesville. Mandy's older brother, Rebecca's father. We'd concluded in our investigation that he was aiding the insurgents.

"And finally," she slid a final photo across the table. "Rebecca Mays. Dating Jim Turville, who you will recall was investigated in an Article 32 investigation last year for the killing of a civilian. One of the events that sparked the war in the first place. We've considered the possibility that she might be using Turville as a source to aid her uncle."

Murphy nodded. "That could still be the case."

Valerie, Avedis and Greenfield all nodded.

Then Valerie said, "I'm not sure I buy it, though. She'd have to be one hell of an actress. She's very distraught. And, if she's lying, why would she come to us now? And with these?" She pointed at the blueprints.

Avedis shrugged. "Lure us into an ambush, perhaps."

Greenfield shook her head. "Sir, with all due respect, I don't think so."

"You willing to bet someone's life on it?" Avedis countered.

She answered swiftly. "Lives are on the line either way. If we act, we face the risk of going into an ambush in the mine. If we don't, then the prisoners face likely torture and execution. I realize I'm a private now and not really entitled to an opinion, but if I were in the General's shoes, I'd err on the side of rescuing those prisoners."

Murphy sat back in his seat and raised a hand to cover his mouth, which had twitched into an involuntary smile. His brother Ken had often spoken of the brash, beautiful and very, very competent company commander who'd served under him. In fact, he'd confessed during a weak moment when the two brothers had put away more than a few drinks that he'd been half in love with her. Murphy could see why. Even after being thrown into a military prison, and now released into the middle of a war zone as a mere private, she was impressive. Privates in the army simply didn't offer unsolicited advice to Generals. The fact that it was so out of line forced him to seriously consider the implications of what she was saying.

Murphy said, "I agree. Lieutenant Thrasher, I want you to get Colonel Redfield with the Fourteenth Special Operations Group on the line. Warning order for a mission as soon as we can possibly launch. You and I are going up there to meet with his command and staff group and brief them."

"Yes, sir," Thrasher said, jumping to his feet.

"Lieutenant Stewart, I'd like you and Greenfield to question Miss Mays. Get all the details you can from her, and prepare a brief—quickly—that we can provide Colonel Redfield. And, just to be on the safe side," Murphy said, "We'll take young Miss

Mays into custody until the operation is completed. Valerie, can you get Bobby to stay with her?"

Valerie smirked. "You'd have to pry him off that girl with a paint scraper, Uncle Tommy."

"Okay. Who in your headquarters knows about this?"

"No one," she replied. "Bobby caught her in the lobby, and brought her straight to me when she told him her story."

"Excellent. We stick with need-to-know from now on. Fourteenth SOG planners, the chief of staff, and those of us in this room. No one else knows about the operation. Clear?"

Nods around the room.

"Dismissed."

FORTY-FOUR

"Get in the back of the truck. Keep your hands behind your head."

Jim Turville followed the instructions. He didn't have much choice. Disarmed, he was surrounded by six armed insurgents, none of them looking happy at all to have he and Phil Nowell along for the ride.

His eyes were fixed on the clearing beside the road. The two Humvees were crashed next to the bluff, one of them crumpled, misshapen where the other had hit it from the side. Billows of white steam poured from the deformed hood of the other. Bodies were scattered around both Humvees.

Across the road from them was a third, his own. Two of the insurgents were getting into it. On the ground near it were the bodies of his friends, Karim Tilman and Jesus Santiago. The man who'd executed them was now towering over Rebecca.

She was on her knees, shock and disbelief in her eyes as Joe Blankenship spoke to her. His face was covered in a balaclava, which was ridiculous. They knew who he was. Another one of the soldiers had recorded the executions, thus the face covering. With a sinking feeling of dull rage, he knew that the video of his friends's deaths would be uploaded to the Internet before long.

One of the insurgents, a burly man in his thirties with a week of facial hair growth, said, "Don't get too comfortable with being alive," then dug out a T-shirt from a bag in the back of the pickup and tied it around Turville's face, blocking his vision. Then he pulled his arms behind his back and bound them with a zip-tie.

His last sight was Rebecca lifting Santiago's upper body to her chest as she wept. Grief and horror was etched on her face.

Blankenship had already walked away from her. At least he had enough humanity left he didn't kill his own niece. For now. Would one of the other insurgents come back and hurt her later? At the thought, Turville almost stood and began to fight. The thought immediately translated to action, and he tried to stand despite his bound arms and blindfold.

"Where the fuck do you think you're going?" a voice said in his ear, shoving him back down.

He felt and heard two more people get in the truck, and a few seconds later it cranked with a deep vibration.

"Where are you taking us?" he asked.

"To hell, soldier. Now shut the fuck up."

He shut up. Jim Turville had one mission in life right now, and that was to live through the next few hours. To live, to return to Rebecca. But he had no idea how to make that happen.

☙

"Rebecca," Karen Greenfield said soothingly, "I want to thank you for bringing us the information you did. I can't tell you how much it means, and we're going to do everything in our power to rescue Jim Turville and anyone else they took prisoner. If you don't mind, I've got to ask you some questions."

"Whatever you need."

Rebecca was focused as she sat across the table from Karen. Sitting alertly with her back straight, ready to answer questions, she was nevertheless shaking with anger and fear. To Karen's left was Lieutenant Calvin Stewart.

She found herself trusting Karen. The redheaded soldier was about ten years older than she was, and seemed sympathetic and understanding.

Bobby Wright sate closer to the door, by himself.

"First... along with Turville, another soldier is missing—"

Rebecca interrupted. "Phil Nowell."

Karen nodded. "Okay. So he was alive when you saw him last?"

"Both of them were being loaded into the back of a pickup truck. They were blindfolded before it drove away."

"Can you tell me what you did after that?"

Rebecca turned her face away slightly. She tried to maintain her calm expression, but she felt her eyes water, and she sniffled a little. Shame flooded through her. Shame for her inaction, her passivity...

"I sat there in shock, cradling Santiago's body, for... I don't know," she said haltingly. "It seemed like forever."

She closed her eyes for a few seconds. Minutes counted right now. Part of her was ashamed she'd spent so long there before she'd finally gone to confront her father.

Karen spoke, gently. "It's okay, you know. Shock and grief and horror are perfectly normal under the circumstances, Rebecca."

"It's just... Santiago was such a nice guy, you know? He was sweet, and kind, and... he was a dreamer. And what's going to happen to his wife and kids? He was working on getting his citizenship."

Rebecca had to struggle now to keep from putting her head down and weeping. She clenched her teeth and squeezed her eyes shut, then opened them and looked Karen in the eyes.

"He was a good guy. So was Tilman. They didn't deserve what happened to them."

Karen nodded. "If it helps any, I know how you feel. I lost some people I was close to during the war as well."

Rebecca shrugged, suddenly irritated the conversation had turned to her emotional state. "My feelings can wait. What information do you need? The important thing is doing whatever you can to save Jim and Nowell, okay? I'll... I'll deal with my horror and grief and whatever some other time with a therapist. Right now, let's do what we need to do to help them."

Karen blinked in surprise, then gave a half smile.

"Rebecca, I think I like you. Okay, let's get practical. How many insurgents were there?"

Rebecca tilted her head, thinking. "Joe, and another guy who seemed to be one of the leaders. There were at least twelve right there, and I saw more at the warehouse. It seemed like about four or five pickup trucks drove off together, along with the two who took Jim's Humvee."

"Okay. Did you recognize anyone else? Other than your uncle?"

Rebecca shook her head. "No. But most of them were wearing ski-masks and stuff." She took a deep breath, then said, "They videotaped what they did to Tilman and Santiago."

"Okay. How did you know to go to your dad? And what was his reaction when you talked with him?"

What was this going to do to help Jim? The thought barely passed through her brain before she said it aloud. "I don't understand what this is going to do to help Jim. What do you care about my dad?"

Karen and Lieutenant Stewart met each other's eyes.

"Rebecca, you seem very sincere. But seem is the operative word. Your uncle is a known insurgent. Your best friend was killed by the soldiers who were ambushed today. You've got every reason in the world to be leading our rescuers into a trap. I want to believe you, and I know Private Greenfield does, but we have to be sure."

Oh. My. God.

"Are you kidding me? You think I'm trying to help Joe and his gang of killers?" Her voice rose to a screech.

"No," Karen responded. "We don't think so. But you understand, we have to be sure."

Rebecca clenched her fists. She didn't have time to convince them, to make them trust her. They needed to move now. "Okay. The reason I thought to go to my Dad. First, he'd seen Joe several times this spring. I already told you about that. He went to Lieutenant Blake and told him to keep Jim from seeing me. It was ... how do I put it? It was really out of character. Not like my Dad at all. Normally he's a pretty reasonable person. He's never just come out and said I couldn't do something with no reason at all. Put that together with Joe threatening me, and the only thing I could think of was: Dad knows something I don't. He knows where Joe is, and he knows that Joe is involved with the insurgents."

Karen nodded, and said, "Okay. So you went home, and... what happened?"

"Well... my Dad freaked. I came on kind of strong I think, and well... you can see what I look like. I wasn't very, um, diplomatic. I told him he was a coward. And that if he didn't tell me where Joe was, I'd turn him in, and then he could deal with someone else asking."

"Okay. So he gave you the map?"

"He told me where it was hidden in his office."

"What happened then?"

"I left. I stopped at a phone booth first, but there wasn't any service, and I saw one of the billboards you guys have been putting up." Holding her fingers up in quotes, she quoted the sign. "'Protect your community. Report rebel activity.' The address was on the sign, and I didn't want to screw around trying to find a working phone somewhere, so I just drove on in. You know the rest."

"Rebecca, how many people in the town are supporting the insurgents?"

"I don't know. Directly, probably not that many. But, I think sympathy is with them. I'd say... indirect support... most of them. I've been at the end of a lot of hostility because I'm dating Jim."

Karen nodded. "Okay. I think we're done. You're a remarkably brave young woman, Rebecca."

She shrugged. "Brave would have jumped in between my uncle and Santiago and taking that bullet for him. I'm not brave. I'm just doing what I have to do."

Karen sighed. "All right. One final thing, and I don't think you'll be happy about this. But we're going to keep you in custody until the rescue operation is complete. I believe your story, and I know General Murphy does too. But we have to take every precaution to protect those soldiers. You understand?"

Rebecca tilted her head. She wasn't planning on going anywhere. "You couldn't force me out of here at gunpoint until he is safe."

Karen gave her a small smile. "We'll see about getting you something to eat then. And some clean clothes to wear."

Karen and Lieutenant Stewart stood and left.

❦

Six Blackhawk helicopters raced across the darkened landscape just above treetop level, the thumping sound of rotors reflecting off the ground below as the trees raced by.

In the lead chopper, Captain Barry McCormack rechecked his final notes. An experienced counterinsurgency officer, he'd spent much of his career in Afghanistan, way too much of it dealing with caves and other underground complexes. He had the feeling he was going to like fighting inside an abandoned coal mine even less. Caves filled with hajjis was one thing. A coal mine filled with pockets of methane gas just waiting for a spark—not to mention radicalized hillbillies gunning for federal troops—was not exactly his cup of tea.

That was the job. You went where they sent you and did what you were told and hoped to make it home to spend some time with your wife and kids before the next deployment to some other god-awful place.

McCormack checked his watch again. Three minutes until the drop. He keyed his headset three times, breaking squelch but not speaking. That was enough to signal the rest of the troops in all six choppers to be ready. The other ten soldiers buckled in with him in the back of the chopper began to stir, and he watched, amused, as Sergeant Wheatley thumped Private Hansen on the head.

Experience had taught them that Hansen fell asleep the instant you put him in a chopper, and he could be counted on to be difficult to awaken. During their practice run, right before they'd boarded for the real mission, he'd never made it off the chopper. Poor kid stood awkwardly during their after-action review, red faced and hideously embarrassed as Sergeant Wheatley chewed him out in front of the entire company.

Most of the troops were still familiarizing themselves with the unfamiliar weapons. Because of the risk of explosions and pockets of methane gas, they were going in with high-powered air rifles. It wouldn't completely eliminate the risk—especially since the insurgents almost certainly had conventional weapons. But every added factor of safety helped.

The coal mine had three entrances to block, plus three more vents big enough to allow humans access, and those had to be blocked as well. One platoon had been detailed to deal with those. The rest were going inside. That assumed, of course, that those were the only entrances. These old coal-mine maps—as their briefing officer had been at great pains to explain—were often inaccurate, missing spurs and entire levels sometimes, not to mention connections to other coal mines in the vicinity. Apparently the countryside here was riddled with them.

McCormack would be just as happy if every abandoned coal-mine complex in West Virginia just collapsed in on themselves. But this time they had prisoners to worry about: two American soldiers had been captured by the hillbillies and were presumably somewhere in the complex. It was his job to get them out, if possible, and kill the insurgents, no matter what.

The pilot signaled thirty seconds. McCormack keyed his radio set six times. The troops began to stand up, readying for the landing.

∾

The voices were low and indistinct, one speaking in short sentences, the other in long, aggressive sounding rants.

Turville slowly opened his eyes, but it made little difference. He was in a dark, rough-hewn room carved out of solid rock.

Thick wooden beams braced the ceiling, and everything was coated with black coal dust. As the men spoke, he lowered his eyelids enough he could barely see them and continued listening.

Against the far wall, near the entrance to the room, was an old wooden table, scarred with age. A small battery powered lantern sat on the table, illuminating a circle of light roughly two feet in diameter. In between Turville and the lamp, two men stood talking with each other. Backlit by the lamp as they were, Turville couldn't make out any features other than the rifles slung over their shoulders.

Turville was in so much pain over his whole body that he wasn't entirely sure where he hurt most. His arms were tied to the chair behind his back, and his feet were bound together so tightly that he could feel the bindings through his combat boots. His head was the worst: his ears rang, and he thought he could feel blood on the back of his head where one of the insurgents had hit him with the butt of a rifle not long after they'd left the scene of the ambush. He didn't know how long he'd been out.

"It's too late," on of the men said. "It was a stupid decision to bring them in here, but now that it's done you don't have any choice. We must execute them."

The other responded, "I'm questioning this one first."

"Fine, Joe, fine. You know as well as I do that he knows nothing of any use. A simple corporal? What value is there in suffering him to live any longer?"

The other man muttered a curse. "You don't get it. It's one thing to kill in battle. It's something else entirely to execute someone in cold blood."

"No! It's no different at all! They are soldiers of Satan! They come to spread their filth and lies! Isn't it true that this one has violated your niece? A simple high school girl? I would think you would be glad to put an end to that, Joe. Not only that... they tell me you allowed her to go free after she identified you. Do you realize how dangerous that is? You've put all of us in danger with your misjudgment, and now you compound that by letting this one live even a moment longer than he should. I'm taking this one out of your hands."

"No! I'm in charge here, Hoover. I decide."

The other man reared back, offense written in his posture. "You are in charge? No! God is in charge here, Joe Blankenship. And in this endeavor, I am His representative. Take care, lest He decide that someone else should be in charge of the tactical leadership."

Turville shifted slightly in the chair, and a tongue of flame shot up his his right shoulder. He groaned, and muttered, "Water."

The silhouette on the right stepped closer, and Turville recognized Joe Blankenship.

The other man said, "You have twenty minutes, Blankenship. After that, we finish it." He turned and stalked out of the room.

Turville's eyes jumped from the man who was walking out back to Joe Blankenship. The conversation had been clear enough. Twenty minutes before the other one came back. Twenty minutes to live. He strained against his binds, but the movement shot pain down his shoulder again and he gasped.

"Here, have a drink, Corporal," Blankenship said. He held a plastic canteen to Turville's mouth and tilted it back.

Turville drank, half of it running down his chin. It was ice cold, and he felt his throat spasm a little as the water went down. He coughed, accidentally spraying water in front of him.

"Slow down, you'll choke yourself."

Turville looked at him, more than a little confused. His manner was, if not respectful, at least kind. It didn't make any sense, nor was it consistent with anything he'd seen of the man previously.

Blankenship looked around, as if he were checking if anyone was in earshot, then said, "I want to ask you some questions."

Turville looked at him, then said, very slowly, "I already know you guys are going to kill me. I don't see why I should answer anything."

"Humor me."

Turville just stared.

Blankenship looked uncomfortable, then said, "Why are you here?"

"I'm sorry, what?"

"You heard me. Why are you here?"

"I'm a soldier, Blankenship. I get orders, I go where I'm told. Weren't you in the military?"

Blankenship shook his head. "This isn't the same."

"Isn't the same as what? Running around in the boonies in Afghanistan or Iraq? Sure it is—it's exactly the same. Except the bad guys here speak the same language you do, and went to the same schools you did."

Blankenship's face twitched, his expression shifting to a glare.

"No. It is not the same. We're fighting for our freedom."

Turville raised his eyebrows. "Like that guy you were talking to? The one telling you I have to die because I violated your niece? He's a fucking clone of Al-Qaeda."

A flash of anger crossed Blankenship's face.

Turville shook his head. He thought about Leo, lying dead in street. Santiago murdered. Tilman murdered. Meigs, shot after the funeral. The little girl killed by a sniper. Blankenship was an utter hypocrite. "Don't get all righteous with me, Blankenship. The fact is, I was planning to ask Rebecca to marry me. You know, she told me about you… and your wife Mandy."

"Don't you dare speak about my wife!"

"Why not? You're gonna kill me anyway. I get it, you're pissed, rightfully, because the feds killed her. They fucked up. But you know what? You're not the only person who ever loved someone else. You're not the only person who ever lost someone you loved. Not by a long shot. And somehow, unless she's a very different person than Becca told me about, she's up there wondering what the hell you're thinking, going around killing people and causing even more pain and loss for others."

Blankenship responded with an inarticulate snarl, then punched Turville in the face.

His head flew back and he screamed. All he could see was white as pain shot from the base of his neck down his spine and shoulder.

Blankenship hit him again.

When he opened his eyes, all Turville could see was the giant opening at the end of the barrel of Blankenship's rifle. He froze, and slowly swallowed. This was it. Everything he'd gone through, everything he'd tried to accomplish, it was all going to end in this shithole right now.

"Go ahead, Blankenship," he whispered. "Do it. Give Rebecca the same pain you have. Isn't that the plan? You're hurting, so you're going to make everyone else hurt just as much as you?"

The barrel wavered, then came back to him.

"I ought to just kill you now."

Turville sighed. It was too late. It didn't even matter if he somehow magically convinced Blankenship, because when the other guy came back, it would be all over. "Whatever, Blankenship. Do your worst. Just remember this: When it came down to it, you were no better than the people who hurt you. No different. I'm not some jack-booted oppressor taking over your country. I'm just a guy like you, going where they send me, trying to make it through life. If you can live with yourself after this, then go for it."

Blankenship lowered the rifle. He didn't look angry any more. He looked like he was about to cry. "Mandy ... she didn't deserve to die."

"No, she didn't," Turville said. "And for what it's worth, I'm sorry."

He flinched at the sound of gunshots, loud, echoing. First a small burst, then more and more. Blankenship turned away completely: the shots were coming from out in the tunnels.

"Son of a bitch," Blankenship muttered.

Hoover ran back into the room. "Time's up, Joe! The feds are here! We're evacuating!"

Blankenship looked at Hoover, eyes wild, then back at Turville.

Hoover raised a pistol toward Turville. "Prepare to meet your maker, Corporal Turville."

Blankenship leveled the rifle at Hoover and two shots rang out. Turville gasped as Hoover collapsed, blossoms of red spreading out on his shirt.

The shots in the tunnels were getting closer. Blankenship stared down at the body, then looked at Turville, his expression shifting between rage and grief.

"Rebecca deserves better than to be married to a soldier, Turville," he muttered. "If you get out of here alive... take good care of her. Don't fail like I did."

Turville met Blankenship's eyes and nodded slowly. "I'll do my best," he replied.

Blankenship turned and ran out of the room, leaving Hoover's body and a bewildered Jim Turville.

FORTY-FIVE

B OBBY Wright sat in a hard plastic chair, eyes closed, hands in his pockets, legs extended and crossed at the ankle. Four tense hours had passed since the he and Rebecca had been brought to the small conference room where they waited—Rebecca to be held in custody until the rescue operation was complete, Bobby keeping her company.

She was a bundle of pure nervous energy, pacing back and forth across the room, talking nervously about herself and her boyfriend. Every twenty minutes or so she opened the door to ask the two soldiers outside if there had been any news.

She was driving him crazy. On the other hand, he couldn't help but wonder what it was like to be Jim Turville—to have someone so passionately in love with him.

There hadn't been any news, no matter how many times she went to the door. Rebecca threw herself into a chair and said, "How can you sit there so calmly?"

Bobby shrugged. "I guess one of us has to stay calm."

She nodded, then laid her head across her arms on the table. "I'm afraid, Bobby," she said very quietly. "I'm so afraid he'll... get hurt... or... or..."

Bobby sighed, sat up in his chair and put a hand on her shoulder. "I know this is terrifying. But I'm sure they'll do the best they can to get him out of there."

She began to sob.

The door opened. Bobby looked up sharply, and Rebecca jumped to her feet.

It was the redheaded soldier, Karen Greenfield. She entered the room quickly, her expression guarded.

"Ms. Mays, Corporal Turville was found and he's going to be okay. They're flying him to the hospital right now."

Rebecca began to wail, tears of relief pouring down her face. She hugged Greenfield. "Oh my God, thank you, thank you!"

Greenfield returned the hug, her expression unreadable. When she pulled back, she put her hands on Rebecca's shoulders. "I'm afraid your father is also in the hospital, Rebecca."

"What?" Rebecca shrieked.

Greenfield nodded. "Apparently he had an attack of angina. It's not a heart attack, but they're keeping him under observation. You uh... you understand he's going to be taken into custody by DHS when he's released from the hospital?"

Rebecca nodded soberly. Her voice bleak, she said, "It's my fault."

Greenfield shook her head. "No," she said in a no-nonsense tone. "It's his own fault. To be blunt, even if you hadn't come to us after the ambush, your father would have been arrested within the next couple of days anyway. We'd just about finished our investigation and knew he was cooperating with the insurgents. Don't waste your time blaming yourself. He's an adult and made his own choices. And so you did you. You chose to save someone's life, kid. Don't ever feel bad about that."

"When... what will happen to my dad?"

"I don't know the answer to that, Rebecca."

Rebecca nodded, her face an odd mix of relief and sadness. "Can I go see Jim?" she asked.

"Of course. There's no reason for you to stay here now. Lieutenant Stewart and I are returning to Whitesville tonight—we've still got some work to do. We'll drop you at the hospital on the way. And Bobby, we'll get someone to give you a lift home."

"Actually, I've got my truck over at the law enforcement building. If you can take me there, I can take it with me. I um... might need a jump start."

∽

At the door to the hospital room, Rebecca stopped short. She was shaking. Greenfield had told her Jim wasn't seriously injured, but after all, her uncle had killed his friends—taken him prisoner. Would he even want to see her?

She took a deep breath, closed her eyes and calmed herself. She reminded herself that he loved her. She reminded herself of his eyes just before he was blindfolded and driven away. She reminded herself that she loved him, and that absolutely nothing in the world was going to get in the way of that. Then she pushed the door open.

Jim was asleep. She stood in the doorway for a few moments, looking at him. An IV dripped fluid into his arm, and his face was horribly bruised and swollen. He looked as if they'd beaten him. Dried flakes of blood were on his face and neck, and she founded herself wanting to find a wet cloth and clean him up gently.

Slowly, trying to be as silent as possible, she stepped into the room and sank down in the chair beside the hospital bed.

Jim let out a little groan and opened his eyes. Very slowly, he turned his face toward her and smiled. "Hey, beautiful," he whispered.

Oh my God, he's okay. She leaned forward and took his hand in hers. "I was so afraid for you," she whispered.

She tried to stop the sudden tears than ran down her face. Stupid! He doesn't need to see that!

"I'm okay," He lifted his hand to her face, wiped away a tear. "I'm okay," he whispered again.

"I didn't know what to do when they took you. I was afraid…." She stopped, then said in a rush, "I was afraid they were going to kill you."

"They were, but your uncle saved me, believe it or not," he replied. "Right at the end... I thought I was going to die. And somehow the Special Ops guys found us pretty quick."

Joe saved him? It didn't make any sense. Why would he execute Tilman and Santiago, then let Turville and Nowell live? She looked at the floor. "I got the location from my Dad. He was helping them. I turned him in. I don't know what's going to happen, I think they're going to arrest him."

He gently smiled "You saved my life, then."

"I had to."

"I guess that means we really are meant for each other," he said, grinning. "No other girl's ever saved my life."

She couldn't stop the stupid smile spreading across her face. "What other girls?"

He smirked a little. "We all have our secrets. But really, there's never been a girl before you."

She swallowed, her mouth suddenly dry. Shaking just a little, she said, "Where... where do we go from here?"

"Well... You're going to college. We have to figure out a way for you to be able to pay for the Academy. And... I go on being a soldier until my enlistment is up. And from there, well... when I get out of here, Rebecca... will you marry me?"

She started to cry and laugh at the same time. Then she whispered, "Yes. Yes, I'll marry you, Jim," and leaned forward and kissed him.

FORTY-SIX

"Have you read the papers yet?" Ambrose asked Valerie the moment she answered her phone.

Valerie leaned back in her chair, shifting the phone to her other ear.

"Yes," she said. "New York Times. You were right about getting those packages out. The big question is, what happens next?"

This morning, the New York Times had broken the story of the two different versions of the report from Hamilton Biomedical, named JD Roberts as the author of the modified, official version of the report, and quoted several unnamed officials from the FBI who said that Roberts had killed the investigation into the Arlington bombing.

"I don't know. But Roberts's web is going to unravel a little now. I expect he'll be forced out of his job by the end of the day. I made some calls this morning to Washington. There's likely to be Congressional hearings within the week."

She sighed. That didn't mean she was safe yet. But it was a lot better. "That's a relief."

"You still need to be very careful. A lot can happen in a week."

"Yes, I know." A week could change everything, and she still had no certainty that DHS wouldn't come after her. If anything it seemed more likely now.

"All right. You ready to set our trap?"

"I'll be moving on that shortly."

"All right. I've got the teams ready. Lay your trail, and let's see what happens."

"I'll call you shortly."

Valerie Murphy hung up the phone, then picked it up again and dialed another number. "Wade, can you come in for a moment?"

Nervously, she tapped her fingers on the memo on her desk and waited for Davis to arrive. She had less than an hour before it would be time to leave for the press conference—six hours before Vice President Hamilton's plane arrived in Charleston.

"Come in," she said at the knock on the door.

Wade Davis opened the door and stepped inside.

"Good morning, Valerie," he said with a smile.

"Good morning, Wade."

She stood and walked over to sit at the small conference table. Davis sat to her right and she slid the memo across the table to him, then pointed at the first of three options listed on the memo.

"I just got the word from the Secret Service; they're using route number one here."

Davis nodded. "Lee to Washington Street."

"Yes. Can you get things moving?"

He nodded.

The next part was going to be difficult. Having three different people call the state patrol and giving conflicting orders was going to make a mess. She leaned forward. "Wade... listen, I'm getting ready to call Hatfield... and I'm going to be giving him a false route. That may cause some confusion for the state patrol, but we'll just have to deal with that."

He shook his head, looking confused. "I don't understand."

"I want to see if he takes the bait. He's our leak, and I intend to prove it."

Davis's eyes widened.

"I see," he said. "Good move. How will you know for sure?"

"I have some assets watching him."

He smiled.

"Okay," she said, "I've got a lot to do to get ready for the press conference. Let's get this moving for the Vice President's visit. And Wade... let's keep the actual route as quiet as possible. You know what to do."

Davis nodded and stood. "I certainly will, Valerie. Do you want me to come along to the press conference?"

She shook her head. "I don't think it's necessary. I'm not expecting to do anything but be visible. General Murphy will be doing most of the talking."

"All right, then."

Wade left the room. She watched thoughtfully for a moment as the door closed behind him, then sent a text message to Ambrose Hall.

Davis has Route 1.

She picked up the phone to call Hatfield, trying not to dwell on the possibility that Wade was the traitor. She'd trusted him implicitly. But as Ambrose had said as long as she'd known him, you couldn't trust anyone in Washington, or in politics. You can have allies and friends, but trust? That had to be limited to a very few people.

❧

Wade Davis stepped out of Valerie's office and walked to his own. He was about to take a terrible risk, but it was time to move, and quickly. For nearly a week he'd been hoping to get a hint of the intended route of the Vice President.

Back at his office, he said to his assistant, "Mary, can you hold my appointments for the next hour? I've got to go down to the Enforcement Division."

"Yes, sir," she said.

He folded the memo and put it in his coat pocket, then quickly walked to the elevator and pressed the button. He tapped his feet impatiently until the slow elevator arrived, then hit the button inside for the ground floor. The Enforcement Division was on four.

At the lobby, he quickly exited the building, paying little attention to Valerie's cousin who sat lounging in a corner, tapping on a mobile phone. In the last week he'd wondered if that was something he could use. She'd been sheltering what was basically an underage runaway in her apartment, and given him an internship at that. The papers would make an interesting story out of that one. Today, however, he was too nervous to even think of Bobby Wright as he walked right past him.

Bobby, on the other hand, noted Davis. He immediately texted Valerie.

Number three has left the building.

On the street, Davis turned left and walked up Quarrier Street to the northwest. It was only three blocks, but he walked quickly. He didn't especially want to be noticed out here, and he wanted to be back in the building before anyone noticed he was gone.

Harry's Hog House was a popular barbecue restaurant three blocks from the office. Now, given the state of the economy and ongoing pileup of disasters in West Virginia, it was barely hanging on. Inside, it was dark and cool.

Harry Digby, the owner, was in the back office when Davis walked in. Davis stepped into the office and slipped into a seat.

Harry leaned back in his chair, looking nervous.

"I've got some information," Davis said without preamble. "This is top priority; it needs to get to Channing first thing this morning."

Digby leaned forward and put his hand out impatiently. Davis passed him the memo he'd been handed by Valerie, the finalized route circled on it.

Digby read it over, then looked up. "This is verified?"

Davis nodded. "Secretary Murphy gave it to me ten minutes ago. When I get back, I have to get the state patrol moving into position."

"All right," Digby said. He scratched notes onto a loose sheet of paper, then handed the memo back. "I'm on it."

Davis stood and turned toward the door, then recoiled. His way was blocked by two men, one of whom he recognized: Trooper Dennis Henry. The other man wore a dark suit and tie. Both their weapons were drawn.

Davis looked at Digby, who had backed up away from them. He looked calm, and not at all surprised.

"Wade Davis," Henry said. "You're under arrest."

FORTY-SEVEN

VALERIE Murphy slowly hung up the phone. Her expression was fixed in place, impassive, but inside, her emotions were roiling.

Despite Ambrose's repeated warnings that he suspected Wade Davis, somehow she'd convinced herself that there was no way he could be a traitor. She'd found considerable comfort in his tears when they'd discussed her father. She'd believed him, and trusted him. And the entire time, he was leaking information. There was no way to know right now what the extent of the damage was: had he also been responsible for the leaks to the media? The incredibly damaging character assassination?

The video of her and David had gone viral, and there was nothing in the world she could do to take that back. Every time she testified before a congressional committee, the old pervs on the dais would have that picture in their minds. Every public act she did for the rest of her life would be tainted with the very public knowledge of a very private, intimate moment.

David had repeatedly tried to contact her since their very brief discussion during the break in her confirmation hearing. She'd refused to answer his calls. While he might not be responsible for letting the video out—though she had serious doubts about his claims, repeated multiple times in the media of a hacker getting into his computer—the fact was, he'd taken the video without her consent or knowledge. He'd humiliated her in front of the entire nation, smeared her name and most likely cut her career short, all for his own deviant enjoyment.

She fought to control her tears. It was just too much. In less than a year, she'd lost her little brother, her father, and been imprisoned. She'd been hideously and publicly humiliated and betrayed by not one, but two trusted friends and allies. She didn't even want this job, and despite that, she'd allowed herself to be maneuvered into throwing herself into it with reckless abandon.

A knock on the door interrupted her thoughts, and she quickly took a tissue from a desk drawer and blotted her eyes. "Come in."

The door cracked, and Ambrose Hall leaned his head in the door.

"Not a bad time I hope, Valerie?"

She smiled, a bittersweet expression.

"Not at all, Ambrose, I'm just... making some last minute notes for the press conference. Come on in."

Ambrose opened the door fully and entered the room. As always, he was impeccably dressed, today in a charcoal pinstripe suit, with a flashy red and gold tie. His eccentric handlebar mustache, remarkably unusual in a big city like Washington, DC, was oiled and expertly trimmed. She'd laughed at the shocked looks in people's eyes when they saw him in conservative Charleston.

"I'm glad to hear you're working, Valerie. I was concerned I would find you brooding."

She tilted her head and tried to suppress a flash of annoyance. "And why would I be doing that? When have you known me to brood?"

Ambrose raised his eyebrows and gave an enigmatic smile. "I know you, Valerie. You've had… a truly horrible year. And I know you very much wanted to trust Wade Davis."

She deflated. "What do you want me to say, Ambrose? I'm heartbroken? It's not as if I'm unfamiliar with betrayal by now."

Ambrose rolled his eyes. "Dear, I didn't make you pick politics as a living. Unfortunately, it does go with the territory."

"I suppose. I guess I didn't see this one coming. Davis… He seemed to be genuinely loyal to my father, if nothing else."

"Yes, but which side of your father? The hardworking, patriotic man who raised his children here in West Virginia, or the leader of a failed revolution aimed at severing the state from the rest of the nation? Perhaps Davis's loyalties are a little more complex, and he saw you as an obstacle to your father's goals."

She shrugged. "I suppose that's possibly it. I mean… don't get me wrong. I want to know why he did what he did. But in the end, it doesn't matter. What matters is that I trusted him, and he used that. That's politics anyway. But it's not just that… it's…."

She stopped, frustrated, struggling to express the mix of shame and humiliation and rage she was experiencing.

Ambrose leaned forward. "It's really about David Brown."

Sometimes she hated it that Ambrose was so perceptive. But he was right. She nodded slowly.

Ambrose gave a droll smile. "Let me tell you something about men, Valerie. I'm aware you're a bright, up-and-coming political operative and despite the idiots in the newspapers, you're doing a fantastic job running this department. But when it comes to men, you're still a babe in the woods."

She laughed involuntarily. He was right again, and that was kind of sad.

"Men mostly think with their reproductive apparatus. Men are visually stimulated. David's video was... an unfortunate product of that combination."

Her eyebrows raised and scrunched together, she shook her head.

"What?"

Ambrose rolled his eyes. "Do I have to spell it out, Valerie? He was thinking with his little head, not his big one."

"Oh, God," she said. "Ambrose. He did it without my consent. Do you understand where I'm coming from with that? I never had a chance to say no, never had a chance to make any kind of decision regarding this. I feel... violated, like I've never felt in my life. Everyone I meet for the rest of my life is going to be looking at me, but inside their heads they'll have that video. He didn't have the right!"

Ambrose nodded. "Very true. Though I have to tell you, this will blow over with time. It's not like you're the only person who has ever had private photos or videos leaked. You just need to be patient right now and weather the storm. To be honest, I don't even think it's going to affect the committee vote on your confirmation. Your shock and anger was quite visible to the committee, you know, and Wade's arrest is going to go a long way toward convincing them of your abilities."

"I don't even want this job. I only did it as a favor to Al."

Ambrose leaned forward again. "Come now, Valerie. Be honest with yourself. This is exactly what you've always wanted to be doing. You're right in the center of things, making decisions, trying to make your world a little bit better. What could be better than that? You need to shake off the distractions and bullshit, and charge forward like you know you are perfectly capable of doing."

Valerie stared back at her friend.He was right again. What else would she be doing, if she wasn't here? Her mother had raised her to try to make a difference in her world, and her father had show in every way an example of just that. Would she be happy somewhere selling real estate? Teaching? Crunching numbers for a financial firm? Not a chance. This was where she belonged. She looked at her friend and gave him a wry smile. "Thank you, Ambrose. You know, I think you may be just what the doctor ordered this morning."

"Good," he said firmly, then stood. "I'll get out of your way then; you've got a press conference to prepare for. Just keep this in mind, dear: if you find yourself feeling isolated and alone… remember you've got people who love you?"

She nodded. "Thank you."

ভ৲

The capitol press room was packed with reporters when Governor Al Clark entered, flanked by Valerie and General Tom Murphy.

Clark strode the lectern. "Let's get this thing going," he said. "Thank you all for coming this morning. I have a couple of developments I'll be covering, and I'd like you to hold your questions until the end."

He waited a few moments while the reporters settled down, then began speaking. "I'm here today to give you an update on events here in West Virginia. As you know, when I took over as governor a little more than a month ago, West Virginia was faced with a crisis of greater proportion than the state has ever faced. Four months ago, in an act that committed the state irrevocably to war, the West Virginia legislature enacted a declaration of independence from the United States of America.

"I'm not going to discuss the rights or wrongs of that decision today. The fact is, at the time the majority of residents of the state supported the action—in fact it was wildly popular due to a series of events which took place last year."

"Regardless of how it came about, the fact is that in January a three-day war devastated this state. Thousands were killed. Tens of thousands were displaced due to the widespread destruction in the areas where ground combat took place.

"Nearly two million residents were left without power or heat through most of a truly brutal winter. We still don't have a clear accounting for the death toll as a result, but hospitals reported nearly three times as many flu-, pneumonia- and other cold-weather illness-related deaths this year than normal.

"Close to a majority of the state's first responders took part in combat actions as members of the National Guard, and have remained in custody since the end of hostilities. Even if they had been free at this time, the state is bankrupt and unable to pay for more than a tiny minority of its former employers.

"In February, the state defaulted on its debt. In short, when I came into office, we were in the midst of a first-class disaster, with challenges that virtually no state government has had to face since Reconstruction."

As Clark spoke, Valerie looked out at the audience of reporters. She recognized many of them, and had frankly avoided dealing with any of them since her hearing just two weeks before. Her own leanings, plus the advice of the public relations people at the department, had been to simply ignore the burgeoning scandal around the video.

That hadn't quashed it in the news: in fact, media attention had increased, especially after the revelation that David Brown had controlled the blind trusts of several members of congress, including Mark Skaggs, the scrappy Republican from Kentucky who had authored last year's so-called Fiscal Responsibility Act. The Securities and Exchange Commission had seized David's computers and were investigating whether hackers had gained access to confidential details of those accounts.

Despite the fact that the press conference had absolutely nothing to do with her sex life, the subject would likely come up today. It was obvious the reporters were delighted to have her as a target for questioning.

Their goal today was to turn that around. Turn the reporters away from scandal and toward the very real progress they needed to make. People were afraid, especially people who lived near the insurgent operations. Today, they needed to be reassured, desperately, especially in light of the news that biological agents had been stolen.

Clark continued. "I convened this press conference today to cover two major developments, but I want to preface it with some words about our major concerns, and the progress we are making."

He fidgeted for a few seconds before continuing. "Regardless of whether you believe that independence for West Virginia was the correct course of action—and I firmly believe that many principled people on both sides of that debate hold genuine arguments for and against independence—but virtually all of us agree that certain actions are beyond the pale. Terrorism. The targeting of civilians. Torture. Murder.

"Unfortunately, a tiny minority of criminals who hold on to the belief of independence have taken to exactly these tactics. In the last thirty days, they have attacked military patrols. They have assassinated the sheriff of Boone County and a prominent Baptist minister. Just forty-eight hours ago they ambushed a US Army patrol, executed several members of that patrol and took two others prisoner. Their actions have gone far beyond that of well-intentioned patriots. In fact, they are terrorists, fanatics and criminals. No civilized society can tolerate such actions.

"With this background, I'd like to introduce West Virginia Secretary of Law Enforcement and Military Affairs Valerie Murphy, who will brief you on a key action that is part of our response to these terrorist activities. She will be followed by General Tom Murphy, commander of the US Army presence in West Virginia, who will address Tuesday's ambush and its aftermath."

Heart pounding, Valerie took the lectern, meeting Clark's eyes just for a second as she did so. He looked reassuring. She wasn't sure she was ready for this. She'd faced reporters fifty times before, but never in the context of them going after her personally. She faced the reporters and began to speak.

"Ladies and gentlemen, in a few moments one of my staff members will hand out a packet containing all the information we are prepared to release regarding today's arrest and the preceding investigation.

"For some time now, we've been aware that a senior official in the Department of Law Enforcement and Military Affairs was leaking information to the insurgents regarding troop movements and other sensitive issues. Immediately on becoming acting secretary, I ordered an investigation—in cooperation with the U.S. Army's 352 Military Intelligence Battalion—into the Department of Homeland Security and the governor's office. The newly appointed special prosecutor is investigating the case for the governor's office, as well.

"Approximately two hours ago, the West Virginia State Patrol, in cooperation with the United States Secret Service, placed Mr. Wade Davis, chief of staff of the department, under arrest for a number of charges. The Secret Service and the xpecial prosecutor will finalize charges as the investigation continues.

"The arrest took place in Charleston today after Mr. Davis was provided false information relating to the visit by Vice President Hamilton, scheduled to take place this afternoon. Mr. Davis was tracked and observed handing over that information in an attempt to put it into the hands of terrorists."

She took a breath. The reporters had stirred substantially at the news of Wade's arrest. Would they follow that lead? It was starting to look that way. "General Tom Murphy will now brief you on last night's operations against the insurgency."

The hushed pack of reporters roared as she finished her statement, shouting questions as she stepped away from the lectern. The news had hit like a bomb, and she had the feeling it was going to go a long way toward distracting the political reporters from the intrigue surrounding her appointment. Uncle Tommy's announcement should make an even bigger impression.

Tom Murphy took the lectern. He wore the Army combat uniform, the single star of a brigadier general muted on the button flap of his uniform blouse. His hair was going grey at the temples, and the lines in his face were more pronounced than they had been just a few months before.

"My name is General Tom Murphy; I'm the commander of the military forces currently operating in West Virginia. As you all know, our mission here is primarily focused on restoring security and essential services to the people of West Virginia. That mission has been significantly hampered by the activities of insurgent groups operating primarily in Boone, Jefferson and Mingo counties, as well as some other cities."

He took a breath and continued.

"The day before yesterday, insurgent forces conducted a well-planned ambush in Whitesville. US forces were caught in crossfire from the hills overhead and blocked by two large trucks from entering the town. Twelve soldiers were killed in action, and two were taken prisoner by insurgent forces."

A hush fell over the room as he spoke.

"As many of you know, we have been working assiduously not only to provide security for the civilian population, but also to engage their cooperation and assistance. This is critical in any counterinsurgency operation. A resident of Whitesville came forward almost immediately following the incident and provided the location of the insurgent forces and their prisoners."

"At approximately nine p.m. eastern time, special forces conducted a raid on the closed Eagle coal mine just outside Whitesville. Their mission was to rescue the prisoners and engage and destroy the enemy."

"I'm happy to report that the mission was a complete success. The prisoners were released, and twenty-two of the insurgents were killed on the scene. Five insurgents were taken prisoner and are now being questioned by military intelligence and Department of Homeland Security personnel."

"I want to be clear that this is only a first step. However, it is a significant blow against what we believe is a small and dedicated force of fanatics. In order to continue that fight and restore peace and prosperity to the people of West Virginia, we must continue to have cooperation and information from the people of West Virginia who are being harmed by these fanatics and terrorists.

"That completes my statement. Questions?"

A roar went up in the room as reporters scrambled to be first.

The first question left no doubt that the New York Times's news would be the story.

"General, can you comment on the New York Times story detailing links between the Department of Homeland Security and the insurgents?"

Tom grimaced. "All I can say at this time is that my understanding is that those links are being looked into by Congress and the Federal Bureau of Investigation. Obviously we're concerned."

"A follow-up—if the insurgents have obtained samples of avian flu from Hamilton Biomedical, what are you doing about it?"

"Okay, first, that's a really big if. We don't know exactly what happened at Hamilton Biomedical. We're working with local and state authorities to develop contingency plans. These are being coordinated with General Wells of US Northern Command as well as the federal government."

Valerie took a deep breath. Her uncle's answer was completely devoid of facts. But it was just about all they could say.

Another reporter raised a hand, and Governor Clark acknowledged her.

"General, are there plans to distribute a vaccine?"

Tom turned to Valerie. She stepped up to the microphone. "At this time, there are approximately 100,000 doses of an experimental vaccine in the United States. The vaccine has not been tested, nor FDA approved. Basically, the vaccine is a nonstarter at this time, except for certain high risk personnel, such as first responders, emergency room doctors and nurses. We're focused on prevention efforts, and if that fails, quarantine."

A murmur rose across the room as the reporters spoke amongst themselves, and a number of them began making phone calls. Finally, one of the reporters said, "What are you saying? That if the insurgents release this stuff, there's nothing you can do?"

Governor Clark looked out at the room, his face impassive. "I'm sorry, no more questions. Thank you."

He walked off the stage, Valerie and Tom trailing him, as the reporters shouted their questions in vain.

FORTY-EIGHT

THE map of downtown Charleston was heavily detailed. A cluster of silver pushpins marked the location of the ruins of the Byrd Federal Building, and specifically the known and guessed positions of the Secret Service detail already at the site. In a broad ring around the site, extending for about three blocks, blue pushpins represented US Army units that had blocked streets, occupied rooftops and established covering positions on top of buildings surrounding the site.

The red pins—representing the state patrol and local police details, were more sparsely spread throughout the downtown area, ranging from twelve to fifteen blocks away from the site.

Valerie was troubled by this. Police had been diverted from the rest of the city, and much of the surrounding communities, in order to provide security for the vice president's visit.

Protecting the vice president was of course incalculably important. But public safety was also important, and the complete absence of any police presence anywhere else in the city presented a major problem.

It was, unfortunately, a problem she could do little about.

"All our units are in position," Hatfield said as she studied the map. Both of them stood in the large conference room, which had been turned into a temporary operations center during the Vice Presidential visit.

"With luck no one will think to rob a bank or commit any other crimes elsewhere in the city," she said.

Hatfield muttered to himself, then said, loud enough for her to hear, "Not much chance of that. This dog-and-pony show is going to cost us, somewhere."

She nodded, glancing up at the clock. "The vice president's flight should arrive in about twenty minutes."

Hatfield didn't respond. He continued to study the map, his jaw set, looking grim. She bit her lip. All along she'd believed he was the leak. She sighed.

"It seems, Mr. Hatfield," she said awkwardly, "that I owe you an apology. I misjudged you, thinking you might be working with the insurgents. I hadn't even imagined it was Davis, even though Ambrose pointed me toward him several times."

Hatfield shrugged. "You gotta do what's necessary, Murphy. I get that. I'm just glad you took that bastard down."

She looked at him, an eyebrow raised. "Honestly I expected you to have much more mixed feelings, Hatfield. Your brother's in custody, isn't he?"

He met her eyes, then said, "I could say the same to you, considering your father's fate. But I can tell you, my brother would never support a bunch of amateurs running around killing civilians. Somehow, I don't think Ken Murphy would have, either."

"No," she said. "Not in a million years. But that doesn't change the fact that the bigger issues they were fighting for are still very real."

He nodded glumly. "That's a job for another day, Murphy. Right now we need to worry about getting the vice president in and out of this city alive."

"Yes."

An aide approached. "Ma'am, there's someone here to see you from the Department of Homeland Security."

Valerie met Hatfield's eyes and raised her eyebrows, suddenly nervous.

"Send them in, please."

Surely it wasn't JD Roberts, the same day he'd appeared on the front page of the Times. A wave of anxiety passed over her, even though she couldn't imagine he would make a scene in front of all these witnesses. But who knew? DHS had the power to walk in her own headquarters and arrest her with no warrant, with no resource, no appeal.

The tall black woman with long straight hair who entered the room a few minutes later rendered her thoughts moot. Nearly six feet tall, in a light brown suit, she approached Valerie and Hatfield and extended a hand.

"Miss Murphy? Mr. Hatfield? I'm Latanya Jackson, with the Department of Homeland Security."

Valerie shook her hand.

"I wanted to come over and introduce myself. The president appointed me as acting special agent in charge just this morning."

Hatfield was expressionless. For nearly the first time since Valerie had met him, he was actually maintaining a poker face. His words were friendly enough. "Nice to meet you, Jackson. Where is Mr. Roberts?"

Jackson frowned. "That's the million-dollar question today. He didn't show up for work this morning, and given the nature of concerns we have about him, we checked out his apartment. He's packed up—gone."

Gone? Valerie thought. That quickly? Someone must have tipped him off.

"I'm sure you are aware of the unfortunate headlines this morning. We've been investigating Mr. Roberts for some days, due to some information brought to the president's attention by General Wells. I understand that was brought to Wells by you and General Murphy, yes?"

"That's right." Valerie nodded.

"If it's all right then, I'd like to get together and talk some time in the next couple of days, so I can get some background."

"Sure," Valerie said. "Most of what I know is speculation at this point, but I'm happy to help."

"I appreciate that." She hesitated a moment, her eyes jumping between Valerie and Hatfield. "Look, Ms. Murphy," she said. I'm aware that Roberts threatened you. I happen to believe in the mission of my department, and anything that reflects badly on it, well... let's just say I'm not happy about any of this. I intend to do everything I can to make things right."

Valerie wondered if that meant she intended to anything she could to cover it up. Time would tell, she supposed.

"I'm glad," Valerie said. "If there's anything I can do to help, just say the word."

"I'll be calling you. In the meantime, I know you've got your hands full, so I'll get out of the way."

They shook hands again, and Jackson left.

Rarely did Valerie have an encounted with DHS where she wasn't disturbed by the arrogance and power of the organization. This was strange, but she wasn't prepared to trust. Not a chance of that happening. Valerie said, "Well, that was ... unexpected."

"Weird, you mean," Hatfield said. "She didn't make me want to check my wallet or watch for snipers. Odd for DHS."

Valerie snorted and shook her head.

∾

Three nearly identical motorcades were lined up next to the runway at Yeager Airport just outside Charleston. The day was warming up, but a cool breeze still blew through the area as the cars sat waiting.

Terminal B, the only one with a direct line of sight to the runway, had been shut down for the morning, and all flights in and out of the city had been halted. Above, a combat air patrol, consisting of a flight of Air Force F-16s, had been patrolling above the city, turning away small and private aircraft. The airspace above Charleston and the surrounding 100-mile radius had been closed by the FAA since midnight.

The press, gathered in a crowd not far from the end of the runway, stirred as a plane came into sight on its final approach. No other flights were coming into Yeager that morning. Photographers jockeyed into position as the 747 rolled down the runway.

The vice president's arrival was anticlimactic. Quickly whisked by the Secret Service into the waiting vehicles, the vice president did nothing more than wave at the reporters before he was out of sight in the armored limousine. The three motorcades rolled out of the airport one by one, each taking a different direction out of the airport.

∽

"The vice president is rolling," said one of the dispatchers in the temporary operations center.

Valerie nodded. "Thank you," she murmured.

Everyone in the center tensed. For the next three hours, the vice president of the United States would be in the West Virginia capital, which had existed on the edge of chaos for months. The massive presence of police and military forces in the city would hopefully suppress violence, but it couldn't eliminate the seething anger that simmered just below the surface. Valerie had little confidence that the forces she had on hand could do anything to protect him. She hoped the Secret Service had prepared a lot more than she knew.

"Time to go, Miss Secretary," murmured Henry.

She nodded. "Let's go. Hatfield, keep me informed please."

☙

Governor Al Clark arrived at the site of the destroyed Byrd Federal Building at 3:55, after clearing the multiple checkpoints. He exited the limousine and, flanked by aids, entered the cordoned-off clearing in front of the ruins.

The sun was shining brightly: it was turning into a beautiful spring day—not a cloud in the sky.

"This way, Governor," said one of the Secret Service agents. Clark allowed himself to be led to a large dais in front of the growing crowd. A small row of chairs was arranged to the left of the podium. Clark took a seat.

"Wait here, sir," the Secret Service agent said. "The Vice President will be arriving shortly.

Clark looked out at the crowd. The front three or four rows consisted of the press. In front of them, kneeling on the ground, sat at least two dozen cameramen and women. Behind the media, one hundred hand-picked guests waited in chairs. It was a quiet crowd of politicians, Republican party activists, fundraisers and businessmen. Clark knew that each of them had been checked out both by the FBI and the state patrol: none of them had any known connections to insurgents or rebels. It was a crowd of loyalists, of course, people who would welcome a visit from the Vice President. No danger there. But if there was anything he'd learned in his years in politics, it was that you could never trust appearances.

He was tense. Things were bad enough across the country, and especially in West Virginia. If something happened here today… it was difficult to imagine the possible complications.

∽

Silence blanketed downtown Charleston, a tense, almost palpable blanket of tension. Valerie, escorted by Dennis Henry and two other state patrolmen, walked the three blocks from headquarters to the ruins of the Robert Byrd Federal Building. No vehicles disturbed the odd quiet: traffic in and out of downtown had been blocked by the Army since six a.m. An outer ring of security was provided by the state patrol.

Here in the center of downtown, the US Army blocked each intersection. God only knew what was going on in the rest of the state: from what she understood, the Army had pulled three battalions of infantry to Charleston. A squad of eight men blocked the intersection as she approached the federal building, two arranged at each corner, oiled and loaded weapons held at the ready. Few pedestrians were to be seen as they walked the short distance. The residents and workers who normally occupied this part of town had found other places to be on this day, and she could hardly blame them.

"Weird, isn't it, Miss Secretary?" Henry said. "I can hear the river from here. I've never known downtown to be this quiet, except in the middle of the night."

"Sure is," she replied.

A young Army sergeant approached them quickly. "Secretary Murphy? Wait here please."

Valerie and her escort stopped walking.

To the north, she heard sirens, then the sound of engines approaching them. She paused as two black sports utility vehicles pulled into the intersection, then two more. Behind them, a long armored limousine pulled in and stopped in front of the federal building, then two more SUVs.

Secret Service agents fanned out, weapons held at the ready. They meant business. She'd attended a number of functions in the past where either the president or vice president had spoken, and she'd never seen that many agents with side-arms at the ready.

಄

Three blocks to the north, with a clear line of sight to the federal building, three men waited impatiently, out of sight of the window that faced the street and the federal building. One of the men listened carefully to the Bluetooth headset in his right ear.

Two of the men were young: patriots, loyal to their leader. They wore oddly formal clothes—suits and ties—as if they were attending a reception rather than an assassination operation.

Their leader, who sat slightly apart listening to the Bluetooth headset, was as different as could be. A former officer and Iraq war veteran, John Channing was his father's right-hand man and a believer in bringing America back to the Christian nation it was founded. He agreed with his father that doing so would require the blood of some unfortunates. Channing and his two assistants had waited patiently and silently in this vacant office for nearly three days, well before the Army and Secret Service blocked off downtown.

They'd watched as the Secret Service cordoned off the area, then the Army moved in. They'd watched multiple snipers position themselves on rooftops; they'd watched as ground floor shops were entered and checked seven stories below. But the fact was, the Secret Service couldn't do everything. They didn't have the manpower. The day before, the state patrol had swept through this building. As planned, the team leader for the state patrol was a friend, and when they couldn't open the office doors here, he'd personally "checked them out" and pronounced them clean.

Channing smiled. Let Blankenship run his sideshow down south, shooting it out with the Army. He suspected it would only be a matter of days before Blankenship was dead. The rebels down there were on the run, with a massive US Army presence about to descend on Boone County. Which was perfect, because the main action was right here.

If they pulled this off, his father was in a position to begin to make real change, starting with a friendly face in the vice president's office. And who knew what they could accomplish from there?

Channing jerked into position as a text message appeared on his disposable cell phone.

"Time," he said. "The motorcade is pulling up now."

&

The FGM-148 Javelin Missile, fielded by the US Army in 1996, was a fire-and-forget automatic guiding anti-tank missile. Designed with a soft-launch feature, the rocket motors were designed not to engage until a safe distance from the operator. This had the bonus of making it safe to fire from indoors, and helped hide the position of the operator.

After its construction by Raytheon Corporation, this particular missile had made its way into Army stores and eventually been brought to the US Army weapons depot in Morgantown, West Virginia at the end of the abortive civil war in January. In March, when that depot was destroyed by insurgents, this missile and a dozen others like it fell into the hands of insurgents.

Channing didn't delegate the duty of firing it. Neither of the two kids assigned to him had any real experience with weapons, much less a weapon like this.

As the motorcade pulled into position in front of the federal building, he raised the shoulder-fired missile and locked in on the target. He waited fifteen seconds, let out a breath, then gently squeezed the trigger.

❧

Valerie watched as the doors of the limousine opened less than one block away. The vice president exited the vehicle, surrounded by the Secret Service, and began to move toward the cordoned area.

Heads turned at the sudden whooshing sound from the north.

The Secret Service agents did not hesitate. They threw their charge to the ground and surrounded him, weapons drawn, searching for targets.

"Get down!" Henry shouted, pulling Valerie to the ground.

Four seconds—each second seemingly forever—went by. She could see the agents shouting into their radios, as they searched for the source of the noise. At the last second, one of them saw something, and bodily lifted the vice president in an effort to pull him away.

It was too late.

The missile struck the armored limousine on the driver's side with a massive explosion. The five-ton vehicle flipped on its side and rolled, crushing everything in its path, including the Vice President and his protectors.

Valerie heard screams from the crowd. In shock, she watched as the Army and Secret Service fanned out, searching for the source of the missile.

"Oh, Christ," she said, looking at where she'd last seen the Vice President. The burning limousine was there, on its side, huge clouds of black smoke pouring from it.

Al! She reached for her cell phone and dialed Al Clark. It rang twice.

"Valerie," Al said. "I'm all right. You saw?"

"Yes," she answered. "I'm just a block away."

"All right. I don't know how much we can do, but... well, do what you can. All right?"

"Yes, sir."

"Talk with you later."

He hung up with no further word. She stared at the carnage, feeling ill equipped to be here. The Secret Service probably wasn't going to be letting anyone near the site, but she stood and approached anyway to offer the assistance of her department. It was going to be a very long day.

FORTY-NINE

ROLAND Channing snapped the telephone shut. It was a few minutes after sunset, and the valley below them was already dark.

"Gentlemen, we have success."

The announcement was met with silence from the small circle of men. Joe Blankenship looked at their faces. Grins and smiles. They were happy, but they weren't in a position to make much noise.

Blankenship stared down at the town. He was troubled, but could not pin down any single reason. After the raid the night before, he and a small team of men had escaped to one of their rendezvous points. From there, they'd taken a vehicle and cleared out of town.

It would be difficult to reconstruct his company. Several of them had been captured, he knew. That meant known caches and safe houses were no longer approachable: the men would be interrogated, and he had no doubt they would talk, and quickly. He was lucky he'd made it this far.

Early this morning he'd picked up another disposable phone and called Reverend Channing.

Channing kept the conversation very brief.

"Meet me in Whitesville, on the access road above the dam. Sunset."

"I'll be there," Joe responded.

And here he was, with two of his men. Channing brought with him a dozen of Nathan Wyatt's rebels from up near Morgantown. They had pulled their vehicles deep into the woods off the access road, in sight of the top of the dam. Whitesville was spread out below them at the bottom of the hollow. From here, the buildings of his childhood home looked like toys.

He only had two of his men left with him. Ethan Judson, his second in command and friend for more than fifteen years, was dead. Yet another score to settle with the feds.

"Tell me again what happened to Hoover," Channing said. He appeared angry and grief stricken at the loss of a friend.

Joe shrugged. Channing could look grief stricken all he wanted: Joe had grave doubts about his sincerity, and he wasn't about to admit that he had killed Hoover. "The Army came in fast. Very fast. Special Forces, I think. Hoover was questioning one of the prisoners, and was shot. I didn't wait around; I got the hell out of there as quick as I could."

Channing nodded. "I see. Well, he is another martyr for the cause. You'll see, Joe. I know you're distressed about what happened last night, but it was unavoidable. We'll still have our success in the long run."

Joe shrugged. He his doubts about Channing were running higher than ever. Maybe it was time to walk away. Walk away from the partnership, walk away from the insurgency. Maybe walk away from the country. He didn't know anymore what he wanted, or what he should be doing.

Channing checked his watch. "Our friend JD should be here in a few moments. Then we'll talk."

They waited in silence as the darkness thickened. Joe stared out over the valley, his home. He had no idea what had happened after the raid. Was Rebecca all right? She must have been the one to turn them in. Bob Mays didn't have the moral courage to do it, but his niece? She had the courage to do just about anything. In a lot of ways she reminded him of Mandy. Running up to a bunch of men with guns and demanding they stop shooting was just… crazy. And courageous. His mouth curled up in a half smile.

God, he missed Mandy. He remembered the day they'd reunited. The day his life had regained it's meaning—the day which had been a disastrous tragedy for the rest of the nation, and the best day of his own life.

❧

September 11, 2001

Joe Blankenship unfolded his handkerchief, found a clean spot, then mopped the sweat and coal dust out of his eyes. The cloth came away black. The noise of the continuous miner and air scrubbers was infernal, a crunching, grinding sound right out of Hell. Thank God another shift was over.

"Come on, Joe, let's get out of here. I've gotta get changed and get to class."

Blankenship nodded. Bob was religious about school. The moment they got out of the mines every day, he rushed home, showered, then drove into Charleston, where he was attending night classes at Marshall University. Joe didn't know how he managed it. After an exhausting day in the mines, it was all he could do to collapse on his couch, grab a beer, and sit in front of the television.

He followed Bob down the dark tunnel, the noise of the miner receding behind him. Above, steel arches supported the tunnel as they traversed the two thousand feet to the elevator. Even as they reached the elevator shaft, he could feel the vibration through his boots. He could almost feel home ahead—and a shower.

At the elevator, the men were whispering, somber. Blankenship frowned. Normally, there was a good bit of roughhousing and laughter as the shift ended.

"What's going on?" Mays asked.

"You didn't hear?" asked one of the men. "Fucking terrorists. Someone crashed planes into the World Trade Center and the Pentagon this morning. Where the hell have you guys been?"

"At the bottom of a coal mine, asshole," Mays responded. "How bad is it?"

"Pretty fucking bad. World Trade Center collapsed—both buildings went down. Everybody died—nobody even knows how many. They're saying the goddamn Arabs did it."

Terrorists attacking the Pentagon? And New York? He would have thought it was a joke, but the serious mien of the men in the elevator made it clear this was no joke.

"Jesus H. Christ," Mays said. "Mandy could have been there."

Blankenship nodded, not trusting himself to answer. Mandy had come back from New York in June, with her bachelor's degree from the City University of New York. She'd taken the summer off here in Whitesville before looking for work.

He'd avoided seeing her—difficult in Whitesville, a town of only a few hundred residents. Doubly so, considering Bob was his best friend. But seeing her—sometimes it just hurt too much.

Mays glanced over at Blankenship, muttered something under his breath. Maybe an apology for mentioning her. Maybe not.

Blankenship didn't look at his friend. It was easier to just focus on the steadily rising elevator. Halfway up, he rubbed his ears and yawned as his ears popped. The coal face was just shy of two thousand feet underground.

Three years now, he'd worked for the Eagle Mine, only the last year as a continuous miner operator. Pretty good pay—he made near enough to twenty dollars an hour since he'd been running the machine, and the day shift at that. He knew he should consider himself lucky. But it was also three years since he'd kissed Mandy goodbye, three years since she'd left for New York. Three years since she'd announced that under no circumstances would she stay in Whitesville, waiting for an accident; a fire, collapse or damp to take him away. She'd have nothing to do with a husband who mined coal for a living, and he'd just have to suck that up.

And who could blame her? Mining accidents were fewer and fewer these days—last he'd heard, there had been less than ten fatalities nationwide so far this year. But when accidents did happen, they were pretty serious. She still had the memory of her father as an example. Nearly five tons of rock had crashed down on his legs; doctors had amputated them and saved his life, but could do little to settle the angry, bitter and drunken man.

Blankenship would never forget her slightly drunken voice, wavering, as they sat on the hood of his dad's pickup after the junior prom.

"At least," she said, "We didn't have to worry about beatings when he was drunk. He couldn't really chase us from his wheelchair."

The elevator reached ground level finally, halting with a crack, and the men walked, still mostly in silence, to clock out.

"Come by tonight," Mays said. "I'll be home from class by nine."

Blankenship frowned. "I don't know."

"Oh, damn it, Joe. You're going to have to face Mandy someday. She's heartbroken she hasn't seen you since she came home."

"Bullshit," Blankenship replied. "She doesn't want anything to do with me."

Mays shook his head. "You're dumber than you look, if you think that."

Shrugging, Blankenship said, "Maybe I don't want to fucking see her, all right? You may be all happy cause Zoe's got a baby on the way, but it's not for me. Okay? I'll meet you at Willard's."

Mays shook his head. "No. No bar for me, not tonight."

Blankenship clocked out, then walked away from his friend without answering.

But when he arrived at the gate she was there, and that pretty much fucked everything.

How to describe Mandy? It was like trying to capture a sunrise in the mountains with nothing but a diaphanous net of inadequate words. The curve of her hips, the subtle and warm smile. Her sometimes racy sense of humor. He'd watched her grow from a spindly little tomboy to a beautiful rose.

But last time he'd seen her—three years ago—she'd broken his heart. And, to be fair, he'd broken hers.

She was flushed, the reddened skin of her neck contrasting with the white sweater she wore. Her face was framed by blonde hair cut shorter than he'd ever seen it, ending abruptly at her jaw. She breathed in short, shallow breaths, and her eyes were wide as she watched him approach

"Joe," she said. Her hands were shaking.

Blankenship struggled to control his face, but without much success. He thought he was going to start crying then and there.

"Mandy. I—didn't expect to see you here."

"Did you hear about the twin towers?"

"Yeah."

Her face crumpled, and she started to cry. "My roommate Nina works at Windows on the World, as a waitress. I—she won't answer her cell phone..."

He closed his eyes, trying to shut out the sight of her grief. Then he thought he would die when he heard her next whispered words.

"I guess coal mining ain't the only dangerous thing in the world. Can—can you forgive me?"

Now the tears did come, and he made a peculiar, horrifying choking sound: the closest he was capable of coming to crying.

"I'd forgive you anything."

She came into his arms, not even noticing the black coal dust that permanently stained her white sweater. Both of them wept. Wept for the lost time, for those who were gone, and above all, for joy. They hardly noticed the crowd of miners—all of them familiar with Joe and Mandy's relationship—who crowed and cheered, a small circle of light on that darkest of days.

Of course, only fairy tails end with "they lived happily ever after."

Two weeks after September 11, a footnote of news that would have been a major story at any other time shook the small community.

As Mandy and Joe sat in her brother's little house, watching the September 11 memorial service at Yankee Stadium, another disaster was unfolding in Brookwood, Alabama. At the Blue Creek Mine No. 5, falling rock slammed into equipment and sparked a methane explosion, trapping Gaston Adams, Jr. under rock, much as Mandy's father had been in 1992. This time, when a dozen fellow miners came to his rescue, a second methane explosion killed them all.

As it often did in the small, tightly knit communities around a coal-mine, word spread quickly, though the rest of country barely noticed in the aftermath of thousands dead in New York.

The four of them—Joe and Mandy, Bob and Zoe—were sitting around a cheap card table playing hearts when word of the disaster arrived on CNN. It came as a silent heartbreak—the ticker of breaking headlines across the bottom of the screen.

Mandy, completely incapable of keeping her eyes off a television if it was turned on and in view, went suddenly still, then started shaking.

Immediately, the others asked her what was wrong. She simply pointed.

Zoe, who shared Mandy's fears, reached over and gripped Mandy's hand. "It's okay," she said. But her other hand curled around her stomach, instinctively protecting the baby she'd carried for nearly nine months.

Bob sighed, looked across the table at Joe. Joe knew that in the end it changed nothing—tomorrow morning, he'd get on that elevator and ride it nearly half-a-mile into the bowels of the earth, just as he did every day.

Mandy knew it changed nothing, as well. She stood, her face frozen, expressionless, shook loose from Zoe's hand, and walked out.

But she didn't break it off. Even when he enlisted in the Army, then spent more than four tours in Iraq. She stayed with him, healed him when he came home wounded to his soul. She was his life.

And then, on a random day, for no reason whatsoever, the federal government just … took her away. Killed her. She was a bystander in the wrong place at the wrong time, and that was all it took to end a lifetime.

ᥫ᭡

Blankenship heard JD Roberts's vehicle before he saw it. Sound carried a long way at night through these mountains, and with all of the violence of the last few days, people didn't venture out at night if they could avoid it. Some didn't venture out at all.

The four-door sedan pulled to a stop. Blankenship waited, listening, as the door opened, then slammed shut, and Roberts approached, his feet crunching on the gravel.

Channing approached him. "Welcome back, brother."

Roberts's face was grim. "It's for good this time, Reverend. I was tipped off this morning by a friend. The FBI has a warrant out for my arrest."

Channing sighed, but looked understanding. "We knew it was only a matter of time. The important thing is, you've accomplished nearly all of our goals."

"I've been listening to the news. They're in full-on freak-out mode now in Washington. I'd expect a brigade to be deployed here by tomorrow. We need to move forward."

"Yes," Channing said. His voice was grim. "It's time."

Blankenship stared at the two of them, doubts rising. What the hell?

Roberts pointed directly at him. "What about him? Is he on board?"

Channing turned and looked at Joe. "That's what we need to discuss right now."

Joe rose from his crouch as the two men approached. He kept his face impassive, but his heart was pounding.

"Joe," Channing said, "it's time you became a full partner in our enterprise. If you are ready." His expression was guarded.

"What exactly does that mean?"

Channing smiled, the grim smile of a man fully engaged in his work. "We're going to make a gesture tonight. An important one, which will signal our seriousness to the Federal Government, as well start the wheels turning toward replacing our godforsaken government."

"And what gesture is that?"

Roberts answered instead of Channing, harshly. "Blankenship, I've had my doubts about your commitment from the beginning.Your motivation is suspect. You aren't doing this for God. Or for your country."

Blankenship clenched his fists. "I'm doing this for my wife!" he spat.

"That's right," Channing said. "What we want to know is, how far are you willing to go?"

"How far do you want?"

"We're going to blow the dam, Blankenship. That's the first step."

Joe was dumbfounded. There were six towns downstream of this dam.

"Are you out of your fucking minds?" he asked in disbelief before he could stop himself.

Roberts shook his head gravely. "Reverend, that's exactly the reaction I expected."

"No," Joe said. "That is going too far. There are innocents downstream. They'll drown."

"No!" Channing shouted. His eyes were wide as he spoke, almost as if from the pulpit. "It is not too far. The only way the people will embrace the change is if they know that their corrupt federal government won't shield them." He pointed down into the valley. "They betrayed the movement, Joe. Your niece was the one who did it! All because of her lust for a soldier!"

"Most of them are just going about their lives!" Joe shouted in horror. "They want nothing to do with you or the feds!" They were crazy. Ethan was write. He remembered him saying, If God tells them to kill everybody, then they'll go do it.

"Then we show them the error of their ways, Blankenship," Roberts said coldly. "The tide of history is on our side. In a year, none of them will recognize the country they're living in. Sometimes the greater good requires sacrifice. Just like Dale Whitt. Alive, he was useless. Dead, he became a martyr for our cause."

Joe's blood froze. Whitt? "What are you saying, Roberts?"

Channing said, "You didn't realize? After all this time? Of course we killed Whitt. He was a loose cannon who had served out his purpose by bringing the independence referendum to the public. In death, he did his greatest service to his own cause, by ensuring voters would approve the referendum."

"That's it!" Joe shouted. "You're both crazy. I'm out. I'll have nothing to do with this. Jesus Christ, what's next? Are you going to tell me you're planning to release some plague you stole from the biomedical plant?"

Roberts and Channing looked at each other, then back at Joe. Both of their expressions were fixed in place, impassive.

"Oh, dear God," he muttered.

Mandy, he thought. I'm so sorry, I didn't know.

"You're out," Channing said coldly. "What exactly do you plan to do now?"

"I've no idea. But I won't... I can't have anything to do with killing innocents. With blowing dams, or releasing plagues or whatever other crazy fucking ideas you have. Jesus Christ. You're both insane."

Channing sighed, as if he'd run out of patience. "Brother JD, I'm afraid you were right."

Joe started to turn away, took one step, then heard the words that sent him into a dead run for the trees.

"Execute him. He's a traitor."

༺༻

The Montgomery Energy dam in Whitesville began construction in 1990 when the energy conglomerate began removing the surface of Boone Mountain. For three decades the company dumped slate, dirt and rock across the valley floor as part of its mountaintop removal operation, slowly building a massive construction of earth and rock 954 feet high, blocking the valley and holding back a blackened lake of poisoned water and coal slurry. A lake containing more than 8 billion gallons of coal waste sludge filled the valley behind the dam.

Community activists and environmentalists had raised concerns on multiple occasions. After all, similar dams in West Virginia had been lost before. In 1972 the coal waste dam in Buffalo Creek had failed, washing away more than sixteen towns in the narrow Buffalo Creek Hollow. Stronger rules and regulations designed to prevent any reoccurrence of the disaster were brought in by the federal government following the disaster, but those rules had been severely weakened in the first two decades of the twenty-first century. Regulations were bad for business, after all. Since President Price's election in 2016, federal agencies overseeing mining operations had been effectively neutered by a combination of funding cuts and politically driven directives.

The insurgents knew this dam, and they knew its weaknesses. Carefully placed to weaken the center of the dam, when the first detonation went off, coal slurry and water began to soak through a line in the center of the dam. First a small stream, then a torrent, pushed through with the pressure of twenty thousand water hoses.

The second explosion was midway up the face of the dam, and weakened the central structure. Rock, then small boulders, were driven out of the way, and within five minutes, an opening the size of a small building had been torn through the center.

The final explosion, at the back side of the top tier of the damn, shifted the entire center of the dam forward nearly three feet. Black water began pouring through the gap, taking rubble, the guard shack, and tons of shifted earth with it. The torrent almost immediately increased as the pressure of nine billion gallons of water and sludge tore out the sides of the gap. A wall of blackened water, coal slurry and debris four hundred feet high collapsed onto the town below.

FIFTY

REBECCA Mays smiled as her phone rang. She reached over and hit "answer" without looking away from the twisting mountain road.

"Didn't we just hang up five minutes ago?" she asked, giggling.

"Rebecca... it's your mother."

Oh, shit! "Mom! Um... wow. That's um... wow."

"Where are you?"

"I'm on my way home, Mom."

Her mother didn't answer. The silence weighed between them, a thousand unasked questions and answers.

Rebecca didn't say that she'd told no one she was leaving. Greenfield had insisted Rebecca notify her if she left the hospital, out of fear Joe would harm her. But she couldn't be accompanied by guards everywhere she went, and she had to see her mother. In person.

She finally sighed. "The police told me Dad had something not quite a heart attack. Is he... is he okay?"

Her mother sniffled into the phone, and Rebecca realized she'd been crying.

"Yes. Your father will be fine, health-wise."

"I'm glad, Mom."

She'd reached the stop sign in Racine and put on her left blinker. There was no traffic; there had been none all night. She turned left onto the Coal River Road.

"Rebecca..." her mother said, then stopped.

She swallowed. Her mother was going to tell her to never come home. That she hated her for turning in her father.

"I understand why you did what you did. It... it was the right thing to do."

Rebecca let out a sob. "Mom, I'm so sorry."

"I know, hon. But your father made his own choices. And... you saved that young man's life. Whatever happens to your father... whatever happens... you need to know that I'm proud of you."

Rebecca couldn't answer. Tears were running down her face.

"Berry... will you come home? Not back to the motel, but home?"

"Yes, Mom. I love you."

"I love you, hon."

"I'll be home in about thirty minutes."

"Okay. I'll be waiting."

With a click, the call disconnected. She drove on in the dark, driving slowly and carefully. She'd soon be at the roadblock. But would it even be there? Just about everyone in Jim's platoon was dead.

She sighed, then jumped when the phone rang again.

"Hello?"

"Hey, beautiful."

"Oh God," she said, starting to cry again. God damn these waterworks! What was wrong with her that she couldn't go five minutes without crying?

"I talked to my Mom."

"Oh, crap," he said, his voice dropping. "Was it that bad?"

"No," she whispered. "She… she asked me to come home. She said she understood. And that she was proud of me."

She could hear the smile in his tone as he responded, "I'm proud of you too. You're a hero, you know."

She passed the sign reading "Whitesville." There was no sign of the roadblock. Her truck was now at the bottom of the valley, and she'd be home in just a few more minutes. But was it even her home anymore? She guessed not. Too much had happened. Her home would be with Jim, in the end. But he was still in the Army, and would be for two more years.

A lot could happen in two years.

"Jim… what happens now?"

She pulled to a stop beside the road, leaving the truck running.

"Well… they just told me I get to go on leave when I'm released from the hospital. Thirty days. If you'll have me, I want to marry you. Now."

She exhaled, relieved. "Right away?" she said.

"We don't really have to wait, do we?"

"No." She didn't want to wait. Not a year, not a month, not an hour.

"Good. Then… well, I've still got two years to my enlistment. And you go to college."

"I don't know," she said, sighing. "I don't think my Dad's going to be paying for college any time soon. He's probably going to jail for a very long time."

"Oh, hell, Rebecca. I'll transfer my GI bill to you. You're going. I want to come to see you dance. In New York. No arguments, all right?"

She leaned against the window, feeling scared and warm and wonderful all at the same time. She couldn't stop smiling.

"I'm picturing us in New York together."

"We'll get an apartment. With a dog."

"Cats. Definitely cats."

"All right, whatever. Cat's aren't exactly fitting pets for heroes, though."

She giggled. "I'll get them little capes."

"Girl, you are ridiculous. I need a big, manly dog."

"You're going to be walking the big, manly dog. And cleaning up its poop."

"Details. Maybe I'll go to college, too. Do you think they could make anything of a blockhead like me?"

"I think you can do anything in the world, Jim."

"With you, I can."

She thought she was going to melt into her seat, so she answered, "Oh, barf. You are such a dork."

"I love it when you say things like that."

She giggled. "You're my dork."

"And you're mine. But I'm gonna have to go," Jim said. "Nurse is looking daggers at me; I guess I'm not supposed to be on the phone this time of night. You'll come back and see me tomorrow?"

"Of course," she said. "I just need to get some of my things... what's that?"

She jerked her head up at the flashing light in the distance.

"What's what?" he asked.

"I dunno," she said, puzzled. "Some kind of explosions from up in town."

Ten seconds later, she heard explosions, rumbling and cracking and echoing across the ridge line. It sounded like a strange thunderstorm, the echoes crashing back and forth, a continuous low rumbling.

"Something's going on," she said, trying to peer through the darkness up the valley toward Whitesville. She turned the engine off and rolled down the window so she could better hear.

The low rumbling came from the distance, getting louder and louder by the second. She saw another flash of red-orange light.

"Something's really wrong, Jim," she said, fear creeping into her voice.

"Get out of there, babe, right now. Just go, then call me back!"

In the darkness, nearly a mile up the valley, she saw it. A massive wall of water, twenty feet high—possibly even higher—mowing down everything in the valley. Oh my God. There were houses riding on top of that wave. Cars and trucks were twisting and rolling end over end. She saw a bright flash as a house was lifted off its foundation and began twisting sideways in the water.

She let out a scream. "Oh my God, somebody blew the dam!"

She turned the key, trying to start the engine. Nothing happened.

"Rebecca, get out of there! Go! Go!"

She tried to crank the engine again. It whined, and the starter clicked, but it wouldn't turn over.

"It won't start!" she cried out.

"Rebecca, get out of there!" he shouted.

She opened the door of the truck and ran for her life.

❧

Karen Greenfield jerked awake at the sound of an explosion. Without conscious thought, she rolled out of the bed and began pulling on jeans. As she threw on a shirt, she realized her hands were shaking.

By the time a second explosion rattled the windows of the flimsy Whitesville motel, she was up and dressed.

"Jesus Christ," she muttered. She threw on her boots and quickly laced them up, then stepped out of the room. It was a cool night out, a slight breeze lifting loose hairs that had escaped the rough bun she'd put it in before bed.

Lieutenant Stewart was already exiting his room. He looked as disheveled as she felt.

"You heard it?" he asked.

She nodded, but didn't speak. They stood on the second-floor walkway of the motel. Lights were turning on across town as the third explosion rang out. They saw the flash this time, high above the town to their left, in the direction of the dam.

"What the hell?" Stewart said.

She shook her head.

A massive bass rumbling sound came from the west, and the ground began to shake.

"Whatever this is...." She trailed off, and then shouted, "Oh my God, get to the roof!"

A huge wall of water and rubble poured down Main Street directly toward them, lifting houses and buildings off their foundations and sending them careening against each other. In the midst of the debris she saw a school bus from the elementary school, floating sideways and crashing into the roofs of the buildings three blocks down.

Karen sprinted for the end of the walkway, where a cast-iron decorative column stretched to the rooftop. Without a word she began climbing as fast as she could, scrabbling for purchase against the edge of the roof. Her heart thumping in her chest, she grabbed the gutter, praying it would hold, and lifted herself until she could heave her upper body onto the roof. She flung her leg up and swung herself onto the roof just as the crashing water reached the hotel.

The roof shifted beneath her as the west wing of the hotel was lifted off its foundation and began sliding downstream. Below them, in the water, cars, houses and tons of debris shifted and churned against each other in the darkness.

She shouted something inarticulate, then threw herself flat on the roof and reached for Stewart's wrists. He was still hanging from the gutter, his knuckles white, one hand beginning to slip as the water dragged at his legs.

Something hard banged against him and he lost his grip just as she got her hand gripped around one wrist. For a second she thought her arm was going to be yanked out of its socket, then—worse—that she was going to be pulled off the roof entirely.

"Throw your leg up! Do it!" she screamed.

He swung one leg up and got it over the edge of the roof, then reached up and grabbed the gutter again with his other hand. His face was clenched, desperate, teeth showing in a fierce snarl.

"Come on! Pull!" she shouted.

Finally, he heaved his entire body onto the roof.

By this time, the hotel had shifted at least two hundred yards north, amidst a jumble of other destroyed structures.

The rumbling to the west grew even louder. Greenfield looked up in time to see another wall of water approaching, at least twenty feet high, lifting buildings and houses and tons of rubble at its crest.

"Hold on!" she shouted, grabbing onto whatever handholds she could find.

The wave hit the hotel and she felt a huge lurch in her stomach as she went weightless, hurtling downstream on the rooftop.

FIFTY-ONE

I T took Jim Turville nearly twenty minutes to finally get clear of the hospital, which he finally accomplished by simply walking out when the doctors wouldn't discharge him, then renting a car with an insanely high deposit because he was under twenty-five. The clerk at the car rental agency had looked at him with extreme suspicion. Turville supposed the mass of bruises and contusions on his face didn't add any trust.

He drove south toward Boone County as fast as the crappy little car would take him, frantic to reach Rebecca. She still wasn't answering her phone, and he was long past panic. Calls to her house didn't ring at all. He got only an "All circuits are busy" message.

Twenty minutes into the drive south, he was forced to pull to the side to let a series of emergency vehicles by... ambulances and military police. He fell in behind them, taking advantage of their speed.

On the final turn over the pass into the Coal River valley, he hit the brakes in shock and stared down at the devastation below. The sun was rising, the valley washed in pale light that illuminated the horror below.

Whitesville was gone. The town had been replaced by a mud flat, slick and black, two hundred feet across the narrow hollow and extending as far as he could see downstream.

Frantically, he followed the hairpin turns down the mountain. He could feel severe pressure building up in his chest, fear of what he would find below.

Details began to emerge as he drove further down the slope: the underside of a car, flipped over and buried in the mud. He hadn't quite reached the high water line yet, but it was obvious how high the water had come. A rooftop, seemingly untouched, but disconnected from any structure, resting on the mud. Not far from the rooftop, a lawn chair lay on its side, smeared with brown and black mud. Here and there, along the edges of the mud flat, stunned survivors stared out at the wasteland that had been their home.

At the bottom of the hollow, Turville brought the car to a stop and got out. It was overwhelming: there was no way he could drive into the hollow without sinking into the stinking black mud, and there was no way he could know how far the flood had travelled. Miles, most likely.

Here, where the road entered the valley and disappeared under the black mud, must have been where she'd called. Now, at the edge of the mud flat, a dozen ambulances and fire trucks were parked beside the road. Emergency workers were staring in shock, apparently unsure where to begin. A helicopter hovered overhead.

Upstream in the distance, he could just make out the head of the valley and the dam, where downtown Whitesville used to be. Now there was nothing in the center of the hollow, nothing at all.

He tried to imagine what she had seen. Her truck pulled to a stop somewhere near here, she'd looked upstream and seen a wall of mud and debris and water rushing at her. Did she stay in her truck, or run for high ground?

He began walking downstream, just at the edge of the mud flat, trying to avoid the debris, downed trees, upended vehicles and random flotsam scattered everywhere. He passed an open refrigerator lying on its back, completely filled with black mud. Leaning against it, a subcompact car, upside down.

It was a nightmare, and went on for what seemed like hours. Skirting the edge of the mud flat, searching through the woods at the edge, he saw bodies washed up on the edge of the flood. Houses crushed to splinters. A million details of people's lives scattered everywhere.

After nearly two hours, smashed around the huge trunk of a tree, he saw the bottom of a dull red pickup. The truck was mostly buried in the mud, but enough was above the surface for him to identify it.

Jim ran toward it, his feet sinking into the mud nearly to his knees. Breathing heavily, he reached the truck and confirmed his fears. The windshield was spiderwebbed, but intact. That hardly mattered, because fully half of the cab was buried in the black sludge.

He slumped to the ground and tried to wipe the sweat off his face, but only managed to smear mud on himself. His mind raced through a thousand possibilities: that she'd drowned, been crushed, or worse. He closed his eyes, shaking, still weak from his injuries and more so from his fear. He had to blink back tears when the thought passed through his mind that he might never find her at all.

Please God, let her be alive. Please.

He kept moving downstream. A woman sat shivering in the trees in her nightgown to his right; two fire-fighters were leaning over her, speaking urgently.

That's when he heard the whimpering.

He looked up, suddenly alert, and listened again. The sound had come from further downstream. He began to walk in that direction, and he heard it again... a faint crying of someone in pain.

Turville called out. "Hello?"

He walked quickly, approaching a small copse of half-submerged trees. Several of them had toppled, creating a tangle of trunks and branches. A stop sign carried by the waters was deposited crazily against them.

Tangled in the branches, one of her legs twisted in impossible directions, covered in mud and too much blood, was Rebecca Mays. He ran to her, sinking up to his knees in the mud.

"Jim?" she whispered.

"Oh, Jesus," he said. "Rebecca...."

No more than a quick glance at her shattered body terrified him. Her leg was twisted almost in a knot, and blood soaked through her jeans. Her face was bloodied and bruised, and a small trickle of blood bubbled at her lips.

He was afraid to move her, afraid to touch her.

"It'll be all right, Rebecca," he whispered, and gently put his arms around her.

"I tried to get away," she said, her voice nothing more than a wisp. "I couldn't get to high ground fast enough."

"You'll be all right, I promise," he said. "I'll get help."

He dug for his phone, then remembered it was gone. The phone had been turned off, in the barracks, when they'd been ambushed. It was washed away in the flood.

"Rebecca, I'm going for help. I'll be right back, I promise."

She looked at him, suddenly panicked. "No... please don't leave me, Jim. Please."

"I won't be long. We need to get you to a hospital, babe. You... you're hurt pretty bad, okay? Let me go get help."

Tears ran freely down her face, mixing with the blood, and she whispered, "Jim, I'm afraid. Please hold me. Don't go."

He nodded, then yelled, as loud as he could. "Hey! Somebody help! We need help over here!"

There was no answer.

He shouted again. "Help! Somebody! Over here in the trees!"

The helicopter passed over them, and he stood and waved his arms at it. He couldn't tell whether they saw him.

"I'm so cold," she said.

He kneeled next to her, and put his arms around her as gently as he could.

"Rebecca, I love you. I won't let anything happen to you. You'll see... we'll get married, and get that apartment in New York, and I'll buy you fourteen cats if you want, and get capes for all of them. We'll go find someplace safe and happy and I'll protect you. I won't let anything in the world hurt you. Oh, God, Rebecca, just hold on until help gets here. Please."

"Thank you for finding me," she whispered.

"I still owe you for rescuing me, babe," he replied.

She leaned her head against his chest and shivered, her entire body shaking. "If I wasn't all screwed up like this, I could stay in your arms like this forever," she said.

"Now who's being a dork, huh?" he asked. He was trying desperately not to cry.

"Will you tell my mom and dad I love them?"

"Oh shit, Rebecca. You're going to be able to tell them. You're going to be fine, you just have to hold on a little while, okay?"

"Don't let me go," she whispered.

She coughed, and a light splatter of blood sprayed across the front of his uniform, her whole body convulsing.

"I'll never let you go, babe. No matter what."

She looked up at him. "I don't think I'm going to make it, Jim. But I'm glad I got to... I'm so glad I got to know you, and love you."

He began crying, struggling to hold it back. "Damn it, Rebecca, you're going to be fine. Do you hear me? We're going to walk away from this together. Don't give up. Please, please, please, don't give up."

She whispered, "How can I give up? I have everything I ever wanted in the world right here."

She closed her eyes, her breathing shallow, and he screamed out again. "Somebody help! Please! Anybody!"

He heard responding voices in the distance.

"Over here! In the trees! Please help!"

His voice broke. She wasn't breathing. Oh, God. Please, Rebecca. Don't go. Don't.

"Stay with me, Rebecca," he whispered. "I love you."

He wept freely as he realized that he was already too late: that his dreams of a safe, warm place where he could protect his love were just as dead as the lovely young woman he held in his arms.

ℭℌ

"I owe you a thank you," Lieutenant Calvin Stewart said.

"Huh?" Karen asked, shivering.

"For pulling me up on the roof. I... I might not have made it."

"Sure," she said. She was too numb to think.

The two of them were still sitting on what was left of the roof of the Highview Motel, huddled together and shivering. The roof itself had broken up into smaller fragments as the building broke up, but somehow they'd survived, floating downstream almost three miles.

It was sunrise now, and they'd been sitting in the cold and dark for hours. Around them, in the narrow hollow, was the devastation the flood had left behind. Bodies in the mud. Fragments of wood and trash and the jetsam of the lives of a thousand people.

She stared at the devastation and was absolutely numb.

"You know, I think I liked prison better," she said.

"It's hard to blame you," he replied.

"The insurgents did this."

He nodded.

"I just wish I understood why," she said. "I knew Joe Blankenship. It doesn't make any sense. What the hell were they trying to accomplish?"

Stewart shook his head. He looked lost.

"Look," she said, pointing.

A line of Humvees was carefully threading it's way along the side of the mud and debris, moving downstream. Field ambulances were mixed in with the column.

"I bet they've got coffee," he said.

She nodded. "And maybe a blanket or something."

"Let's go," he said.

"All right."

They stood and walked toward the approaching Humvees.

FIFTY-TWO

"Ladies and gentlemen. The President of the United States."

As the shout rang out, the combined chambers of the US Congress rose to their feet as one. One side of the chamber naturally applauded louder. Cameras flashed as the President entered the room flanked by Secret Service agents. On the way to the raised podium, he stopped, shaking hands with a number of members of Congress and Supreme Court justices.

President William Price was in his prime at forty-six years old. A huge smile on his face, he took the podium and waved at the assembly. It took nearly two full minutes before the applause died down enough that he could speak.

"My fellow Americans," he began.

The applause in the chamber began again, and he grinned.

Stupidly, Valerie thought, from her vantage point in the back of the room. In Washington to wheedle funding from the Department of Homeland Security, she'd been passed an invite to the presidential address by a friend in Senator Wilson's office.

President Price waved again, then tried to speak again as the applause died down. "My fellow Americans, I come to you at a time of national tragedy."

The room quieted down quickly, as the President talked about the war of secession in West Virginia, the following insurgency, and the events of the last month.

"Have no doubt that the criminals and terrorists who would seek to undo this nation believe that they have accomplished a victory. With the assassination of my friend, the vice president, and the devastating flood that has killed more Americans than any other terrorist attack in history, they think they've taken a step forward. They think they have us scared. They think they have us on the defensive.

"But let me tell you, the enemies of freedom will never win. They cannot take away the unique qualities that make us American. They cannot win.

"So this message is for the terrorists. If you seek to damage American freedom, you will fail. If you seek to hurt Americans, we will hurt you back.

"Today I am committing all of the resources of our nation to rooting out the terrorists. We will find them, whether in the coal mines of West Virginia or in the mountains of Afghanistan. We shall achieve a victory for freedom and for God."

The men and women in the room spontaneously rose to their feet, cheering. Valerie felt a chill. A victory for God? Something about his wording chilled her to the bone.

She missed the next few words, as Price shouted over the still-noisy crowd. They began to quiet again and she heard, "… and that is why I announced today a state of insurrection not only in West Virginia, but in the surrounding states where the insurgents have hid themselves. This state of emergency extends to Virginia, Kentucky, Tennessee, Ohio, Pennsylvania and Maryland. Tomorrow morning I will transmit to Congress a body of proposed laws which will allow us to shore up our security, root out the terrorists, protect our religious freedom and save our country."

He paused, as the audience broke into applause again.

"Additionally, I have decided on my nominee for the next vice president of the United States—a member of this august body, Representative Mark Skaggs of Kentucky."

Valerie felt as if the air had been sucked out of her lungs as the cheering in the room rose to a fever pitch. Mark Skaggs!

Skaggs had been the author of last year's Fiscal Responsibility Act, which had gutted the federal government and precipitated the war. As chair of the House Committee on Homeland Security, he'd had oversight over DHS and its excesses. It was hard to imagine a worse candidate for national office. Yet there he was, striding to the front of the chamber, a grin on his face.

He shook hands with the President, and the roars from the crowd rose unbelievably higher as President Price pulled Skaggs into a bear hug.

Valerie stood, her thoughts in disarray, feeling nothing but dread. There was no doubt from the tone of the chamber that Skaggs would be confirmed as vice president. But that raised a tremendous number of doubts about the future. She quietly made her way to the exit.

Once she exited the Capitol building, she thought about waving down a cab, but decided to walk instead. It was only a few blocks up Pennsylvania Avenue to her hotel anyway, and she needed the quiet. As always, Henry tagged along with her, but he'd learned her moods well enough that he stayed a few yards back, leaving her at least the illusion of privacy.

Her mind passed over the events of the last year of her life. A year ago, she'd been dating David Brown and working for then-Congressman Clark right here in Washington. Almost exactly this time last year, a series of bombs in Arlington, Virginia had set off a chain of events that resulted in a war. Bombs she was now convinced were set by confederates of Roland Channing, then aided by JD Roberts and possibly others from DHS.

Roberts had been missing since the morning of the New York Times story. In the aftermath of the assassination of Vice President Hamilton, then the destruction of the dam in Whitesville, the scandal at DHS had somehow been buried in the headlines. Hearings had been scheduled in Congress to investigate, and Valerie was disturbed to remember that Mark Skaggs was slated to chair those hearings. She wondered who would be running them now.

Her father, a brave and courageous man who had refused to back down from his principles, had ultimately been killed by those principles. Executed by lethal injection. She couldn't help but think he'd given up, that the loss of his wife and son had been too much for him to tolerate living any more. His last words to his brother had been to look out for her.

She'd been betrayed by her former lover. That betrayal was followed by the betrayal of someone she thought of as a friend and confidant.

Valerie couldn't help but ask herself what it all meant. Yesterday, during her interview on Washington Talk, she'd been peppered with questions about the sudden spike in flu cases in major cities on the east coast. Did she believe the assurances of the White House, that it was a normal series of flu cases, or was it somehow related to the avian flu stolen from West Virginia? Half a dozen deaths in New York and Atlanta had already been reported.

Would they go that far? Had Channing and his confederates released a deadly virus on their own country? If so, what was their goal? What in God's name were they trying to accomplish?

In God's name, indeed, she thought. Because that's what it was all about.

On her right, she passed the FBI headquarters, on the corner of 10th and Pennsylvania. Somewhere in that building she'd been held prisoner for three months. She shivered at the sight of the building, and crossed the street so she didn't walk too close that building; no matter that it made her walk a little further.

In the morning she would return to West Virginia, empty handed. She'd received nothing but vague reassurances. Certainly no funding for law enforcement, quarantines, or anything else her state so desperately needed.

She could see the hotel now. When she got home, she'd start work again in the morning. Not work she'd chosen—not this time—but it was a continuation of her life's work, of her father's.

So far, on a large-scale level, both she and her father had failed so far. But that didn't mean that she wouldn't keep trying, and keep fighting. Not because she was completing her father's legacy, or taking care of Al Clark, or any other reason other than this: it was the completion of who she was. She would never be content to just get up and go to work every day, and let her country to go to hell. No matter what, she'd keep fighting, she'd keep trying to do the right thing.

☙

Bobby Wright breathed a sigh of relief when the seat belt lights turned off and the cabin attendant said, "You may now turn on approved electronic devices. Please remain in your seats with seat belts fastened unless you are going to the restrooms."

Someone a few seats down from him groaned and broke into a sneezing fit.

Bobby felt a chill go down his spine. He'd read the material in Valerie's package, about the virus stolen from Hamilton Biomedical. Worse, he'd read most of the contingency plans her department had developed to deal with the potential of an epidemic.

Bobby was no idiot. His Google alert for H5B1 had sent him a dozen news articles in the last four days. Cases of H5B1 had been reported in Washington, DC, Atlanta, New York and San Francisco, all within a day of each other. Several patients had died.

The media wasn't really paying attention yet, but he was, and he didn't like what he saw.

What was going to happen? All he could do was fulfill the promise he'd given cousin Val: to go home. Two more years of high school and he'd be free. He could survive two years of anything, even his Dad.

As it had many times in the last two weeks, his mind drifted back to Rebecca Mays. What a fascinating, beautiful girl. And there was no question she was head over heels in love with her soldier. What he wouldn't give to inspire that kind of devotion. All it took was closing his eyes to see her dark eyes, her lithe form, and the passion in her eyes.

Someday, he thought. He still had a lot of life ahead of him. For now, it was time to go home and face the music. He'd apologize to his father and mother, go back to school, and do everything he could to get into a good college.

One thing he'd learned in the last three months made everything else make sense. No way was he going to be like his father, buying and selling real estate, or something else pointless. Bobby was going to make something of his life. He was going to make a difference. He was going to continue the work Uncle Ken had started, starting by publishing Valerie's packet on the Internet. He had the keys to DHS's network in his hands, and the skills to make use of it.

Whatever else happened, he would do everything he could to make sure they couldn't skulk around in the darkness, ruining lives unnoticed.

∾

The officers in the command center, including Brigadier General Tom Murphy, stood at attention at the entry of Lieutenant General Richard Varley, commander of Seventeenth Airborne Corps.

Varley, at six foot seven, was a former West-Point basketball player, and had led a combat brigade during the 2003 invasion of Iraq. A hardbitten, no-nonsense soldier, he'd been a mentor to Tom for many years.

"At ease," Varley said.

At that, Tom stepped forward and passed Varley a clipboard. It contained orders for Varley to sign, assuming command of the counterinsurgency in West Virginia.

Varley signed.

"Welcome to your new command, General," Tom said. He had mixed feelings at Varley's arrival. On the one hand, it meant that somebody in Washington was finally taking the insurgency seriously enough to bring in large numbers of troops.

On the other, it meant that he, personally, had failed. With a higher ranking general bring brought in to combat the insurgency, Tom would likely be passed off to some meaningless job. This moment might well spell the end of his career.

"Good to see you, Murphy." Varley looked serious.

"And you, sir."

"I have news for you."

"Oh?"

"General Colson is retiring, effective immediately. General Wells and I agreed, and forwarded to the President, your nomination to take command of the Third Infantry Division. The President agrees."

Tom gasped.

"That is… unexpected, sir." Unexpected was a serious understatement. He was stunned.

"You've earned it. You probably know Third Brigade is currently in Wisconsin. The remainder of the division is en route to West Virginia now."

Tom thought about that for a few moments. He'd known as soon as the president announced that all of Eighteenth Airborne Corps would be deploying to quell the insurgency that he would lose his command. That was fine. A division! He'd expected to eventually get there… in maybe another five years.

"We'll go over my expectations in detail later, Murphy. For the time being, you can join the division advance team in Morgantown; they're already on the ground establishing a headquarters. My staff is putting together the formal operations order now, but I've got your warning order now."

Tom looked over the proffered one-page order. It was chilling. Close all highways to interstate traffic and establish quarantine centers. He exhaled slowly.

"Sir… is this what I think it is?"

Varley nodded. "Yes, Murphy. The news hasn't caught on yet, but we're in deep trouble. Somebody released bioweapons, and we're already seeing the first casualties."

"I'd better get to my new headquarters right away, sir."

"Yes, go. Keep me informed as you get settled in. And make it quick, Tom."

"I will, General."

∾

Karen Greenfield sat down across from Lieutenant Colonel Cory Avedis, Lieutenant Stewart sitting beside her.

Avedis looked at them. "You two did an excellent job in Whitesville."

Stewart frowned. "Not good enough," he said. "Not enough to save those lives."

Karen nodded, silently agreeing with Stewart. If they'd moved more quickly, they might have prevented the flood. No one even knew yet how many had died, but estimates in the media were already ranging in the several thousands.

"There was little you could have done to stop that," Avedis said. "I got some news this morning that you'll find interesting. It's why I called you in here."

Karen raised her eyebrows.

"The investigation team found out where the insurgents had been right before they blew the dam. And what's interesting about it is there were some spent shell casings there... somebody was shot, and left a lot of blood behind. Blood matching Joe Blankenship's DNA."

"Blankenship's dead?" she asked. She found herself having mixed feelings. There were still too many unanswered questions, too many things that didn't make sense.

"We don't know. No body's been found."

"Some kind of internal power struggle?" Stewart asked. "Maybe they just dumped the body. Given the chaos there, we might never find it."

Avedis sighed. "Think for a moment, Lieutenant. If Blankenship was shot at ... then by whom?"

Karen met Avedis's eyes. "Presumably, his allies. Turville told us during the debriefing that Blankenship killed someone named Hoover during the raid. His words, I think, were that Hoover was a religious fanatic." She thought for a minute. An internal struggle made sense. Blankenship was a complicated man, but religious he'd never been.

Avedis nodded.

"So what's next for us, sir?" Stewart said.

"Well, first of all, we're all being reassigned. The battalion is being attached to Third Infantry Division. I've already spoken with the new division commander. You two are going to keep doing exactly what you are doing. Follow up the leads you developed. I want to know exactly who Blankenship's allies were. Who shot him, and what are they up to? Where is he? If he's dead, find his body. If not, find him. What happens next? It's your job to find out."

"Yes sir," Stewart and Karen said simultaneously.

∾

"You know, Jim... I was never much of a dad. And I'm sorry for that. For what its worth, I kind of get what you're going through now."

Jim Turville felt the hand on his shoulder. He shuddered, took in a deep breath, and said, "Thanks, Dad."

Jim had been on leave for ten days. Fourteen days since she had died. The fourteen longest days in his life.

While it was still dark this morning, they'd set out in his dad's car from Falls Church, Virginia and driven west. Back to what was left of Whitesville, West Virginia. Back to the ruins of his life.

He stood defiantly in his dress blue uniform, daring anyone to question his right to be there. A few dozen surviving townspeople stood in a ragged circle at the base of the destroyed dam, near the ruined elementary school.

A somber Catholic priest from Charleston gave the address. He talked about the sacrifice of innocents. He talked about grief, and loss.

Jim listened, trying to make the connection between the priest's words and his own grief. He knew somehow that the words were meant to comfort the survivors. But they didn't provide comfort. The only comfort he could imagine was gone, washed away in the flood. Instead, he looked out at the destruction and thought about Rebecca. Whitesville was transformed, the center of the town completely washed downstream. Only homes on high ground had survived the deluge.

He thought about Rebecca and the day they'd met. Even during that chaos, she'd been courageous, getting her friend inside and under cover. She'd sought him out three days after they'd arrived in Whitesville. He remembered her beauty, her thin, lithe frame. The fascination of watching her dance at her rehearsal in Charleston. The beauty of her single-minded focus on perfection.

He thought about the feeling of her lips on his. How her simple touch on his arm had been enough to make him lose his mind.

He thought about their dreams together, washed away by the flood just as her home had been.

One of the townspeople stood and began to read the names of the dead. The confirmed dead. They still didn't know for sure how many were gone.

Rebecca and her mother were both on the list. Her father, currently confined in federal lockup, was not.

At the sound of her name, Jim felt as if he'd been punched in the gut. His face twisted.

His father squeezed his shoulder.

Eventually, the painful, ugly, but strangely cathartic ceremony came to an end. No one approached him. Instead, the survivors slowly scattered, each in their own haunted way.

Jim stood for the longest time, staring at the ground.

"She agreed to marry me, Dad," he whispered. "Right away, while I was on leave."

Pat Turville sighed.

"I don't know how to go on," Jim said. "You don't know... I... she was everything. For the first time in my life, everything made sense."

"I get it, son."

"What do I do now?" Jim said, tears rolling down his face. "What do I do?"

His father answered, slowly. "You just go on. You try to make the best of it. And you remember her. That's all you can do."

Turville stared off, down the valley. How could he just go on? What did it matter, if he couldn't give her life, her death, some meaning? It was too much.

What he knew was this: the events that had started a few days after he finished basic training, the bombing in Arlington, had somehow led him here. Led her, and countless others, to their deaths. It couldn't be meaningless. He wouldn't let it be. Rebecca was never going to dance again, she would never going to share that passion with him again, but maybe he could turn that passion into something else.

"Dad, I'd do... anything to bring her back."

"I know."

"This is... it's not what I signed up for. I wanted to defend my country, Dad. I wanted to be... honestly I wanted to be like you. A hero."

Pat Turville choked up, trying not to sob. "I'm no hero, son."

"I promised her I'd keep her safe, Dad. I promised her... I'd protect her."

Jim looked at his dad, the man who had once saved a little girl from a fire, the man who'd come home broken from his own war, and whispered, "I failed her."

His dad shook his head. "No. You did what you could. You did everything that was possible. No one can control everything out there. Especially not in war. Kid... I know what you're going through. Yeah, it wasn't your mom I lost, but... I understand guilt. I lost guys in my squad, guys who were closer to me than my brother. And I let that... that pain... that guilt... tear up my life. I let it hurt you, and your mom."

Jim shook his head, trying to stop his father, to tell him not to blame himself.

"Dad... you don't have to do this..."

"No. Son, listen to me. Please, please, listen to me, just this once. You... you have to forgive yourself. You have to move on, and do what you can. Make your life a good one. Make it one she'd be proud of. Do you understand me? Make Rebecca proud. Right now, you've got a choice. You can let this eat you alive, or you can be a better man than I ever was. Make her proud. Make me proud."

Jim sobbed. "I will, dad. I will."

"Come on, kiddo. Let's go home."

Pat Turville put his arm around his son's shoulders, and together, they walked back to the car, leaving behind the barren devastation of the war.

THE END

AMERICA'S FUTURE WILL CONTINUE IN

FRACTURED

BOOK 3 OF AMERICA'S FUTURE

FEEDBACK

Thank you for reading Insurgent.

I'd like to encourage readers to post a review on Amazon. com, Goodreads, or tell your friends on Facebook and elsewhere—whether or not you liked the book. Word of mouth is what makes the publishing world go round, and for independently published authors all the more so.

If you'd like to contact me with feedback, or want to find out when the next book will be released, please feel free to get in touch!

www.sheehanmiles.com
http://www.facebook.com/CharlesSheehanMiles
Twitter: @CSheehanMiles